CRYSTAL FALLS

CRYSTAL FALLS

BRAD WALSETH

GERYON PUBLISHING
TWIN LAKES, WI

GERYON PUBLISHING
NEW YORK, LONDON, TWIN LAKES

ISBN-13: 978-0-9986904-1-4
ISBN-10: 0-9986904-1-4

Second Printing 2017
This edition published in the United States of America by:
Geryon Publishing
1919 Sycamore Street
Twin Lakes, WI 53181

First published in Australia in 2014
by Satalyte Publishing

ACKNOWLEDGMENTS

I would like to acknowledge my wife Melody, my kids Angela, Dustin and Dylan, my brother Dean, Stephen Ormsby at Satalyte, Phil and Tony Bonyata at Concertlivewire.com, my coworkers at Vance Publishing and DMI, Darrell Harvey, Carl Hoberg, and all of my friends, teachers and professors.

For the Street Kids

CHAPTER ONE

Fall not into the grip of desire, lest, like
fire, it consume your strength;
Your leaves it will eat, your fruits
destroy, and you will be left a dry tree.
For contumacious desire destroys its
owner and makes him the sport
of his enemies (Sirach 6:2-4)

When it came right down to it, I was surprised to discover it really wasn't as hard as I thought it would be to kill Jesse Ray Hawkins.

I guess it's strange when I think about it—and I do think about it often these days with a considerable degree of disbelief. After all, he was my best friend, hardly someone whose life I would have ever believed myself capable of terminating. I can assure you that planning the task had cost me long tumultuous nights of sweat and strain, twisting in bed unable to sleep; agonizing over every small and potentially overlooked detail; torturing myself endlessly with the ramifications and moral justifications of such an action; contorting my body like an insect impaled on a pin—one hanging suspended over the crackling flames of Hell fires sure to be my reward for committing so gross a sin as cold blooded murder.

I remember the night well: the cold, the quiet; my fear.

Lead me, O LORD, in thy righteousness because of mine enemies; make thy way straight before my face.

How can you do such a thing to a friend—maybe your only friend—the only one you really ever had or ever will? Friend and foe, deliverer from harm, tempter with the winning smile beaming with sin and delirious evil. As joyous and natural as the north wind sweeping down from Canada, as base and cruel as the lowest snake with its fangs sunk in your flesh, I both loved the boy and hated the

man he became. But, despite the hatred, to kill him...? Yes, I know
Moses struck down the overseer and buried him in the sand, but he
was God's chosen to lead his people into the desert. David had Uriah
killed for the lust of a woman—that's more my taste—but he was
God's favorite, the beloved of the Almighty. I am just a pipsqueak,
a dust mote in a windstorm. No voices have I ever heard reply,
despite my endless tormented prayers addressed into the void.

*Oh let the wickedness of the wicked come to an end; but establish
the just: for the righteous God trieth the hearts and reins.*

In the end, my panic subsided, and it was as smooth and easy as
swinging out free, hanging suspended for an eternity, as the seconds
ticked away, and then letting go of the rope to fall into the cool water
below, just as Jesse and I had done so many summers before, down
at the Paint River. It just seems that now the peaceful river of our
youth has flooded its banks, its rapids rolling turbulently over
uneven boulders, sweeping me further downstream and away from
the safety of shore.

Out of the depths have I cried unto thee, O LORD.

I can see it now in my mind: just as Cain slew Abel, the long
simmering sin of envy burst forth between brothers. And that is how
I considered him, despite our not being blood related, and yet the
bloody results were the same as in that oft-told bible story, so clearly
documenting the first of so many similar crimes that have occurred
over and over again throughout history.

My defense is of God, which saveth the upright in heart.

Sad to say to my patient listener, the mortal blow when struck
was more mundane than heroic: an anticlimactic end that registered
more as Buster Keaton deadpan than a John Dillinger jailbreak on
the excitement scale. Hands shaking, heart throbbing, I stilled my
nerves and advanced with eyes of hard steel and unstoppable
resolve, and when the moment came, I was cool, calm and
completely in control. I can point with pride to my focus and
determined manner in the face of the unthinkable: for once, the
coward did not flinch.

*His mischief shall return upon his own head, and his violent
dealing shall come down upon his own pate.*

A second of silence, then a sharp crack; a flash in the dark under the stars; the singed smell of gunpowder in the air; a dark circle oozing between his surprised and angry eyes; the fall to the ground that seemed to echo even louder than the thumping in my chest; and then it was over but for the calm of the lapping waters, the chirring of the insects and the mournful howl of a solitary wolf in the distance as I made my way back beneath a mere sliver of moon to the shore and the arms of the angel I had forever longed for—the one who waited unknowingly for her deliverance from evil at the hands of an unseen protector in the shadows.

The LORD lifteth up the meek: he casteth the wicked down to the ground.

At least that is how it was supposed to happen; but, as is to be expected around here, things never happen like they are supposed to.

CHAPTER TWO

The seasons pass here in Crystal Falls: people are born, people die, but it never really changes. Time stands still here in the U.P.—that's the Upper Peninsula of Michigan in case you don't know—and we like it that way. You've got to wonder what it is that makes people live in remote places like these, seemingly away from the advantages of civilization, but truth be told, that is exactly why we live here: we want to be separate, to be alone, to live apart from the rest of society. It is a place to hide, a place to be reborn, a place to hunker down and pretend it is still the great frontier to be tamed and settled, or maybe to just disappear into. Strangers, the dark-skinned, and city folk with their big city ways aren't necessarily welcome, and are often eyed with a wariness that may take time to overcome, but if you're a friend we've got some pasties in the oven, a cold one in the cooler and an extra seat at the card table for a round of rummy, cribbage or canasta.

There's bingo at the Legion, the community theater's presenting "Annie," and it'll be grouse season soon. Around here it's back to the most basic of human instincts—kill or be killed—hunters and prey, just as God and Nature intended. Pick up your muskets and tackle, because the deer are running, the wild turkeys are in the bush, and there are muskies as big as your arm down in the cool, dark depths of the Michigamme Reservoir.

Despite the modern trappings: the gas stations, convenience stores, and occasional fancy house built by a wealthy retiree, the town itself feels old—almost as if the white men had run the Ojibwa Indian tribe off to the reservation on the point of a bayonet only yesterday. If you drive into town along Route 141 you'll pass through some of the newer subdivisions, primarily populated by retirees from down south in Illinois and Wisconsin.

Turning right and heading north, Superior Street rises steeply—so steep you could roll a quarter down it and it wouldn't stop rolling until it rolled clear out of town—up to the Iron County courthouse that is at the epicenter of the town, lined by weathered brick buildings that appear to be the same bland and unappealing style as just about any Midwestern town I've ever seen. Dominating the town is the bell tower of the courthouse, with a bell whose tolling can be heard for miles, and an onion-shaped water tower erected between the courthouse and the school, which can be seen from considerable distance, and whose ascendant manifestation lends a foreign, fairy-tale/science-fiction, almost Soviet-style appearance to the village.

Aside from the soaring building and water tower at the top of the hill, the town features what is generally just a solid and respectable looking main street, complete with bank and hardware store, the drugstore, a gas station, the post office, the Lutheran church, the remodeled theater—the pride and joy of the local artist scene--a pub, bar and grill, pizzeria, bowling alley—now closed, the dinky library and a creaky museum. Unfortunately, the times have hit the main street hard, and many of the businesses have closed up shop, or have turned to selling old, thrown away items as antiques, and the visitor is greeted by several 'For Sale' signs hanging in the windows along the avenue.

If you happen to glance down the side streets off the main route, you will see large oak and aspen trees spreading their branches skyward alongside sleepy rows of wood frame houses and log cabins in various degrees of repair—many with for sale signs themselves, or lonely garage sales in operation—their collected goods, furniture, toys, cars even, spread out across the yard in sad resignation. The omniscient courthouse meanwhile, proudly displays a ring of tall pines that suit its gothic verticality quite well, while from its cornice, looking down over us all, watching as if imbued with maternal interest, sit the three figures of Law, Mercy and Justice, whose unchanging marble gaze falters not, as they cast their view solemnly earthward toward their lowly subjects from this lofty pinnacle.

Yes, as I'm sure you will ask, there once were actual falls north of the town, on the Paint River out on the Iron Range Trail near Power Plant and Rock Crusher Road, but the river has been dammed and put into use by the utility company to light up the town, and the falls only appear during the spring runoff. But aside from the town founders' proclivity to perch their town on a bunch of rolling hills, and the recently discovered proximity to the world's largest mushroom—the 30-acre Humungus Fungus located in nearby Mastodon Township, I suspect that most visitors probably remember most the beautifully colored leaves of fall and the underlying chill that permeates the air in all but the hottest days of August and in turn makes this place a haven for snowmobilers and ice fishermen in a winter that seems to last nearly half the year.

Fishing, hunting and drinking are about all that is left to do for the Finns, Cornish, Italians, Germans, Pollocks and Swedes who migrated here to work in the iron mines and lumber mills before most of the industry disappeared overseas. My family, the LaPointes—my name being Nate LaPointe—on the other hand, were French Canadian on my father's side, and his father came down from Ottawa after World War I to work the iron mines. Our northern heritage and mandatory, albeit nominal, Catholicism was yet another matter that served to mark us as outcasts among these predominantly Northern European and Protestant settlers.

I too am a mortal man, the same as all the rest, and a descendant of the first man formed of earth... And I too, when born, inhaled the common air, and fell upon the kindred earth...

My mother was an Ojibwa—a pretty, dark-haired waitress who ran off with a lumberjack shortly after I was born. I never knew her, although I have a couple of photos and have often wondered what became of her and whether she ever thought about the boy she abandoned. There was a rumor that she headed off for Alaska, but I never heard a word, her silence never ceasing to reverberate through the empty hallways of my life.

The stable parent, my father, was a high school science teacher, until his drinking got him fired when I was about ten. He did some odd jobs around town after that—selling Amway and working part time here and there, but mainly just spent most of his time scrounging drinks in the taverns and picking up a string of divorcees and widows, who would keep him in the chips for as long as the relationship lasted. Eventually, he slowed down a bit, and then mainly just spent his days in front of the TV, watching sports, endlessly putting together puzzles and reading cheap detective novels in between sneaking drinks when he thought no one was watching.

I inherited my mother's dark hair and eyes and my father's tall, thin build, as well as his love of reading and books. I learned early to avoid my father's dark moods and foul humors, especially when he had been into a bottle, but he was generally content to leave me on my own, as if I were a mistake he knew he had to live with. Undoubtedly, I received as a gift from him my jaded outlook on the world and sardonic sense of humor.

My father still lives in the small house I grew up in just a few blocks from the high school where he worked, but I rent a place of my own out near Runkle Lake and the city cemetery. I try to stop in to see him on Sundays for lunch and make some small talk about the high school sports teams and what fish are biting, but we really don't have much to say to each other, and my visits have become more infrequent as my attentions have become more distracted. He doesn't seem to miss me.

It's pretty quiet around here most of the time, although the tourists drive us all crazy during the summer months, hiking and biking and canoeing and asking us how to get to the Porkies—what we call the Porcupine Mountains—further on west, or where Kelso Junction is—it isn't. But I guess it's good for the local businesses— we'd all be on welfare without them, instead of only 50 percent of the local population. Of course, there are other opportunities up here in the north woods for those with a more entrepreneurial bend as well, as my association with Jesse Ray Hawkins was clearly to prove.

CHAPTER THREE

The building was dark and shuttered as the car pulled slowly to a stop in the alley behind the mini mall. Jesse and I slid the ski masks on over our faces.

Jenny climbed out of the passenger side and got behind the wheel. Reaching into her purse, she extracted and handed Jesse his pistol, which he tucked into the waistband of his pants. Kissing her on the forehead, he hissed final instructions: "We'll be right back. Be ready to haul ass as soon as you see us come running."

We climbed out and he opened up the trunk, and I reached in and pulled out a sledgehammer, a couple of flashlights and two duffle bags, and then we strode silently, but purposely, around to the front of the store.

Sweat ran down my forehead and into my eyes, blood pumping through my veins, supercharged, throbbing with adrenaline. It was a warm night and we were wearing gloves, as well as the baseball hats and hoodies that Junior had suggested, telling us they were the type favored by the Latinos down in Green Bay and would help throw the authorities off our trail.

Traffic was sparse on the streets on a Sunday night as we suspected it would be. A lone pickup truck with one headlight out and a bad muffler lurched to a stop at the light before turning unsteadily and, belching gray smoke, rattled slowly up the road and out of sight.

Emerging from the shadows, we scrutinized the empty street in both directions as far as we could see. The breeze was crisp, but I was sweating nonetheless. Quiet hung in the air; while the neon sign announcing the word *Drugs* illuminated our silhouettes in blue.

"Go for it, Preach," he directed in a whisper.

I raised the sledge above my head and swung the cumbrous end with violence at the front door, shattering it, spewing a shower of dust and glass particulates into my face.

An alarm immediately punctured the night air with a shrill

scream.

I lifted the hammer to swing again, but Jesse held my arm back and leapt through the opening like a rat into a hole. "Let's go," he shouted back at me as I followed—glass shards crunching under my shoes and the twisted metal frame tearing at my arms as I distorted my angular limbs and clambered through.

Inside, the essence of decades of stale cologne, mothballs and antiseptic creams struck my nostrils. Staggering forward cautiously, my eyes struggled to adjust to the darkness, the interior lit only by the rays of our flashlights, reflecting off the displays of postcards, cardboard eyeliner supermodels and super-size condoms. In the back, the pharmacy area shimmered with florescence. We headed that way.

Jesse sprinted down the aisle and bounded with one leap like a deer over the counter. Frantically, he tore through trays and boxes and bottles—scattering their contents across the counters and onto the floor.

"What do we need again?" he screamed over the wailing alarm and waved his arm wildly for me to search the other end of the racks. "What's the shit called?"

"Pseudoephedrine? It's in the sinus shit!" I responded with frustration. I'd been through this with him too many times before to have to worry about it now.

"Yeah, yeah, I remember," he said while ripping open cabinet doors and yanking the contents out.

I hoped so. *How many times did we go over it?* I wondered with irritation.

Jesse checked the time on his watch. "One minute," he screamed—rising excitement evident in his voice.

I scrambled into action at the opposite end of the pharmacy area. Heart throbbing violently, I fumbled with dozens of bottles, my shaking hands knocking several off the counter, spilling mounds of yellow and pink pills across the floor.

The alarm continued its ear-splitting attack.

"Where are you hiding it, you motherfuckers?!" Jesse yelled as he slammed the contents of a bin to the floor. Grabbing the telephone in frustration, he smashed it against the wall sending plastic shards flying everywhere.

I glanced up over my shoulder and saw with apprehension that I was looking into the lens of the security camera. It knew that it couldn't see the details of my masked face, but it could see into my eyes. I felt its gaze staring back at me; it felt like God himself was looking deeply into my soul and judging me.

Search me, O God, and know my heart; try me and know my anxious thoughts.

"Minute and a half!" Jesse's voice skirted the edge of the abyss.

My legs wobbled as I scrambled around the pharmacy work areas—upending stools, swinging open cabinets and emptying drawers, shining my light into the recesses of shelves and cabinets, peering quickly within to determine their contents.

The alarm wailed relentlessly; they would be coming soon. I could see the sad eyes of my father gazing at me through the bars of a jail cell. We had to get out now.

Suddenly, I spotted the familiar red and green colored boxes in the glare of my flashlight.

"Here!" I shouted. Using both hands, I scrambled, stuffing armloads of the boxes into my bag.

"Jackpot!" Jesse cried out in delight a second later and dancing in a circle held up a bottle triumphantly. "I found some Oxycontin. We are going to be very popular motherfuckers when we get back home," he giggled in giddy enthusiasm.

"What else should we grab?" I asked while shoving the final boxes of sinus meds into the duffle.

"You tell me, you're the answer man," Jesse snapped.

"Okay, I guess just lithium batteries and blister packs if you see them."

"Two minutes, dude. We don't have time. We got what we came for already, so just grab as many pills as you can—the dead heads back home will take anything for a buzz. Fill the bag with whatever, just make it quick."

Frantically, I stuffed my bag full of whatever bottles of pills I could reach, arms pumping at a rate of speed I didn't realize I possessed. Jesse banged open the cash register with his fist and grabbed a handful of bills from the interior as he flew by.

"Two and a half!" he yelled. "Time to rock and roll!"

Vaulting over the counter, we ran hard for the door—knocking items off the shelves as we blurred past—a display of sunglasses crashing to the floor in our wake.

Reaching the exit, Jesse launched himself through the hole to the outside like a bullet from a gun. Following close behind him, I stumbled and fell as my unwieldy body clambered through, tearing my jeans and cutting my knees on the debris. Crying out in pain, I reached out and grabbed Jesse by the heel, and he whirled back, and, grabbing my arm, dragged me back to my feet and we hurtled down the pavement.

Regaining my balance, we sprinted around the corner and dove into the car, the wail of the alarm still echoing in our ears.

"Drive!" Jesse shouted.

The tires squealed as Jenny hit the gas.

"Not so fast! Take it steady and slow! We don't need any attention!"

Jenny slowed the car to a legal pace and we slipped softly like a ghost for a couple blocks through a quiet, residential neighborhood, before switching the headlights on and picking up speed. Jesse screamed at the top of his lungs, "That was fucking awesome!" and pounded on the dashboard.

I slouched down in the back seat and guiltily watched for red and blue lights in the rear view mirrors, panting in dreadful anticipation at getting busted, until at last, we took a final turn and cleared the town. Breathing heavily, laughing, relieved and quite pleased with our take, we turned on the tunes, fired up a jay, and— taking the winding back roads that we had scouted before—were out of Iron Mountain and on our way home in less than five minutes.

CHAPTER FOUR

I first met Jesse Ray in first grade; I remember it like it was yesterday: that's when he saved my life. School was a frightening and lonely place that year, and I admit I was a bit of a pussy—a shy, quiet, pale kid, trembling and confused, almost to the point of chronic nausea, lurking in the shadows like an alien from a faraway planet, terrified by the bizarre rituals of humanity and just trying to make sense of my tumultuous surroundings. Meanwhile, Jesse was regarded by everyone from teachers to fellow students, as a terror on two legs—a devil with a winning smile and a bad reputation, well earned. He was a fearless, non-stop dynamo—part bully, part clown: feisty, bold, coarse and roguish, yet lovable even then.

His rescue of yours truly occurred one morning when I was sitting in a stall in the bathroom outside of Mrs. Montag's classroom at Forest Park grade school. I dreaded taking a crap at school as the bathrooms were notorious for gangs of older boys roaming unsupervised, and engaged in mischief, often resulting in shoes, shorts or smaller kids dunked in the toilets, garbage cans or worse, but this was one of those times when I really had to go and was simply out of options.

I slipped in as quietly as I could, but the heel of my sneakers squeaked on the polished floor and two vicious-looking third graders spotted me, and I knew in the pit of my stomach that I was in for it. I had already encountered one of the boys' older brothers—a member of a group of hooligans, who had jumped out of the bushes en masse and pummeled me when I was walking home one day only a week earlier. These two may even have been present as well, I wasn't sure. The whole thing was a blur of surprising violence—one of several that had turned my attitude toward life from sunshine and lollipops and televised happy endings to one of fear and bewilderment even at a young age.

I had learned to walk quickly home with quick eyes constantly searching for movement, avoiding certain streets, street corners, houses, alleys, lanes, shacks, bushes, parks, cars, businesses, empty lots, playgrounds, yards, parking lots, bridges, paths, walkways, riverbanks and deer trails, and by doing so, manage to mostly stay clear of the rough and rambunctious cadres of young males, and admittedly some scary, and presumably female, females, who ran in packs looking to pick off strays. All in good fun, an essential part of growing up I suspect you say.

In any case, I remember well that my adversaries saw the fear in my eyes as I slunk quickly into a stall and I was shaking as I rapidly pulled down my pants on that fateful day. Noticing movement, I watched with horror as two sets of tennis shoes advanced to the door of the stall, accompanied by a hideous whispering and giggling that sounded to me like a cross between a pair of hissing vipers and the utterances of two cave dwellers having spotted a baby rabbit with which they meant to club: this clearly foretold of no possible good to come. The hallway door opened suddenly, and my heart nearly leapt over the high walls; but my pitiful hope that, by chance, a random teacher had blundered upon the devious plot and come to my rescue was crushed when yet another, even smaller, set of tennis shoes joined the devious duo, the chuckling and evil whispering increasing proportionally.

I'll never forget those shoes as long as I live: dirty white canvas high tops. The cavalry should issue those shoes to their bravest soldiers for rescue missions.

Through the crack of the stall door, my pleading eyes spotted one sparkling, wolf-gray eye peeking through, and then I heard him laugh out loud and say:

"Aw, you guys don't want to do (unintelligible) to him. He's alright... He's an artist."

The voice sounded like a pint-sized Jimmy Cagney, Bronx accent and all, echoing off the tiles, but it sounded to me like the Hallelujah Chorus in full swell. No doubt, it probably wasn't Jesse Ray's size or reputation that deterred those boys off from whatever they were planning to do, but I suspect it was rather his clever reasoning and the force of his spirit and personality. I still shudder wondering what they had in mind. He was always a sawed off little runt—short and shaggy, but tough as a bobcat—with long, wild, dirty blonde hair and crazy eyes; but although wiry and muscular, he was never physically imposing. Still, he had a strange charisma; a natural force that had to be respected, like fire or gravity: even to the end.

His two older brothers: Jake, tall, dirty, greasy-haired and nasty, with a long, cratered face looking like a cross between a T-Rex and a dog (a *gorgonopsid* to those dinosaur freaks), and Jared, wide-bodied, hairy, filthy in body, mind and spirit, grunting, spitting and ever psychotic, evoking the thought that saber-toothed, serial killing Neanderthals must have bred with skunk apes somewhere in his prehistory, were both certainly to be reckoned with. Indeed, both were bigger and meaner than most by far, and almost feral in their predatory nature—no doubt they were in the band that savaged me, but Jesse didn't have to call on his family renown to get whatever he wanted. No, even then that smiling little badger with the magnetic grin and glimmering, frosty-paned eyes simply exuded with effervescent charm and a life spirit that attracted everyone, old and young alike, and held them spellbound as he performed his act.

The artist thing—well, that came about because I was pretty good with the creative stuff, although I never really got the grades for it because I had considerable trouble coloring inside the lines (yeah, I know—same old story). Despite the teacher's displeasure that year with my lack of discipline and natural sloppiness, my diorama featuring a cartoon dog with a thought balloon rising from his head displaying a pithy comment like those seen in the funnies was a surprising hit with my classmates, while, my construction paper tom cat wearing lederhosen and carrying two beer steins had been a true sensation throughout the entire grade, eliciting smirks, mumbled chortles and even a few appreciative glances. Lord knows where I got such ideas—my endless hours on my own at home reading weird shit, or zoning out in front of the T.V. perhaps.

In any case, I had no idea that the popular—and to me quite frightening, ruffian Jesse Ray Hawkins even knew who I was, let alone that he had noticed any of my products. On the playground, he was always a dust devil of action and misdirection, running hither and yon a kilter with a football or snowball, knocking down a kid in the dust with a tackle, throwing rocks at birds, pushing, screaming, yowling, whirling, whizzing and howling away in the center of all action, while I kept myself busy amusing some other lesser regarded souls by drawing a picture of the teacher with chalk on the pavement and trying to stay out of the way of the hoopla.

A frightening little demon of fearless energy, Jesse Ray tormented the teachers, confounded the principal, pestered the bigger kids, bullied the smaller ones, badgered the lunch ladies, perturbed the janitors, titillated the girls and entertained the rest of us with his jesting, his antics, his enthusiasm for the daily battle, fighting like hell even with the most feared third, fourth and Good Lord, *even fifth* graders, earning school wide renown as a dirty fighter who wouldn't hesitate to bite, claw, pull hair or grab a rock or stick in the clutch.

When someone pointed out that he was cheating, he just shrugged and said with a smirk, "My daddy says, 'All's fair in love in war.'"

Nobody mentioned the fact that Jesse's daddy—the feared patriarch of the Hawkins family, old Jude—was currently serving another stint in a correctional facility. In and out of prison for years—his final stay, several years later was for, among other things, manslaughter. Prison was where the old bastard would die many years later from stab wounds received in a fight in the prison yard; or maybe it was cancer—there were a lot of crazy stories and nobody ever really knew, even Jesse himself.

But back to the toilet, shall we? After Jesse talked the tormentors out of whatever they had in mind, I waited until they left before daring to slink out and back to the classroom. Despite my gratitude for my benefactor's surprising intervention, I was too shy to express any thanks out loud, and remained in my place on the fringes of the scene, trembling, yet hopeful at the thought that someone important and admired may even some day talk to me. He had, after all, expressed some notice, if not admiration, of my talents. Our unusual friendship officially started a few days after the bathroom incident, when a cocky Jesse Ray zoomed by me at full tilt, then hit the brakes hard, stopped and spun around to my desk, where he hovered for a moment like he had something in mind. Finally, he announced nonchalantly in a voice that sounded like a nasal, 1st grade version of Al Capone, "Hey Pointy, why don't you draw me some knives?"

Now this was pre-Columbine mind you, and the teachers at the time never seemed to be around to monitor everything we did like they seem to these days. Although, alarmed by this sudden attention, I was secretly pleased. I was one of those kids who actually dug the library and had devoured books on knights and weapons, making the arcane study of guns and swords and such one of my particular specialties.

I rapidly worked up a page of various knives drawn to scale from memory and labeled from a Bowie to a broadsword to a dagger to a fencing foil and even threw in a mace and pike to boot. My perspective was poor—I remember some of the blades more closely resembled bananas, pregnant guppies or crescent moons—but in the end, the results could not have been more impressive and rewarding.

Jesse Ray took one look at my scrawled page and his mouth burst into a huge grin. Snatching the paper from my hand, he waved it around the room, and ran from group to group showing it to the other boys who looked at the page with glee and appreciation. Some of the girls even gave me a look as if I actually existed, and I blushed as I basked in my first glow of the warmth of human goodwill.

He hadn't thanked me, and in fact, seemed to forget about me for the next few days, but I had felt the subtle touches of acceptance for the first time in my life and the tingling, like a first kiss, lingered still. After my success, I was even asked to join in a few football games, where, although ponderously slow and heavy-footed (my first nickname, "Turtle," I thankfully outgrew, becoming more of an ostrich if one must compare to the animal kingdom), I performed just well enough to not be shunned, while also being careful enough not to outshine some of the "superstars," whose talents were often less super than their mouths. But I wasn't even real comfortable with even the edges of the spotlight, and felt I might be just about to slide back into my comfortable, yet invisible status for good, when something occurred to cement our friendship forever.

This time Jesse Ray didn't ask.

"Draw me some guns," he commanded.

CHAPTER FIVE

*A*nd Jenny, ah Jenny.

Behold, thou art fair, my love; behold, thou art fair; thou hast doves' eyes.

Behold, thou art fair, my beloved, yea, pleasant: also our bed is green.

"You probably don't remember the first time we met, do you?" she asked as we lay entwined in the darkness of her bedroom together.

"You're right," I said, trying to remember. "I know your family moved to town half way through second grade from like Pittsburgh or something."

"Close enough—Allegheny County. My stepdad's cousin thought he could get him on with the logging company he worked for. Nothing ever came of it, but he picked up a job driving truck and we kind of got stuck here." Her voice was soft and drowsy.

Thy lips are like a thread of scarlet, and thy speech is comely: thy temples are like a piece of a pomegranate within thy locks.

"I can't say I remember an actual first sighting—so no love at first sight, I guess. I was too busy trying to maintain my own equilibrium to notice the comings and goings of anyone else."

"Yeah, I was a scared rabbit in those days myself. New kid and all. The local girls weren't exactly members of the Welcome Wagon."

"I thought you looked more like a deer in the headlights myself."

"Oh, thanks a lot!" She slapped my arm.

How beautiful are thy feet with shoes, O prince's daughter! The joints of thy thighs are like jewels, the work of the hands of a cunning workman.

"I mean a cute little doe, of course—with those long skinny legs and pretty big brown eyes. I started paying attention the more I saw you, and it was love even then."

"You're nuts, little kids don't know what love is."

"I don't think you're giving me enough credit; I was very advanced for my age in some ways. Certainly not socially—I was a retard in that area, but I knew about love and romance even then. Probably all those books on knights and chivalry."

"You always were a bookworm, Preacher."

"I wish you wouldn't call me that. I never liked that nickname," I said sulkily.

"Okay Nate." She rose up on one elbow and continued seriously. "Actually if you want to know the truth, I thought you were kind of annoying back then."

"Really?" I asked, raising an eyebrow.

"Yeah, you were always tagging along after Jesse."

"He was my best friend."

"Yeah, it was always the three of us—down at the Tastee Freeze, swimming in the river, at the movies."

"You two smooching it up, yeah don't remind me. I hated being the third wheel, but Jesse always insisted I come along."

"He was a demanding jerk even then. Don't know what I ever saw in him."

"Yes you do. Same thing I did. Same thing everybody does even now. He's a charming son-of-a-bitch, even when..."

"Yeah, I know, and handsome as hell is right. That cocky, macho attitude makes me sick; but that shining smile he has, those fucking blue eyes—he still makes my knees weak when he smiles and winks, and says "Hey Darlin',—the prick."

"So you still love him?"

"Oh Nate, of course I do, despite his being a total asshole. You're sweet, and this is wonderful, don't get me wrong. I love how you are so gentle. You're almost like a brother to me."

"A brother?" I said choking.

"Well, a brother that I sleep with," she laughed quietly.

"But the way he treats you..."

"Listen Pre—sorry, Nate—sometimes people are made for each other. That's the way it is with him and me. We're like different parts of the same person that only exists when we are together. Now, you I like—"

"Like?"

"Well, more than like. I love you too, but..."

"Yes?"

"Oh Nate, don't make this more complicated than it already is. Besides, you need to get going—we don't know when he may back."

"He won't be back. He's down in Green Bay with one of his sluts," I snapped moodily.

Her hurt eyes flashed in the dark. "Thanks Nate. Tell me something I don't already know. But you know he's so goddamn unpredictable—he likes to show up unexpectedly and accuse me of sleeping around. Gets worked up and turns into a jackass, breaking things and... Plus, I don't want to wake up Jeremy—it was hell getting him down to begin with and I'm exhausted, but I've got to get this house clean and laundry done before he gets back..." She motioned around to the mounds of clothing stacked on the floor around the bed.

"Are you sure you don't need some more brotherly love?" I asked and reached over to embrace her, but she pushed me away.

"Stop it. I said you need to get the hell out of here. Don't you ever listen to me, dummy? We're taking enough chances as it is. I told you before, Jesse's brothers have taken to driving by here sometimes—I think he's got them checking on me. In fact, I was going to tell you... I don't think we should do this anymore." She climbed out of bed violently and flipped on the light.

"Don't even say that," I said, getting dressed. "We'll just have to use my place or a motel or..." Standing, I pulled her close and whispered in her ear. "I'll think of something."

Thou hast ravished my heart, my sister, my spouse; thou hast ravished my heart with one of thine eyes, with one chain of thy neck.

The lamplight...

How fair is thy love, my sister, my spouse! How much better is thy love than wine! And the smell of thine ointments than all spices!

The curtain rippling in the night breeze...

Thy lips, O my spouse, drop as the honeycomb: honey and milk are under thy tongue; and the smell of thy garments is like the smell of Lebanon.

The hunting rifle propped in the corner...

A garden inclosed is my sister, my spouse; a spring shut up, a fountain sealed.

"Just get out. But before you go, you promised me a taste, Nate. You know the bastard locks it up when he's gone."

She stood up. I could see she was shaking. Her face was pale and I thought I noticed some of her teeth had started rotting. An open sore on her cheek. God she was skinny; I could feel her ribs when I held her.

"You don't need it," I said. She wavered like she would fall, but caught herself.

"Fuck you." Her eyes were dark and hard as oil-stained concrete.

The bastard was killing her. He and the drugs both. Her ashen complexion shone cadaverous under the lamplight, her ivory skin mottled with scars and bruises. For a moment I saw her how she really was and was shaken to my core. I closed my eyes and the instance passed, corporeality faded, the glass and beads fell gently into place, into interlinked symmetric patterns, the pulsing light refracted through the pieces, and then her beauty overwhelmed me once again. She had never seemed more vulnerable and beautiful, but she was being destroyed and I was helpless to stop it.

I would lie, cheat and steal for her. I would kill for her.

"Give it to me now."

"No. It's killing you, Jen."

"Preacher—give me the fucking crank." Raising her voice. "You fucking promised!" She was scratching her arm now. I could see the track marks were infected. I looked away.

"Jen, please—"

"I'll scream and wake the neighborhood. I'll call Jesse and tell him you raped me. Don't think I won't do it. Give it to me now you fucker!"

"Okay, okay." I pulled a baggie from my pants pocket and tossed her the rock.

Hurriedly, she bent over a card table, broke off a piece and put it in a glass pipe. I leaned over her back and put my arms around her.

"Just get out." She stiffened coldly as I worked my way down her neck with my lips. Her focus intense on keeping her trembling hands steady, she lit the pipe and took a long draw, closed her eyes and shuddered with a pleasure that sadly I had failed to produce in her earlier in bed, as the rush filtered through her body.

I stepped across the cluttered floor to leave when she suddenly spotted something out of the corner of her slitted eyes and, reaching under the bed, pulled out an old paperback book and tossed it at me. I turned just in time to catch it as it hit my chest.

"Hey, here's that book that you loaned me. You can have it back."

"No shit. You still had it after all these years?" I said, turning over the battered pages in my hands. "I forgot I loaned it to you. Did you ever read it?"

"What do you think? More than once even." She reloaded the pipe.

"Did you—?"

"Understand it?" Thanks a lot. You must really think I'm stupid don't you?" She lit the pipe again and inhaled deeply, her energy returning in surging ecstatic waves behind her hooded eyelids.

"—I was actually going to ask if you liked it?"

She blew a blue-tinged cloud out of her rose petal lips. "Yeah. Yeah, I guess I did... But I don't know why you thought it was so sad, it all comes together in the end and everybody is happy."

"It comes together, but I'm not so sure everybody's all that happy. They've all been cheated and been beaten down by life. It's pretty apparent that the reality of life is that it isn't exactly fair or kind."

"Maybe not..." Her eyes drifted to the walls of the room. "But that's just the way it is, isn't it?"

"That's the way it is." I replied softly, and rolling the book, shoved it into my back pocket.

She got up and hugged me. I could feel her heart pounding. She was filled with nervous energy and ready to face the housework if she didn't get... distracted.

"Be careful, Preacher, okay?" Her eyes were shining. "And thanks."

"Don't mention it. And don't worry, everything will be alright," I lied.

"We've got to be more careful."

"I know."

"It's not just Jesse—"

"I'm not scared of him... or his nutcase brothers."

She looked up and stared hard into my eyes and spoke softly but firmly.

"You should be."

CHAPTER SIX

"What's that thing called?"

"An Iron Maiden."

I held the book closer so Jesse could see. His icy eyes sparkled, while both of his rapidly moving hands expertly tied a firecracker to a grasshopper.

"Damn, that's sweet!" he said and whistled in veneration. Snapping the lighter open with a crazed grin, he lit the fuse. As it sizzled, we ran for shelter, diving onto the ground behind the trees in a fit of maniacal giggling just as the explosion went off, sending a shower of dirt and pine needles scattering into the air. Excited, we returned and searched the debris, but there was no blood and guts to be found, much to Jesse's disappointment. Not one to give up, Jesse painstakingly searched the ground closely, eventually finding one spiky gray back leg, which he held like a trophy above his head while whooping and dancing an exaggerated war dance.

Several victims—including ants, earthworms, beetles, a dying bumble bee and a garter snake—later, our fireworks cache was depleted. Finding a cool secluded spot, we sat in the shade of a red pine tree and paged through the thick book I had borrowed from the library. Jesse was thrilled by the pages upon pages of weapons: cannons, pikes, blunderbusses, bayonets, broadswords, catapults and suits of armor, but he was especially excited by the pictures and descriptions of torture devices and methods.

"Hot oil poured over their heads—that's awesome," he exclaimed. "Sure wish we could try a few of these."

"Like on 'Mini-Hitler'?" I suggested, referring to our beloved gym teacher by the nickname we had recently bestowed upon him.

"Ha! That prick'd be one of the first to get it." We had been forced to run extra laps for goofing off in gym the day before and were none too happy with the diminutive, albeit muscular, Phys-Ed instructor.

Finished paging through the illustrations, I yawned, closed the book and put it aside, and we both lay back and gazed silently at the streaky clouds sifting softly across the robin's egg blue sky.

"So what are you going to do when you get older, Nate?" Jess finally broke the silence.

"I don't know."

"Maybe be a teacher like your old man?"

"Hell no!" I sputtered, annoyed at the thought. "Astronaut would be cool."

"Heck yeah," he agreed. "But I hate to say it; I can't really see you in rocket... maybe in the control room..."

"Yeah, I suppose. Okay, maybe a scientist, or an explorer or a guy in an office. I've even thought about being a... preacher."

"That's... cool, I guess," he watched the sky thoughtfully. "Me, I think I'd like to join the Army, only... I don't want any half-assed, donkey-dick drill sergeant telling me what to do."

"Yeah, that would suck. Doing pushups and stuff and getting screamed at."

"The guns would be pretty cool though."

"Yeah," I said a little nervously.

"Bombs, grenades, mortars... You get to shoot people and get paid for it. Maybe even get a medal."

"Sure. Shoot the bad guys... but you do know, they shoot back, right?"

"They'd never hit me," he chuckled, "I'm too quick and wiry, like a small, fast moving target. I'd be on their back cutting their throat before they even knew I was there. Like a Navy Seal with mad ninja skills." He leapt to his feet and pantomimed the action as he described it, and Nate could almost imagine the look of surprise on the sentry's face when Jesse slipped softly from the shadows and caught the Russian guard unaware with a sharp and serrated blade thrust into the jugular.

"Do you ever think about it, Nate?" Jesse asked suddenly, after collapsing back down to earth.

"Think about what?"

"Killing someone," he said flatly, twirling a piece of grass.

"Are you kidding?"

He didn't answer. Pulling a pinecone off the tree, he crushed it to powder in his hands. Finally, he spoke:

"I do."

"Really?"

"Yeah, I think about it. Mostly my dad. I can still remember the bastard's face when he whipped me half to death for pissing my bed. Man, he scared the living crap out of me. Smelling like whiskey, with a red face and eyes like a devil. I was scared of him then, but I ain't now." He puffed out his chest and flexed a bicep, but despite his braggadocio I could glimpse a tiny glimmer of fear in his eyes.

"You wouldn't really kill him, would you?" I asked, shuddering, feeling a chill in the air, like when a bashful sun hides itself behind a lacy curtain of cloud.

"Sure I would. I'd put him in an Iron Maiden if I could."

"I suspect if you did, you'd go to Hell," I said after a pause, appalled at his disturbing lack of conscience.

"Where'd you get that idea?" he scoffed, annoyed.

"It's in the Bible."

"What? Does it really say that? I thought it was just people who didn't believe in Jesus that went to Hell. You're supposed to smite your enemies and shit aren't you?"

"Well it says 'An eye for an eye,' but it also says 'Thou shalt not kill.' I'm not sure it says for sure you'd go to Hell, but I think that's what it means. I'll check in my copy and see when I get home if you want me to."

"Do what you want. I don't believe any of that Sunday school crap anyway."

"Jesse!"

He rolled over onto his stomach and ran his fingers through the pine needles on the ground beside him.

"I'm just curious about it," he said at last.

"What do you mean?"

"I just wonder what it would be like?"

"To kill someone?" my voice choked.

"Yeah. Just pop 'em in the head or something. What would that be like, I wonder—to be able to just do it?"

"Someone who deserved it? Like an enemy soldier in a war?"

"Naw, just someone at random. If you could do that, and get

away with it, you'd think you could get away with just about anything."

"Wouldn't you feel guilty? I mean someone's momma or brother or something—"

"I don't know," he said blankly. "I'm not sure that I would. I don't feel nothing when I shoot a squirrel or a rabbit, or gut a deer. So with a human... I kinda wonder if I would feel anything."

"You gotta feel guilty. Everybody feels guilty when they do the wrong thing."

"I don't," he stated dully.

"You don't?"

"No. Weird, isn't it? I don't give a shit about nothin' or nobody. Maybe I've just got a different way of looking at things. Who knows?" he smirked.

"But killing someone?"

"Might be fun."

"Man, you are going to hell for sure."

"Good, who'd want to float around on a cloud singing and playing a harp anyway? Hell sounds more like my kinda place— blood and guts and pain and screaming—fun and excitement's better than boring any day."

"Be quiet Jesse, God's gonna hear you," I whispered.

"Fuck God."

"Jesus Jesse!"

"Yeah, him too. I got this whole church crap figured out—it's just a bunch of malarkey they worked up to scare little kids into behaving. You believe what you want, Nate, but humans are just another kind of animal, and just like out in the woods, some of us are like the wolves and some are like the deer. And I don't plan on being no deer."

"No," I said after another disturbing pause. "I don't think that's right. God gave us rules."

"Way I figure, rules are for the cows and sheep. They stay in the pen and next thing you know they're hamburgers or lamb chops. I don't follow rules and that way ain't nobody ever going to grind me up for chow."

"What if you're wrong, Jess? You're talking about your eternal soul."

"Fuck Nate, you're sounding more like a preacher every day," he snapped with a glare, but then quickly switched to a laugh. "Aw, fuck it anyway."

Jumping up, he bent and picked up a rock and flung it as hard as he could toward a distant tree, where it thwacked off the tree trunk— a dead bulls-eye. Tipping his head back, he brought forth a powerful howl from deep inside his chest that rattled through the branches and hung echoing in the treetops like the roar of some wild beast screaming out his life and death in a single moment.

"Besides," he said with flashing eyes, "Hell can't be no worse than it was living with my ol' man."

CHAPTER SEVEN

You might think I'm crazy, but I say I'm just lucky, because I am one of those rare individuals who lack the addiction gene, or whatever the heck biological trigger that is necessary to turn me into an alcoholic, coke fiend or crack head. I know, it doesn't make sense with my father being a full-fledged alcoholic, and my mother's Native American blood, but it's true. Their particular sins must have skipped a generation, or maybe I just experienced enough of their bullshit and it scared me off.

But the old man told me that my granddad on my father's side was a teetotaler, so maybe I got something from him. Not that I'm against it. I mean, I enjoy a toot as much as anybody. I like getting plastered and will even sample the goods when required, but I am not driven by strange compulsions or inner demons to imbibe, nor do I miss it when it is not available. Stick a can of soda in front of me and I'm just as apt to drink it, even though I hate that sugary crap, as if it was a glass of fine wine or a shot of Tequila. What can I say; I'm just a thirsty guy. I probably enjoy my reefer more than anything, but even that I can take or leave because of the paranoia feelings it can produce, making you think everybody's out to get you.

Jesse thought I was nuts. Of course, he was just the opposite. I give him credit: he started off mostly pretty good, keeping his fingers out of the dope, staying out of it as much as he could, but eventually he discovered the joys of combining whiskey and beer with coke and reefer and then... he graduated to even harder stuff, finally getting himself trapped completely in a messy tangle of conflicting addictions like the snakes in the bottom of the pit in your nightmares. The dreams he had for making money to get the hell out of the U.P. just dissipated, and he started dealing mainly just to pay for his tastes and his debts.

Jenny thinks I'm clean because of my, so called, spirituality, but she, on the other hand, lost it more and more every day, and when she lost it, I lost it.

The only true clean one of the bunch, as far as using went, was Junior. I guess I haven't said much about Junior before, but besides being a truly unique creature, he was a crucial element in the success of our little venture.

Roy Pultz, Jr., aka Junior, was a few years older than us in school and the son of the former Iron County Sheriff. His dad, Old Roy Sr. was a popular fellow with the local businessmen throughout the region. He was known as being a good old boy who was friendly with the locals and hardnosed against vagrants and lowlife criminals, but that was only half the story: in fact, he only jailed those who failed to provide him with his share. And the wheeler dealer criminals who run the town were his best buddies, who got away with just about anything they wanted, including, it was rumored, rape or even a murder or two. The story of his death from a heart attack in a motel room, in the company of a woman known to be paid for her services, was both legendary, as well as expected for a man in his position and was generally applauded by his peers.

Junior himself was a bit of an odd duck. To start with, he inherited his mother's small but piercing blue eyes, nearly luminous pale skin, and yellow wavy hair that he kept piled high in a pompadour style that we all thought made him resemble more a poodle than a man. Puffy and pear-shaped, with small feet and hands, the chubby man resembled a parade balloon more than a cop; but despite his limitations in appearance, Junior was a star athlete in high school, who made honorable mention as a light-hitting, defensive-minded catcher for the baseball team, as well as second team all-district in basketball—both pretty big deals around here. With his large thighs and ample buttocks, he was adept at blocking the plate, and he was hard to move around in the paint on the basketball court. He was deceptively quick and agile, and could jump surprisingly high considering his rotund, dough-boyish appearance.

In fact, it was his quickness that won him quite a bit of the acclaim he received. He had an amazingly fast first step; if a defender tried to guard him, Junior would just blow right past him on the way to the bucket, leaving the startled victim checking his jock to figure out what happened. Junior scored a lot of easy baskets that way, but the problem, was that he cheated. You see, you're not supposed to take a step before you dribble the basketball. But Junior figured out at an early age that if you take the first step and then dribble, nobody is going to be able to stop you. Of course it's illegal as all hell, but most of the time nobody said anything, and the refs here in Crystal Falls looked the other way—not wanting to earn the ire of Roy's dad by calling his kid for traveling.

Of course, some of the folks from the other towns got up in arms about it, and he didn't get away with quite as much on the road, but that quick first step was so fast—like a snake striking—that the refs were often too slow to call it, and the team was on the way back the other way down the court before they even knew what had happened. I know myself how he did it because I got stuck guarding him in some pickup games, and after having this chubby demon zip past me like a freaking zephyr multiple times, I finally gave up. In fact, it got so nobody would play with him anymore, so he moved on to other pursuits: handball, golf, running drugs.

Junior wasn't only an athlete—who, by the way, never drank or smoked—but he was also a noted dancer. His Mom made him take tap lessons as a kid, which often made him the butt of jokes, but admittedly must have helped him with his balance and agility. We smirked and mocked him for it—especially when were out in the streets and we would see him go past in the back seat of his mom's big old Cadillac dressed in some outfit covered in sparkles and fringe—but he was quite a hit with the ladies, who found his graceful motions on the dance floor, along with his puke green GTO and rumored family money stash, enough to overcome the distractions of his pudgy appearance and sometimes unusual behavior.

But although he was voted to the Homecoming Court and had plenty of dates, Junior rarely took any of the girls up on their offers of kindness, instead choosing to maintain a close, and some would say, unhealthy relationship with his mother as the years went by. In fact, Crystal Falls' most eligible bachelor seemed content to escort the widow Pultz and her matronly friends to and from church and the Ladies Auxiliary meetings, while gaining a reputation as a dependable and courteous young man about town.

Surprisingly, after high school, and despite his success—albeit tainted—in sports, Junior received no scholarship offers. Perhaps, the scouts knew he would lose his advantage once he left the confines of his father's dominion. So, following in Roy Sr.'s footsteps, Junior briefly joined the service, serving in Guam and the Philippines with the military police. A couple of years spent dealing with drunken soldiers nearly satiated his sadistic streak, but his enthusiasm for cracking heads began to wane, especially since those big old boys sometimes liked to hit back. He longed for the comforts of home and easier prey, so when his father died, he returned home like a good son, to dutifully take care of his mother.

His reputation and family name was gold in the eyes of those who run the town, and he was quickly added as a deputy on the force, thus beginning a successful ascent up the ranks of law enforcement to someday replace the current sheriff, maintaining the continuity of town's renown and adding additional golden braids and ribbons to the legacy of his beloved father. Only it was taking too long, and Junior was an impatient fellow who felt constrained waiting for the sheriff to retire. Like I said, Junior was quick; he didn't wait around for things to happen.

It was a bright and beautiful sunny afternoon, about a year or so after he got back to town, that he pulled up next to Jesse at the park one day, rolled down his window, took his sunglasses off and gave Jesse a long look—or so Jesse told me. He knew the cop was up to something sneaky, and as Jesse was carrying a half pound of smoke, he was a little shaky, but, as was his usual approach, he decided to act like he didn't give a shit.

"What's up Porky?" Jesse called nonchalantly in Junior's direction. He had just finished handing over a dime bag to Little Pete a minute earlier, and as was typical of the little twerp, Pete had been a little too careless in flashing the money he had handed to Jesse in front of the eyes of the world. When he noticed Junior's cruiser had slid silently in behind him, Jesse began to mentally give Pete hell for being stupid as always. No doubt he hated the little shit right then and was thinking he was going to nail that dumb fuck but good if he got busted.

Junior leaned lazily on his arm out the open window. Munching on a fast food burger, he daintily wiped the ketchup off his lips with a napkin between his pudgy fingers and took a long draw on a pink milkshake before answering. "Watch the smart mouth, Hawkins, or I'll run you in for loitering," the cop threatened, only half seriously.

"In your dreams, Pultz," Jesse scoffed and shuffled his feet nervously. Out of the corner of his eye, he saw Pete reach the far edge of the park and start to cross the street headed north. Jesse breathed a sigh of relief and thought maybe he'd just maybe take a meander south, but when he turned to leave, Junior's stopped him with a strident, official voice.

"Hold up a minute, punk."

"What for?" Jesse turned. He knew it; he was busted. Fucking Pete.

"I got something I want to say to you."

"So say it. But make it quick; I gotta be somewhere." Jesse lit up a cigarette.

"Oh, I think you got time for me. Stick around for a few. I want to have a chat."

"What the fuck do you think you and I could possibly have to talk about?"

"Well now Hawkins, I've been doing some thinking and I've got an idea."

"That would be a first."

"You're a real comedian." Junior finished his burger and neatly folded the wrapper, placing it carefully into the bag next to him. Overhead, a cloud slid ponderously in front of the sun, covering the two in shadow. Licking his lips, the cop spoke again, this time lowering his voice and swiveling his head to search in both directions. "Seriously kid, this could make us both a lot of money if you're interested."

"Yeah right, I know what you want." Jesse never did care for authority in any guise. "You want to me work for you?" Spitting on the ground, he continued with a snarl. "I don't know what you are thinking, but I ain't no narc, Pudge"

"Just hear me out, scumbag," the cop retorted angrily. "I don't need any fucking narc."

Jesse kicked at the ground. "Fine. So spit it out, Roy. What do you have in mind?"

Junior slurped on his straw and swallowed before continuing. "You've been selling shitty weed to the kids for a couple years now, huh Jess?"

"Fuck you. You don't have anything on me."

"Well now, I don't know about that." The cop blew his nose. His eyes were red from hay fever, and his took his time putting drops in them before continuing. "I believe your buddy heading up the road probably still has the bag of grass you just sold him. He's a little weasel as you know, and he likes to talk. A lot. I'm sure he'd enjoy chatting with me all about it. And I'm sure I could find some of your other... clientele, who would be happy to assist local law enforcement in keeping the streets safe... for a reward, of course."

The sun emerged again and shone down on the pair. Jesse, sweating and uncomfortable, was on the verge of making a break for it, but instead gave Junior a cool stare and stood his ground. "So what's it to you? Don't you have better things to do than hassle me? I don't know that kid from Adam; he just asked me for a match. Go do something worthwhile, like catch somebody speeding or running a stop sign or something."

The officer grimaced. Junior hated traffic stops and Jesse had struck a nerve. Groaning, he took another sip of milkshake and looked into the distance for a moment like he was remembering those faraway islands and, so disgusted with his current lot, was contemplating going back to breaking up fights and picking up bar girls, before he hiccoughed and regained his composure.

"Listen," he softened his tone smoothly. "I've had my eye on you for a while, kid. You're a tough little shit. You've got grit. I like that. But you're working at such a low level: a little speed, a chunk of hash if you're lucky. That ragweed you're pushing is small time stuff; I've got a better way."

"I'd say you're trying to set me up."

"Now why would I do that?" Junior hissed with disdain. "I put you in jail, what do I get? Sure, maybe some goodwill from the church ladies for putting a troublemaking twerp like you in the hole, but where's the real payoff? Busting a low rent dealer like you is just a waste of time and energy is how I look at it. No, I'd like to... help you out... in exchange for a piece of the action."

Jesse scuffed his shoes, his eyes downward as he thought it over—I can almost see him do it like he always did when he was thinking through some crazy scheme—before he looked up and caught Junior in the sights of his two gun-barrel eyes and responded. "Now why would I ever do that?"

"Come on, Jesse; think about for a bit and maybe even a dumb ass hick like you will figure it out. I'm a good guy to have on your side—the best guy as a matter of fact. And on the other hand, I'm pretty sure you don't want me on the other side against you."

Thoughtfully, Jesse's brain balanced the calculations like a jeweler sizing up a stone and judging the flaws in its facets. "So I got no choice?"

"Of course you do. Everybody's got a choice, Jesse; but I'd think real hard about what I'm offering. And in the end, I believe you'll come to the make the right choice."

Jesse kicked a rock. It skittered across the pavement and rattled across the street. "Okay, I'm listening."

"You ever cook up bathtub speed?"

"What's that? You talking crank?"

"Yeah, or ice, crystal or cat, whatever you want to call it. So you know how to do it?"

"Naw, 'fraid I don't know nothin' about that." Jesse's eyes narrowed and he pondered his options. The clouds covered the sun again. "But I might know somebody who could figure it out." He said later that even then he had me in mind, and I don't for the life of me doubt that he was telling the truth. "Why do you want to know?"

Junior smiled with a snakelike mask of a face, his voice dripping with oily venom. "Check into it and let's talk again... real soon, Jesse."

"I'm sure you realize that I'm still not too sure I should trust you, Junior."

"That's okay, kid. You're right not to. You shouldn't trust anybody. Ever." Taking another sip, the officer shuddered with delight as the cold sweetness slid down his throat. "But Jesse, understand, I know how to work things. Learned it from the old man. We play our cards right, you and me, and we could own this town."

"I'll think about it," Jesse growled sullenly, acting indifferently on the surface, but in his mind he was already calculating the odds, weighing the risks and rewards of the partnership deal being offered to him.

Junior put his shades back on and stared into the distance. His character changed and he spoke in a hollow, distant manner, like a cop again. "In the meantime, move it along, Hawkins. This is a public park, and I might just have to search your backpack for whatever illegal substances you might have on you."

"Right, I get the hint; I'm on my way, Chief." Jesse started down the street quickly, but nonchalantly, not like he was in a hurry or anything, calling back over his shoulder. "Maybe, I'll see you around."

"I'm sure you will," Junior muttered quietly under his breath, then after blowing his nose loudly, he finished off his strawberry shake with an extended slurp. Tires squealing, he pulled out of the parking lot in half-hearted pursuit of stray tourists in minivans who might roll through a stop sign in this, his town.

CHAPTER EIGHT

I lay flat on my face on the oily pavement in the shadow of the garbage can, waiting anxiously for him to pass, Jenny lying still beside me, her body shoved up tight against mine. Holding our breath, fearing the worst, we watched with rapt attention as he moved toward the parked car in the driveway, our muscles tensed tightly, ready to run at any moment.

"Let's go, Nate," she whispered nervously and grabbed my arm.

"Where is he? Can you see him?"

"Over there. He's on his knees looking under the car. I think we can make it."

"No, don't run." I said peering around the can. "Not yet. Wait until he gets around to the other side.

"He won't catch us."

"I don't know about that. He's big... and fast..."

"Don't be a wuss. We can make it."

"Shhhh..."

We watched nervously as he cocked his head. Maybe he heard us? Burying our faces into the ground, we sought to stifle the sound of our breathing with the hard and gritty cement.

He looked the other way. Pulling her long legs in and curling into a ball, Jenny scraped against some loose gravel on the pavement. Hearing the sound, he turned abruptly and moved in our direction, sensing our presence, stalking us, advancing rapidly toward our location, when...

A noisy commotion suddenly burst out in one of the bushes next to the house, and the stalker quickly reversed his steps and pounced into the brush, emerging a moment later pulling a small child out by the scruff of his neck. The boy howled, half in pain, half in laughter, while a small white terrier yapped and leaped around the legs of the pair.

"No fair, Skippy licked my face," the smaller boy protested.

"Now," I whispered, and Jenny and I clambered up and started to run toward the light pole. We were home free.

"Jeneeeeeeeee!"

A sickeningly familiar masculine voice bawled loudly from the distance, cracking the night air and stopping us in our paths, brokenhearted. Figures emerged from all shadows and corners, groaning and complaining.

"Sorry guys, I have to go," was all she said, as always, and turning, she bolted like a long legged colt off to her corral, leaving the neighborhood gang of kids to carry on the game without her.

I watched sadly every time as she sprinted toward her backyard, only to disappear for the night behind the gate, where a red faced man stood in the half-light smoking, his snarling face flush and angry, as it seemed it always was. Seeing me watching, he would give me a wink, and raising his arms as if he held a rifle in his hand, would aim his invisible gun and slowly and patiently shoot the skittering Skippy again and again, chuckling with satisfaction as every imaginary bullet struck its mark. Finally tiring of the game, he would toss his cigarette butt over the fence, turn away and stagger inside, following the girl into the house. It was the usual nightly ritual, but certainly not one that lent any comfort to my melancholic gloamings.

As you can probably tell from the way I begin spitting and cursing whenever I mention him, I never did care much for Jenny's stepfather Al, a stocky, redheaded and usually unemployed truck driver with a lazy eye and a penchant for killing the neighborhood dogs. He didn't actually shoot them—as far as I know poison was his usual method. The aforementioned Skippy ended up dead under our porch not long after, no doubt due to Al's handiwork. As for poor Jen, we never knew what the punishment would be meted out for her not going home immediately, but it must have been pretty bad because she never even considered waiting for a second call. As such, our nightly game of hide and seek was always one that was fraught with anxiety over when the dreadful shout would come that would chill our hearts and take our Jenny away from us, leaving only the growing darkness and emptiness of our lonely eventide.

Yes, I know I said earlier that I had no friends, and that my peers were all ursine, edacious cretins who roamed the streets like barbarians at a slaughter, but this was clearly not entirely the case. As you will see, my memory is not all it once was, for various reasons, and I suspect I have a tendency at times to play loose with the facts. But I can assure you, that I did feel the way I told you I did in 2nd grade when Jesse's shoes arrived and saved the day. And there obviously were other kids in the neighborhood, who played relatively harmless games of tag, capture the flag and hide and seek, even as Jesse and his brothers had games of their own and would have found our tame little games tedious and childish.

But, back to Jenny's family. Most agreed that the red faced brute Al and Jenny's mom made a strange pair. Jenny's mother was devout Jehovah's Witness who used to go door to door distributing *The Watchtower*, while her husband was drinking highballs down at the tavern with Junior's old man—a relationship that allowed him to escape prosecution for his slightly eccentric hobby of dispatching wayward canines for years.

Jenny lived a couple blocks from me and sometimes we used to play in the kiddie pool in her backyard. When Al was off the road, he would pull up a lawn chair, throw a slice of lemon in a tall glass of beer, light up a Winston and pretend to read while he checked out the little girls with his cocked eye as they splashed each other in the pool. Gave me the creeps. Only time he wasn't yelling for Jenny or screaming at us to shut up so he could take a nap was when a coterie of half-naked, underaged nymphs were frolicking around on the slippery slide.

I still shiver a bit when I remember him with his flabby, sunburned body, his auburn-colored hairy arms and legs, wearing nothing but cutoff jeans and flip flops, sitting there reading the sports page over and over, coughing, belching and licking his lips. Even as a kid I hated him, without knowing why, and felt guilty about it because adults were to be respected and were always right, weren't they?

Jenny's mom, on the other hand, was prim and proper, quiet and uptight and rarely, if ever, cracked a smile. Whereas, Al would treat Jenny to ice cream and candy, Jeanne frowned at anything more radical than lemonade or carrot cake. She was always feeding us her damn carrot cake. Thick and dry enough to make you darn near choke. Thank God for that lemonade. She seemed to wear the same gray dress and shoes and no makeup and kept her stringy corn silk hair tied up in a bun most of the time. Jenny always got into arguments with her mom over clothes and her hair, and then after the storm had burst, Al would end up taking the girl in to town for an ice cream sundae and a new dress.

How her folks ever got together to begin with was a matter that baffled just about everyone who knew them. I asked Jenny about it, and she said they had met in church during a time when Al was on the wagon and tending to his personal demons through a sudden, short-lived and, more than likely, court-ordered religious conversion. The love of a good woman was just what he needed to see the light. He, on the other hand, was newly clean cut, semi-sober and employed, and didn't seem to mind that the young widow— Jenny's real dad having choked to death on a piece of steak when she was two—had a cute young daughter in tow. Not unexpectedly, the relationship between the married couple grew volatile, as Al fell from grace almost immediately, but had settled into a strange sort of stasis over the years, whereby Jeanne's slippery slide into her religion was effectively counterbalanced by Al's giving himself the freedom to do just about whatever the hell he wanted. Were they happy? Who is? They got by.

Of course, when Jenny started showing up at school with bruises on her arms and legs, nobody thought much about it. Jenny was a tomboy who ran with the boys and was always getting into scrapes. When we asked her about it she'd just say, "Oh, I tripped jump roping and fell," or something along those lines, and nobody really paid any attention. Child rearing was a personal matter, best left behind closed doors in those golden times.

Must have been that this all happened before teachers were told to pay attention to that kind of thing, or they were just pretty clueless or afraid to say anything because none of them ever let on that they noticed. My Jenny took to wearing jeans and long sleeves instead of dresses and shorts. She still seemed happy enough, but it was about this time she started getting moodier and distant, even with me. She no longer wrestled with the boys on the playground during recess, but instead sat in a swing, swaying back and forth by herself, watching the distance as if she could see a squall line approaching just beyond the edge of the curve of the earth. Most depressing of all, she even quit joining us for our nightly hide and seek ritual, leaving us newly-bonerized boys just standing there in the street, staring longingly at the light on behind the curtains in her house, hoping to catch her peeking out at us, so we could wave and holler at her to get her skinny ass out there to join the fun. Frankly, the game wasn't the same without her and after a few weeks we all drifted apart and quit our nightly ventures for other pursuits. As you will see.

She started developing quickly around that time and we all looked on in amazement as she grew into a young woman before our eyes. But when we saw her at the ice cream parlor or the carnival with Al—her mama shunned such events—she would quickly look away and pretend she hadn't seen us. Those were times I dread to recall—times when it felt as if an icicle was being shoved slowly through my heart. I am ashamed to admit that I cried myself to sleep beneath my blankets; perhaps it was my dread of abandonment resulting from my mother's hasty flight from our north woods Sodom and Gomorrah (no pillar of salt, she) raising its unattractive head and merging with my fears of losing my dear friend, girl, friend. As if in a fever dream, I took to sneaking out while my dad slept it off at a girlfriend's house, or on the couch or bathroom floor, and spent hours pacing back and forth past her house late at night, hoping for just a glimpse of those soft, brown velvet eyes again.

My heart overflowed with sorrow and loneliness, like a bursting dam overrun by love and longing. I could take it no longer.

Once in the dark of night, Inflamed with love and wanting, I arose...

And softly opened the gate and snuck into her yard... again, and walked past the tree where I once sat and watched an angel bathing. Al's truck was parked outside, but the lights were out. Driven by mad urges, demons, lusts, reverence, who knows... I took the chance and broke off a small branch from the tree and brushed it gently against her window until she finally opened it.

"Nate?" she whispered, peering into the dark.

"Yeah Jenny, it's me."

"What do you want?"

"I—" I started, my voice cracking.

"Shhh... my stepfather will hear you."

"I wondered if... well, if you maybe wanted to go for a walk down to the river like we used to?"

A pause. "I don't know. I really shouldn't..."

"Come on, Jen," I pleaded, displaying a face that must have radiated with ultra-toxic levels of despair and desperation. "I haven't even seen you in so long. It'll be fun."

"Alright," she said after a moment, perhaps sensing I was just off-kilter enough to do something utterly random and unpleasant, like wake up Al with a display of loud weeping and gnashing of teeth, and so she closed the window. A few eternal minutes later she whooshed noiselessly out the back door and we made our way, shivering some in the frosty air, in silence, with heads down and chattering teeth, down the hilly street to the empty park, where we skipped along the wooden boardwalk and stepped with soaked tennis shoes squishing noisily across a damp grassy field to a spray paint emblazoned concave hollow under the spans of the gray Paint River bridge, a place we used as a hideout of sorts when transients or older kids making out or partying weren't around.

It was empty, and we sat together, battered and battened down, partially concealed from the sharp wind which rushed along the riverbank slitting the air like a steel blade through a soft wrist, huddled up on the cold stone riverbank beneath the painted cartoon image of a smiling mushroom, with the words *Get High!* splattered in fat, childish letters that dripped from the wall in black uneven script, the names and initials of lovers and persons long forgotten swathed across the curving arch bent high above and behind us in swirling red and black and blue and yellow gunk, pronouncing a message of life and love and joy and death in a kaleidoscopic galaxy of aerosol-inflicted layers of shapes and letters and hieroglyphics, fields and sections of solid color spattered and strewn on the gray concrete bulwark as if to mark, confront and assail this unnatural cement and steel affront to the timeless river like a taunt from the wall of an Altamira cave, freezing for those who dare to venture below a precious moment of rebellion and the last remnants of youth in time until the years or the seasons, the chiseling away of entropy or the efforts of solid citizenry and moral certainty would wipe it away, listening to the water trickle by and the echo of the sound of the occasional car or truck overhead, passing through or getting out, escaping this tattered attempt at a town in haste, wheels on the road rumbling and booming reverberantly amidst the bowing incurvation of arches and spandrels and across the heavy air of the stone enclosure, skipping, pirouetting lightly on downstream, carried rippling over and on the water's surface with the rushing, bittersweet laughing tinkling of the silty prehistoric current.

The lights from the town at the water's far edge and the passing vehicles overhead flickered dully with an unhealthy yellow, red and white luminosity, illuminating our faces with a pallid pinkish hue—as if we sat alone together and abandoned, in the heart of the forest of our darkest wood, prophesying our fates in the sparks and cooling ashes deep within the dying embers of the last fire of the season.

"So what did you want, Nate?" she asked as she fiddled with the drawstrings of her parka.

"I dunno. I guess I just wanted to talk. You know, like we used to. "

"So talk," she said and looked away in the direction of the cold and remote stars.

"We just... well, we miss you... I miss you. Hide and seek just isn't the same—"

"Hide and seek is a kid's game," she snapped moodily.

"You used to have fun—"

"That was then... in case you haven't noticed I'm not a kid anymore like you." That hurt.

"I just... just... I'm worried about you."

"No need. I'm fine," but her lip trembled.

"Jenny, I..." I tried to touch her arm, but she flinched and moved away.

"Don't touch me, Nate."

"What's wrong, Jenny?"

"You really want to know?"

"Yes."

"You can't tell anyone, Nate. You have to promise," she spoke softly, her eyes moist as the evening dew.

"I promise."

She slowly pulled her sweatshirt and pajama top off, revealing her bra and bare skin. Purple marks stretched across her back, red welts rising in eruptions on the skin. I gasped.

"Who did this to you, Jenny?"

Sobbing slightly, she painfully worked the sweatshirt back over her head, covering her scarred body again.

"Jenny, if that creep stepfather of yours has—" my voice rose with fear and anger.

"Shhhhh."

"You have to tell somebody—"

"I can't..."

"That dog killing pervert son of a bitch—"

"Nate—"

"We have to tell the police."

"The dog killing pervert's best friend is the Sheriff, remember?"

"We have to find someone. The FBI..."

"You don't understand."

"What is there to understand? He has to be stopped. First Skippy and the other dogs and now he's hurting you—"

"No."

"What do you mean, no?"

"You don't understand, Nate."

"You have to tell someone. We have to turn that bastard in to someone and get you out of there."

"It isn't what you think, Nate."

"What do you mean, Jen?"

"I can handle Al," she stated flatly with a glint in her eyes. "In fact, pretty soon I don't think I'm ever going to have any trouble from him ever again..."

"So—"

"It's my mom, Nate," she choked. "She sees me changing and says I'm wicked. She uses coat hangers to beat me. To beat the Jezebel spirit out of me, she says. She only does it when Al's on the road or after he passes out at night. He stops her if he's awake. My own mom, Nate, can you believe it?"

The looming giants of authority: police, teachers, the President, Superman and God himself stood and watched wordlessly and without the slightest hint of intervention as two children shivered against the wind in the lonely shelter beneath the concrete arch.

CHAPTER NINE

"**D**id you get the *gingerbread*?" Jesse asked harshly, his eyes flashing sharply as he looked up from the scratched up old desk we had rescued from a dumpster and placed in his shed, which he now called his office.

"Yeah," I replied sullenly and dropped into a chair in front of him.

"Any trouble with the witch?"

"Naw."

This was the first time we found ourselves in the middleman business. We had been cooking the stuff for several months now, but Junior warned us that the Feds might get called in if we kept blowing things up and leaving our trash around to be discovered. So we found ourselves a friend of a friend up in Canada who took care of the production end of it, and I got selected to make the pickup over on the shores of the state forest over near Sault Ste Marie.

The job was easy as walking the dog, or cat if you like— "cat" being the term used for meth around here in those days, although we preferred to use the childish nursery rhyme term gingerbread for our product. We giggled lots over that. On this trip, like the others, I just followed the bread crumb trail to the gingerbread house—a secluded harbor where a boat arrived and traded me a cooler for a bundle of cash—I don't know how much and I don't care—money never meant anything to me. Drove four and a half hours through a whole lot of nothing—trees and farms—only to sit for an hour at a windy beach and then turn around and drive home all night, obeying the speed limit of course. Was a bit boring most of the time with just a few nerve wracking minutes until the hard-looking, silent Canucks finished counting up the cash, handed the goods over and took their ferry home. Everything went pretty smooth and easy and I was pretty pleased with myself for not tripping over my shoelace and making a mess of the job.

"Did you check it out? How's the quality?" he snapped,

squinting up at me.

"Better than our usual." I pulled the package from the cooler and threw it on the desk.

I had to test a bit of it, of course. Just to keep myself awake. Good stuff, pure and potent. I could see why people liked the buzz. I could see myself as a baseball star or great writer, a gangster, or.... the world's greatest preacher—maybe the messiah himself. When I took a hit everything changed for me and I became invincible. That was its charm; that was its danger.

Switching on a black light lamp, he greedily tore open the wrapper. Holding a crystallized rock sample under the phosphorous glow, Jesse smiled hard, nearly splitting his face with his black light jack-o-lantern grin, while he cackled like the gingerbread house witch stirring the pot with anticipatory pleasure.

"Nice, this is the shit, baby! We can cut it up real nice with some MSM and get it down to the Spanish Monarchs in Green Bay by Tuesday if you are up for it."

"Let me think about it," I said. I still felt jittery and full of energy. The buzz wasn't winding down a bit even after the long drive home and I had plenty to do at home. But I was worried. "So what do you think Junior's going to say about this?"

"Colonel Blimp ain't gonna know nothing. This is strictly our deal," Jesse huffed.

"You don't think he's going to hear about it?"

"He probably will. So what?"

"He'll want a cut, Jess."

"What he wants and what he gets are two different things. He can't prove anything."

Sighing, I argued, my voice rising. "We're better off bringing him in on it. He's too dangerous to screw with. He can make it tough for us."

"Fuck him!" Jesse slammed his fist on the table and glared at me.

"Whatever. It's your call. I gotta do my laundry." I waved my hand and turned to go.

"Hey Nate—stop!" Jesse's voice commanded

I paused at the door, a chill rising up my spine. I turned and saw him looking at me kind of sideways, his eyes fixed on my face,

"Just want to thank you for keeping an eye on Jenny," Jesse said, mumbling. "Jared said he saw your car over at our place the other night when I was out of town. Nice to know she ain't whorin' around. I appreciate you keeping her occupied. She has a tendency to get... independent at times."

He leaned over and reached into a drawer, pulled something out and tossed it at me: a baggie with a rock of crack in it aimed at my face. I reached up and snatched it out the air.

"Give her a little of this when she needs it," he snarled. "Don't give her the whole thing or she'd use it all up in one night." Chuckling to himself, he muttered. "Don't ever say let it be said that I didn't give her anything."

Dismissing me with one last sour glance, Jesse turned his attention to the dope at hand. Rumpelstiltskin-like, he bent his wiry frame over the table and attentively tended to his treasure, his form melting into his black-lit realm, as, seething, I retreated back out to my car, stuffing the baggie into my pants pocket as I went.

CHAPTER TEN

We skipped high school that day and a bunch of us knuckleheads headed out into the woods, as always with the valiant and intrepid Sir Jesse leading the charge.

The caravan of rusty pickups and muscle cars cruised up north, roaring, racing, passing each other, screaming and throwing beer cans at each other out the windows, before eventually turning off on a rutted dirt road that led us, clanking, rattling and spewing up dust, to an abandoned quarry, where some deep water, perfect for swimming and diving awaited us. While Jenny and the other girls scampered, tittering gaily, behind a rickety wooden building to change, the guys built a campfire, hauled the coolers into a semicircle, lugged over the boom box and began to bellow and holler like a circle of chimps. We were young and free and itching to go wild.

"Told you I could find this place," Jesse said with a pleased smirk. "My brothers brought me up here to party one time. And you guys wanted to drive all the way to the Porkies." Actually I had been the one to navigate, but humbly kept my silence.

"Yeah, yeah—so you were right—it's a pretty cool place. What do you want a medal or something?" Hal Turner growled, his acne-inflamed face scowling as he cracked open a beer.

"Pretty creepy," Tommy Berglund offered while looking around at the empty structures. "You think maybe it's haunted?"

"There ain't no such thing as ghosts, right Nate?" Jesse queried. Despite the frivolity of the proceedings, I kept my distance, hovering nervously around the periphery, not being a fan of football star jerk Turner and his heavy fisted ilk.

"Well, there's a lot of stories out there," I said cautiously, "but nobody's ever come up with any actual verifiable scientific evidence for paranormal phenomena—"

"Fuck you, Brainiac, my cousin saw my grandmother's ghost fly out of the fireplace up at our cabin on Lake Superior," Hal raged.

"You're not calling him a liar, are you?" He spat on the ground and glared threateningly. I said nothing.

"Don't know why we have to put up with your little shadow, Hawkins," he muttered darkly. "If it was up to me I'd kick his smart ass but good."

"Leave the kid alone. He's got more brains than all the rest of us combined," Jesse intervened, coming to my rescue as always. I was tall, getting taller by the day, but skinny as a fir tree, and Hal had about a hundred pounds of muscle advantage and a rosaceatic, cratered and excrescent face that, Medusa-like, could nearly kill a person just by looking at you.

"Bet you I could knock his brains out in about two seconds flat," the furuncled lummox grumbled nastily.

"You'd be swallowing your own nuts in one second if you ever try, pal," Jesse said. He smiled as he spoke, but his fearless eyes glinted with the promise of unrelenting vengeance, pain and blood feud. "I guarantee it." And he did.

The two eyed each other like two tigers sizing each other up, until Hal finally blinked and, angrily grabbing another beer from the cooler, rapidly changed the subject to sports. Last I heard of Hal, he was an insurance salesman in DePere and had been married three or four times. Good for him. A real swell guy.

To break the tension, Tommy belched loudly and goofy Rolf Malinowski crushed a can on his head and everyone laughed and things went back to the normal pecking order of things. Then the girls came back, looking good, real good, in their bikini tops and shredded cutoffs.

"Hey Darlin'!" Jesse said and whistled his approval.

Launching up like a hormone powered V-2 rocket, Hal snatched his tiny girlfriend into his arms and raced toward the water-filled quarry with the girl kicking and squealing in mock terror. The other girls ran screaming toward the water with Rolf and Tommy in pursuit, while Jenny and Jesse and I remained at the campfire.

"Don't you want to swim?" I asked Jenny, but she just shook her head.

"Not really."

"Not with those jerks anyway," Jesse motioned toward the sound of splashing and shrieking: they sounded like six-year-olds at a pool party. "I'm sorry I brought them along. They're ruining my buzz."

I switched on the boom box and the thump of pounding rock music filled the air. Jesse relaxed, pulled out a joint and lit it. I looked around, embarrassed to find myself the odd man out again, and hoping Jesse and Jenny wouldn't sneak back off to the car to make out too soon, leaving me alone to be used and abused by the heathens. I had some books with me, including my Bible, which I had just started carrying with me, so I hastily scanned the region for a spot in the shade to sit and read.

"Sorry about that creep hassling you, Preacher," Jesse said. "Those clowns can't even read off their cereal box without stuttering and they want to give you shit? Don't worry; I'll keep them off you. But you know you gotta stand up for yourself sometimes. I can't always be watching your back."

"Preacher?" Jenny asked.

I blushed.

"Nate's been reading the Bible lately, along with his usual textbooks, novels and assorted encyclopedia sets. Says he's thinking about taking the veil or something."

"You found religion, Nate?" she gently teased. "Are you born again?"

"Bored again most likely," sneered Jesse.

"Yeah well..." I started. "There's some interesting stuff in there. Lots of wars and battles and blood and curses and plagues and sin and murder and begetting..."

"Huh?" Jesse asked, his interest piqued.

"Sex, dummy," she chuckled.

"Wow, really? Maybe I should check it out," Jesse laughed. "Naw, I'll stick to Spiderman comics. That Heaven and Hell stuff will warp your brain, Preacher."

"Quit calling me that; I'm not a preacher."

"His daddy was a teacher, Natey is a preacher," Jesse mocked, half singing. "Hey Darlin', I made a rhyme."

"Leave him alone, I think it's nice." Jenny defended me.

"Shoot, it is nice. Nate's such a nice guy and all and you know where that leads." Jesse 's taunts stung, but he grinned his crooked smile and passed the joint, and in the end, as usual, all was forgiven.

"Tell Jen about the apostles, Preach—that's kind of cool." Jesse said squinting into the sun and blowing a smoke ring.

"What does he mean?" Jenny asked.

"Oh, he's talking about how the apostles ended up — most of them got killed pretty bad in the end. Stephen and Matthias were stoned to death—"

"Not a bad way to go as long as you're smoking good shit," leered Jesse.

"Peter, Andrew, James and Simon were crucified. Some of the others had their heads cut off or were burned alive—"

"Ain't that the coolest! Some were stabbed and their eyes gouged out—" Jesse chortled with excitement.

"Yuck! That's just gross," Jenny said and grabbed my arm. "Better watch yourself, Nate or you'll end up like that."

"That's why I love this dude; he just knows the weirdest stuff. Anyway, one of the main reasons I brought you along, Preach," Jesse continued, as the sun beat down warm and we started feeling a nice buzz coming on, "was that I know you read a lot of history stuff and I was wondering if there's any gold up here?"

I looked around thoughtfully. "Well yeah, there could be. I know they used to mine for copper and iron up here, and I think a bit of silver and gold too."

"Copper's worth something, ain't it?" Jesse asked.

"Well yeah. Price goes up and down, but usually you can get something for it at a scrap yard I think."

"Like selling aluminum cans for beer money? That's small change. Gold would be better. What would you need to find the stuff: shovels and pick axes...?

"Metal detector, maybe," I suggested.

"Awesome," he said grinning widely. "You know where to get one?"

"I suppose I could check into it. I think they sell them in the back of the Spiderman comics."

Jenny laughed, shining like a sunbeam. We all laughed, but Jenny... she was laughter itself incarnate.

"Didn't you tell me one time, when we jumping trains, about a train robbery?"

I sat back thoughtfully and tried to remember, "Yeah, there was a train robbery happened up here somewhere back in the day. Around the turn of century, I think. They never did find the loot. I told you the whole story."

"Yeah, yeah, I remember a bit about that and have been thinking we should get cranking and find that shit. See Jenny, I told you I'm gonna be rich. Me and Preacher Nate here are going to find some buried treasure, and we'll get the hell out of Crystal Falls and take you to Paris or France on our private yacht."

"Paris is in France," I corrected.

"Thanks for that bit of information. That's why I need you around, bud; to keep me from getting lost. Speaking of which—watch this Jenny—which way is north, Preach—Nate?"

I shook my head, annoyed, and pointed.

Jesse howled. "You see that! I don't know how he does it. He always knows the direction. How do you do it?"

"I've told you before. Where's the sun?"

"Over there."

"So where should it be this time of day?"

"I don't get it. It's where it is."

"Yeah, what's the deal?" Jenny added.

"Well if the sun is down there and it's two in the afternoon," I said pointing, "then that direction has to be north, understand?"

"No," said Jenny pouting.

"Crazy isn't it?" Jesse grinned. "Dude always knows where he is. He can't ever get lost."

"That isn't true, Jesse. I get lost plenty."

"What happens when the sun goes behind the clouds?" Jenny interjected.

"Perfect example, or in thick woods with lots of trees where you can't see the sun."

"Or at night?" she asked with smirk.

"Well, then you've got the North Star. Unless the clouds are in the way, in which case—"

"Why don't you just use a compass?" asked Jenny.

"They don't always work properly around here because of all the iron in the ground," I replied.

"Yeah, that's crazy, ain't it? Love it when some stupid tourist gets lost because his compass went haywire," Jesse jumped into the conversation, jealous of the attention I was getting from Jenny.

"You just have to take the right path. Did you ever hear that Robert Frost poem? *Two roads converged in a yellow wood, And sorry I could not travel both—*"

"Who cares," Jesse cut me off. "Why don't you quit reading all that sissy, fruity stuff and get on the stick finding out where our missing gold is?"

"Well, I was going to tell you," I countered, reddening "that they found a three-thousand-pound copper boulder up north years ago. Scammed it from the Indians, who considered it sacred. It's in the Smithsonian now."

"No shit? But that's just copper. I want gold. I can see myself strolling into town with a gold nugget the size of a watermelon. Put on the biggest party that loser town of ours ever saw. Bet I'd get some respect from the idiots then."

"But that train robbery wouldn't have had stuff like that, Jesse. I said loot, remember? It was a train robbery, so probably was cash, maybe some gold and silver coins, but probably bills, old bills."

"Whatever, gold, silver, money... I don't care, just get that egg-headed brain of yours working on something worthwhile for a change it and figure out where it is, okay?" he commanded, and dismissing me, turned his attention to Jenny, ready to get busy.

"Okay okay," I said, feeling I had been assigned my duties and given leave to depart. "I'll check into it."

"We got to treat our sweetheart with style, don't we, Darlin'?"

Jenny and I both blushed as Jesse grabbed her around the waist and gave her a big sloppy kiss. I looked away. Down at the water, the boys and girls squealed.

"What a bunch of idiots splashing each other and playing grab ass," Jesse growled. "Those turds don't know what real fun is. We, on the other hand... " He reached into his backpack and produced a handful of M80 firecrackers from within.

"No way," Jenny said with a grin.

"Way. The Amazing Jesseroo, his lovely assistant Jennifer and the always entertaining Preacher Nate are about to give our unsuspecting friends over there a little surprise to remember."

When he dropped the M80s down the mine shaft a few minutes later, the reverberant blast frightened our victims nearly to death, almost causing Hal Turner to shit his pants, while we screamed in jubilation, our bodies detonated in tremors of laughter. The story of Jesse's prank passed freely from person to person like a river rushing over smooth stones, ultimately helping to cement the legend of, and at the same time erect the community's statue to, the youngest Hawkins boy as being, without a doubt, the craziest son of a bitch in the entire county.

CHAPTER ELEVEN

"Hey there, Nate." My father didn't look up from the puzzle he was putting together as I came in the back door and entered the living room from the kitchen. It was dark inside the room and it took a moment for my eyes to adjust. The shades were drawn, only allowing a thin stream of sunlight to course through a haze of dust motes, whirling and flickering, which were driven into vibrancy by a fan rotating noisily in the corner. The room still looked the same, although the disrepair grew with every visit, the result of entropy turning my childhood home into dust before my eyes, not unlike my life itself.

At the nearest end of the room, Dad bent forward intently, perched like a gargoyle on the cusp of his fading, faux leather recliner, leering with focused gaze at the scene below. On the side opposite the window, a patched, blue and tan twill couch cantilevered, teetering precariously, held aloft on one end by a tower of bricks. Along the cobwebbed wall above, an empty gun rack and mouldering deer head, inexplicably minus half its horns, hung sadly. Interspersed on the walls were several framed and faded Norman Rockwell prints featuring scenes of family life involving apple pies and turkey dinners, jolly mothers and fathers and grandparents, and smiling children and policemen with lollipops and other such amusing fantasies which I found so alien and exotic when I was young, dangling crookedly on the castaneous, paneled walls. The haphazard arrangement next led the offended eye to a heavy wooden bookcase, whose appearance nearly groaned aloud like a dying mule, as if it would collapse at any moment under the weight of stacks of dusty books and magazines it was forced to carry.

As usual a newer model television set, enthroned at the altar near the front door, chattered and harangued loudly, producing a constant stream of bile nearly as effective as white noise for only half the cost (if you act now). As I moved closer and peered over the top of his inclined cranium and slouching shoulders, parting the reddish sea of strands on my father's thinning pate, I discovered my adventurous father was deeply submerged in what appeared to be a sun-drenched, tropical ocean scene, and, judging from the looks of it, had gotten himself tangled up in the seaweed.

"Hi Dad," I said. "How'd you know it was me?"

"It's Sunday isn't it? Who else would it be?"

I could think of a few of his floozies, but as far as I knew he wasn't seeing anyone at the moment, so he had me there. He tried a piece in all four directions, but couldn't force it into place.

"Damn."

"How you doing, Dad?"

"Not bad. Could be worse." His eyes never left the pieces on the card table in front of him. "You?"

"Well, I—"

"There are some TV dinners in the freezer if you want one. I'll have the turkey, and get me a soda pop. There's bologna and cheese if you want a sandwich instead."

I went back into the kitchen and cooked up his meal in the microwave. I wasn't hungry but got myself a glass of tap water out of the tap and threw in a couple ice cubes.

He reluctantly slid the ocean to one side, the curved shape of the diving bell giving him one last moment of ponder, and cleared a space for the plastic tray on the coffee table in front of his recliner. I laid down his meal and can of soda on the TV tray in front of his recliner. Sniffing the food with a grunt, he stirred the gravy around over his potatoes and corn with a noticeably trembling hand. Blowing on it first through his ill-fitting dentures to cool it down, he greedily shoveled a fork full of corn kernels into his mouth.

"See Stewie Roberts had another good game Friday," he said through the mouthful. "Team lost though."

"Yeah, I saw that."

"Don't know why they can't beat those jokers from Iron River. They aren't any more talented. I blame the coach. He doesn't handle that pitching staff right."

"Nope, never could." I sat down on the couch.

"When I was assistant coach, I took down all the statistics on all the pitches that got thrown during the year so when we got to tournament time we were prepared and knew how to use our pitchers."

"Uh huh."

"Almost beat Iron River that year."

"Yup, almost did."

He had helped the baseball coach as an unofficial assistant for one season until a parent complained that he was showing up drunk for the games, so they banned him. I didn't remember him coaching as it was before my time, but I had heard the story, sans the dismissal part, often. Very often.

"You know that Roberts boy?"

"Nope, don't know him."

"You went to school with his brother, didn't you?"

"Leroy. He was a couple years older than me. Didn't know him either."

I sipped my water. Dad took a bite and chewed it slowly, his attention still fixated on the watery panorama before him. A friendly mermaid wearing a crown waved from the sandy sea bottom.

He sighed and I tensed. It was coming. The same familiar subject. Again.

"Don't know why you never played baseball in high school? You could hit the ball and could run a bit too. You had some ability; you just never worked at it."

Here we go again. "Dunno, Dad. It never really was my thing." Another familiar topic. I had learned to muffle my anger even as he mulled over his disappointment of me out loud again and again and... "I was pretty slow too. A little too gangly, I guess."

"Yeah," he said absently. "That's too bad. You could hit the ball alright. No power of course, but a good eye at the plate. Your coordination wasn't the best... but it just takes work. You have to focus and work at what you want and never stop until you get it. Ah!" Triumphantly, he reached over and completed a section of green sea grass and looked up finally.

"Are you okay? You don't look so good," he asked with some concern.

"Well—"

"You have to take care of yourself, son. Eat right and get some exercise. Get a haircut. You look shaggy. Are you getting enough exercise?"

"Probably not."

"You're pale. You need to get some sun. You always were more of a bookworm. Took more after me than your mom, I guess. Of course, I liked to play ball too. I was a hell of a catcher and I played some right field when the teachers had that softball team. I saved the day that time... I made the catch... we almost beat the... we should have won the game... the ump... that was a terrible call, a terrible call..."

A story I'd heard a thousand times before. I listened silently, but my mind wandered in and out. There was a layer of dust on the shelves that I swear was three inches thick. There had been dust on the shelves as long as I could remember. *What would it take to just run a rag over it once in a while?* The old man rambled on for a time, his mind deep in his memories. He paused and cracked open the can of diet cola and took a sip before continuing. I knew what was coming next and braced myself.

"Remember when you and I used to play catch? Back when you were a boy. Then you missed that one and..." He frowned and waved his hand as if to return the unwanted memory to its distant hiding place.

He's right... sort of. We did play catch a couple times, but once when I was nine or ten he was drunk and hit me in the face with a wild throw and I had to go to the hospital with a black eye and a cracked cheekbone. We didn't play again after that.

He paused until the memory faded away and then the next reel caught on the sprocket and the old black and white film of his memory sputtered and began again.

"Your Granddad was a boxer you know?" I did. "And a fisherman before..." A pause and then another reel change. "Yes, like I said. Sports and exercise and eating right—that's the key. That and... beets. I read a study the other day that says beets are the new wonder food. That red color means it's full of Vitamin-C. Prevents cancer they say. Vitamins and fiber and stay off the booze and cigarettes. Don't be like me, kid. You need to take better care of yourself Nate, you really do."

Here I was pretty confident the conversation would continue down the usual pathway without much variation and, like the magic show clairvoyant who knows where all the cards are, I knew where it would lead.

"Are you working?" he asked.

"Here and there." Sure enough. I'm good.

"Always good to have a job. Idle hands are the devil's hands. I always had a job, all my life, until..."

He hadn't had a real job in a decade. He never would again. Disability for the treatment of alcoholism, school district retirement, social security—his house was paid for. He was screw-up, but he had it made and didn't even know it. He may have been considered a loser around town, but he didn't have to worry about where his next paycheck was coming from.

"You are such a smart kid. I just don't get it. I don't know why you quit school." His rant began to pick up speed. And intensity.

Why do I play this game? "I didn't quit—they threw me out, remember?" That was just being nasty, but he didn't notice. He continued headlong down his one track.

"You had it made. You could've had a career. An accountant or maybe a pharmacist or a teacher—"

"Like you?" I was losing it. Have to pull it back in. *Roll all the anger into a ball. Turn the anger into a pure white dove. Release the dove into the open blue sky. Watch your anger mount into the air and flutter away, forever...*

"You had brains like me..."

I had tuned him out years ago, but it still annoyed me to have to play my part in this charade masquerading as a relationship.

"You could've been a lawyer or a professor—"

"Or a preacher?" That threw him momentarily.

"I suppose... Not much money in that though."

"What about helping people?" That shut him up. He chewed his food thoughtfully, his feelings obviously hurt by my disrespect. Perhaps, I ventured to imagine, some tinges of guilt at being a failure as a parent were gnawing at him from the depths of his delusions.

"Don't worry, I'm making some decent bread," I added helpfully.

"Doing what?"

"I guess you'd say I'm an entrepreneur."

"That's a tough way to make it these days. No insurance, 401-K—"

"I'll mention that to the boss," I said sarcastically.

"Thought you didn't have a boss?"

"Everybody's got a boss."

"Yeah, I suppose so. Just remember, the customer is always right. Well as long as you're keeping busy... You still living over by the cemetery? Your car running okay? You got a girlfriend?"

"No... I mean, I am still living by the cemetery, the car is running fine and no, I don't have a girlfriend—"

"Too bad. What ever happened to that little cutie, Janice something...?"

"Jenny Ruthven?" I sighed.

"Was that her name, Ginny? You always liked her, didn't you? She still with that Hawkins fellow? Never could figure what she saw in him. Nothing but trouble that one... his whole family was nothing but trouble... What's he up to these days? You ever see him?"

"Yeah, I see him, and yeah, Jenny's still with him. They're around." I didn't elaborate further.

He took another bite of turkey and mashed potatoes and wiped his lips with a paper napkin before motioning with his plastic fork toward the front window. "Well, as long as you're here. You see that tree out front?" he asked.

I looked out the window. "Which one?"

"The one with the branch hanging over the fence. Over the sidewalk."

Behind me, reflected in the glass, I watched as he pulled a bottle of whiskey from beside his chair and poured it into his diet soda.

"You want me to trim it?" I waited to turn around until the bottle had been hurriedly replaced in its hiding spot. No need to hide it, Dad, I smelled it as soon as I walked in. Like always.

"If you could, Nate, I'd appreciate it."

I stood up and went to the garage and found a rusty hand saw and used it to cut the branch back a bit. I checked the yard. The lawn could use mowing, but wasn't too bad yet. Give it a few days. Didn't look like rain anyway, better to keep it long and not let it get scorched.

When I returned, the food was finished off and the TV was still on, but now at a volume level that could be used to peel paint in industrial applications. I washed my hands and face in the kitchen sink and wiped the sweat off with a dish towel.

"You get that branch for me?" he shouted as I came back into the living room.

"Yeah. You need anything else?" I responded, struggling to make myself heard over a marching band selling cars to the beat of a hideous Sousa march on the TV.

"Nope. Aha!" He finished the chest of sunken treasure with a flourish. "You going to stay a bit?" he asked, not looking up. "The Brewers will be on in a few."

"I should probably get going. I've got some things I should get at."

"The lawn—?"

"Yeah, I'll come by in the next couple days. Or maybe next Sunday. It doesn't look too bad yet."

"I'll do it myself. You always put off for tomorrow what you should do today!" he snapped angrily, but the threat was empty. He started to rise from his chair, but seeing a pattern, sat back down and placed a piece of the fin on the dolphin swimming happily beside the mermaid queen.

I picked up his dinner tray and threw it in the garbage.

"Love you, Dad," I said softly beneath the jingle barrage and headed for the exit.

"Don't forget the lawn," he called as the screen door slammed behind me.

CHAPTER TWELVE

Everybody started calling me the Preacher officially because, when I was a senior in high school—at the height—or more accurately, depths—of my sinfulness (or so I thought at the time), I nearly overdosed on a combination of pills and alcohol, and somehow, out of this event, I found the Lord. I'd been reading the Bible for a few years by then and Jesse's nickname told hold for good after I had my conversion experience.

We'd been out in the lumberyard whooping it up and I guess I overdid it some. Jesse said I was barely breathing, but he and his brothers dragged me to Jenny's house, and in between Jesse slapping me silly, she managed to pour enough coffee down me to bring me back to life.

When I awoke to her beautiful face looking down at me from above with loving concern, I felt as if I had received a shocking revelation, as if the Lord God had spoken directly to me, although I'll be damned if I remembered what she said. I had a vague feeling that I had been touched by grace, and I knew then that I needed to diverge from my path of temptation. I stopped drinking stone cold, quit drugs and partying and began attending church regularly, seeking to straighten out my life.

I'd been reading my Bible off and on for a couple years, but after my conversion, I started studying it pretty steadily. I told Jesse that I didn't care much for the path I was going down and needed to take a break, but he just laughed and said I'd be back.

I didn't go back to the Catholic church I had attended two or three times as a young child with my father, but instead found myself sitting in the back at the Lutheran church. I can't really say that I was welcomed with open arms: the congregation as a whole eyed me suspiciously, and any of the few kids my own age, especially the girls—knowing my wayward reputation—avoided me as much as they could. Eventually, some of the older ladies took a chance on the sad puppy-dog-faced loser in the back row and gave me a bit of much needed mothering, and I actually put a few pounds on my bones with all the cookies and coffee cakes they fed me.

The shepherd of the flock, Pastor Carlsson, was a small-boned, pale, middle-aged man with beady blue eyes and a thinning thatch of blond hair. I made him nervous, especially when I queried him on some of the finer points of religious dogma. He was used to telling his congregation how it was and having them nod their heads, open their hymnals and, after a good song and prayer routine, they would all go home feeling emotionally satiated for another week. My questions then, regarding important issues like: where did Cain and Abel get their wives? Or do unbaptized babies who die go to Hell? And why does God allow sin and violence in the world? all delivered with earnest innocence and youthful energy, noticeably disturbed him, causing him to recede quickly away upon viewing my imminent approach.

In turn, my embarrassing confession, in which I revealed that I had considered becoming a pastor myself, caused the frail fellow's cheeks to redden brightly, while inducing in him a convulsive fit of coughing that took a cup and a half of water to quell. Lisping slightly through lips that, combined with his stony eyes, made him resemble a landed trout, he sat behind his oaken desk in his austere office, and patiently explained that my years in the wilderness had put me at a disadvantage with regards to being accepted as pastor in the Lutheran faith. He added that youths of their faith are baptized and instructed in the church doctrine through years of catechism classes staring at an early age, and that it was unrealistic to expect that I could catch up so quickly.

"Are you saying I can't be a pastor?" I asked, hurt.

He sighed and shifted nervously behind the desk. "As you are a lapsed Catholic, Nathan, you can't be expected to immediately understand the complexities of the true, original Protestant faith. You see, as I think we have discussed before, we Lutherans believe that God himself has predestined us all into our roles here on earth and we must accept them. Your path may not coincide with that of the churchly pursuits, but your life is no doubt unfolding as it was been preordained. You must accept that you are a sinner, my son. We are all sinners. But the elect—those who have accepted Jesus

Christ as their savior—are the only ones who will ascend into heaven. Tell me son, have you accepted Jesus Christ as your savior yet?"

"I'm... I'm not sure," I stammered. "I mean, I admire his teachings about the meek and sharing the loaves and fishes with the less fortunate... But if I did, would that make me 'elect'?"

"Naturally, conversion is permitted upon sincere repentance for sins—"

"In that case, I can change—"

"Yes, I am sure you feel that you can," he purred. "However, Nate, as I explained in our previous discussion, it is the belief of our church that all of humanity exists in a state of... total depravity, without any free will until spiritual regeneration occurs. I am convinced that your intentions may be serious and sincere in your own mind, and that you are surely a... well-intentioned young man at heart, but your state of spirituality at the current moment may be somewhat... stunted."

"But Pastor Carlsson, I think I feel the spirit moving within me. I want to help people to feel God's love as I have..."

"No doubt your feelings are heartfelt, and as the Lord guides the universe, he may indeed have spoken to you in your time of need. However, you did say this *epiphany* occurred during an extended overindulgence in alcohol and illegal drugs?"

I blushed. "Yes, but like I told you before, I'm through with all of that now."

The pastor shook his head thoughtfully. "God works his wonders through all things, and both good and evil exist only through his benevolence toward mankind. Adam and Eve's disobedience corrupted God's perfect world, and the sin of theirs in attempting to become gods themselves has tainted us all. You seem determined to pursue a course toward salvation, and for that I applaud you, I truly do, but I would suggest that your... talents... may be put to better purpose in one of the less exacting congregations—the Methodists perhaps?"

"Are you saying I can't be accepted into the Lutheran church?"

"I truly hope you won't take my advice in a negative way. We are certainly open to any and all who are in need. It's just that... you asked me for my opinion and I am speaking to you as an adult to a young man on the cusp of adulthood. And in all honesty, I have to admit that I fear your learning curve may be too steep to ever become a full-fledged member, let alone a... pastor in our church. A learned layman perhaps someday, a trusted member of the church, possibly... yes, perhaps.... but this is a process that would take years of focused study and hard work to attain, and it is not the kind of decision one can base on one... rough weekend."

I stared at his frozen smile. His red mouth seemed painted onto his petrified wood face.

"So, what can I do?"

He tapped his fingers on his chin. "You are a senior in high school. Is college in your future?"

"I hope to go. My grades are good enough. Of course money is tight."

"Hmmm.... perhaps you could take some religious studies course, study theology in college and you can see if this newfound interest of yours is more than just a passing fancy. Take some classes in public speaking. You'll have to get over your shyness to preach, you know."

I hadn't thought about that. I've never been comfortable speaking in front of people. I just wanted to learn the Truth and share it with others.

"I'm not real good with that speaking part," I admitted.

"Hmmm yes." Leaning back in his chair, he closed his eyes and thought hard, before sitting up with a lurch. "You know, I just had a thought..." His eyes brightened. "Have you perhaps ever considered joining... the CIA?"

"I... I... well no, never—" I stammered.

"You know they are always looking for young men such as yourself."

"I really don't think—"

"You could do a great service to our country. Keep your friends and family safe from the Godless curse of Communism. You know, that's nearly as important as preaching the faith. Maybe more so."

"It hadn't crossed my mind," I admitted, confused.

"It's something I considered when I was younger, quite

seriously... the adventure... the intrigue... but my path was already laid out before me." He sighed, his eyes shining as he tilted his head back as if remembering a pleasant dream. Opening a drawer, he searched through several folded scraps of paper. "My time to serve our beloved nation is unfortunately past, but you are still young and free to take a risk. I have a friend in the agency. I could make a call if you would like."

"I appreciate it, but really I don't think so."

"You don't want to join the CIA?"

"No."

"Why don't you want to join the CIA?" He was hurt.

"I don't know."

"I could make a call. I have a friend." He pulled the paper triumphantly from his desk drawer and reached for the phone.

"Honestly, I am not interested, thank you," I said more forcefully.

"But Nathan, what could be more Christ-like than the service you could provide your country by serving in the CIA? Don't you see? Just think of the converts that could be made. I'd even go so far as to say that it is very possible that our Lord and Savior Jesus himself would be an agent of the CIA if he were alive today—maybe even the director, relentlessly spreading the power of American-style Christian faith, democracy and capitalism among the heathens worldwide through preemptive coercive action."

"No," I squeaked and shook my head emphatically. The pastor stared in disbelief.

"Very well," he stated finally in a deflated voice. Noticeably shocked and disappointed, he slipped the slip of paper back in the drawer. "You know, it has come to my attention that one of the primary problems with the youth of today is a lack of willingness to sacrifice," he muttered irritably. "You have to learn to sacrifice, Nathan, to be willing and able to sacrifice everything for that which you love and believe in." Rising mechanically, he offered a delicate bony hand, signaling the end of our interview.

"Let me know if you need a letter of recommendation for school," he stated, absentmindedly. "I will of course be happy to help. And of course, my friend... if you change your mind. The

CIA—"

Embarrassed, I reached out and hugged him, and felt his cadaverous body stiffen as I wrapped my arms around him, a dank wave of coldness emanating from his skeletal body. He gently patted my back limply with one emaciated fin as I released my grasp.

Thus ended my brief association with the church of the elect. I stopped attending after that and did manage to find my way to college, where I studied, among other things, theology. But I did it on my own, and never troubled my sanctimonious mentor for his kind, and no doubt quickly forgotten, offer to provide a letter of recommendation.

CHAPTER THIRTEEN

Jake locked the door as Jesse and Jared forced the trembling teenaged boy to his knees on the apartment floor. The kid's eyes glanced nervously at the window. I slid over in that direction and blocked his view, holding the rifle across my chest. From my vantage place, I could see the top of the stadium and wondered if the Packers were going to be any good this year. The boy's nervous breathing was audible as Jesse paced the floor nervously in a half circle around him. Reaching over, I turned a knob on the radio and filled the room with the sounds of a tremulous tenor yodeling a plaintive love song in Spanish.

"You don't have to do this," the boy said in a trembling voice. "My uncle is coming soon. He can straighten this all out."

"I'm not sure I believe you. That chicken shit uncle of yours ain't coming," Jesse snapped with a glare.

"No really, I talked to him earlier and he said he'd be here around five." We checked the clock hanging on the wall. The black and white, bow-tie-clad cat's eyes went back and forth as the tail swung in time: it read 5:17.

"He's running a bit late," I offered. Jared snorted at the comment.

"Yeah, he's just running late that's all," the boy pleaded. "They probably kept him... at work."

"That's a load of crap and you know it. There ain't no 'work.' The only time your uncle gets out of bed is when he goes down to the liquor store to cash his unemployment check."

"That's not true—"

"Oh that's right; he can't collect unemployment, because he's a *stinking illegal*."

The boy bit his lip and looked at the ground.

"Look kid, we drove all the way down here to freaking Green Bay to talk over a few things with your uncle. The least the fuck head could do is show up on time for our meeting."

"He'll be here, I swear it... and soon. Real soon."

"I hope so. Jared there gets bored easily." Jared gently tapped his baseball bat on the tip of a plaster statuette of the Virgin Mary. It cracked and crumbled into a pile of dust and pieces on the coffee table.

A flurry of rapid voices aggressively jabbering a commercial in Spanish erupted from the radio.

"I don't know how you can listen to that shit," Jesse snarled. Reaching over, I tuned the radio to a rock and roll station and Jesse relaxed back into his chair.

Waiting, waiting; the cat clock ticking away. The apartment was quiet except for the kid's heavy breathing and Jesse's humming and air-guitaring along with a classic rock triple-play. Jared rummaged through the fridge and helped himself to a Corona. Moving his hulking body contentedly over to the couch, he flopped down, kicking his dirty boots up onto the coffee table, and began slurping his beer loudly. The minutes passed with the boy frozen in fear on his knees in the center of the room.

Finally, a squeal of tires came from outside. Pulling the shade aside, I checked the street three stories below. Two cars and a truck pulled to a stop, and nine or ten men emerged from the vehicles carrying bats and guns, hurrying toward the entrance like a SWAT team answering a call.

"He's here," I said glumly, "and with a few friends." I took the safety off.

"I told you he was coming," the boy said proudly from the floor where he was crouched. "Now you're going to get your asses kicked, gringo."

"I wouldn't be so sure about that, 'Taco,'" Jake snarled, "we still have you."

Clamoring voices and heavy footsteps echoed from the stairs and hallway, followed by a loud pounding striking the door with a boom and a voice calling out: "Jaime, are you in there?"

Jess prodded the boy in the side with his foot. "Answer him."

"Yeah Jesus, I'm here."

"Let us in."

"I'm... not alone."

"They are with you inside?"

"Yes."

"How many?"

The boy hesitated. "Go ahead," Jesse said and kicked him again, harder this time. "We don't want to keep any secrets from anyone."

"Four."

"With guns?"

"Si."

"Let me talk to them. Let me talk to... Jesse."

"I'm here, *Hey-Zeus,*" Jesse snarled. "We were getting tired of waiting outside, so we invited ourselves in. Hope you don't mind. We've been enjoying your Mexican brand of hospitality. The beer's nice and cold and your nephews been keeping us amused cooking tacos and burritos and telling us some real funny stories and all... something about your mama and a donkey show. A real riot. But time's wasting and we're all busy people, so let's talk."

"I am thinking there must be some... misunderstanding here, Jesse. Your message to me... something about one of my people crossing into your territory... I don't know what it is you are talking about."

"Sure you do, you ass clown. Don't play dumb. My brother caught him selling crack in Escanaba two days ago. And that's not something we look upon too kindly."

"And you think I had something to do with this?"

"No, we KNOW you had something to do with it. Your amigo gave us your name after we had a little... chat with him."

"What did you say this person's name was?"

"You know who it is, your boy Chavez. Orlando Chavez."

A pause and some muffled mumbling outside the door, before the response: "You are mistaken; I've never heard of this Chavez."

"Oh, we're pretty sure you know him, Jesus," Jesse chuckled sardonically.

"The man is a liar. I have never heard of any Orlando Chavez."

"Quit with the games. How do you think we got your phone number, you moron? No, he's one of your peons alright."

There was a pause and angry voices speaking in Spanish outside in the hallway before Jesus continued.

"So where is this... Chavez now?"

"We left him walking home somewhere around Marinette. Or maybe crawling was more like it. He didn't look so good when we saw him last. I wouldn't wait up or anything. Might take him a few days to get back home."

Jared chuckled. Another pause and muffled voices from outside the door.

"And what exactly is the meaning of your visit today, Jesse?"

"Jeez, I really gotta spell it out for you, Jesus? You don't understand English too good or something? Look, it's bad enough they let you wetbacks in the country to fuck everything up for the rest of us. And you know, whatever you want to do down here in the city is your own business, because this city is a shithole already, but... when you send your guy up north with your shitty powder, and your pants down to here, undercutting our prices, stealing our customers and... well, we just have to remind you to stick to your own neighborhood."

"Is that so?"

"Yes that's so. And get it through your skull, you tamale-eating, tequila-pissing, dog-fucking scumbag: You keep your boys out of the great white north—that's our property, you got that? Keep in your own lane and maybe everybody stays happy and healthy."

"And if I don't?"

Jesse laughed. "You don't even want to go there, *hermano.*"

"Well, Jesse, I admit that I don't see how you sons of whores think you have the *cajones* to dictate conditions to me, but let's just say I agree to consider your proposal; what's in it for me?"

"Besides keeping your balls attached to your body, you mean?" Jesse chortled. "Well, who knows *Hey-Zeus,* maybe we work something out and do a little business together sometime? I have good sources, safe and reliable, and good product—way better than your Drano powder shit. But my problem is my market is expanding and I can't keep up with demand. I could use another supply channel. We are getting out of production ourselves—too much trouble, but I hear you Mexicans are cooking it up like crazy down south of the border these days. So we work it out and I take some of your product off your hands—not the low-grade stuff you push on the local junkies—I want the top notch shit, and we distribute it in our territory, split the profit and everybody's happy. What do you say, *compadre*, we got us a deal?"

"Hmmmm... your proposal is... interesting, but I think I will have to... pass. I don't need partners, especially not crazy gringos who do such foolish things as to come into my house uninvited, insult me, hold my family hostage and make demands. After all, we are ten and you are four. So... I believe my friends and I will just take what territory we want and now we will teach you disrespectful, cocksucking, *Yanquis* a lesson or two as to who is in charge around here while we are at it. Is that a deal?"

"I wouldn't try anything rash," Jesse replied calmly. "Remember, we have your boy." He kicked the young man hard in the ribs. The boy cried out in pain.

"If you hurt my nephew, you will never make it out of here alive."

"Oh, I think we will." Jesse bent over and unzipped the duffle bag he had placed on the floor. "In fact..."

The boy screamed as Jesse started the chainsaw. Our safe escort out and subsequent business agreement were thus quickly arranged.

CHAPTER FOURTEEN

" Hey Darlin'!"

When Jesse and Jenny first hooked up, it felt like I got shot up with a needle full of Novocaine, only it wasn't just my cheek and teeth and gums, but all over my body and to the depths of my brain that went numb and festered with a dull, throbbing ache. Then as the realization of the reality of my infinite solitude seeped through my skin, absolute emptiness engulfed me, and I felt like I was just like an old hollow tree, with the wind blowing right through the big open wound where my heart used to be.

She was everything good and eternal to me: all blue unclouded skies and shafts of sunlight through cool green bowers arcing above; the rippling waves caressing the shore, a cascade of sparks shot from the lightning in a summer storm, burning the prairies with the intensity of the wildfire of her divine life force. Whatever was good in our world belonged to her. She was its source. All charity, all peace and kindness and love and grace; all hers and hers alone.

But that was not all...

Fireflies flickered in her honor, the stars glowered in envy of her beauty, the sun did not rise nor set, the wind did not move across the waters, the sea itself did not move, nor did the earth rotate, but at her command. The universe itself humbly bowed its knees as a thousand songbirds sang in effulgent harmony within even the quietest whispers of her voice. In the deep depths of the dark woods, steeped in blackness thick as eternal night itself, haunted by evils and threatened by peril and deadly despair, she shone forth like the effervescent light of a thousand atom bombs, banishing all dread and despair, shattering the silence of my eternal prison of seclusion and lifting me with burnished feathery wings up, up to the heavens in rapturously tormented ecstasy. Her eyes sparkled like azure gems in a crystal pond, her lips were like absinthe. Wait a minute... YOU know what absinthe tastes like?

I digress...

How could she do it?

How could I blame her? Jess had all the looks and charm and he swept her off her feet with all the attention he gave her. The kid never grew much past 5'7" and 155 lbs or so—hell, Jenny was taller by an inch or so—but he was handsome as fuck, I hate to admit. Long tousled dirty blonde hair and an often unshaven stubble on his chin, framing those glimmering ice blue gray eyes, that twinkled like the Pleiades in an early autumn night, and that damn smile of his that could charm a snake, or even worse, a Sunday School teacher. His charisma was potent, intense, pervasive, and his damn energy was just hellacious, brutal, relentless, and I could only watch in misery and horror as I saw her submit and give way to his pursuit like a lily plucked and trampled by a barbarian, a brutish fiend. But, it was as if their relationship was preordained—maybe Pastor Carlsson was onto something after all. The attraction, like gravity or electromagnetism, was a fucking force of nature, and nothing and nobody could stop it, let alone the supporting player lurking in the shadows as the drama unfolded.

She was my first kiss you know. The first and the best. It's like they say: nothing ever comes close again. Jesse put her up to it, talked us into playing spin-the-bottle; but he sure got pissed off when I won the first spin and she planted a wet one softly on my lips. The world exploded and nothing was ever the same again after that—not for me anyway. I felt like somebody slapped me in the mouth, but in a good way like with a fist made of silk and cotton candy and then clamped a car charger to my heart because everything just blew up and got real intense all of a sudden. It's like that scene in the Wizard of Oz where the color comes on; I felt like someone turned on the lights in a dark room and I suddenly knew what it all meant, what I was here for, what I wanted more than anything.

But Jen was Jesse's girl, and I watched helplessly as they progressed from subtle looks of longing, teasing, hand holding and finally, to intense kissing sessions in Jesse's brother's car, with me acting the part of driver and mute witness to their increasing passion.

I was insane. I couldn't bear to watch them sucking face, but I feared being left behind more than anything. One night I couldn't control myself and snuck into her yard, my heart throbbing like a jackhammer, and climbed a tree to where I could peer in her windows. I watched as she went into the bathroom and... I thought I saw her... she stripped off her clothes and turned the shower on. The curtains were drawn, but I could make her out vaguely through the lace, her slim body arched, her breasts hanging like a pair of luscious peaches as the drops of water beat upon them and caressed her pink skin and I reached into my pants and...

Or maybe it was just a dream?

Meanwhile, the determined and resourceful Jesse even stopped Jenny's mom from beating her. He just told her flat out that there would be no more of that, and that was all she wrote, and so the mystical sadist Jeanne retreated further up the stairs into her tower to heaven. Al, on the other hand, liked Jesse, whom he thought of as being a younger version of himself—fat chance. He wasn't happy about losing his precious little girl, but Jesse's sharp eyes and fearless confidence scared the older man enough to back off, and he made the best of it by offering Jesse a can of lukewarm beer and slurred fishing stories whenever Jesse deigned to spend time at Jenny's house.

He did it, and credit must be given where it is due: Jesse saved her from her miserable existence—something I could never do. I prayed for a second chance—for my arms to sprout muscles that I could use to beat Al to a pulp and scare Jeanne into submission as Jesse had done, but it was too late, too late... My fate was already sealed, and I was doomed to be nothing more than the sidekick, the third wheel, the one who seethed in anguished misery when he was dispatched to the store for snacks, cigarettes or to bum beer whenever the chosen couple wanted to be alone.

Why me? Why was I appointed to be an attendant, and not the leading man in the play? Some are just born to be the star, while the rest of us gawk and mope from the wings, running the sound and lights and prompting the players, secretly envying the action onstage. Know your place, my father says; blessed are the meek, Pastor Carlson preaches; but just look what timidity and meekness gets you: an uncomfortably hot seat smack dab in the middle of the front row viewing an endlessly looped presentation of the

Technicolor, surround-sound, full-blown love scene to end all love scenes, brought to you in vibrantly vivid 3-D, and without commercial interruptions, by the sponsor Himself.

Even now, even after all these things have come to pass, the sound of their passion, their muffled giggles and hurried breathing coming from the back seat as I drove them around for hours on end, seething, jealous, angry, alone, so alone... haunts me with a stinging pain that burns inside me like a sampling of what I can only imagine to be Hell's finest and most decalescent torments.

CHAPTER FIFTEEN

We sat in Jesse's old beater in the corner of the Eagles Club parking lot in Iron River, watching as the crowd arrived in large-finned Caddies and newly polished Oldsmobiles that probably spent their lives in their garages and had less than 30,000 miles on them. The arrivals, mostly elderly, in colorful outfits seemingly pulled from closets last opened in 1942, many enfeebled, supported by canes, walkers or the arms of helpful escorts, emerged from their shining chariots with their trifocals on, their bow ties spiffily tied and wigs, hairpieces and freshly-blued hair piled high, and shuffled their way slowly into the hall from which loud throbbing music emanated.

"It's like the dance of the living dead, ain't it?" Jesse sneered and passed me the joint. "Fuck, shoot me now, before I start wearing white slacks and listening to Lawrence Welk."

"Hey Larry Elk's got a pretty sweet band. Accordions of death metal and all."

Blaring into the night every time the door opened, the music, through its heavy ONE, two, three, ONE, two, three-beat and syrupy melodies drew the revelers back, further in time, and closer to their romanticized, genetic memories of the Old World. Jesse was jittery, so I tried to calm him with the rock and roll station on the radio, but the resulting cacophony was worse, so we just sat suffering to the sounds of polka music, trying to make the best of it.

The door opened again and heavy tuba and accordion oompawing filled the air. A clarinet squealed as though someone inside was bending a cat.

"No wonder they all need hearing aids," Jesse scoffed and took a toke.

Wearing a too-short-for-her-age skirt, a tiny, timorous titmouse of a woman in thick horn-rimmed glasses, rotting peach-colored wig piled high atop her head and a string of pearls you could skip rope with, climbed out of a shiny gold behemoth that had beached itself nearby. Her escort—a withered, white-haired martinet in a plaid, lime green sport coat, held the car door for her and took her hand as though he was handling a delicate and priceless artifact. Warily glancing at us out of the corner of his eye, the septuagenarian lothario puffed up his chest as he took her arm and, with a stiffly limping step, ushered his date proudly and protectively into the ball.

Jesse and I looked at each other and burst out laughing.

"Check out the tough guy. Ain't nobody gonna mess with him."

"I'm scared, Jess. Can we go home?"

Howling with laughter, I opened the cooler, cracked a beer and handed it to him, and grabbed another for myself. Our laughter trailed off and we sipped our beers in contemplative tandem.

"Kind of sad, though," I said in a quiet voice, seeking to break the discomfort.

"What's that?"

"Oh, all these old folks dying off. It's like they are endangered species or something." I took a sip and motioned to another group limping their way painfully to the door. "It's like we're watching the dodo go extinct before our very eyes."

"They're dodos alright," Jesse chuckled. "What do you care about these ancient creeps? You're joking, right?"

"Naw, I'm serious. This whole polka thing All the whirling around and the *oom pa pa* and the frilly dresses, and capes and top hats and shoes with spats are going by the wayside. These people die off and it's just gone: a whole tradition disappears. It's like some ancient ritual that nobody will understand when the aliens dig up a rusty old accordion someday, when they are sifting through our junk on an archeological dig in a future millennium."

"There you go again, getting all philosophical on me, Preach." Jess took a long drag and tossed the roach into the ashtray. "It's just the way it is. You get old and you die. You think people are going to be listening to rock and roll in a couple hundred years? We're going to be sitting in the old folks home with the tunes cranked and they'll be laughing at us like we're laughing at them. That's just how it is—the young eat the old."

"I guess you're right."

"Of course I am. That's why I keep telling you that you gotta grab what you can, while you can. 'Cuz nobody's gonna give you anything unless you take it, and you never know, you could be dead tomorrow."

"Amen to that," I said and took a drag. *Man is like a mere breath; his days are like a passing shadow.*

We sipped our beers wordlessly, while the thumping continued in waltz time. I occupied myself by tracing a smiley face in the dust on the dashboard.

At half past, the white caddy we were expecting finally arrived and glided smoothly into the lot a few spaces away from us.

"Well, it's about time," Jesse snarled and flashed his lights.

Junior, dressed in a too-tight, pale blue sport coat that clung uncomfortably to his doughy torso, climbed out and went to the passenger side, pointedly ignoring Jesse's attempts to summon him. Adjusting the crocheted shawl over an older woman's shoulders, the portly cop led her gracefully to the door of the club, where he bent and whispered in her ear, motioning to the parking lot. She nodded and continued in alone, while the deputy strode toward us lightly on feet that were strangely small compared to his ample body. We climbed out and stood as he approached,

"Hey Darlin'. Nice date you got there," Jesse said with a leer.

"At least I know where my momma is, and she ain't sucking dicks down at the Lakeside." Junior's fat lips spat out the words angrily, his tiny eyes boring a hole into Jesse's face. "No offense meant, Preacher," he added as an aside.

Jesse's mother was hardly a mother-of-the-year candidate, so this was a sore point. Although she was only in her fifties, Old Sal Hawkins looked at least seventy. She had a coriaceous face that could stop a sundial, and she had been passed around from man to man like a bowl of pretzels at a Super Bowl party ever since Jesse's dad had been sent up. She had been known not to come home for weeks at a time, and her regular haunt, The Lakeside, was perhaps the sleaziest bar in the county—one avoided by all but the most desperate and degenerate.

Jesse's fists balled up and I thought for sure there would be trouble, but then he shook it off, relaxed and smiled.

"You'd know best. She's probably been sucking yours, since

you seem to go for gray pussy."

The eyes grew colder on both sides. "What the fuck did you want, Jesse? I don't have time for your crap right now."

"Just wanted to check in—see if you got any ideas where to start the ball rolling on our little project?"

"You're ready to go?" He directed the question toward me. I nodded. We had his attention. "You got a place?"

"Yup," Jesse said. "My daddy had some property outside of town. Said it was for logging, but don't think he ever did any. It's got a couple trailers—think he used to take his sluts up there and put 'em to work entertaining his friends."

"How far out?"

"Far enough, but close enough that we can get back to town quick enough if need be. It's fenced off and hidden away pretty good so nobody will find it we don't want them to."

"Hmmm. Sounds okay. Fine. And how are you set for supplies?"

"We were hoping you could give us a little direction there."

"What am I, the fucking Yellow Pages?"

"We were thinking maybe the drug store on Superior Street."

"Morons! Why am I even talking to you imbeciles? Didn't your daddies teach you anything? You don't shit in your own nest. You got plenty of towns around here. Norway, Iron Mountain... Use your imagination."

"Well, we were kind of hoping you'd help us out with the alarm or something."

"Yeah, and risk losing my job? What the fuck is wrong with you two? You gotta use your brains. You pick a place, choose a good time, smash the window and grab as much as you can in three minutes."

"Three minutes?"

"Might take the cops four or five to get there, but I wouldn't chance it."

"How the fuck are we supposed to get what we need in three minutes?"

"Not sure if I'd go much more than two-and-a-half, but that's just me. But Preacher knows what he's looking for, and I seem to remember you were always good at running away, Jesse."

"What is that supposed to mean?" Jesse tensed again.

"Roy, are you coming?" Junior's mother suddenly called out from the doorway where she had reappeared.

"Yes Mother, I'll be there in a minute."

"Mommy's calling, Roy Boy," Jesse said with a snicker.

Junior whirled around in a flash and hissed, "You know Jesse, it's obvious that nobody ever taught you any manners, much less any sense, now did they? Keep it up sonny, and you're going to end up in the slammer like your old man."

"Fuck you, Pultz," Jesse sputtered bitterly. Junior ignored him and went on.

"You really don't get it, do you? You've got to learn to lay low and don't attract attention, you fucking cockroach. Cut your hair, fix your muffler. You think a beat-up, piece-of-shit Chevy in a lot filled with Lincolns doesn't stand out? Get a fucking clue. You want to work with me? Then you better get your act together, you understand!"

"Don't flip your wig, Matilda," Jesse said smirking.

"Listen up, punk, and quit with the smart mouth. I am the fucking professional here and you are just some dumb yokel who I am trying to help, but you're just too damn stupid to listen. Do I really have to explain everything to you? Listen up and learn for a change, you smartass punk. You do what you have to in order to fit in with these people. They are just a bunch of dumb sheep. You know that and I know that, but you're so stupid and lacking in subtlety that you're going to let those clods beat you in the game."

Jesse sulked as the puffy cop's face grew redder as he continued his tirade.

"It's like hoops. You play their game, but you do it your way. If you pretend to play by their rules you earn their trust. If they trust you, you got them right where you want and can do whatever you want. But you don't do it obvious like you do, dumb ass. You don't put a sign on yourself that says *criminal* and march down the middle of the street. You've got to keep it quiet. Patient. It takes time. Years sometimes. You work your way in to the middle of things, that's where it all comes together, don't you see? I learned from the best. Unlike yours, my daddy did it right."

"What, dying in bed with a whore?"

"Hell yeah. Better than dying in prison with Bubba Joe's dick up his ass."

Jesse's hand reached behind him to where he kept a .22 pistol stuck in his belt. I clutched his arm tightly. Pultz was on a roll, getting Jess more and more riled, but killing a cop would do nothing but stick Jesse and me as roomies with his old man and his buddies up the river.

"You gotta fit in, asshole," the flabby deputy continued with a sneer. "Act like you care, like you're one of them. Listen to their sob stories and cry with them when somebody croaks and pat them on the back and laugh with them when they win a pot at poker or a stupid baseball game. You go to the games and the church dinners and the polka nights and the square dances and you work hard making a show about being a solid citizen and contributor to the community and you earn the respect of the clueless fools, and then when they aren't watching you make your move, and that's when the rewards start to come your way. You don't really have to listen, just smile and nod your head. You don't have to really like them; you just pretend to give a shit about their pathetic little lives. You bide your time and keep up appearances and pretty soon you've got all the strings and you're in charge of the whole fucking puppet show."

Jesse relaxed and let go of the gun, so. I released his arm.

"Whatever," Jesse said with a forced smile. "So you got our backs or what?"

"I'll give you fellows one shot to impress me, but be real fucking aware that if it comes down to it, I don't know you and you don't know me. I only keep helping you out as long as you get with the agenda at hand and don't get stupid, sloppy or greedy. And whatever you do, don't ever think about fucking with me, or I promise that you will find yourself lying in a ditch filled with your own blood some night. You got the picture?"

"Oooh, I'm scared."

"So where do you think we should start?" I quickly interrupted.

Junior eyed Jesse up and down slowly, glaring, and then turned to me.

"Alright, but this is my last bit of advice for the evening. Write it down, Preacher. Try the drug store on Route 141 in Iron Mountain. Late at night. Make it a Sunday. Should be relatively easy pickings and a good first test for you clowns. The guy working that shift for the police is a little slow on the draw, if you get my drift—might buy you a couple more minutes, but don't count on it. Bust the door down and snatch and grab the shit. Don't dick around. Get out quick; I can't stress that enough. Three minutes, maybe four tops. Get your girl to keep the motor running out back. Drive away smooth and slow and act like you're heading south out of town. Slip over on Highway N and come back up through Florence on the back roads."

"Maybe we could have Jenny make a call about something going down on the other end of town and get the cops headed in the wrong direction," I suggested.

"Hmm, good idea... I like how you think, Preacher," Junior said thoughtfully, "but no, don't use it the first time. Save it for next time you want to hit the place. You don't want to use that one too often. That's good though. Real good... But no, first time on a Sunday night—should be quiet enough and you don't want to be stirring up a hornets' nest. Good shit though, Preacher; Jesse's lucky to have you on the team."

"Yeah, yeah, he's my starting shortstop," Jesse said sourly. We ignored him.

"Anything else," I asked scratching away at my notepad.

"Yeah. Dress like gang bangers and cover your fucking faces with ski masks or something—they have security cameras, you know."

"And you're going to back us right?" Jesse asked petulantly.

"Let's see how you do first. Do okay and I might throw you a little help from my end—no promises, but if something does go wrong, we never had this conversation."

"Roy!" An impatient female voice emoted weakly from doorway. "They want to know if you want any raffle tickets."

"I'm coming, Mother!"

Turning on his surprisingly light toes, Junior pranced off toward his impatient mother and his exciting evening on the dance floor, calling over his shoulder as he left:

"Try to keep him in line, Preacher. And remember, Jesse, you cross me and I'll shoot you myself without a second thought, and I don't think anybody in the town would even give a damn about it. *Hell, they'd even probably give me a medal,* he thought with a chuckle.

"Mother, you look so lovely tonight," he said, turning his attention to his date. "Tell them I'll take a dozen raffle tickets if they play that last polka again and I get to dance with the prettiest girl at the ball," he crooned in a honeyed voice and kissed the Widow Pultz on the cheek as she blushed in the moonlight.

CHAPTER SIXTEEN

The sunshine showered down on my Jenny and she seemed to soak it all in and glow brighter than a sunbeam.

For she is fairer than the sun and surpasses every constellation of the stars... Compared to light, she takes precedence...

We were standing around in Jesse and Jenny's new backyard. He had just finished putting the money down on the place and we had spent the day moving furniture in. We had pretty much done all we could for the day, so a bunch of us were celebrating with a few icy beers and shots of whiskey and some tasty cheeseburgers sizzling on the grill.

It wasn't much of a house. I was pissed that he didn't do better for her, but he did get a decent price on it as it was a foreclosure. The guy building it skipped town and left the better part of the siding off one whole side of the house. Jesse swore he'd have that on there in a week or two, but he got distracted and never did get to it.

There was no sidewalk leading to the front steps, the driveway was dirt and the garage was just an unfinished frame next to a rickety shed. There had been a problem with the pipes freezing and the unfinished basement had flooded, leaving a musty smell that they never did get rid of. But it was a house, with a big yard overgrown with weeds that Jeremy could run around in, and it got Jenny and the kid out of her mother's house.

She was looking good as always. Despite having the baby, she was still skinny as a twig. Some women are lucky that way. She was wearing those short, short cutoffs right up to her perky little butt, and a loose fitting halter top, and I could see having the kid had given her more of a chest than she had before. She always was pretty small, but those pale orbs with their rosy nipples under her blouse gave me unsettling dreams for years. More than mouthful is wasted anyway, as Jesse used to say.

"Hey Darlin'," Jesse said in that sickening, albeit seductive drawl, as he kissed her on the cheek and left to go talk to a couple of friends inspecting the splintered back fence that tilted heavily to one side.

The kid, Jeremy, must have only been a little over a year old, but he was already running, stumbling and stomping around the yard wearing a diaper and with a bottle in his mouth—glaring with ferocious eyes at the people assembled. Every so often he'd fall down and cry and Jenny would rush over and pick him back up, or he'd drop the bottle and turn his face to the sky and howl like a banshee. He was a real terror even then.

Jenny beamed with joy, proud of her status as a new home owner, although she wasn't officially married to Jesse or listed on any of the papers. Her boyfriend also whooped with pride, occasionally grumbling in mock annoyance to the guys that *his bitch* made him spend his hard earned money on this home that was sure to turn out to be a money pit. The house was on the end of a little dead end side street and traffic was rare; if and when a car did pass by, Jesse would scream and wave his arms and the startled driver would flee back the way he or she had come.

A loud wail burst out as Jeremy ran into the picnic table and fell and let out a holler. Quick as can be, Jesse did a handstand and everyone laughed. The toddler stopped and stared. Jesse grabbed his son and flipped him over to attempt a handstand of his own, and Jeremy howled with laughter.

"Jesse, don't do that!" Jenny said, but she was laughing too.

Jesse pushed the kid onto the grass, and the youngster whined and stood back up holding his arms out and asking for more. Grabbing him up, his father swung the tyke around in the air wildly, with Jeremy yowling away with childish merriment. Jesse threw the kid higher and higher into the air, the boy laughing louder with every toss. Finally, tiring of this, Jesse deposited his son on the ground, and rubbing his arms, announced the little fucker was getting bigger and heavier every day. The wild child's unhappiness with his father's abandonment subsided when he spotted his bottle under the table, and he retreated under there to lie down in the shade and suck on the nipple, momentarily exhausted by his exertions.

Popping open our beer cans, we sat back in lawn chairs and watched as the shadows of the trees stretched across the lawn and the sun continued its lazy afternoon descent toward the western horizon. Jeremy belched loudly and fell asleep with the bottle still between his lips, while Jake and his latest girlfriend left to go home and watch porn. Jesse jumped up, waving his arms around, full of energy, deciding to give Jared and a couple other dudes the grand tour of the basement, leaving me alone with Jenny and her sleeping tot.

"You're looking great these days, Jen," I said squinting at her through my sunglasses.

"Thanks, Preacher. It's good to see you too. I'm just glad you made it back alive from the big city."

"You don't have to keep calling me Preacher, you know. That's all over and done with. I bombed out."

"Oh, you know you'll always be 'Preacher' to me, Nate. You have to promise me you won't ever change and that you will always be my friend and Jesse's." She reached across the table and I took the hand she offered, smiling weakly.

"I'm just glad you came back. I knew big city life wouldn't suit you. I never knew why you wanted to leave anyway, you've got everything you need right here." She motioned around the yard and leaned back, letting go of my hand. "What more could you want? We've got the sun and the shade trees and that nice breeze. We've got this awesome house and this killer yard and I can raise a whole bunch of kids and have parties with the friends and we can all grow old together, right Nate?"

Within my dwelling, I should take my repose beside her...

"Sure," I said.

"Of course, we have to find you a girl too, but not one who's prettier than me, or I might get jealous. Hmmm... how about Cindy?"

"Pete's cousin? The one with the wooden leg?"

"Oh you! " I ducked, the napkin she tossed at me just missing my face. "You know that's not true. She just walks kind of funny— one leg is longer or something, but she's got some big titties."

"More than—"

"Don't you even say that," she said and threw a beer can, this time nailing me square in the face.

"Ow," I said rubbing my nose, and watched like a hawk as she, pleased, adjusted her top.

"Well, Superior isn't exactly a big city, you know," I said.

"Bigger than this hell hole."

"Hell hole? I thought you said you liked it here?"

"I do, it's just..."

"What?"

"Oh, sometimes I think it would be nice to go someplace like Paris. Like in that book—"

"You mean my old Balzac?"

"Yeah, Paris sounds romantic—or maybe Hawaii or Florida. I get sick of getting stuck indoors in the cold for months at a time. I could just sit out there in the sun under a palm tree and stick my feet in the ocean."

"And let the alligators bite you?"

"There aren't alligators in the ocean are there?" She looked alarmed. I chuckled.

"Don't think so."

"I hate when you tease me." Pulling a metal pipe out of her pocket, she took a hit and passed it to me, coughing a bit as she did. "So what do you think of me? A mom!" Her eyes sparkled.

"I think it's great," I lied.

"And Jesse doing the right thing and trying to be a dad."

"That is going to take some supreme effort on your part, I would think."

"I told him we couldn't be cooking up any cat in the new house. No crack, not with the baby. You guys are going to have to do that shit up on his Daddy's land."

"Good call."

"That was fun the other night wasn't it? I got such a rush. I make a good getaway driver, don't I?"

"You're a natural."

"It was such a surprise for me when Jesse told me you were back in town. And then this whole thing with Junior. We have money! We even have our own house!"

"I think he could have got you a nicer one."

"Oh, this is more than good enough. And he says he'll fix it up.

And it's got such a big yard for Jeremy to go crazy in."

"Good thing or that kid might tear up the house. He's a baby Hercules."

"With Jesse's energy and a mean streak like his daddy's. You know he bit me on the arm the other day."

"He's got teeth?"

"Only a few, but they're sharp as hell."

"You've got your hands full, that's for sure."

"So Preacher, honey," she asked with concern in her eyes, "we really haven't had a chance to talk until now. I'm curious, what exactly happened in Superior anyway? Jesse says you got thrown out of school, but you won't tell anybody why. You can tell me. I won't say anything."

"Nothing really. I hit a guy—my professor."

She burst out laughing.

"Oh my God, that's—I mean that's not funny, but damn that's hilarious. You're the biggest wimp I know. You've never hit anybody in your life, and you get yourself into college and all and you studying to be a preacher and you... hit... your... professor." Tears rolled down her cheeks as she laughed loudly. "It's just too... unreal."

I sipped my beer and stared at the ground.

"So why did you hit him?"

"He made a pass at me."

"No!" She roared with laughter. Jeremy woke up and started squalling. Jesse and friends emerged from the house.

"What's so funny, Darlin'?" he asked squinting his eyes in the sunlight.

Jenny couldn't stop laughing.

"I just told her a dumb joke. You know how blondes are."

"You got that right," Jesse snarled. "But grab that kid and get in here. I've got party favors and an ultra-special surprise for both of you."

Jenny picked up the boy, who snuggled against her chest, eliciting jealous rumblings on my part, and we followed Jesse inside to where he had some of our product laid out on a tray. Breaking off a piece of the rock, he placed it theatrically into a glass pipe and lit it and we began passing the pipe around. The rush of adrenaline was immediate; I was beginning to like the buzz I got from the crank: I felt like I had enough energy to go all night long, and my mind was as clear and precise as a snow covered winter meadow lit by the light of a full moon.

As soon as we were satisfactorily endowed with a heightened state of awareness, Jesse jumped up like a court jester ready to entertain the court. Whipping a tarp briskly off a rectangular object sitting on a stand in the living room, Jesse revealed an aquarium filled with an assortment of brightly colored tropical fish swimming frantically around in circles.

"This is for you, baby!" Jesse said proudly. "Angelfish for my angel."

"Oh Jess," Jenny said with a scowl, "they're beautiful, but who's going to have to clean that thing?"

"Oh it will be worth it, believe me," Jesse said as he pulled a plastic bag from behind the couch and held it above the tank. "Watch this. You gotta check this out."

Moving close, we huddled around and watched as Jesse opened the bag, dumping the golden contents into the water with a plop. Wasting no time, the fish in the tank sensed the newcomers' presence and attacked aggressively. Dazed, the goldfish frantically struggled to escape, banging against the glass walls only to turn back into the roiling water and razor teeth of the hungry angels and striped clownfish, who vigorously tore the flesh from their victim's thrashing bodies in chunks and long strips and crimson ribbons of shredded fat and muscle, the churning water now streaked with crimson plumes as I watched the unfolding in increasing horror.

Jesse roared with laughter, and everyone joined in, delighted at the spectacle. Jared held the wide-eyed baby up to the glass to get a closer look. I turned to look at Jenny.

She was laughing along with the rest.

Gagging as the vomit rose up through my throat and into my mouth, I stumbled across the room and made my way outside. Falling to my knees, I threw up on the lawn, the sound of my retching accompanied by the hysterical laughter erupting from the house behind me.

CHAPTER SEVENTEEN

Hearing the faint rap on my window, my heart leapt, hoping it was her, but already knowing that it wasn't. Climbing out of bed, I pulled the shade up.

He stood in the dark looking lost and forlorn, with red eyes and his white face streaked with tears. "Can I come in?" he asked sheepishly.

I nodded. "Meet me at the back door."

I unlatched the door and let him and we moved silently through the dark house.

"Your old man home?" he asked softly.

"I don't think so." I yawned. "Was the Dodge in the driveway?"

"I didn't see it, but I came up the alley."

"I don't think he's home then. Think he's got a new girlfriend. He left a note. Said he was going to be late. Left me some hot dogs in the fridge."

"You got any left?" he asked in a hopeful voice.

I shook my head. "Sorry, I ate the last one."

"That's okay."

"Got some peanut butter," I said. His eyes brightened.

I led him back into the kitchen and got the peanut butter and jelly out of the refrigerator and some white bread out of the bread box. I made him a sandwich and poured him a glass of milk and he ate and drank greedily.

"Thanks," he muttered as he washed the last bites down, his eyes downcast, ashamed of his hunger.

He placed the plate and glass in the sink and we stepped down the hall to my bedroom.

"Were you sleeping?" he asked.

"No. I just laid down."

"I'm... I'm sorry... I..."

"No biggie, I wasn't asleep yet."

I clicked on the small television on my dresser. A late night comic was performing his monologue. "Want to watch some TV?"

"Yeah, okay." We sat on the end of the bed. The monologue ended and a stream of commercials commenced. I switched across another few channels searching for a war movie or horror flick, but found nothing but more commercials, an infomercial for a new exercise machine and an old movie with Cary Grant kissing a girl.

"Yuck," we both said in tandem.

I shut the TV off. "Nothing on," I said. He nodded sadly.

He stood beneath my Superman poster—the Man of Steel glowering down as though Lex Luthor had showed up unexpectedly at the Fortress of Solitude—and toyed with a set of figurines of knights arrayed in full battle on my dresser, as I shuffled my homework off my desk and into my backpack.

"You want to stay?" I asked.

"I guess so," he said meekly.

"Your dad again?"

He nodded.

"Won't he get mad at you?"

"He's already mad at me. This won't make it any worse."

"You sure? I mean won't he or your mom miss you?"

"Naw, he won't remember anything in the morning. And she don't care none."

I pulled the covers aside and climbed into bed. Jesse took a pillow and climbed in opposite me as he had done many times before: his head at the foot of the bed, his feet up near my head.

"I ain't no queer you know," he muttered and rolled over and faced the wall, as I turned off the light.

"I know." I replied.

"You know, do you ever try praying?" I asked softly after a few minutes in the dark. "I mean about your dad?"

"I don't think God would like what I would be praying for," he responded angrily. "And besides, how can you really be sure that if something happened that you prayed for, that it was God that was the one that answered your prayer and not the devil?"

I didn't know.

"G'night Jess."

"G'night Nate."

CHAPTER EIGHTEEN

It didn't take long. I knew it wouldn't.

They caught me in Lefty's, a sleazy little diner on the outskirts of town. I'd been avoiding my own place and Jenny's as much as I could, sleeping in my car and keeping to the back roads. But I ran out of supplies and hadn't eaten in almost two days. A guy has to eat, right?

I was sitting in a corner booth, chowing down on a greasy blue cheese burger, and washing it down with a chocolate malt. It was hot and stuffy in the diner and the ceiling fans groaned as they tried their best to push the thick air around. I was uncomfortably sticking to the plastic seat, when suddenly I swear I felt a cold chill. When I looked up they were standing there looking down at me in all their manifest ugliness.

"Hey guys," I said half-heartedly and raised my fist for a fist bump. Neither took me up on the offer. They weren't smiling. Jake, his prehistoric sloth facial features twisted into a malignant scowl, drooped down into the chair across from me, stretching his long legs into my territory under the table. His loutish counterpart, Jared grabbed a chair in his meaty paws and slammed his beefy frame down backwards in it, blocking the aisle. The elderly waitress scowled at us but didn't dare say anything about this egregious violation of the fire code; instead she disappeared into the back for what seemed to me to be eons. In the booth on the other side of us, the older couple ceased their conversation and began searching frantically with their eyes for someone to bring them their check.

My ravenous enemies beset me; they shut up their cruel hearts, their mouths speak proudly

"What's up," I asked nonchalantly and took a bite. The tangy burger suddenly seemed sour in my mouth.

"Been looking all over for you, Preacher," Jake began. "You seen our brother lately?"

"Jesse?"

"What other one do you think?" Jared snapped. He was not in a good mood. He never was, of course, but today his mood seemed even more off balance than usual, if possible. His hard eyes flickered off and on like dangerous bonfires as his synapses crackled and fizzed within the thick jawed shell of his solid skull. "We were supposed to go fishing yesterday, but he never showed up."

I doubted the fishing part, but I'm sure they did have plans of some sort. Swirling my fries around in figure eight patterns in the catsup, I looked Jake in the eye.

"Naw, haven't seen him in days."

"Is that right? Since when have you two not been attached at the hip?"

"Ah well, we don't really hang as much these days."

"Really? What's up with that? You guys have a lover's spat?"

Jared chuckled. The kind of chuckle a butcher makes when he tells a dirty joke while chopping off a limb.

"Funny," I said. "You should do stand up."

"What's that supposed to mean?" Jared's meaty fists clenched.

Their steps even now surround me; crouching to the ground, they fix their gaze

"Lighten up, Jared. It was a joke." My expression of indifference was an inspired performance. I bit off another bite of burger, proud of my coolness under fire.

Picking up the mustard dispenser, Jake beat it thoughtfully in his palm like a blackjack.

"It doesn't make any sense that he'd disappear and not tell us. So you really don't have any idea where he is?"

"Come on guys, you know Jesse. He's always got something going."

"Yeah. But it's pretty weird. He ain't answering his phone."

Thinking quickly. "I think he said it wasn't working. It fell in the toilet or something."

"You shitting me?" Jared smirked at the thought of his brother's accident.

"I wouldn't shit you, bro, you're my favorite turd."

The older couple in the next booth shifted nervously and gestured with their hands for the waitress to bring their check. A fly buzzed my cheek; I brushed it away.

"I'm sure he'll turn up," I said calmly, trying to keep my heart in my chest. "Jenny can tell you—he's been disappearing for days at a time lately."

"You know what he's been doing?"

"The usual. Deals. Poontang. You check with any of his girlfriends?"

"Just Jenny. She's worthless as usual."

I felt my fist tighten under the table. The fly landed on my plate. I shooed it away.

"She says you two were doing some treasure hunting," Jake said, watching my eyes for any hint of a vein of gold.

"Jenny said that, huh?" I finished my malt with a slurp and took a deep breath. "Yeah, we've done a bit of that. Not much luck though."

"Jesse always said you were gonna figure out where that stagecoach money went. You figure that out yet?" Jared licked his lips and slid his chair closer. I could feel the heat of his mammoth body.

"Ha, I wish." *Train, you dummy. Not a stagecoach.* I chewed slowly, the last bite of hamburger sliding tightly down my throat. "If I had found the money, would I be eating in this crappy place?

"True." Jared spit on the floor. The old man in the next booth rapidly waved his hands in the air like he was sending a distress signal via semaphore. The waitress emerged briefly, looked the other way and retreated rapidly back to safety behind the swinging door, ignoring the gesticulating patron's plight.

"So when'd you see him last?" Jake asked, a tattooed arm brushing his long greasy hair out of his elongated face.

I leaned back thoughtfully. "Oh hell, it's been a few days. When was that? I don't really recall. A few nights ago, I guess. We were pretty trashed."

Jared chuckled. Jake was straight-faced. The fly landed on his forehead. He frowned and waved his hand absently to chase it away.

"He say anything about going anywhere?"

"He might have. I was pretty stoned. You guys know how that goes. He's got some new friends... connections, I mean. Some guys in Detroit I don't know. Some Mexicans, some Canadians—he's like a corporation now—he's going big time—international."

"Yeah, he's a regular Kenfucky Fried Chicken all right. I don't suppose you got names or numbers for any of these guys?" Jake asked pointedly.

Throwing a twenty down on the table, the old man and his wife escaped, stepping gingerly, but hastily, and without a backwards glance, the bell jangling on their way out.

"Fuck, Jesse don't share nothing like that with me." I couldn't finish my fries and pushed my plate toward Jared. "You want some?"

"Yeah, all right. If you aren't gonna eat 'em."

The fly buzzed in a circle, flying past Jared's eyes.

Like lions hungry for prey, like young lions lurking in hiding

"He's always talking about some new pussy down in Green Bay. Matter of fact he's probably banging her right now," I offered. I'm a helpful fucker.

"Wish it was me," Jared said with his mouth full, ketchup running like blood down his chin.

"No number for her either, I suppose?" Jake picked up the knife and gently stabbed a napkin. Repeatedly.

"Naw. I think her name is Lisa or Tina or maybe—"

"You're fucking worthless too, Preacher, aren't you?" Jake shook his head. "No last name or address or nothing, huh?"

"Afraid not." I sipped my water glass and took a long breath. "Aw you guys are worrying about nothing. Jesse's tough as hell. There isn't anybody stupid enough to mess with him, you know that. They'd end up messing with you pricks, and I don't know anybody who is that stupid or suicidal. He's just off doing his thing and he'll probably come walking through that door any minute with his shit eating grin, laughing at us and telling us we're a bunch of pussies for checking up on him. You'll see."

Jake leaned forward, his hair hanging over his eyes like an oily mane, and whispered, "You're probably right, but that kid don't have a fearful bone is his body and that means he is just crazy enough to get himself in trouble. He's been making deals with people we don't know: *Internationals,* like you said. And I'd guess Junior probably knows that he's been cutting side deals—"

"Fuck Junior," Jared said loudly."

"—and he's already got that asshole Big Pete's gunning for him."

"Fuck Big Pete," Jared said even louder. A heavy set, bearded man in a baseball cap at the counter—the only other customer remaining—finished his coffee quickly and headed for the exit without a word.

"Pete's got a legit beef. He thinks Jesse capped his kid brother."

"That punk was a waste of oxygen anyway. If Jess did it, he had it coming."

I had never truly noticed and fully appreciated the swirls of coloration on the surface of a diner table top before. They were fascinating—the surface was so smooth, yet the graduations made it seem as if there were mottles of texture, an uncanny appearance of deviations in depths—motion even, despite its 2-D reality: an enchanting multi-hued pattern, coiling, serpentine, fractal-like— almost hypnotic. I held my breath.

"So did he do it, Preacher?"

"I only know as much as you do, fellas. Of course, I've heard the rumors."

"Rumors say you were there too, asshole."

I looked down at the table top, studying the design intently. The arrangement looked like clouds—blue clouds in a white sky— clouds somewhere far away from this place. I gripped the ridged aluminum grooves on the table edge tightly and said nothing.

"And who knows jack shit about these Canadians," Jake continued, "let alone the lowlife spic bangers and druggies you guys have been playing around with? Jesus, you gotta have more common sense, Preacher. I know Jesse ain't got none, but you've always supposed to have been a smart motherfucker. That's your job, ain't it? You should be keeping his ass out of trouble."

Rise O Lord, confront them and cast them down; rescue me by your sword from the wicked…

"I ain't Jesse's keeper," I explained impassively, "and you guys know as well as I do, that there ain't nobody that can keep Jesse out of doing whatever the fuck he wants—least of all me." I picked an ice cube out of my water glass and tossed it in my mouth. My eyes returned again to the marbled display adorning the tabletop. We fell into silence.

"Well, you hear from him, tell him to call us, ASAP!" Like a reanimated zombie, Jake stood up with a lurch and towered over the table threateningly. "Tell Jenny too."

"Fuck her," Jared added.

"Yeah, I'll do that," I responded to the first statement. To both statements.

"And don't be a stranger, creep."

They started away. I held my breath and stared at the clouds on my table. Crumbs. A water ring. They suddenly paused and turned back.

"I just have a bad feeling. Jesse's made too many enemies." Jake muttered. "You sure about his cell phone?"

I shrugged. "I'm pretty sure he said there was a problem, but I can't say how it happened."

"Fell in the shitter, I'll bet," Jared laughed as he stood. "What a dumb ass"

His eyes suddenly focused. Quick as a boxer, he thrust his beefy right hand out and caught the fly in mid-air. Giggling like an imbecile in a fun house, he crushed his prey and threw the remains of the mangled insect onto my plate, sending a light sprinkling of ketchup splattering onto the tabletop.

Jake's eyes narrowed as he bent closer to my ear and hissed. "You know, Preacher, you've been a hard cat to reach the last few days. We usually see you hanging around Jesse and Jenny's place around the clock. What have you been up to? Doing some business, yourself?"

"Not really. Been kind of under the weather. Hanging out. Here and there."

"Like your old man," Jared interjected and grinned as he pretended to pour a bottle down his throat.

I felt the rage rising from deep within. I wanted to kill him then and there.

Instead, I smiled and nodded.

"I guess," I said.

CHAPTER NINETEEN

Keen hunger, sharp and stinging, drove the longing, carried the long legs forward, pushing off with wide padded feet, galloping atop the snowdrifts like spectral gray streaks, moving swiftly amidst the dark shadows, the pack hunted. The pungent smell of the deer filling their nostrils, their blood rising in torrents, snapping and snarling and growling with anticipation through jagged toothed jaws, as they burst though the heavy brush of thickets, over and down embankments and across meadows, led onward by their addiction to the primal odor that hung in the cool night air, under the moon and stars and massive whirling snowflakes, the scent calling relentlessly to them with a promise of the satiating taste of blood.

Twisting, the crooked trail twined its way into the heavy forest, and as the runners crashed through the brush, the trees laden with ponderous drifts, which bent the branches low with their weight, were shaken and, as if joyous to be freed of their burden, unloosed cascades of snow onto the fur of the racing beasts, who only felt their velocity impeded and not the cold and damp through their thick coats.

Near the back, the smallest and youngest wolf—the only black one in a family clothed in tan and gray fur—breathed heavily, struggling to maintain the pace of the rest of the pursuers. Ahead, he saw his father, the Alpha, leading the way, followed by his brothers and mother, in close pursuit of an older buck. The buck suddenly veered hard about, and, turning quickly, the black wolf felt his back leg slip, and he stumbled, yelping and whimpering softly as he fell and slid hard against a fallen log. His mother turned her head slightly and he saw her brightly shining eyes for a moment glance back in the darkness at him, as he struggled rapidly to his feet with a jerk and redoubled his speed to catch up with the company.

Heart thundering rampant in his chest, the black wolf reached the clearing as the circle slowed and halted, surrounding the panting, panic stricken deer, near where they knew by scent a human den was located. His mother growled and poised to pounce, when abruptly there was a flash and the thunderous blast of an explosion, shaking the woods as if an earthquake had struck, initially stunning, then scattering the wolf pack and their prey into every direction. Escaping the flames from which rose a plume of smoke and sparking ashes, the black wolf fled, oblivious to the shouts and laughter of human voices in the distance, as he took flight, sprinting far away into the tenebrous refuge of the night.

CHAPTER TWENTY

The small town of Channing was quiet in the mid afternoon as Jesse drove through the dusty streets slowly surveying the layout. A few lonely trucks and cars were parked at the post office, the train station and at the bar across the street. Jesse eyed the cratered parking lot with concern before deciding not to chance the suspicions of the locals.

"We could go in and buy a beer and ask to park for a few hours, but that's just asking for attention. They might ask for an I.D. You never know about these small towns. Some of these jokers are poor and desperate for business, but they won't take a dime if they think you're under age," he explained. "My great aunt Beryl lives a few blocks away. She's senile as you can get and she won't even notice if we park in front of her house. Anyone says anything; we were visiting the old bat."

As he pulled the car into place in front of a small, weather-beaten house, I thought I saw the front curtains move slightly, but it may have just been the wind. Jesse waved in case anyone was watching and we walked quickly away.

"Keep it cool," Jesse hissed. "Act like you belong."

Strolling quickly down the road and out of the small town, we stayed along the edges, skirting the main road. From here, we could see the yard and noted that it was not empty: a metallic clanking of machinery rang out across the fields and a flutter of human activity persisted, proving once again that Jesse's experience could be relied upon.

Once we were a safe distance from what there was of a town, we crossed the road and ducked into a field of tall wild grass and sat down on a bank.

"How long do we have to wait?" I asked nervously.

"It shouldn't be too long. They don't stick around this shit hole any longer than they have to."

Clanking sounds clattered down the line from the direction of the station and we could hear shouts and laughter carried by the wind that rippled the stalks and stems around us.

"What if they catch us?" I asked with concern.

"Hell, they don't give a shit about us. Just don't be obvious. Even if they see us, they're too lazy to do anything about us. It's guys like the bull up in Marquette you gotta look out for."

"The bull?"

"Railyard police. Usually a bully who is too fat to be a regular cop."

"What does he do?"

"Well, he'll beat you silly with a club if he catches you for starters. Fortunately, he's slow, but if he does manage to get a hold of you... it ain't pretty."

"Does he arrest you?"

"He might hand you over to the cops after he's done having his fun with you. It's private property, so you're taking your chances. Better to get off before we get to the yard."

"You ever see him?"

"No, but my brother Jake did. He barely got away. Says he watched him damn near kill some Indian who was too old and sick to run away."

The clouds glided slowly, gauzily across the light teal canvas of the sky, while the sunlight filtered down warmly onto the top of our heads, and the light breeze tickled the tops of the weeds and wildflowers in the grassland surrounding us. My mouth was dry. Jesse cracked a beer and passed it my way. It was lukewarm and hit my stomach and soured.

"I don't know, Jesse. Maybe this isn't the best—?"

The train whistle sounded. Jesse's body tensed as he moved into a crouch.

"Get ready, Preach."

In the distance, the wheels begin to turn slowly, picking up their impetus with each rotation, and the locomotive started to move ponderously down the tracks toward us like an enormous metal trilobite.

"Don't move until I say so."

The clattering grew louder as the train approached, the tortoise inexorably becoming the hare, picking up speed as it grew closer, its arrival more imminent.

"Don't let the engineer see you; he could call ahead to the bull. Watch for a boxcar with an open door."

As I watched, he bent and picked up a rock and slipped a stone the size of his fist into a pocket. I did the same, puzzled.

Charging forward, the train was nearly upon us now as the roaring engine and whine of the steel wheels on the rails grew to deafening levels. As it became adjacent, I looked closely up into the cab to see if the engineer noticed us, but his dull eyes betrayed nothing as he looked steadily ahead at the track stretching out ahead of him.

A blur of freight cars appeared before our eyes. Jesse stood up; I followed.

I pointed at the ladders on the side of the cars, but Jesse shook his head.

"No good," he shouted. "That's only if you want to get on top."

"What about those," I asked, pointing at some empty open air metal cars.

"Those are flat cars," Jesse said, shaking his head. "They ain't no good except for freezing your ass off on a ride."

The cars whizzed past with more velocity now, a few tankers, a handful of hoppers, the rush of the cars went past at increasing rhythm, inciting dizziness and an uneasy feeling in my guts, where the sour beer churned in my stomach and I nearly retched. Jesse's frustration mounted as a line of cars loaded high with the bodies of felled trees swung past. Reaching into his pocket he tensed as if ready to fling the rock at the train and call it a day, when suddenly he spotted it: an open door on a standard boxcar.

The opening appeared toward the rear of the train. There was a chance the brakeman could see us from the caboose, but Jesse was determined.

"Come on," he shouted and burst out of the bushes and up the berm toward the tracks. I scampered after him, my feet sinking in the soft earth and slipping on the loose gravel.

"Here it comes. Jump!" In one smooth motion Jesse bounded into the darkness of the car.

I grabbed at the dusty floor of the boxcar, but there was nothing to grasp. Running alongside the train as fast as I could along the uneven rocky surface next to the track, panting, I felt myself losing ground, my long legs loping as I tried to keep up. The engine sped up with each turn of its iron wheels: it was leaving me behind. I caught a glimpse of those clanking metal wheels whining below and knew that just one stumble and it would be over. The train's tempo picked up even more as the whistle sounded again.

Pushing myself up with my arms, I hung suspended in the doorway, legs swinging frenetically toward the whizzing wheels below. I could imagine the feeling of the sharp steel cutting through my legs. The blood, the pain; the tears of my father. Would Jenny cry? Living the rest of my life in a wheelchair. Would she nurse me in my infirmity? That's if I lived, that is. A big if. I could bleed to death, or simply be dragged underneath to be chopped and pummeled into an unrecognizable trail of blood, gore and bone.

Then, like the buoyant float of a life preserver to a drowning man, I felt Jesse's hands under my arms, lifting me up, pulling me in with all his strength. With a desperate burst of adrenaline, I pushed off, and propelled myself into the dark interior, landing hard on top of him, both bodies rolling to the other side of the car, to where, after sitting up, and shaking the dust out of our hair, we erupted into relieved laughter.

"Man, I thought you were a goner," Jesse howled. I laughed hard as well, exhilarated and relieved to still be in one piece.

We slid on our asses over to the doorway and sat on the grimy floor, watching the scenery streak by. Still breathing hard, we looked out through the open door as we traveled through long open fields and marshlands, dotted with the occasional farm house, and a road that often paralleled the tracks. At intervals we entered thickly wooded copses, with trees on both sides of the track branching up and across, creating a canopy of leaves that wove together overhead like a tunnel of lush emerald verdure.

"Wahoo!" I screamed and Jesse's voice joined with me. No one could hear us above the rattling tumult; and at that moment, we didn't care if they did.

We whooped and hollered for a while, but soon grew quiet, and fell, mesmerized, into a kind of trance, lulled into an inner quietude by the passing hills and trees, and the rumbling clamor of clanking cars.

Jesse pulled the rock out of pocket and rolled it back and forth between his hands.

"What's that for, anyway?" I asked loudly over the nearly deafening din.

"Couple of things," he shouted back at me. "Sometimes you run into somebody who ain't real happy to share his car with you. Or he's got some weird ideas like he wants to take your money; or something even worse, like a hobo queer who likes boys."

He placed the rock securely in the door opening.

"And even more importantly, you always have to make sure the door doesn't close on you when the train stops. I've heard stories of people getting stuck in a car for days and freezing to death. They find 'em later and they're turned blue and half eaten by rats."

I shuddered at the thought of dying in a filthy, rolling tomb like this. The rushing air whipped past our faces as the train barreled along. Jesse noticed me shivering.

"Don't worry, we didn't bring any heavy clothes, so we won't ride all the way to Marquette this time."

"So then where do we get off?"

"We'll see. I don't much like the look of the guys at the yard in Republic, so I guess we'll have to jump out just before we pull in there and try to catch a ride back."

"Jump?"

"Don't worry buddy, the train won't be going that fast and a few cuts and bruises won't hurt... much," he said, grinning widely. "Just be sure to roll—away from the tracks that is—and try not to bite your tongue or land on your face. Although in your case it might be an improvement."

We both laughed and sat back silently to enjoy the ride, wind rushing past us as the train advanced clamorously on its northeastern journey.

"Hey, didn't you tell me there was a train robbery around here back in the day?" he abruptly shouted at me through cupped hands.

"Yeah, it was some pretty crazy stuff," I yelled back at him.

"Back around the turn of the century or so, some guys chopped down some trees onto the tracks and caused it to stop. They robbed the payroll for one of the mines and they think at least some of them might have got away with it."

"No shit. So what happened to the loot?"

"They never found it. Some people said it was Jesse James or the Younger Gang, but most of the experts think that's bullshit. It was more likely just some hungry locals looking to feed their families. Times were hard in those days."

"But they never found the money, so it could still be out there somewhere?"

"So they say."

He sat facing the landscape we flew by, reflecting on what I had said, his visage flickering in mercurial streaks of shadow and coruscating particles of sunlight.

"Why do you suppose it never turned up?" he asked finally.

"Well, according to the story, the guard shot at the guys who robbed the train as they were leaving. They thought he might've hit a couple of them. Maybe those two didn't make it. They thought they might have caught another three of four of them and dealt with them, but they never found any of the cash."

"None?"

"Nope."

"Maybe they hid the money and were going to go back for it later—?"

"And got caught—"

"Or one or two of them escaped and took the money with them to Mexico."

"Or two got away and they got greedy and killed each other for it..."

We sat in silence for a while, pondering.

"We find that treasure, we split it 50/50, right?" he blurted out.

"Damn straight."

"You know I trust you, Preacher. I trust you with my life."

"You can always trust me, Jesse."

We shook hands.

"We got a good team here; we gotta keep it going, you and me."

"You know it."

"I mean it Bro; you're like my brother, my best brother."

"A brother is a better defense than a strong city, and a friend is like the bars of a castle."

"You make that up?"

"It's from the Bible... Proverbs, I think."

"You and that damn book," he said with a snort. "A friend like the bars of a castle, I like that!"

A few miles later, I survived the jump from the moving car with just a twisted ankle, bloody lip and a ripped shirt to show for my efforts. In the following months, I jumped trains with Jesse several times—even making it to the outskirts of the Marquette rail yard one time, before the game became too tame for us and we moved on to pursue the more stimulating adventures and all-consuming passions of adulthood.

CHAPTER TWENTY-ONE

She wasn't sure when it first began, when she had first noticed him standing in the shadows in her bedroom late at night, a beer in one hand, his other one fumbling at his crotch as he watched her in her bed. She could feel his eyes staring at her as his breathing grew heavier and with a final grunt, he retreated back to the living room. He never touched her, not yet anyway, but it confused her and grossed her out nonetheless.

After he left, her teary eyes would look around the posters and pictures on the walls where beautiful cartoon princesses twirled and danced, smiling happily in their wonderful Neverlands. A prince would surely rescue them from their ogre someday; it was promised, but was it really to be for her?

For years her prince never came, and as the time went by her ogre grew bolder. Sometimes clothing went missing. There was extra touching. A hand on the shoulder or the knee. Uncomfortable conversations. He tried to show her a magazine once; it was men and women together, naked. She covered her eyes and ran and hid. She was afraid and could see in his eyes that he was examining her developing body with interest. It was only a matter of time.

Her mother couldn't help but notice Al's attraction to his stepdaughter, but she simply took what she believed to be the high road, blaming Jenny, whipping her for dressing too provocatively. Even worse, she sometimes took sleeping pills now, seemingly giving her husband the green light to do his nocturnal creeping. And still Jenny's prince never came despite her prayers: she was on her own.

Finally, one night the moment she had been dreading arrived. She awoke, shuddering, her body tightening as though she had rigor mortis, as she felt his weight lower onto the bed, his breath reeking with alcohol and cigarettes as he tried to kiss her. She tried to fight him off, but he just laughed. She started to scream, but he covered her mouth and groped her breasts, his huge belly pinning her to the bed.

"Come on baby girl, you know you want it," he slurred as he reached between her legs.

"No, don't...

"You want it. I know you do."

"No, please," she whimpered between his fingers over her lips.

"You've been teasing your Daddy, haven't you? Showing him that sweet little body of yours. I know you want it, don't you?"

"Yes, yes..." she panted, overcome at last. He pulled her panties slowly down her long smooth legs. "But... please... can I have a beer first... Daddy?"

"A beer?" Al was startled. "What for?"

"I want to get drunk and fuck like Mommies do, Daddy. Pweeze."

"You'll do what you're told?"

"Yes Daddy." The big eyes looked up at him.

"Well, okay. That's more like it." He got up and left the room.

Climbing out of bed quickly, she knelt and pulled the bottom drawer of her dresser completely out and laid it on the floor. Reaching into the dark opening below, she retrieved the Mason jar she had taken from Al's cabinet in the work area of the garage. Remembering the demise of Skippy, the cute little terrier, whose dying gasps she had witnessed as he lay drooling his life away, she poured some of the contents of the jar into Al's half empty beer can that he had left on her desk, returning the jar to its space below the bottom drawer and replacing the drawer just as he was heard singing in a low voice as he staggered back down the hallway.

She looked at him with moistly submissive eyes and suggested in a childish voice that he show her how it was done. He drained his beer, as she pretended to sip, and then she lay back down on the bed and closed her eyes.

"Call me Daddy again," he slurred as she felt his weight press down upon her.

*****

Later, at the hospital she whispered in his ear as he lay pale and nearly comatose: "If you ever even think about touching me again, I promise you that you won't wake up the next time. And I will never call you... Daddy."

    The doctor claimed that had never seen such a violent case of food poisoning and warned Al that he was a lucky man to have survived. The dog killings stopped shortly afterwards.

CHAPTER TWENTY-TWO

The horses snorted and quivered nervously as they stood stiffly on the top of the escarpment, four men in a row mounted astride them, the men keeping their eyes focused into the distance down below the ridge and to the south. Mist rose from the dew soaked brush in the hollow below, turning the morning sunlight into a veil of haze, which enveloped the men and their horses as they waited tensely.

The youngest broke the silence. "Can you see it coming?" His voice was a whisper, but his eyes betrayed the excitement of youth.

Merrick noted the lad's fresh face and felt a twinge of apprehension for allowing the young man to come along. Young Sam was the dark bearded leader's nephew, an energetic and industrious youth, who, having unexpectedly learned of the plan at hand by hiding behind a door and listening in to the men's heated, late night conversations, had begged to be included. Merrick was hesitant—justly so, he felt—to include a novice in this dangerous endeavor, let alone a relative; but he was desperate for a fourth man—especially one he could trust, and he hoped that his sister would eventually forgive him. Clearly he would have to keep a close eye on him; his nephew was a good lad and could be developed in time, but he was practically jumping out of his boots this morning.

Gwynn took the initiative, barking at the boy in mock anger, "Shut up, you silly pup. You might hear it, if you'd just keep quiet."

Merrick's dark eyes sparkled as he surveyed his half-brother taking charge for a change. Although the elder brother was considered the handsome one of the family—with long ginger curls and mustache and a chevron of a beard below his bottom lip—he usually deferred to his dark haired and stocky younger brother. In gang matters it was clear: Merrick was in charge.

Sullenly ignoring the exchange, the fourth member of the group—the ever silent Teague, meandered his horse lazily down the slippery ridge and into the misty shadows to see if he could spot anything. Merrick didn't want him to be noticed and thought about calling him back, but paused. He didn't know Teague well, nor did he trust him. In fact, if he regretted anything more than bringing his nephew along on this dangerous endeavor, it was that he had to rely on a brooding, ill-tempered man who had grown up in the slums of Cornwall, and one who no one in these parts seemed to know much about. What was known, or at least whispered, was that he had killed a man in Nova Scotia waters while sailing aboard a whaler, later escaping the noose and fleeing westward, followed close behind by a bounty on his head, something Teague steadfastly refused to confirm or deny.

Merrick stretched his neck. The man's muscles were stiff; they had been in place for hours. Much earlier—before dawn, they felled and dropped several trees onto the tracks in a position that gave them enough room to operate, and then they simply sat back and waited for it to come. The train that is: the train carrying the payroll for the mine.

Yes, Merrick admitted that he felt some remorse for the families who would have to wait for their pay. Maybe some would even go hungry. But Merrick and his family were hungry too, especially since they had been blackballed from working the mines, charged with instigating trouble: in other words, organizing the men and demanding better pay and treatment. He'd lost everything for standing up for the others, and now he and his family were on their own. If they could just pull this off, they could not only strike a blow against the mine owners, but it would be enough to get them a new start, maybe out west somewhere.

Shaking the reins, Teague turned his horse back and lazily rode up the bank. "I heard it. It's coming," he said calmly.

"Get ready," Gwynn snapped at young Sam, who looked to Merrick for confirmation. The man nodded his consent, and the boy gave a kick and spurred his horse off at a gallop southward along the tracks.

"And stay out of it when things get started. You ride on back home and we'll meet you there," Merrick couldn't keep from shouting after the rapidly retreating figure. The boy waved a hand back toward his uncle as he drove his horse away in a fury.

"Don't know why we don't just let the train crash and pick up the pieces," Teague growled once the boy had disappeared.

"We don't mean to kill anyone, Teague. They tend to hang murderers around these parts, as you may have heard. And I hold no grudge against the men working the train; they are just working to feed their families as we all must." Eying the man to gauge a reaction, he received nothing but a cold, blank stare in return.

"We talked it over and Merrick... er, we decided: the less mess, the better, right brother?" Gwynn added. "While the crew is distracted by the fallen tree, we slip in and out with the cash. No shooting or anything."

"More's the pity," Teague snapped. "How much was it again?"

"They say it's near twelve thousand," Gwynn replied. Merrick's eyes blazed. He knew Teague already knew how much was onboard—they had gone over it several times before.

"Four-thousand apiece," the stranger mused.

"Now Teague, you know it's more like three— a little less even—"

"You pay the kid out of your share."

"That was not the agreement."

"I'm thinking it should be... or maybe I should just go back home to the warmth of my lady's bed and leave you good fellas to your... fun."

Gwynn moved toward his pistol. Teague already held his aimed at Gwynn's heart.

"Four-thousand, Teague," Merrick said dully. "Not a penny more."

"But Merrick—" Gwynn protested.

"Eight thousand is more than enough for the three of us and our families. But Teague, you had better be worth it."

Teague holstered his pistol. "Well, sir, I'd say that I am proud to have left no unsatisfied employers behind in most of my previous engagements. I'm sure you will find me to be well worth the price."

"I hope so," Gwynn muttered and looked away.

"And Teague, another thing—there will be no shooting unless I give the say so. You understand?"

"There will be a guard," he replied, his cold eyes sparkling.

"Yes, there no doubt will be," Merrick said softly.

"He may need persuading," Teague grinned.

"I don't doubt that he may."

"If you'll leave that to me, my good sir, I'm quite sure I can find a way to make the devil talk." He fingered the gun at his side.

"We will see—" The sound of the train approaching stopped the discussion. The men tensed in their saddles.

In the distance, Sam rode full speed alongside the tracks, furiously waving his arms and shouting at the engineer to stop. The driver had already slowed the train and his puzzled face peered out of the window of the cab.

"There's a tree down on the tracks! There's a tree down on the tracks! Stop the train! Stop the train!" the boy pleaded frantically.

His efforts paid off. With brakes shrieking like a flock of banshees, the train slowed to a halt in a secluded grove where several tree trunks lay stacked across the tracks.

"Well, what the hell?" The engineer stammered. "Thank you, son—" But as he turned to speak to him, the boy's silhouette could just be seen receding into the distance as he and his galloping horse raced back up through the trees and over the ridge and disappeared.

CHAPTER TWENTY-THREE

My experience in the big city was as brief as it was disappointing. Although my grades in high school were good enough for acceptance to college, they weren't all that good, and there was no scholarship money available to assist me. So I took out a loan, and my father even pitched in a few bucks, and I was accepted to college in Superior as an undeclared undergraduate, but with hopes of majoring in religious studies. It was with considerable fear and excitement that I loaded my beat up little Nissan and navigated my way to a place farther away from my home than I had ever been in my life.

There I discovered a whole new world, and I can tell you that my new life living in the dormitories was a true revelation. Expecting to find the same fresh-faced, studious and well-mannered student body depicted in the colorful school brochures and catalogs, I was instead bombarded with screaming, shouting and loud music at all hours, shrill exhortations by shit-faced frat boys to partake of beer bongs, and unbridled exuberance over the daily adventures of the *Fighting Saints,* our Division III runner-up football team, all such frivolity actively pursued in lieu of any actual attention to studying. In other words, maybe it wasn't really so different after all: it was just high school all over again.

Turned out, several of the kids were fairly well off, with trust funds and family businesses to inherit at some point in their well-oiled futures, and, with no real need to take learning seriously, the temptation to overindulge on their first extended stay away from mommy and daddy simply proved too much for them to resist.

Meanwhile, the authorities clearly understood just how much business the students and their families brought to the local bars, hotels and restaurants, and for the most part looked the other way at the shenanigans, as long as no property was damaged. I, on the other hand, had already sown enough of my oats, culminating in that aforementioned and forgettable sojourn in the lumberyard, and wished for nothing more than some peace and quiet, spending most of my time at the library or a local coffee shop, where I managed to take a part time job sweeping up and emptying the trash at the end of the night.

Needless to say, my relationships with my fellow students, which began on a sour note when I vehemently declined a spirited request from a rowdy mob to appear wearing a 'fighting saint' costume at the initial pep rally, only managed to deteriorate further with my continued absence from such supremely important social events. I see now, looking back, that I could have perhaps extended a bit more of myself in the direction of the playful mood of the general public and maybe saved myself the painful experiences I endured of loneliness and occasional ostracizing that my antisocial behavior brought upon myself. I suspect they took me for somewhat of an oddball, and I wonder myself nowadays whether I would even have cared to share a beer or cup of coffee with the dismal, sneering little creep I no doubt was in my former life.

Certainly my half-hearted dreams to meet a girl who could help me forget Jenny and start a new life were doomed from the start to be unfulfilled. 'Strange' is not usually a primary character trait most women look for in potential mates, and combined with a lack of money—nor the prospects for any in the future—is generally considered the kiss of death in the romance arena. Nor were my looks any boon in this matter: I had the tall and dark part down, but was sadly lacking in the third requirement.

My religious studies classes were of course, no help in this regard. Aside from one or two blonde, albeit vapid, virgins (who only dated the football stars), most of the women resembled pop-eyed Russian peasant women, complete with lumpy misshapen bodies like sacks of potatoes, unwashed hair, prodigious facial warts and drooping jowls like basset hounds. One bespectacled, heavy-thighed religion class doyenne invited me to her room for tea one evening, but her insistence on assailing my bewildered senses with a reading from an arcane selection of mystical mutterings culled from the Gnostics, a sect whose presence until then I had not even been aware of, combined with the insect repellant taste of Earl Grey tea and sickeningly sweet aroma of patchouli incense, nearly drove me from the room even before she rammed a sloppy tongue in my ear; my escape made only successful by using the timeworn excuse that I did not wish to "ruin our friendship."

Hard as it is to imagine, my relationships with professors were possibly even worse than those with my peers. Seemingly, one of the requirements for obtaining employment as an instructor at this particular institution was to endeavor to always exhibit an abundance of arrogance and self-importance, as well as an imperious attitude toward students, staff and other such lackeys. Perhaps it was an unspoken belief of the faculty that in order to ready the student for the harsh realities of the outside world, rudeness and contempt were to be directed toward the students in their classrooms in order to embarrass them and remove any semblance of innocent ignorance through the time tested rites of trial by fire. This harsh treatment was especially essential if a student showed any sign of weakness or a lack of confidence. As a shy, unconfident fool, who had the most unfortunate habit of blurting out his thoughts at inopportune times, much as someone lobs a soft volley just over the net to a waiting tennis pro, I was a frequent victim of many gleeful slams from my superiors as a result.

The religious studies professors were somewhat more tolerant by nature, yet their behavior was generally condescending toward me, and I found myself bored with their endless lecturing, dry pontifications and pedestrian directions of study. Meanwhile, my love of books and reading was undergoing an unpleasant transformation through the grinder of the Fine Arts Department. One literature professor, who hummed Mozart arias in front of the classroom and then taunted us that we were unfamiliar with the great musical works, was the worst of my tormentors. This tenured terror, whose neatly pointed beard was rumored to be matched by a pair of cloven hooves within his shoes, took particular joy in mocking me, once delighting in deriding my timid mention of Steinbeck's religious themes, while amusedly telling the class that my problem, as well as the author's, was that "we believed that all poor people were good."

Brusquely rejecting my idea to do a paper on the nature of tragedy in Shakespeare, he instead demanded that I write my report on the use of the letter 'S' in paragraph five of Act Four, Scene Three of *Richard II,* or some such nonsense. I sweated over the paper for days and, upon turning it in, was barely given a passing grade. His denunciations of my grand pronouncements and breathless manner of argument were sharp and witty, scrawled in a quick and careless hands as though written when he had nothing better to do, while I managed to garner praise only for a section that I blatantly plagiarized from one of his more well-known contemporaries, whom I suspect he had failed to read.

Meanwhile my clever, or so I thought, opening paragraph for my report on Richard III, in which I mentioned that recent research into serial killers had noted that these individuals seemed to lack what we call a conscience (not unlike my pal Jesse Ray), elicited gasps of horror at my audacity from my classmates, and howls of derision from the professor for daring to call the beloved Shakespearean villain a serial killer. In my defense, I said no such thing, but as with all things my entire life, I was misunderstood again. Sweeping the floors at night, watching the ease at which other people glide through their lives, listening to the bubbling laughter of coeds I would never have the nerve to talk to, replaying the latest round of insults and rejections over and over again in my mind, my despair grew nearly to the point of suicide.

One gloomy night at the coffee shop, my pedantic nemesis arrived alone and took a seat nearby without noticing me, where he commenced to peer over his reading glasses at a thick tome. Swallowing my fear, I took a deep breath, and forcing myself to take the initiative, approached him warily.

"Hello professor," I announced cautiously, in a suitably respectful tone of voice.

"Hello," he responded sullenly without looking up from the book he was reading.

Nervously I continued. "I was wondering if you could let me know if there is anything else I can do to improve my work in your class."

Without looking up, he addressed me with no enthusiasm and in clipped tones. "I keep regular office hours. Please make an appointment with the department secretary. Thank you."

I was dismissed, but too stupid and desperate to know better. "Well, you see," I continued, "I am a bit worried about the upcoming exam—"

"If you must insist on interrupting my reading, at least have the courtesy and initiative to fetch me some more tea: chamomile with a touch of sweet milk," he demanded, glaring furiously over his reading glasses. Hurriedly, I ran to fulfill his request and returned with his tea, which he sipped without pleasure.

"Not fully steeped and a tad heavy on the milk, but it will suffice. Now what may I assist you with? And do be quick about it."

"Well, I don't seem to be doing too well in your Shakespeare class—"

Examining me closely for the first time over his half lenses, he gave a snort of recognition. "Ah yes, Mr. LaPointe, our amateur psychoanalyst. I'm afraid even the Bard of Avon would have to be impressed with the ahem... creativity you displayed in your keen and penetrating analysis of his sublime anti-hero Richard. Yes, one of the finest characters to evolve from the mind of true genius, reduced to a mere Richard Speck of dust by an upstart undergrad who is still just learning his letters."

"I think maybe I was misunderstood—"

"I suspect that if that is the case, it may have been due to your immaturity and undeveloped communication skills. Or quite simply it was merely your initial ill-formed and illogical premise that was the culprit in that particular case. Don't be alarmed, with better effort you may find a way to do better next time. As for the upcoming exam, simply prepare yourself as you would do any test, put your nose to the grindstone and spend some extra time on your notes and I am confident that you will perform to the best of your abilities. Now, my tea grows cold, my eyes are tired and I still have considerable reading to do before I can repose in the welcoming arms of Morpheus."

I started to move away, but something in his kingly manner made me respond angrily.

"*Voi avete un cor fedele.*"

"What's that?" He looked up again from his reading.

"*Voi avete un cor fedele*—You have a faithful heart. That Mozart aria you were humming the other day in class. I knew it, but you didn't even give me the opportunity to say what it was before you told us we were all musical illiterates."

"Well now, I am surprised. And how may I ask…?"

"My father had a few classical recordings in the house when I was growing up."

"Well then, perhaps there is hope yet. Now if you will—"

I refused to let it go. "Why don't you like me, professor?" I blurted out.

"I can assure you that there is nothing personal—"

"I don't believe that."

"I see." He took off the reading glasses and smirked as he stared at me. "Pray go on with your analysis of my character."

"Well, I just get the feeling you don't like me and I'm not sure why. I love reading and great literature, I try hard… tell me, what it is I am doing wrong?"

"Well, Nathan," he said with a sneer as he dramatically waved his spectacles at me, "love of literature is no guarantee of success in school, you know. We may all enjoy picking up a good book now and then, but your so called *love of reading* must be converted into results, or you are simply someone who… likes to read a little. Such as a truck driver or factory worker who may enjoy reading for leisure during lunch breaks."

"Do you see me as a factory worker?" I asked in a fury.

He stared at me with his cold eyes and said bluntly. "I have been a professor for more than twenty years, Mr. LaPointe, and I believe that I have earned the right to consider myself a more than competent judge of which students will succeed and which will… simply fade away."

"And you don't see me as succeeding."

"To begin with—if I may speak frankly—please understand that it is not your fault, but primarily a matter of your antecedents: your background, your genetics, so to speak. Look at the facts. You are a country boy, from a rural small town, with, I would imagine, poor to average educational standards and facilities; peers no doubt of low level intelligence; indulgence in drinking and perhaps even drugs, a broken home I suspect…" he squinted in the candlelight as he plumbed the depths of my guileless face for its mysteries. "...yes, a father or mother missing from your life; a lack of fortitude, energy, insight; a needy, weepy, bookish child raised in an intellectual wasteland—*Voi avete un cor fedele* notwithstanding, with a brain packed full of television, religion and other superstitions.

"No, Mr. LaPointe," he continued, "surely you must have read the news that it is a difficult world out there and one must be tempered like steel to take it on. It takes the courage of a lion to achieve anything of value in the literary field, or in that of any other I might add, and there are times when you simply must face the fact that you don't exhibit the necessary requirements. My duty as a professor is to help young men to see the light, to see their limitations and to prepare them for what their lives will become. In your case, I foresee you making your way, as a... schoolteacher. Yes, that's it. Your father was a schoolteacher for a time, if I remember correctly. I can see you following in your father's footsteps. Nothing wrong with that. A noble profession, teaching..."

I trembled and bit my lip, but said nothing.

"Freud, my child," he continued pompously. "As I constantly entreat my charges in the classroom, the key to all of the mysteries of life and humanity can be found in Freud, the Upanishads and Wittgenstein. Read and master this holy trinity and you will learn all you need to know in life."

"But as a teacher?" I said, choking.

"You may, with some considerable effort and the possible attainment of wisdom and maturity through the years, be able to succeed on that level. There are always school districts looking to hire, I am told. But clearly you will need to work hard to overcome your limitations before you should be allowed to bend and mold the minds of our pliable youth. It may be that teaching itself may also prove to be beyond your capabilities, and, as I am not sure what else you can do with a background in literature, you may wish to consider perhaps looking into alternatives, such as trade schools.

"I was thinking maybe of preaching."

"An... interesting choice," he said with a cocked eye.

"And I had read in the Wall Street Journal that businesses are looking for people with written communication skills."

"Indeed? Well, that is welcome news to me. But don't let me rain on your parade. If you read it in a newspaper it must surely be true."

"You make it sound like I shouldn't even be in school. That I am wasting your time."

"I'm sorry to be blunt, but you must know that I am an exceptional judge of aptitude, and I feel that I would be doing you a severe disservice if I encouraged you in following such unachievable... fantasies."

"And you don't think much of my... aptitude."

He sighed. "You must learn not to take things personally. We are all products of forces beyond our control. Our DNA and so forth. One of the greatest lessons we must all learn is to accept the things that we cannot change."

"So you are telling me... to know my place."

"Well done, Mr. LaPointe. You are learning something. And if you must know what initially confirmed my diagnosis of your abilities was your actions on the first day of class," he went on ruthlessly. "Do you remember where you sat that day?" His eyes twinkled merrily.

"No..." I stammered. "Maybe the second row?"

"Yes, that's it. Exactly. The second row: second best. Do you understand the concept? I have taught students for many years and from close observational analysis have developed an extremely accurate theory about the level of achievement that my students will be able to attain. Would you care to hear it?"

Without waiting to hear my answer, he continued. "You see I have closely examined the careers of my past students with considerable interest and have determined that where a student sits on the first day of class tells me what grade the student should receive. Students in the front row will almost always tend to receive the A's, while those in the second row earn the B's and so on. I have watched the results for years and years and I can assure you, the formula almost never fails."

"So because of where I sat on the first day—"

"And your antecedents of course, but yes, your seating was most unfortunate." He patted my arm in consolation. "Still, a B student is not so bad and should provide a good basis for a possible future teaching career."

I was shocked and began to protest, but he waved me away with the back of his hand.

"Now please leave me in peace. You have unfortunately wasted five minutes of my time; time that I can never reclaim. Really, I have asked the management here in the past not to allow me to be disturbed. I will let this infraction on your part pass, but only this time. You will learn some day. Youth is never aware of how valuable the time allotted us truly is until it is too late. And my time... the time of someone with real meaningful work to do, is especially at risk of being disrupted by mundane and trivial interruptions. So Mr. LaPointe, let us make an end to this evening's unexpected conversation. Calm your fears of impending tests and make yourself into a shadow, and I in turn, will bid you goodnight and forgive your youthful impertinence." He put his glasses back on and reopened the book.

As I turned to leave, tears welling in my eyes, he delivered one last message: "Besides, I believe it is nearly time for you to empty the garbage."

I don't remember much except for swinging my arm, and the sharp feeling as I cut my knuckles on his glasses, the crunch as my fist broke his nose, and the horrifying, yet almost comical way in which his form flailed in slow motion, crashing through the glass window and falling outside onto the sidewalk below.

CHAPTER TWENTY-FOUR

They came for him in the night, long after the television had been shut off, and after he had fallen deeply into sleep. His brothers roughly pulled the still groggy boy unwillingly from the warmth of his bed and dragged him to the backyard, where he stood, rubbing his eyes and shivering in his pajamas and bare feet on the damp grass, under the gaze of his father, whose whisky-soaked breath nearly staggered him.

"I want to sleep," the boy whined. His father's rough hand slapped his face and dropped him to the damp ground.

"Shut up, you little piss ant!" His father's voice rumbled like thunder. "Pick him up!" he commanded, and Jake and Jared pulled their brother up by his arms. Their faces grim; they knew what was coming.

"Your mother says you've been playing around in school, you little cocksucker. You like games? Let's play some games." Jude's voice was slurred, his eyes glowing red in the dark. Jesse looked around for an escape: the plank fence rose high around the yard like an impenetrable wall, Jared's bulky frame blocked the only gate like the moon blacking out the sun in an eclipse. Whimpering, Jesse looked to the house for help, a curtain fluttered in his parent's window, a silhouette appeared in profile, and then quickly disappeared.

"Mom—" he started to call when the fist hit his stomach and he doubled over and fell to his knees.

"Shut the fuck up." Raising his voice like a salvation show preacher, the angry man shook with rage as he stared into the skies indignantly and shouted, "This ain't any of her concern. These are my boys and I'll make sure they learn what's what."

"I... I... Dad, don't...." Jesse forced the words out.

"Get up, you little prick. Get up and get what you've got coming." The man's weathered face burned crimson with hate, a hate that had only a little to do with his boy's behavior, but had as its source the fires of self-hatred and anger at the world, fueled by years of failures, disappointments, pain and alcohol abuse. Jesse pulled himself slowly to his feet.

"You want to play games? Let's play some games," his father muttered as he paced.

"Jake, you and Jesse go first."

"I don't want to, Dad," Jake said in a quavering voice.

"You don't... want to?" The eyes burned, the voice hissed.

"He's too little."

"That's bullshit, boy. You have to start when they're young. Like my Daddy did. Like I started with you and Jared."

"Yeah, the kid's turning into a pussy," Jared snarled.

"Now you either give him the treatment, or I give it to you. What's it going to be?'

Jake reluctantly posed in a boxing stance with both fists up in front of Jesse.

"Hit him," his father ordered and popped open a beer.

Jake tapped Jesse on the chest.

"That ain't hitting. You better hit him, or I'll be hitting on you."

Jake swung and popped Jesse's arm.

"Owww," Jesse cried.

"That still ain't worth shit, Jakey. The kid needs a smack in the kisser. A bloody nose and a fat lip will wake up the smarty-pants."

"Get your fists up, dummy," Jake whispered to his stunned little brother.

"Hey, no fair giving hints," his father said and threw the empty beer can against Jesse's forehead. Jesse's head snapped back and the tears came streaming down his cheeks.

"Daddy, I'm sorry..." Jesse wasn't sure what he was sorry for. Glancing again at the gate, he considered making a run for it, Nate's house wasn't far, but Jared read his thoughts and mouthed *don't even think about it.*

"He's sorry, he says he's sorry. Look at the little baby crying that he's sorry. Yeah you are sorry alright; you are one sorry little..." He fished out another can of beer from the cooler and took a swig, sitting down on the cooler with a thud. "Now I want to see some fighting here, or I am going to get mad. Hit him, Jake!"

Jake swing and caught Jesse in the nose. Blood spurted in all directions as he fell hard to the ground.

"Hoowee! Yeah, that's how you do it!" His father hooted and slapped his knee. "Pick him up. Jared, it's your turn."

"No, Jared—" Jesse cried, but the beefy fist struck his stomach, knocking the wind out of him. His body curled up and he drooped to the ground.

"Ha ha! That's the way, son. Work the body. Soften him up for me. That's how we used to do it to queers in the army. Your turn again, Jake. Hee hee, this is fun, huh? I love playing games. I could watch this all night long."

Jake swung, but Jesse ducked and the punch only grazed the top of his head.

"Goddamn it, Jacob!" the old man howled, his face crazy, wolfish in rage. Cuffing Jake's ear, he proclaimed loudly, "He's learning, he is. Getting tricky like a mouse. You missed him, dummy. Give it another shot and this time you better connect like good."

Tears of anger brimming in his eyes, Jake hauled back and unleashed, hitting Jesse in the jaw, sending him flying back onto his back on the lawn, where he lay sobbing.

His father strode over and pulled him up. "You disgusting little crybaby. Are you going to let these two pussies beat you all night, or are you going to fight back?" Jesse growled and rose to his feet. Lowering his head, he charged full force into Jake and knocked them both down. Swinging his fists blindly, he struck his older brother with rapid bursts of his tiny fists.

"That's it! That's the way you do it. You don't let anybody knock you around without knowing they're going get something in return. You may be smaller, but it ain't the size of a dog in a fight, it's the fight in the dog. You gotta let 'em know you ain't gonna take it lying down. Bite him, pinch him, scratch him, hit him in the nuts, do whatever it takes to win."

Jake grabbed both of Jesse's fists and pinned him squirming to the ground. "Quit hitting me," he screamed.

"Aw, is the little kid picking on the big, bad brother? Looks to me like he got you good there, Jake. You going to let him get away with that?" Grinning, his bony features giving his face the appearance of a glowing skull, the man stalked relentlessly in a circle around the fight.

Finally pulling the two apart, he shoved Jake out of the way. "Jared's turn," he sang out. "Let's see if the little mouse can take the fat one. I'm betting that he can. My money says the little one might just give Chubby a run for his money."

Jared's eyes glared like his father's as he raced toward Jesse ready to do damage. This time, Jesse's small fists were raised.

The games continued for hours, sometimes several days a month, sometimes for reasons of punishment, often times not, until his father at last made a mistake and got himself thrown into prison where he ended up stabbed to death not long after. Until that time, and true to his plan, the brothers would soften Jesse up for his father, who with a leer on his face that haunted Jesse for the rest of his life, would then proceed to remove his belt and bring the games to an end.

CHAPTER TWENTY-FIVE

O ur cooking career basically came to an end one snowy night in the forest. At that time, we were still novices at our newfound trade. Our first attempts were painfully shoddy, but the product still sold surprisingly well. Junior was pleased and pushed us for more. In my greed and elation, I had forgotten what the Bible says — *Ignorant zeal is worthless; haste makes waste*, and I allowed myself to ignore my usual caution as I drove myself ever faster down our newfound path to Hell. We knew it was dangerous, but that only heightened our sense of excitement.

Anyway, it was damn cold that night and the roads were slick, and if we would have had any sense we would have stayed home, but greed makes you do stupid things. Jesse, Jenny and I took his brother's truck and loaded a couple of snowmobiles and headed out to his property. Jenny's mom was watching Jeremy that night. The place wasn't far from town, but we slid all over the slippery roads and by the time we got there it was well after dark.

The road into the woods hadn't been plowed, but there was a spot we could park the truck just off the road, and we got on the snowmobiles and headed up the trail. The snow was deep, wet and heavy, but the wind was strong enough that the flakes blew swirling around our heads, ice crystals sticking on our faces and stinging our cheeks. Jesse roared far ahead with Jenny riding bitch and screaming into the storm with delight, but I took my time—visions of hitting a tree stump and launching myself through the air face first into a tree trunk gave me pause.

When we arrived, Jesse and I hurriedly climbed into the travel trailer where we kept the chemicals and mixed our batches, while Jenny headed across the lot to the full-size trailer to turn up the heat and see about some coffee. We planned on spending the weekend cooking.

Meth is easy to produce—anyone can do it. Trust me, I'm no chemist, but you can get all the info you need out of books or on the internet. Once inside, Jesse switched on the lights and flipped on the space heater. We kicked the slush off our boots and slipped into our slippers, and then I started things off by opening up the boxes and grinding the cold and allergy pills into powder in a dish with the flat head of a claw hammer.

After I had smashed up a good portion, we poured the powder into some wood alcohol in a plastic jar with a lid and started shaking it. You have to shake it for a good twenty minutes or so, so Jesse and I took turns. We were focused on what we were doing and didn't really say very much. I turned on the radio, but it had a broken antenna, and with the storm, we could only pick up static, so we shut it off and the only sounds were the wind howling through the trees outside and the rhythmic shaking of the jar.

Jenny showed up with two cups of steaming coffee, spiked with some Chivas—which was our drink of choice those days. We sat on rickety stools under a shop light Jesse had strung up, joking around about what we were going to do with the money we were sure to get from this batch, while we let the chemicals separate and settle— waiting for the good stuff to float to the top.

Even after slipping Junior his share, we'd made a decent amount of change from our first several efforts and were giddy with power. I moved out of my dad's place and into one half of a crummy duplex. Jesse had put money down on their house and bought a used Trans Am and Jenny... well, she got to ride in it. She talked about wanting to buy some baby stuff for Jeremy, but Jesse had bigger plans. He bought the snowmobiles the week before as a Christmas present to himself and Jenny.

We were getting good at this—professional even; and we followed the checklist I devised like clockwork. Next step: put a coffee filter into a funnel, and then carefully pour the pseudoephedrine into a glass dish trying not to get too much of the crap in there to keep it as clean as you can. You have to burn the alcohol off—so we plugged in a hairdryer and took turns heating the stuff. We used Jesse's oven for our first efforts, but the fumes were making Jenny and the baby sick, and she had a fit, so we switched to the hairdryer.

Before we had even put our masks and gloves on we were pretty hungry. We weren't using the stuff ourselves yet at that point, and the coffee wasn't really keeping us going like it should. Jenny said she'd go make us some toasted cheese sandwiches. We had some red phosphorus we extracted from road flares added with hydrochloric acid cleaning solution in another jar, and we added our powder to that, screwed the lid on and started back in on the shaking. We'd talked about finding something to automate this part of the process—maybe a paint mixer? But for now we figured sore arms were worth the financial reward.

After about twenty minutes or so, Jenny came back with the sandwiches and we put the jar aside. She told us that, although she couldn't see a picture, she could get sound, and that the TV said the storm wasn't getting any worse. Of course, it wasn't going to get any better anytime soon either. Outside, the trees creaked from the weight of the snow, while the wind wailed on in big gusts producing surging waves of drifting snow. Our angel delivered hot chocolate this time—and what a treat that was. I was starting to get drowsy, but the hot sweet stuff gave me a much-needed boost.

Soon it was time to add the sodium hydroxide, so Jesse opened the jar and the pungent odor immediately filled the air. Jenny said goodnight and left to go back to the trailer—her mother had to work at the church the next day, so she'd have to get some sleep before picking up the kid. Jesse jokingly called her a wuss for abandoning us. He was just kidding her, but she still got a little mad and stomped off, laboriously trying to walk back in her own footsteps through the drifts to the other trailer.

Suddenly, the power sputtered and the trailer went dark for a moment—the light above us flickering off and on again. Jesse, startled, spilled a drop of acid onto his foot. As it burned through his slipper, he shouted out in pain and kicked his foot out.

Bumping the table hard as he leapt up, he knocked the jar over—its contents spilling onto the table, where the hissing pool of liquid slowly moved toward the edge, where it lingered momentarily, before cascading in slow motion toward the space heater below. Whirling, Jesse's upturned hand struck the work light, which came unloosed and fell, tumbling toward the ground, glancing off Jesse's head on its downward plummet.

Our eyes met for a split second.

I was closest to the door and shot through it with a speed I didn't know I possessed. Jesse was close behind me, pushing me even faster through the exit. Ahead, Jenny's form turned and looked back, eyes wide in terror, as the trailer erupted in a powerful blast.

The impact threw me to the ground as smoldering debris flew everywhere, scattering in all directions. Jesse's shirt was on fire and he ripped it off and rolled screaming in the snow. Jenny stood still, staring at the blast as if frozen in one spot.

The sparkling winter air was filled with twinkling ashes descending intermingled with floating snowflakes, amidst rising noxious fumes and the sounds of pieces of plastic, wood and metal popping and crackling around us. Our ears echoed with the reverberations of the violent blast, but the world around us was still; no sirens filled the air. We were alone—no one heard; no one could help, but no one would prosecute either.

As we stood and watched in horror, flames sputtered and sizzled, and black and gray smoke rose in a thick spiral into the sparkling night sky. And as we realized we had escaped alive, the sound of joyous, uncontrollable laughter surged forth from this trio of very lucky survivors, who were well aware and quite thankful that they had cheated death, at least for the time being.

CHAPTER TWENTY SIX

I guess I always knew Preacher was in love with me. Of course back then he was just mopey little Nate LaPointe—he wasn't the Preacher yet—but he was a serious little shit nonetheless. Kind of a runt too before he suddenly shot up about a foot or two during high school. I think I stood a head taller than him in 5th grade and probably could've knocked the living snot out of him, but we got to be pretty good buddies, playing hide and seek, chasing crawdads down at the river, stealing apples and generally just being typical pain in the ass kids.

I remember a time at the county fair and we were riding on the Ferris wheel and I caught him trying to sneak a peek down my shirt. I threatened to throw him out and twisted his arm behind his back until he yelled uncle, but I wasn't really too upset. I was starting to develop and I didn't mind the attention I was getting from the boys who previously never even threw me a glance except to call me "skinny" or "chicken legs."

Like Jesse Hawkins. Yeah, I admit that I had a thing for him from the moment I laid eyes on him, more fool me. My mother always had him pegged as a worthless creep, but she didn't exactly set the bar any too high herself, so I never paid her any mind. Like Preach used to say, there's only been one man who was perfect in this world and they crucified him a long time ago.

I never thought I could get anyone to love me, let alone Jesse. He was always the center of attention, the ringleader, the class clown, the tough guy—everything you want in a man, even when he was just a boy. I never thought I was pretty. Sure, my stepdad used to get touchy-feely and say some things about me being pretty, but my mama never said it once. She was always on me about how I looked: if I dressed nice I was a slut; if I dressed down I was a slob.

All little girls want to be princesses; it's in our blood, I think. I tried not to be. I tried to be one the boys. I was as tough as I could be, but underneath I was helpless and might as well be trapped in a castle waiting for a knight from one of those stupid stories. I wanted to run away, but without Jesse, I'm not sure I ever would have ever escaped from my tower cell.

There were other pretty girls, prettier than me of course, but I guess Jesse and I hit it off mainly because we could make each other laugh. Man, he made me laugh. He could tell the funniest stories and do the most off the wall stuff. You know, we couldn't ever pass a tree without him climbing way up in the top branches before you could blink. He always drove the teachers crazy, acting up, making jokes, and arguing and talking back just for the hell of it. He knew what his daddy would do when he found out, but he just kept on going, almost as if it was just to spite his old man.

Zero to sixty in six seconds flat, that's Jess, and in fifty directions at once mind you. If you could just bottle the energy in that boy there'd never be any damn energy crisis. His mind just kept going and going, working out all sorts of plans and schemes; of course he usually never did finish anything he started: that's why I think in some ways it was good for him to be around Junior and Preacher — they could kind of keep him on track and headed in a direction, even if the track they laid wasn't exactly within the boundaries of the law.

Yeah, my Jesse kept me on my toes and we had a lot of laughs together, but I truly think the strongest thread that connected us was that we could see each other's dark side. Jesse knew what I had been through, and I knew about his father and him, and we could understand each other in a way that no one else could. Preacher... he had pain too, after all his mama left him when he was just a baby, but he still had hope. He had a father; he had brains and talent and all that knowledge about things from all his reading, and all that positive mental attitude crap from going to church: he could have gotten out, maybe even had a future if he wanted. He just never could understand that it wasn't like that for Jesse and me.

CHAPTER TWENTY-SEVEN

Why did I hit him? I still wonder and replay the scene in my mind. Certainly I had been pushed around, insulted and mistreated many times before but I was always unwilling or maybe just unable to break through the inertia of my life to take any action against my oppressors. But this time something clearly snapped—something within me that had been repressed and tightened to its breaking point over time. I'm sure his beloved Freud would have something to say about it. Although I was outwardly horrified and ashamed by my action, secretly I reveled in it. Yes, admittedly the victim of my outburst was older and smaller than I was—an aged man, almost a cripple, soft and toad-like in body, but my heart still pounded proudly at the memory of the testosterone rising, charging the blood that coursed through my veins and the nerves, triggering the reactions in my muscles that, in an explosion of bottled rage, helped me put that evil incarnate in his place. It felt good.

Naturally, I was appalled and humiliated to be sent home in disgrace. Restitution and a humbling written apology was all that was required, as the professor—to his credit—refused to press charges in the hopes that the squalid tale would fade more quickly away. I was treated as a hero among the few students I ran into while making my escape, and I was greeted sadly by my father upon my return, with his only comment being that he only wished I had shown as much spunk on the baseball diamond. Outwardly, I appeared chastened at first; inside, I longed for the feeling of release that impulsive discharge of fury had elicited in me, and I burned with the fervor to experience it again.

So when I ran into Jesse again, as I knew I would, selling pot in the park, hanging with the other dopers and petty thieves, scheming with his brothers and Little Pete and lately Junior, it was an easy move to fall back into his world. It was clear to me now that the world of fang and claw, blood and flesh, sex and violence were more real than any of the fairy stories they tried to teach me in church or school. Being good offered no rewards, of this I was now sure. Timidly at first, I dipped my toe into the rippling waters and, renouncing my former life as a punching bag forever, dove headfirst into the dark and murky waters that bubbled below.

I was still called "The Preacher," but soon my name was beginning to be mumbled with respect and a bit of fear by my former tormentors, not only because of who I associated with, but because I had changed. I was taller and had grown into a wiry and somewhat more formidable frame, but mainly it was something in my eyes. They were now like Jesse's, hard and with a glint that whispered of an undercurrent of malice that would not be pretty to encounter if goaded to emerge. I had been tested and tempted and now come to the realization that the earthly body was all we had, and that like Jesse always said, we needed to take what we could while we still had the strength to do so. So, I followed my mentor and was his right hand man, and we made quite the team, successful and respected, albeit at the lowest levels of society.

One night I ran into Hal Turner seated alone at the bar. One of the jocks who ran in a pack and used to belittle me, he saw me coming and looked quickly away, visibly nervous and trembling, understanding that he could not call on any backup in this situation. Walking over confidently, I stood towering over him, glaring with hatred, relishing in the fear I saw in his eyes.

Muttering, and giggling, he tried making a few lame jokes. I didn't laugh, but just took a long drag on my beer bottle and asked him where his friends were and if he still thought he could knock my brains out in two seconds. It was stupid; he still outweighed me by a ton, but he saw now that I had no fear in my voice or cold stare, so he just twittered nervously, and his voice got higher, sweat running down his face. Turning away with a sneer, I walked out, leaving him relieved and still in one piece, but knowing that the weights had been shifted on the scale, and that the balance had been forever changed with regards to his relationship with me.

It was only in the hours before dawn when I lay awake that I crucified myself with guilt over what I had become. But I never could decide if it was remorse that kept me awake and troubled, or whether I was tortured because I was ablaze with dreams of Jenny's

arms holding me tight as I fell headlong into the abyss of those
suffocating, funereal nights.

CHAPTER TWENTY-EIGHT

Please sit down. Would you care for a glass of Merlot? Too early in the day? Nonsense. Well, I hope you won't mind if I indulge myself with a glass or two as we speak. I don't have class for a couple of hours and t'will merely provide me some of the vigor necessary to teach the intricacies of Browning's rapturous poetry to the same cretins who would have trouble deciphering the picaresque adventures of one Archie and his stalwart companion, Jughead.

This particular vintage comes from a secluded vineyard I discovered on one of my sojourns to my ancestral home and its surrounds and has become one of my favorite little rewards to myself for bearing the heavy burden of finding myself inexplicably incarcerated—I should say tenured, unto this drab diploma factory year after year. But I sense good fortune may be in the winds: retirement looms ever nearer and I will shortly extricate myself from this fetid Midwestern tomb and settle somewhat nearer the sunrise, eastward across the Atlantic. You see, I have a highly neglected book in the works concerning the lack of Platonic ideals in 17th Century French literature to complete, but I won't bore you with the sordid details of that particular pedagogic endeavor.

Ah, that's better. Served at room temperature—not chilled like the insipid clods around here are apt to do. Now where were we? Ah yes, the Nathan LaPointe incident. I had almost forgotten that ridiculous scene. How is our middleweight champ doing these days? Oh? I cannot say that I find myself surprised.

I'll have you know that I have acquiesced to speak with you regarding this matter only because you have agreed to hear me out and set the record straight at last and for all time. I am perfectly at ease with allowing this unsavory escapade to fade permanently into the void, but certain hostile elements in my workplace have conspired to keep rumors afloat, and I find the pungent odor of this trash rising at times from the gutter where it belongs, reeking and forming itself into ever wilder phantasmagoria which confronts and confounds me with such a stench of utter untruth that I feel I must present what really occurred upon that fateful night.

No doubt you already know the stage on which this tragedy unfolded. I was seated at my usual place in the café, where I had previously observed Mr. LaPointe was employed. Mind you, I had given the management strict instructions not to allow the patrons or staff to bother me—aside from bringing me my tea, as I was engaged in important research for my aforementioned manuscript and could not abide even the slightest interruption. Whether it was due to the fact that he was relatively newly employed and had perhaps not yet received the appropriate instructions regarding my need for solitude, or, more likely, adolescent nervousness over his less than stellar performance in the classroom, the impertinent youth chose to disrupt my thoughts, just as I was pondering an argument I had recently undertaken with Oxford's Professor Teasley over his obdurate and inane assertion that Flaubert was a Marxist (as if!).

The rude behavior in interrupting me was bad enough, but the bothersome child just kept standing there like a shabby scarecrow— gawking, stammering and blinking his eyes as if he were going to burst out at any moment into a fit of theatrical weeping.

You must understand a few things about Mr. LaPointe's persona, if you will. Under his seemingly innocent outward demeanor, he was what I would call a bad egg. I marked him early, and indeed my hunch bore out as it nearly always does. His true self was revealed through his actions as a jittery, yammering, unfocused, nervous Nellie, with little perception, no manners and a sneaky mean streak.

But unbridled enthusiasm in the young is like an untethered puma, and as such, his subsequent flare up was not so unexpected after all. His attendance was, shall we say, spotty at best, and when he did bother to make an appearance, he was often late, sleepy, smirking and possibly... stoned. Yes, I suspect the boy may have been under the influence of illegal substances, as I noted the reeking stench of what I suspect to be low grade marijuana smoke upon his person, yet I did not call him out for such disrespect, only his lackadaisical work habits and shoddy scholarship.

I have three rules that I wish to impart to those in my charge: show up for class, show up on time, and do the work. LaPointe was not alone in his sins; he was really no different than the majority of my students who have been raised to believe they are somehow entitled and must only be treated with gentleness and patience. Balderdash. That is not how the world works, and we would only release them into the wild to be devoured by the bigger and nastier fish that feed upon the slow and the weak. Wasting time on the laggards is unproductive; the unworthy must unfortunately be discarded, while the select few must be tempered into steel through a crucible of fire. We professors are the ones called upon to feed the flames of the ovens.

Of course most, like the aforementioned LaPointe, are simply not suited to succeed and will fall by the wayside. That bootstrap business may work selling pizzas, but unless you are into primitive folk art, the fine arts are the domain of the educated and cultured. It is a simple fact. You play Mendelssohn on a Stradivarius; fiddles are best suited for "Turkey in the Straw."

Shakespeare, you say? Unlikely indeed, that a clodhopper from down on the farm, penned the glorious creations that bear his name. Most well-informed persons agree it was likely Edward DeVere, the 17th Earl of Oxford who wrote that extraordinary canon of sonnets and plays, using the unwitting farm boy Shakespeare as his beard... er bard. Heh heh.

You look at me askance, as if my Ivy League background precludes me from insight into the plight of the lower classes. Let me assure you that I have done my share of hard work. Maybe not slaving in the fields or a factory, but during college I spent my summer years working at the club, and believe me it is no picnic doing laundry and cleaning up after the members. And one summer I even spent several tiring days helping the servants varnish my grandfather's gazebos. But clearly this whole "poor people are holy" message about the lower class can be dismissed as Socialist claptrap. I mean really, have you ever heard of a rich person mugging you?

As for my theory regarding the placement of students based on their seating arrangement, I am unrepentant. I have more than twenty years in this field and I am certainly, by now, entitled to my opinions. Life is not supposed to be fair, and the sooner some of these coddled puppies learn this, the better.

Regarding the punch itself, it was simply too quick and unexpected for me to dodge. Although I am somewhat diminutive in height, and mental stress and the years of academic life have left me in less than ideal physical condition, I was a rower and cross country runner of some note in my younger days, and if given some forewarning, may well have given the headstrong lad a sound whipping. Of course, maturity has long since lessened my desire to throw a roundhouse punch at an adversary, and as a result, his cheap shot caught me completely off guard, leaving me the butt of many an ill-informed jest.

I especially resent the implication that somehow my *cruel* indifference to his sad plight, as well as my allegedly sarcastic elucidations, were somehow enough to propel the boy into a fit of frenzy. He obviously had mental problems to begin with; but if indeed I had a hand in his eruption, I take pride in the fact that the quivering wastrel finally felt strongly enough about something to take a stand. His aimless nature, simpering smile and too eager to please personality were frankly enough to make this highly-trained educator vomit. Allowing him to continue in at the school would have only served to delay the inevitable, whilst taking up the space needed for a more deserving candidate.

So although it ended his college career, for which he was clearly unsuited anyway, at least he took a solid step in the direction of becoming the man he was destined to be. He discovered his true meaning—something many perhaps never do, and I have to admit that I... admire him for it. We need more of that type of self-discovery; there would be less unhappiness due to unmet expectations and unreachable chimeras.

The blow he struck did break my nose I'm afraid. But even that was a blessing as it gave my rather bland face a touch of much needed character that I am told by some admirers is rather becoming. My body shattered the window and hit the sidewalk rather hard, knocking the wind out of me, but I fortunately found myself otherwise unhurt.

Stunned a bit at first, I launched myself to my feet and beat a hasty escape to the nearby college clinic. Rest assured that it was only out of Anglican charity that I turned the other cheek and did not climb back in the ring to thrash him thoroughly. He stood there, clenching his fists, staring with hate filled eyes, and I could not be sure that he wasn't on drugs—angel dust perhaps?—possibly ready to leap upon me like a vicious animal looking to finish the task. So I decided on prudence as the best tack, and here I am sipping this fine Merlot in my well-furnished and comfortable home, so I would suspect you would have to agree that I made the appropriate choice.

I had my nose reset, and took a too short, but admittedly quite refreshing sabbatical to France, while the storm calmed down in my absence. I steadfastly refused to press charges—something I believe has been unfairly overlooked in the accounts I have heard bantered about. The boy paid restitution to the bistro and was dutifully expelled. I could see no purpose served by having him incarcerated, and I quite honestly preferred that this somewhat disconcerting episode did not linger on in the spotlight ad infinitum.

So naturally the gossip lingers even now, and I still suffer occasional humiliations through hurtful comments by unfeeling colleagues; but I am content knowing that I will have the last laugh and soon will leave these yokels and their third rate institution behind me forever. They will be the jealous ones, as they remain behind, shoveling lumps of knowledge to an endless conveyer full of *brummagem* "students," whilst I wander the vineyards and dusty libraries of the Mediterranean region, contented, and still actively engaged in the pursuit of a higher plane of existence in the autumn of my life.

I am surprised to find I am saddened to hear of the young man's end, but my conscience is clear that I was honest with him; perhaps the only one in his life who has been. And, to that end, he was able to find his true meaning in life.

We all have our parts to play in the unfolding comedy or tragedy we inhabit in this universal playhouse in the round. And in fact, I am pleased to learn that my seating arrangement theory has once again been proven right. Perhaps someday, after my treatise on Plato is complete, I will formulate my findings on classroom seating and produce a manual on the subject that can be used by professors everywhere.

But that is getting the cart well ahead of this balky steed; and, as the bottle seems to have evaporated during my telling, I must bid that you leave me now, as I must prepare for my upcoming lecture on *Fra Lippo Lippi*—that delightful poetic vignette—relating the exploits of the loquacious wayward monk and painter, as captured vividly in the midst of his illicit nocturnal excursions, and brought compellingly to life across the ages by the exceedingly brilliant Mr. Browning. *Zooks!*

CHAPTER TWENTY-NINE

In the dusky half-light, sniffing the cool air with keen focus, the alpha male led the pack surging down along the swale and through the fence in a section where the thunderstorm had knocked it down on its side in the tall grass, its electrical spark no longer functioning as an effective deterrent, and across the meadow to where the hapless herd was grazing contented and unaware. Creeping forward slowly, stealthily, they searched the bovines assembled for a suitable target.

It didn't take long. Straying a step too far from the mass of cattle, the calf skittered lightly, its young wobbling legs skipping forward, prancing, attracted the eye of the alpha, and the beast charged ahead urgently in the calves' direction.

Bounding, leaping powerfully forward, he was upon it without delay, sinking his teeth into the unsuspecting babe's nose, taking it down to the ground with a ferocious twist, before the terrified herd had any sense of what was happening. The calf bayed in pain and fright as teeth ripped her face apart. Struggling to regain her feet, a second set of fangs severed the tendons of her back legs and she fell, faltering with a cry. Snarling, a third wolf bit a huge chunk out of her belly, exposing ribs and bloody entrails that the alpha wolf greedily began devouring, even as the calf bawled and the life force drained from her twitching body. Tearing the flesh from the midsection, the alpha voraciously chewed with bloody maw, while the other wolves circled and smacked their lips hungrily.

As the herd scattered, the mother cow moved with purpose toward her calf, but the growling wolves forced her back.

An onrush of deep barking suddenly disrupted the attack, as a pair of white bear-like dogs parted the herd and bolted vigorously into the circle, snapping their jaws, attacking the pack with an ancient, deep-seated hatred of the wild canines, knocking the alpha off the still quivering carcass and taking down one of the other wolves with a surprise bite to the jugular.

As the fallen wolf howled in pain and collapsed to the earth, blood erupting from the severed vein, the other wolves pounced and sank their teeth into the thick hair on the necks of the twin Great Pyrenees, but the dogs wore sharp studded collars that cut the wolves' mouths that caused them to cry out in pain. A massive white paw stomped on the black wolf, pinning him to the ground, but the alpha female sank her teeth into the mountain dog's underbelly, and another wolf gouged the face and drove the beast into a frenzy of anger. Rising and meeting like two boxers in a clinch in the ring, the alpha male and his shaggy adversary stood on their back paws, snapping and tearing at each other's throats.

Wild, panicked human shouts and running footsteps approached, and then the sharp crack of gunshots rang out. A wolf fell hard to the dirt and was silent. Another shot and the alpha female yelped, and fell, spastically striking out with her paws, a red stain on her belly. Lying on the ground next to the half-eaten calf's corpse, her eyes registered pain and confusion as her body contorted in death spasms, before the eyes glazed over and she fell silent and still as well. Struggling to its feet, the bloody, throat-bitten wolf was hit in the leg and limping away toward the forest was struck again and then again and then fell and lay motionless.

Ignorant of the carnage surrounding them, the alpha wolf and the massive dog focused only on each other, striving to tear out the other's throat; fur, blood and pieces of shredded flesh mizzling in all directions from the center of the skirmish, the humans in the distance bellowing and running toward the fray.

Disengaging himself from underneath the fallen wolf's wounded body, the black wolf leapt to his feet and ran hard for the wooded darkness fringing the far end of the field. A bullet struck the ground next to him, spraying a plume of dirt into the air, and he darted abruptly to one side to avoid another shot that sliced through the air near his ear. Panicked, driven by fear and the urge for survival, the young wolf's long legs pumped strenuously, pushing his sleek body faster to the tree line and freedom. Another shot singed the tip of his tail as he reached the edge of the forest, and yet another rang out, its fine honed whir cutting through the air focused and direct, before striking the tree next to him with a sharp shock and sending a shower of wood chips into the air. Without looking back, the black wolf breached the fence and passed alone into the shadows.

CHAPTER THIRTY

I am surprised it didn't happen sooner.

Jesse had done some pretty cruel stuff over the years. He had pummeled guys in fights, and cut a few deadbeats who owed him money with hunting knives, and even threatened a little spic down in Green Bay with a chainsaw—not to mention all those marks he put on poor Jenny. He didn't know I knew, but I saw them; she didn't half deserve the beatings she received. But the kid—Pete that is, really and truly didn't warrant what he got, either.

Another day, another party at Jesse's property in the woods. We still had one trailer left—the one where we cooked the product was just a bunch of charred ruins, but we still kept the other one stocked up and ready for parties. It was so far removed from the public view that if you didn't know where it was you'd drive right past the gate and the *No Trespassing* sign without even suspecting what was down the dirt driveway; only a few of the local druggies and some of our best customers knew how to find it.

This particular day we had a few people over—a few locals and a couple special guests from out of town—prospective customers, I think. I was starting to get into mixing my drinks and drugs real heavy about then, and people were coming and going, so things are admittedly a bit fuzzy in retrospect.

Among the locals was a scruffy straggler we called "Little Pete." Landon Peterson had been a grade behind us in school. A scrawny kid with teeth that kind of went in all directions when he smiled his dopey smile, which he almost always did, Little Pete was one of those guys who seemed to attract trouble like picnics attract rain. A nice enough kid, but one who was constantly picked on by everyone. He hung out with us and, in return, we got him hooked first on booze and then weed and finally the harder stuff. Jesse and his brothers used to egg him on and laugh like fiends when he overdid it and started flailing around like an epileptic before crashing to the floor.

His brother Tate, "Big Pete," was a year older than us and was a big football star who got offered a scholarship to play the offensive line at Eastern Michigan. But he had neither the brains nor the mean streak to succeed and was back home within a month, working at the lumber yard with Jared, hauling wood, lifting heavy things.

Little Pete was one of our crew, but, because he was a little slow upstairs, we only trusted him with selling weed to the grade-schoolers. Even then, we had to be constantly on our guard for fear he would sell it to the wrong person or talk a little too freely about where he was getting his goods. In exchange for his services, Jesse got the kid hooked on meth, which meant the little punk was slavishly indebted to Jess.

To his credit, Pete also worshipped Jenn, and was highly motivated to do well by her, but his nervous, endless jabbering about off the wall subjects, as well as the perceived 'kick me' sign tattooed on his forehead that always seemed to draw attention from elements we hoped to avoid, had us all frustrated with the kid. Jesse especially expressed concerns about his slipping up someday, and had mentioned, only half-jokingly, sending him alone on one of our dicier runs to see if maybe someday he might not make it back.

This particular evening was unusually hot and humid, not the type of weather Yoopers are used to, and the pterodactyl-sized mosquitoes were especially voracious. We only had a couple of beat up fans going and naturally, one broke down. It was almost unbearably hot inside, but the bugs were eating us alive outside, so we suffered as a group, surrounded by smoke and the smell of sweat and warm beer.

We were mostly spread out around the living room, sitting and perspiring on the couch and carpet in a semicircle, while I was ensconced in a battered lounge chair in the corner. Everyone was plastered with sweat from the basketball game we had just finished out on Jesse's dirt court, and he was already annoyed that his team had lost at the last second when Little Pete had fired up an air ball instead of passing Jess the ball. Jenny passed out snacks and drinks. She was looking great as always.

We settled for amusing ourselves by watching the Brewers lose to the Cardinals again through the crappy reception we had on the TV set. Jesse was holding court in the kitchen with a couple of girls from out of town that he wanted to impress, when the second fan groaned and suddenly stopped working.

The kid started kicking it. He never knew when not to push.

"Goddamn it, Jesse Ray, whatdaya gotta buy such cheap shit for?" He was obviously quite high and giggling madly at his audacious impertinence.

Jesse was in a foul temper already. He had started using crystal himself by now, but he was also drinking Scotch, smoking dope and occasionally dropping acid. He had found himself getting more and more in debt to Junior and was paranoid that the cop was playing him the way we played Pete. His outbursts had revealed a more deep-seated anger lately and this one had an especially evil flavor to it. He glared as the kid did a silly dance in the center of the room, accidentally spilling one of the girl's wine cooler.

"Hey, watch it, moron!" she snarled.

Jesse growled and went back to his entertaining, but he was keeping track of events happening in the living room.

Pete started singing in a loud voice. He was higher than I had ever seen him.

"Settle down, Pete," I warned.

"Fuck baseball anyway," he ranted. "Kickboxing's the sport of the future. I'm going to take classes and be a kickboxer one of these days." He began punching and throwing wild kicks around the room.

"Watch it!" a girl snapped.

"Jesse, this cat is getting out of control," Chuck Larson called out to the kitchen.

"Cool it. Don't make us throw you out," I whispered to Pete.

"Okay Preacher, I don't need a sermon." He sat down with thud on the couch, spilling an ashtray and a bag of chips and nearly dislodging one of the girls from her seat.

"Dude, you are fucked up," one of the guys said with disgust. Chuck and some other people left around then, I think. I'm really not sure who was still there. I was really buzzed and sleepy and started dozing in and out.

Jesse disappeared into the bedroom with the girls, leaving Jenny pouting on the couch. Closing my eyes, I watched the colors flicker. I don't know how long I was gone. I think I might have dozed off.

Pete went silent and stared at the game for a while, but couldn't restrain himself and started then bellowing.

"Jesse! Your TV sucks!" I tensed with each shout. He stopped and I took a breath, but he couldn't stop himself—man, he was so high—and began hooting and hollering again. "Jesse! Jesse!"

"Dude," I hissed, my eyes still closed.

"Jesse! Your TV really sucks! You can't see shit. Jesse, you hear me! Jesse!" He laughed uproariously at how his sense of humor had been improved by the cat running through his bloodstream.

He didn't see the gun until it was pointed directly into his face.

Eyes closed, I heard Jesse hastily emerge from the bedroom. When I opened them, I saw him with the .22 in his hand. Shaking with rage, he pointed it at the kid's forehead, his lynx eyes glistening.

"You just don't ever shut up, do you, you fucking pipsqueak!" Jesse screamed.

"I never... I never..." Pete sputtered, his eyes bulging with fear.

"You don't think! You don't think before you talk and you don't ever stop talking." Jesse was furious, out of control. "And I know you've been talking to Junior!"

"Jesse, you know I didn't mean it. You know I didn't," he sobbed. "You know how Junior is. He said he'd put me in jail."

"I know about you. I know all about you, you worthless waste of humanity. I don't have the time to burn babysitting a worthless piece of shit like you. I should do it. Put you out of our misery. I should just pull the trigger." He cocked the hammer and bounced the barrel against Pete's forehead, once, twice. "Nobody would miss you, not even your momma or that stupid ox of a brother."

"Please don't joke around like that Jesse."

"Let's put it to a vote. All in favor of killing a cockroach say aye."

A few voices jokingly said, "Aye." I mouthed the word, but no sound emerged. The kid started to stand up.

"The ayes have it."

Jesse pulled the trigger.

There was a pop and the kid hit the floor hard.

A girl screamed. Was it Jenny? I opened my eyes. I think I

remember people screaming and running out of the door. Smoke from the gunshot hung coiling in the air, the shot still echoing in the silence of the living room.

"Preacher, grab that sheet of plastic from the back room," Jesse said in a quiet voice. The two girls he was entertaining in the bedroom stood behind him, looking over his shoulder with frightened eyes. Closing the bedroom door, they disappeared out the window and were never seen again.

Jesse walked carefully around Pete's body and sat down on the couch. "We'll have to tear up that carpet and make a run for some bleach. Jenny, can you get the mop from the kitchen?" His voice was calm and methodical.

"Jesse, what happened? I..." She stood shaking and looking in horror at the body on the floor.

"He had it coming, didn't he, Preacher."

"I suppose so," I said dully.

"He pushed us too far."

"If you say so."

"Christ, what did I do? Jenny, where is the goddamn mop?!" he shouted and Jenny scrambled down the hall to the closet.

Putting his head in his hands, Jesse stared at Pete's lifeless body. After a few seconds, he started laughing.

"You know I always wanted to pop someone in the melon and guess what? Now I have."

"What are we going to do about it Jesse?" I asked in a whisper.

"Call Junior. He'll know what to do. Yeah, that's it. Junior will help us." Jesse voice came from a faraway place. "No..." he reconsidered, "he's not going to like this. He won't like this at all. We'd better fix this ourselves."

"What about Big Pete?"

"He's a big pussy. He won't do anything."

Jenny returned with the mop and bucket. Jesse walked outside and I heard him announce in a firm voice to anyone still present, "Alright, everyone get the hell out of here. Nobody saw anything. Anyone says a word about this, and they get what Little Pete got, only worse. I'm talking mother, father, whole family dead. You got it? Now get out. The party is over!"

Less than three hours later, under a shroud of darkness, Jesse and I slid Pete's body out of the plastic sheet and over the edge and down into the mine shaft where Jesse had thrown the M80s a couple of summers before. Pete's body landed far below with a distant unsettling thud.

CHAPTER THIRTY-ONE

We skipped school that day and walked down to the water's edge intending to seek new adventures upon the snaking currents of the Paint River. You see, my old man had inherited a canoe when his widowed father, who I never knew, was killed in a freak accident. Story goes, Gramps was fishing one day when he was struck between the eyes by a nesting Canadian goose he came upon in the reeds and accidentally startled, which, in turn, knocked him out of the canoe and into the lake. Weighted down by his heavy wool pea jacket, he drowned in relatively shallow muddy water. Understandably, my dad—who witnessed the event from the distant shore—never overcame his paralyzing fear of waterfowl, and as a result had kept the canoe stored in our garage for many years, never considering using it, no doubt due to bad memories of the unfortunate fatal incident.

Finally, one year when I was about eight, he decided enough was enough and that he was going to face his fears and do his duty as a father by taking his son fishing. He dragged it from the garage, cleaned it up and got it in fine working order and asked a friend of his if he could tie it up on his property. There it sat unused, season after season because my father never did follow through on anything. I brought it up a few times, but something would always come up, like a possible rainstorm or a sick girlfriend, or an important ballgame on the television, and he would nervously beg off.

Audacious adventurer that I believed myself to be, I just didn't think that was right, especially when I had pirates and submariners on the brain; and here was that boat just sitting there getting dirtier and dirtier. We'd drive by it every so often just to make sure it was still there, but he'd just take a quick look and shudder and start sweating and then drive away real quick like. And so the plans for fishing expeditions he'd been so boastful of a few moments before would dissipate away into embarrassed silence and faraway stares evoking memories best not remembered.

But for me and my big mouth, that old boat might have just sat there and rotted away into dust. Of course I had to mouth off and mention it to Jesse one day before school as we were sitting in the cafeteria and talking about the book we had been assigned, *Huck Finn*.

"It's a damn stupid book and pretty much a waste of time in my opinion." Jesse was pontificating as usual. I doubt whether he had gotten past the first few pages.

"Come on, it's cool," I said. "Who wouldn't want to take a raft down the Mississippi? I'd float all the way to New Orleans if I had the chance."

Jesse thought for a moment and his eyes brightened. "Yeah, I guess that would be a riot wouldn't it." He hadn't even cracked the book open yet and this new information caused him to rethink his initial impression and decide that maybe he would skim through the book after all. "Maybe we should build a raft and take it out on the Michigamme."

"That would be great, or..." I spoke without thinking, "...too bad my dad wouldn't let us use his canoe."

"He's got a canoe?" Jesse asked and grinned his evil grin.

I had opened the floodgates; might as well let the water pour through now like the falls. "Yeah, it's an old one. He's got it tied up down on the river."

"No shit?" His eyes sparkled as his mind worked on the details.

"Yeah. The thing is just sitting there," I moaned. "Every time he says we're going to take it out, well... we just never seem to."

"Would he let you take it? Us I mean."

"Who knows? Probably." I lied. "I think... maybe..."

"So what are we waiting for? Let's do it."

"What do you mean?" I asked. Jesse's eyes were flashing the crazy sign.

"Let's split this pop stand and go check it out. I'll be Huck and you can be Tom."

"You know Tom Sawyer is really kind of a sissy creep in this book—" I started to explain with exasperation.

"Perfect," Jesse snickered.

"It does sound great, Jess, but..."

"What's wrong?"

"What about school?"

"Hmmm.... I tell you what, I'll call you in sick and you call for me."

"But we're already here."

"Oh yeah. Hmmm... Don't worry, I'll think of something."

It was one of the first days of May and the sun had finally emerged from behind its winter's mantle of gray. In fact, it was unseasonably beautiful, and damn hard to keep the mind locked into place.

The bell rang and we herded into our first class and took our seats. History with Mr. Gordon; sure to be another yawn, despite my affinity for the subject itself. Gordon was hardly an inspiring instructor and the class was filled with too many halfwits who didn't care and who couldn't even tell you who our current President was, let alone who won the War of 1812. As such, the resulting path through the ages plodded along halfheartedly, wending its way torturously through fits and starts, outbursts and expulsions, and enough battles, uprisings, coups and mutinies to write its own history.

Today's lecture on the Treaty of Versailles was sure to be electrifying. Already some high spirited jokers were busy being disruptive. One clown threw a spit wad at one of the cheerleaders, who scowled and stuck out her tongue. Hal Turner and Tank Martin practiced wrestling moves on each other in the center of the room, sending a chair toppling to the floor with a crash. Jesse was generally a ringleader of the exuberance, but today for once, he sat quietly at his desk, deep in thought. Ignoring a spit wad that grazed my ear, I doodled a picture of Jenny—who was absent from class for an unspecified illness that day—quickly adding dog ears and a devilish mustache, rendering the embarrassing drawing of the girl I yearned for mostly unrecognizable before anyone could notice. The bell rang again and Mr. Gordon finally looked up from his papers, clearing his throat to signal the end to the preliminaries, and that the festivities were about to begin in earnest.

"Settle down. Settle down. Now we were about to begin where

we left off with the signing of The Treaty of Versailles—" he began in a tired and disinterested baritone.

Before he could continue, Jesse suddenly sprang up out of his seat and approached the teacher, speaking in an excitable, rapid-fire delivery.

"Mr. Gordon, can Pre— I mean Nate LaPointe and I be excused?"

"What on earth for, Hawkins?" Eyes goggling, Mr. Gordon's sighed audibly, obviously exasperated by the fact that the day hadn't even yet begun and already one his most troublesome students was already threatening to bust his chops.

"We have to help set up a... slide show... in the auditorium." Jesse glowed with enthusiasm. "We promised... uh, Ms. Donnelly that we would."

"A slide show... I wasn't aware of any..." the teacher sputtered.

"Yeah, nobody knows yet. It's a surprise."

"And you say it's for Ms. Donnelly?" Gordon stroked his chin and pondered the implications.

The Ms. Donnelly in question was the new assistant principal— an unmarried lady of approximately thirty years of age, whose unusual facial features, including a slight overbite and protruding buggy eyes were more than compensated for by her ample breasts. (we estimated a 44 DD cup size.) Her recent hiring had injected a bit more bounce into the step of all of the male teachers, who competed wildly amongst themselves inventing ways to make her feel welcome. As Gordon rubbed his fingers through his thinning gray comb-over, I marveled at the ingenuity: Jesse's plan was a stroke of genius.

"Yes, it's for Ms. Donnelly," Jesse went on plaintively, "and she's going to awfully disappointed if you don't let us go right away. You see, we forgot to tell you before, but we should be there already and we'd really hate to let her down. You understand?"

Gordon understood only too well and weighed the potential ramifications of being the one to disappoint Ms. Donnelly heavily in his mind. Meanwhile, Jesse stood there pleading with wide eyes and his most honest face—one I suspected he kept at home in a drawer and only pulled out on special occasions such as this one. It was a man on a wire, an actor of Shakespearean depth, a rare and marvelous treat to watch his performance.

"Well, I suppose..." Mr. Gordon said slowly, a hint of doubt lingering in his voice. "If you promised Ms. Donnelly, you had best... get going and not keep her waiting."

Jesse waved me over. Trying hard not to burst out laughing, I gathered up my things and we headed quickly to the door.

"LaPointe!" Mr. Gordon's voice stopped me cold in my tracks. "What is this slideshow about?" My jaw dropped and I began to stammer. "What's that?" he questioned, frowning.

"Whitewater rafting," Jesse suddenly interjected, saving my life and forever cementing his reputation with me as the best improviser I ever knew. "The slideshow is about whitewater rafting." He opened his mouth to go on, but thinking quickly, said no more than was necessary, avoiding another possible trap and again earning my awestruck admiration.

"White... water... rafting..." The teacher's voice trailed off thoughtfully. Mr. Gordon was an avid outdoorsman and his eyes sparkled with interest at a subject so near and dear to his heart. *Was Ms. Donnelly into that kind of thing?* he wondered. *What a woman! Mrs. Gordon doesn't like the outdoors herself: she would get cold and bitten by mosquitoes and complain, but if Kate... Ms. Donnelly that is, liked rafting, well... maybe she would like hunting too, and fishing, ice fishing, maybe even night fishing...* He imagined the two of them alone in his little boat with a cooler of beer—Mrs. Gordon only drank wine—and under the stars as Kate Donnelly laughed at his jokes and she took her life preserver off and revealed—

He was hooked and his imagination nearly took him away down a churning, adrenaline-inducing, whitewater stream with a willing, most willing co-adventurer. Just as he reached a waterfall of ecstasy, he suddenly remembered himself and snapped back to attention, returning to that unfortunate reality where he had a room full of miscreants around him and the heavy anchor of the Treaty of Versailles sinking him back into the depths of boredom and lonely misery of his daily existence.

Sighing, he waved at us to go and turned back to face his personal circle of hell. Without hesitation, we sprinted down the hall and were out of the school and running down the street laughing hysterically within minutes.

"You don't think he's going to find out?" I asked, huffing breathlessly when he finally stopped. "He'll be down in the auditorium as soon as he has a break, looking for Ms. Donnelly and her inflatable... rubber rafts."

"He'd like to rub her rafts," Jesse laughed. "No, he won't say a word. He'll be too embarrassed that two dumb kids pulled a fast one on him." Jesse was right about that one by the way: Gordon never mentioned the incident; in fact, he never looked either one of us in the eye again after it had been proven that we duped him.

"I gotta hand it to you, Jesse, that was great, and you got us out of class, but what about the rest of the day?"

He waved his hand in dismissal. "I'll think of something. But first let's stop by my house and grab some of my dad's beer and our fishing gear. We've got us some canoeing to do."

*****

I started having second thoughts, as well as third and possibly even fourth ones by the time we finally got out of town and found ourselves fighting our way through the thick brush to the river bank where the canoe lay tied to a tree. The Paint River is only a short hike from Jesse's house, but it was a school day after all, and we had to cross the bridge in plain sight. My knees were shaking that Junior's old man would spot us and discover the beer, or worse the pot, in our backpacks.

Of course, we were carrying fishing poles, so maybe he'd have let us go anyway, since the noble art of angling carries with it a high regard from some of the old-timers, and even the sin of skipping school may have been absolved in the name of promoting patriotism, fishing and manhood. Who knows? Maybe the sheriff would have even taken a beer from us to look the other way? In any case, we made it out of town unnoticed and began hoofing our way across some rough terrain down along the river bank.

We were already breathing pretty hard from maneuvering our way across an uneven field, heavily rutted with lumpy mounds of soft earth, rocky outcrops, and thick clumps of weedy brush, when at last we reached the tree line that fringed the river. We may not have mountains here like they have in Colorado, but we are rather proud of our woods around here.

In fact, I'd highly recommend to those folks who enjoy trees that they come up here and see for themselves. Our forests are dense and overgrown with as wide a variety of trees as I suspect you'll ever run across, with all sorts of deciduous trees, from birch and quaking aspen to maples, ashes, multiple varieties of elms and oaks; mixed in with a plethora of evergreens, including spruces, cedars and several species of fir and pine, all fighting branch to branch combat for sunlight and space. In the fall, the foliage shines with an incendiary brilliance, attracting a swarming tourist invasion. Most of the visitors are smart enough to stick to the main roads while enjoying the scenery, and the locals make a point of advising against ventures into the woodlands themselves.

Entering a dark grove and attempting to traverse the forests around here are not for the faint of heart. The nearly impenetrable vegetation and sometimes swampy trails makes walking difficult; nasty mosquitoes, no-see-ums and ferocious biting flies feast at will on the hapless hiker; and of course the presence of bears and gray wolves, even in close proximity to human settlements, can be unnerving to say the least. It is easy to lose direction when you can't see the sun through the branches, and even your compass can be worthless in some areas due to the massive iron deposits that inundate the surrounding landscape. Every year people get lost taking a wrong turn down a maze of unpaved roads that seems to just lead deeper and deeper into the forests. Eventually finding themselves confused, they abandon their car and take off wandering into the maze of tangled thickets looking for help. Most get found, but it isn't all that much of a surprise to us around here when someone just doesn't come back.

Fortunately, we didn't have far to go once we hit the woods. The canoe was tied up at the water's edge where the trees had been mostly cleared away. Its white outline was easily spotted whenever we drove down the road across from the river, and it could have just as easily have disappeared over the years. But it is an unwritten rule around here that you don't mess with another man's wife, girlfriend or boat, so although it was tied loosely to a tree and could be seen clearly from the road, there really was very little concern that anyone would steal it. That is, until we came along.

The slithering stream unfolded effortlessly along the horizon like some sparkling silken fabric unfurled by the hands of a patient seamstress; a cool, substantial turquoise ribbon, limned with white cottony puffs, brown and green strands and sinewy tendrils reaching upward as if in supplication, like the arms of the damned rising from their depths below, meeting their drooping counterparts halfway and merging at the mirrored surface, double branches grasping simultaneously skyward and arching into the torsos of bent and convulsed tree trunks lining the riverbank while alternately plunging down toward the sandy, muddy bottom, where slippery, moss-encased rocks held firm against, and foul smelling fronds unspooled languidly within the gentle push and pull of the accumulated watershed. This was a quiet and calm world where delicate, newly hatched insects skated on or floated breezily just slightly above the juncture between the airy and aqueous domains, and dappled minnows schooled and sounded in drops and eddies, shadowed by the overhanging edge of an eroded bank. When approached, the lurid blue hue faded and the river shone instead with a familiar, rusty orange haze, the origin of its name, the product of leaching iron and other minerals seeping from the ground as if the earth were bleeding itself into a river of its own bloody tears.

Slumping on the ground, Jesse tore open a can of beer and, panting, I did the same. The beer was lukewarm (again), but it had that familiar bite and tasted good anyway. Leaning back, we lit a joint and sat wordlessly, catching our breath, inhaling the warm smoke and gazing with wonder upon our prize. The canoe was beat up and dirty; to anyone else it probably would have been a disappointment, but to two crazy kids looking to break free after a long cold and harsh winter, it could have been the Golden Hind. Our minds reeled with visions of adventures to come.

"Awesome," Jesse finally spoke, blowing a smoke ring into the gentle river breeze.

Our river is usually pretty slow moving in the doldrums of

summer, but, on this day, the spring thaws still had it flowing at a fairly decent clip. As the canoe was lying upside down, we flipped it over and brushed out the spider webs and other crud before balancing it on the edge of the bank ready to embark. We had to be careful climbing in; the last thing we needed was to spill the boat and have to explain that to my dad.

"How do we get it back up here?" I only realized we hadn't discussed a return plan as I cautiously clambered over the side and fell with a metallic thump into the aluminum bottom of the craft. Tipping precariously from my weight and the current, it tilted crazily, but I held still and it soon stabilized, buoyant on its liquid base.

"We'll hide the boat a few miles downstream and hitch-hike back. Get Jared to drive us back down and pick it up in his truck. Drag it back here in the dark and your dad will never know it was gone."

"Unless, he drives by here today..."

"You think he might?"

"Probably not."

"Good! Then let's not worry about it." Jesse pushed the canoe off from the bank and into the current from the shore and dove over the edge and into the craft, unbalancing it and nearly toppling it over. I held my breath as the boat shimmied and rocked wildly, and then we pitched and spun sideways and out into the tug of the downstream drift. As the river carried us ahead, I experienced a momentary thrill as I felt that we were no longer tethered to gravity, no longer in control of our own motion, but rather at the mercy of a powerful moving body of water, one that cared not a bit that we had climbed astride its undulating back for a ride.

"Paddle!" Jesse shouted as we thumped against a rock and cantered dangerously astern. Grabbing my paddle, I shoved it against the boulder and pushed us away as a small flood of water spilled over the side. Jesse grabbed the other paddle and together we straightened the boat lengthwise and, with a shout of joyful relief, we steered ourselves, somewhat soggy, but still enthusiastic, into the central flow of the current.

As the sun stood directly above, and we had worked hard to

bring the craft under control, we found that we were sweating already, despite the steady nor'easter that blew in behind us, increasing its power as we reached the river's center and adding to our speed. The pace of the current was steady enough that we discovered to our satisfaction that we didn't need to paddle much except for when we wanted to veer close to the shore for exploring.

Despite the regular but lazy progress of the day, the river was alive with activity. Swallows and flycatchers swooped about on all sides, picking off a buzzing armada of gnats and other insects, while evincing an obvious delight in the demonstration of their flying prowess, veering to and fro, effortlessly besting the best aerial maneuvers the Blue Angels have to offer. Turtles lolled in the sun, propped up on stones or floating logs, tipping and diving headfirst into the water at our approach. A pair of wood ducks swam nervously into the reeds on the opposite bank, while a quarter mile downstream, an otter shimmied rapidly out of the water and slithered hurriedly into a hole in the bank, while Jesse pretended to shoot at it. A snake rippled through the water near our boat, while an occasional lazy fish, or cluster of darting minnows emerged from under the paddies in the shadowy pools that formed under the low hanging branches. Taking our shirts off, we lay back, relaxing in the sun and floating along without a care in the world.

"This is the best," I said with a sigh as I popped open another beer. "Makes you glad to be alive."

"Yeah, or dead," Jesse said with eyes closed and a smoldering joint in his hand.

"What?" I asked, startled.

"I said it's almost as good as being dead. Just think about it: no worries, no school, no girlfriend nagging on you..."

"No fun," I added in disapproval.

"No pain," he said softly.

"No nothing," I countered.

"Yeeeeeaaaaah," he said and blew out a cloud of smoke with gleeful satisfaction.

The tree-packed woodland morphed deliberately into a vast open meadow on one side, where a lone heron patiently fished the edge of a marshy swamp filled with yellow, blue and purple wildflowers, and red-winged blackbirds perched atop the cattails like proud monarchs of their dragonfly-infested domains.

"Are those eagles up there?" I asked to change the subject and pointed at a group of large birds circling in the sky ahead.

"Wow, way cool! I hope we get to see 'em snag some fish in their claws and tear them apart; that would be awesome." We paddled forward, excited, so preoccupied with watching the aerial stunts of the raptors that we hardly noticed that the current had picked up somewhat.

"Hey, we're starting to move now," I mentioned happily upon discovering our increasing velocity.

"Wheee! No shit!" Jesse shouted with gusto.

Ahead, coming closer with rapidity, the marshy prairie came to an unceremonious halt as a pair of craggy, forested abutments appeared in the distance, looming above either side of the escalating stream. Huge bumpy hillocks, creased with wrinkled layers of rock, rose above both sides of the river like the backs of twin tumorous bison, whose bulky bodies protruded with bumps of stone sparsely covered by a shaggy mane of sickly verdigris-colored trees. Like two lumps of mud and rock thrown down by a petulant giant child, the hills darkened the sunlight, while the landscape changed from sunny, flat and serene to shadowy, jagged and ominous. Our initial joy, enlivened by the increased tempo signaling the end of our *Adagio* movement was short lived, and I felt a surge of fear as the water hurled us onward directly into the tumultuous *Allegro agitato* section of the symphony, with our ship lurching and yawing wildly, becoming increasingly difficult to control.

Propelled forward even faster now, we found ourselves hurtled downhill, as if riding a rickety toboggan down a perilous icy slope, but here pulled onward, carried forth by the weight of desperate rushing waters, whose goal of reaching its destination in the big lakes was suddenly impeded, turned, twisted and convulsed by masses of stony impediments. The shoreline flew by quickly, seemingly unreachable, as we frantically paddled and maneuvered the boat between the obstacles jutting from the rocky riverbed in an attempt to run aground ahead of the obstacles and drops ahead of us. But the canoe's motion grew even faster and more erratic, bumping against and over large rocks with a series of unsettling bangs, rattling the aluminum shell of the boat and threatening to tip us into the raging torrent. Nervously, we looked at each other as we swung our paddles with abandon.

Before us, the Horserace Rapids stretched out for what seemed like miles, but we had no time to ponder the memories of our short unhappy lives, as the craft fell like an elevator whose cable has been severed over a drop and into a rush of foam, careening madly, slamming violently against boulders and racing forth headlong in a rush of vigorous gyrations. Blood thumping in my temples, the furious rush of water tossed the boat relentlessly, cold spray splattering our faces harshly, water pouring over the sides threatening to engulf us.

I felt dizzy, like I was falling through the air. Gasping for breath, a surge hit me in the face and I choked as I swallowed the water, my eyes filling with cold water that ran like unstoppable tears. Crashing against a rock, the canoe banged and shuddered to the very edge of capsizing, and flinging our bodies skyward in opposition to gravity. Regaining his balance in time, Jesse lurched across the boat, reached out, and grasping my arm, dragged me back aboard, as I nearly tumbled headlong into the roiling waters.

The breakers of death surged round about me, the destroying floods overwhelmed me... In my distress I called upon the Lord... and my cry to him reached his ears... He reached out from on high and grasped me; he drew me out of the deep waters... and rescued me, because he loves me.

My panic rose as the roar of the savage onrush filled our ears like a locomotive in a tunnel, and we plummeted deeper and faster into the churning, rolling torrent. Regaining the oars, we swung wildly at the array of boulders that loomed like cunning predators ready to pounce from either side. Struggling, slapping the wooden oars against our solid adversaries, we maneuvered around a massive boulder, spun violently against another, and teetered for a moment before prying ourselves loose and sliding back into the channel pathway again like pinball bouncing against bumpers.

Sluicing through a narrow rivulet, we descended through a crack between two rocks, careened and launched up, over and down a waterfall, landing in with a mighty kersplash. The boat, rocking and swaying in a deep and foamy pool, bumped along a shallow strip of ragged rock face that plateaued inches below the water line.

Then suddenly the cascade slowed and we found ourselves again steady and in control in the center of a calm and slow moving flow. We sat and breathed heavily for a moment—eyes still wide and hearts still throbbing, under a sky that suddenly seemed bluer than ever before. And then Jesse stood up and raising his arms to the eagles circling above, shouted at the sky in triumph.

The next thing I knew I was soaking wet, sputtering and shivering and the canoe was upside down in the water.

CHAPTER THIRTY-TWO

It didn't take as long as we hoped it would for them to find Little Pete, and in the end, it wasn't even the authorities who found him. Big Pete and his family and friends had heard some rumors that Little Pete had met a bad end, and had organized search parties to scour the nearby forests and swamps and talk to people, but they didn't find anything and couldn't get any information out of anyone. Most people who knew the truth feared the Hawkins clan more than the Petersens. So although foul play was suspected, the kid vanishing became old news as the weeks went by. It happens all the time where people get fed up with scrabbling around here trying to make a living and just up and leave the U.P. for greener pastures, so many just figured that the little goofball just had enough of Crystal Falls and had gone off and joined a circus or something.

But, as ol' Chaucer once said, 'murder will out.' Tourist season was upon us and our neck of the woods has acquired prime status, not only for hunters and fishermen, but for hikers, birdwatchers and, unfortunately for us, spelunkers. Sure enough, some yuppie kids from Chicago decided to explore the mine and came across the body, and it was then the shit hit the fan.

Junior was on Jesse immediately.

"You dumb motherfucker."

"Who says I had anything to do with it?" We were standing on the boardwalk overlooking the river. Junior, currently off duty and on his way to pick up his mother for a square dance that evening, wore: a striking pair of bright red cowboy boots and matching hat; a tan jacket with fringe on the sleeves; fringed tan slacks that ballooned out on the side;, a dark maroon scarf tied at the neck; and a pale peach shirt, with red and gold colored designs on the shoulders. The poor shirt was stretched tightly across his ample belly and was damp with perspiration. The cop looked more like a reject from a clown college than an officer of the law, but Jesse knew better than to rib him on this occasion. Junior's tan was an artificial shade of orange, but his face turned bright red as he blustered. Emotions were amplified, so we struggled to keep our voices low, as there was an older couple—tourists, I believed—ensconced nearby, watching a cormorant flying low across the water with their binoculars.

"You're the only one stupid enough to do something like this," Junior hissed.

"If I did, you can bet he had it coming. He was talking too much."

"Talking to me you mean? You gotta know that I have to keep an eye on you, Hawkins. I have to protect my investment. So the kid had a big mouth, there are better ways to handle it."

"I don't know about that. He ain't talking much now, is he?"

"This ain't the Pirates of the Caribbean; dead men DO tell tales, you little creep. It's a little thing called forensics. This is a fucking mess."

"Who can prove anything?"

"Was anybody there?" He looked to me. I swallowed hard and nodded.

"I think so," I responded reluctantly.

"Tell me the names."

"You don't need to know—nobody will talk," Jesse snapped.

"If I don't get names now, they will be looking in the mines for your body next."

"Chuck Larson was there," I offered. Jesse shot me a dark look. "With his girlfriend, I think. For a while anyway. I don't really remember. We were all pretty trashed."

"Who else?"

"Jean LeFluer was there," Jesse muttered. "And Bucky Beauchamp, I think... maybe Tyler Hansen and their chicks, a couple of girls from out of town— didn't get their names... of course, Jenny was—"

"Fuck, was half the town there?" The old couple glanced our way. Junior lowered his voice. "Anyone else you can think of?"

"I think that was it," I said. "Oh, Hal Turner might have been there too. But people were coming and going, and like I said, I really don't remember who all was there when it happened." Jesse nodded.

"Your brothers weren't there?"

Jesse shook his head no.

"Well, we can probably be glad of that or we might be talking a full-fledged massacre." The deputy scratched his head and pondered the issue. "He was a stupid little runt, wasn't he?" he said with the hint of a chuckle.

"It ain't a problem. Nobody cares," Jesse snarled.

"Big Pete does," Junior replied.

"Big Pete's a big pussy."

"He's slow and usually pretty easy going, but you wouldn't want to tangle with him when he's riled up. He'd be more than a handful."

"He'd never even lay a hand on me."

"He catches you in a corner—"

"I got my brothers and this—" Jesse pointed to the pistol in his belt.

"You dumb son of a bitch. Is that the same gun? Give me that thing."

"No fucking way."

"You want to go to prison like your daddy and his pals? I'll get you another one, but let me take this. I'll wipe it clean and say we found it at the site."

"What good will that do?"

"We've got to muddy the waters a bit. Give them all something else to think about. Can they trace you to this gun?"

"Fuck no, Jake picked it up from somebody on the reservation and I stole it from him. He thought his buddy Weasel took it when he went on the lam."

"Good. Let me see what I can do. I'll talk to your witnesses—"

"Nobody's gonna talk."

"Somebody always talks. In the meantime, you lay low."

"Yeah, yeah—"

"I mean it. And Jesse," the cop pointed a fat finger at Jesse's chest. "Get double-timing on getting a hold of more cat. You owe me big for getting you out of this mess."

When the official cause of death came out as a gunshot wound to the head, speculation naturally centered on Jesse, who started spending more and more time at his property and away from town, and began making more trips to Green Bay, where he had made a few new friends.

But, Junior tainted the evidence and spread the word that the gun had been found near the body with Little Pete's fingerprints on it, and that in the opinion of local law enforcement, the kid had committed suicide. Honestly, the kid shooting himself in the face before falling into a mine shaft seemed unlikely, and Big Pete howled bloody murder, but stranger things have happened before here in the U.P. and Little Pete was soon mostly forgotten. Mostly, that is.

CHAPTER THIRTY-THREE

The steakhouse was busy, as I suspected it would be on a Saturday night, but we managed to get a table pretty quickly and sat down to sip our beers and wait for our meal, surrounded by the noise of the jukebox and boisterous loud talkers at the bar cheering the baseball game.

"You know we could've gone to the fish fry at the Lakeside last night instead. It would have been less of a drive and cheaper," the old man said.

"You've done enough fish frys in your life. Thought you'd like to do something special for a change."

"You sure you can afford this?" he asked, eyeing the menu.

"Sure Dad, it's my treat," I answered. Business was good these days and my wallet was fat with cash.

"Why don't you let me pay? I get a Social Security check every month, you know."

"You've been paying for me all your life. Let me do it for once."

"Awww," he said waving his hand in mock disgust. "So where'd you get all this cash all of a sudden? I didn't even think you were working."

"I'm doing ok. I do stuff here and there."

"Enough here and there stuff to pay for rent and a car?" he asked in disbelief. "You know you are always welcome to move back in to your old room if you need to."

"Thanks Dad, I'm doing fine. And you've got more room now. You can use my room as an office."

"I don't need an office."

"You always said—"

"That was back when... I don't need an office."

"Well we're both at the age when we need a little more... privacy."

He blushed a little and concentrated on buttering a warm piece of homemade bread. "I always wondered, did my bringing any of my lady friends home ever bother you?" he asked.

"No, but maybe some of mine might."

"You got a girlfriend?"

"I'm working on it."

"About time."

The waitress arrived to take our order. I chose the T-bone and a baked potato; Dad went for a prime rib, rare.

"Make it so runny that I can drink it. My teeth aren't so good these days."

"And two scotch on the rocks to help us wash it down."

"Whoa, listen to the big spender."

The waitress left and the old man returned to the subject. "So you've been working? Doing what exactly? Yard work? Cleaning gutters? It doesn't seem like raking leaves and mowing lawns would pay very much."

"You might be surprised. Besides, I do other stuff: painting houses, putting up fences... walking dogs."

"Eddie down at the smoke shop says you've been doing something with that Hawkins kid. Isn't he the one who's always in trouble?"

"Can't say Jesse's in any trouble that I'm aware of."

"Thought Eddie said something about him maybe being mixed up with some kid gone missing or something."

"Eddie's clueless. I don't know why you even listen to that loudmouth."

"Jesse, huh? I think I had Jacob in one of my classes. Nothing but a pain in my ass, that one. He could hit the ball a mile, but nobody wanted to let him have a bat. The whole faculty breathed a sigh of relief when he dropped out. His old man's the one in prison, isn't he?"

"Was. I think he died though."

"Oh, I didn't know that. Or maybe I did and just forgot. There was another brother wasn't there? What happened to him?"

"He's around. Jared never even made it into high school, so you never had to deal with him."

"I think I've seen him around. Kind of a lunkhead with an evil look?"

"That would be him."

"Saw him get thrown out the Lakeside for a fake I.D. one night. Took several big fellows to do it and they all took their share of lumps doing it. He just kept grinning and coming back for more. You aren't hanging out with those two, are you?"

"As little as possible."

The waitress brought our drinks and he took a sip and sighed. Turning his gaze to me again, he lowered his voice and became serious. "I gotta ask, you aren't doing anything illegal are you, Nate?"

I looked away from him. "No more than anyone else."

"I have to admit that that was not exactly the answer I was looking for. What do you mean?"

Hurriedly placing the salad bowls onto the table with a clatter, the waitress scurried away without a word. We didn't look like the big tipping kind, so she didn't intend on wasting any time on conversation.

With wickedness comes contempt, and with disgrace comes scorn

I stared into my blue cheese dressing as I spoke. "I just mean... look around, Dad. Where do you think any of these people got their money?"

"Where do you think they did? From working their jobs, of course," he said with a knowing chuckle.

"You think so?"

"Or cashing their unemployment or welfare checks. Where else?"

"What about the guy at the bar, over there at the end?"

"Stu something. He works at Josephson Motors. What about him?"

"What does he do?"

"He sells cars. Used cars."

"Rips people off, you mean."

"Come on, that's not fair."

"Isn't it? What do you call taking people's money for a hunk of junk that's had its mileage rolled back and the frame is bent from an accident? Bet he doesn't mention that now, do you think?

"You're being harsh, but I suppose he does cheat a bit. They've got a reputation."

"And the guy in the suit at that table?" I motioned toward a table of men eating steaks.

"I've seen him around. Can't recall the name."

"Let me refresh you. He's the lawyer that helped the school district give you the heave ho."

"Oh Jeez... Guess I should have remembered him. Those times are a bit of a blur. He's put on a few pounds, I see."

"The years have been good to him. Who is he eating with?"

"Um, Jack Fleischer?"

"Who is?"

"A lawyer."

"And a town councilman, right? Now why would they be having dinner together?"

"You tell me."

"You remember that new development they want to put in out on the south end of town?"

"Yeah."

"The one you said was a waste of time and tax money."

"It's a bunch of crap. What about it?"

"Well, those two just got it approved. No doubt this is a victory celebration."

"Are you serious? The bastards!"

"Just two of our finest citizens who deserve congratulations for pushing through their boondoggle of a plan to destroy several acres of pristine forest, prairie and farmland in order to put up a series of crummy town homes and mini-malls."

As if he had heard Nate, the man in the suit looked in their direction. Nate smiled and waved. "Not to mention, he's one of my best customers," Nate said softly.

The man looked blankly at them with no emotion for a moment and then looked away.

"I can't believe they are going through with it," my father whispered. "I used to fish in that pond down there. It'll be gone and for what? That isn't going to bring any business into town anyway. It's like painting a racing stripe on a pig."

"What's the matter Dad, are you against progress?" I mocked.

"Well no, it's just..."

"Stop the whining, start the mining, eh?"

"Well sure. We've got to get people back to work or the whole county is going to be empty pretty soon. They tell me down at the high school that they had ten families move away after the end of last school year."

"And I suppose you don't care if they pollute the groundwater."

"No, no, I didn't say that, but we have to have something around here... I mean even tourism is way down, and hunting—"

"So what? Do we really need more idiots firing guns around here? We have enough crazy bastards who will shoot anything. I mean I heard some little old lady was feeding an orphaned fawn down the street from me, and what do you suppose happened next. Her moron of a neighbor blasted it away one morning—in her yard. Said he likes to eat them young because the meat is so tender."

"—like I was saying," he continued, scowling, "the hunting business is way down since they let those wolves loose. They've been killing off the deer and elk and even people's dogs and livestock. They just shot three or four of them to death attacking some calves over near Golden—"

"Yeah, I heard about that. What a drag. The wolves were here before there were people. We should leave them alone."

"Leave them alone?" he raised his voice incredulously. "They were attacking a man's livestock. He had every right to defend—"

"It was the people that brought the cows into the wolves' territory in the first place, Dad."

"There were no wolves here back then, they've proven that. It's just some crazy environmental freak's idea to mess with everybody."

"They're beautiful animals."

"They're killers.

I took a long sip. "Well let's just agree to disagree on this one."

"Fine. Just don't start putting animals ahead of humans."

"Why shouldn't I? What is so great about humans? How are any of these people any better than animals?" I sipped my scotch and scanned the room. "See the guy with the bad rug on the other side of the bar. He's a broker, and that's exactly what he's doing to his clients—making them broker. And that guy over there in the shadows with the young lady with the big hair is cheating on his wife. He blew his kid's college fund taking his bimbo to Mexico last month."

"You're full of shit," the old man sputtered. "You're making it up."

"You got me on that last one. But I'll bet I'm pretty close. Should we ask them?" I started to get up.

"Quit clowning around, you joker. Sure, there are some miscreants around, but not everyone is like that. What about Sharon Taylor over there? She's a real sweetheart." He pointed to an attractive middle-aged blonde surrounded by a gaggle of giggling women drinking colorful drinks with umbrellas in them. "She owns a flower shop here in Iron Mountain. Plenty of dirt there, I suppose, but not the kind you think there is. She's active in the church, always willing to lend a hand with city activities and is one of the biggest contributors to charity in the area."

I sipped my scotch. "Blood money," I replied. "You know how she got that shop, don't you?"

The old man swallowed his scotch and glared. "No, not really..."

"Your precious Sharon there made a trade for it. Sold herself to... I mean married, one of the biggest assholes in the state. You remember that toy factory down in Detroit that got busted for using toxic materials?"

"The one that got all those kids sick?"

"That's the one. Taylor Toys. Her husband, Lance Taylor, owned it. Big golfing buddy of the governor, mansion on a private island in Lake Michigan...."

"I thought the government shut that company down."

"Naw. They just changed the name to 'Happy Toys' and moved the plant to Indonesia when a citizen's groups started to make it too hot here. They're still making toys for the rest of the world where the safety standards aren't so stringent. Meanwhile, his old factory just got awarded the bid to make the highway signs for the entire state: it's nice to have friends."

"But Sharon... she's divorced...."

"Yes, after years of service, she got a nice little payout when her creep of a husband traded her in for a newer model, but whether she was directly involved or not is irrelevant to the argument. The flowers that she sells are flowers of evil, and she and her friends are just painted whores in SUVs, for sale to the highest bidder."

"Jesus, son. What has happened to you? When did you get so cynical? I thought you had found religion?"

"I have my religion alright. You know what their religion is? *The world is my toilet; I shall do with it as I please. I will piss in the rivers, shit in the ocean, dig up the land and kill all the animals and any and all people who get in my way until the end of my days when my children will take on the duties of rape, waste and destroy. Yea, I walk through the shadow of death; I fear no evil, because I AM the evil. As long as I have a big house with cable TV, a refrigerator full of alcohol and animal flesh to consume, and a four-wheeler truck the size of an aircraft carrier, I will spit the face of those who have less than me and tell them proudly to fuck off because I've got mine.*"

"Well, they do say that whoever dies with the most toys—"

"You're still dead, Dad. You know biology. You know this can't go on. You put an organism in a petrie dish and it multiplies until the point where it runs out of space. It uses up all the resources, and finally drowns in its own waste."

"Well, yes, but humans are more than mere organisms, Nate. We have built a society that is now centuries old, and we have learnt from our mistakes."

"You think we can just think our way out of it, Dad? Come up with a better way, a way to overcome the simple facts of nature. Even if we did, how would we sell it? These people aren't interested in the future, especially if it is somebody else's. If they can't eat it, drink it, sell it, or fuck it in the next ten minutes, you've lost them. And just try to tell them they can't have it all right now. Then you'll see a real armed revolution. These people don't know the meaning of the word 'no', let alone patience, moderation, peace, love... No, you might as well just go along for the ride and get a few chuckles while you can."

"How on earth did you become so bitter?"

"How on earth are you not? In any case, I'm not bitter, just realistic. There is a world of difference between them."

"But Nate, son, not everyone is like that," he protested. "There's Eddie... and old John at the bait shop, and Miss Mooney the school nurse—none of them would ever hurt a fly."

"Maybe they should sometime. Hurt a fly, I mean. Did they try to stop our friends at the other table from ripping off their fellow citizens with their land grab?"

"They signed the petition, we all did—"

"I'm talking about taking a stand, Dad, a real stand. Something more effective than scribbling on a piece of paper. Action demands action, not just good thoughts. I have been told that there are monks meditating for world peace in a cave somewhere in Tibet, but they are just a bunch of lazy cowards if you ask me. If you let people walk all over you, you are equally to blame for not pushing back, and you are just as much to blame for the state of the world. If all you do is just piss and moan about things, but give in, in the end, then you are just as guilty. And if by your compliance you profit— even if you whine and cry and wring your hands in mock disgust, you are still a part of the problem—a smaller part I suppose, but still..."

"Of course, there is no real incentive to someone to fix a broken system if that person gains any profit—however limited the share— through its inequities. I understand how it works now, Dad. When you have nothing to eat but the rich man's crumbs, you are afraid to rock the boat for fear that the rich man will sail away and leave you behind and you'll wind up with nothing. Blessed are the meek alright."

"And me?" he asked grimly, ashen faced.

"And you, Dad," I said softly as I slid the lettuce around my plate absently. "I don't know how you do it. Living here, surrounded by people who look down on you and call you trash."

"That's an exaggeration. I have friends—"

"Your friends are the ones who are probably the guiltiest. They treat you like a joke. You're the town clown for them. They laugh at you because you are too nice. You don't have the killer instinct to stab people in the back or the ability to kiss ass that is essential for becoming a success in their eyes. And I'm the same as you are, Dad. I am my father's son, after all. Only I don't take their crap anymore.

I know how their game works now and I am beating them at it."

"Look son, stop a minute. Please. I know this hasn't been the best of a life for you, but... well, your mother..." He paused and took a drink and wiped his forehead with his napkin before continuing. "I tried to be a good father, but... I really didn't know what I was doing. Look, I'm only human... I guess we were both only human. We had failings, as every human does. You have to forgive her for leaving and never writing, and I hope you forgive me because I know I was weak and I drank too much and didn't do what I should have done to be a good father, but I tried, Nate. Please know I tried... As much as I could."

The man in the toupee put an arm around Sharon Taylor's shoulder at the bar and they shared a raucous laugh over some off-color joke, their mouths gaping wide, exhibiting bright and pointed canines.

"And the school, son... I know you must have had a good reason to hit that man. Lord knows I've wanted to clock a few folks over the years, you know I have. But Nate, you've got to learn how to let it go and forgive. There's still so much good in the world. You've got to focus on that. You just need to trust people, so you can find it again.

"You've got to get back up out of this darkness that is surrounding you. You can't hate the whole world. You just can't. It isn't perfect, but it is the only one we have. And you have to have moderation. You can't just take the good or the bad too seriously. We are all sinners, without a doubt, and those folks you've been talking about, well, they'll have to face what's coming to them someday. They will be judged for their crimes. Your religion tells you that. But when you hate everything and everybody, well... it's just going to tear you apart because you hate everything that's good too, and that's a poison—a poison that you will never recover from..."

"So what's the antidote?

"Not sure about that. Don't think I'd find that in any of my chemistry books," he chuckled nervously before continuing. "No, I think you have to find the solution within yourself. It's like that story your mother once told me. You know, the one about the old Indian chief and his grandson... How they're sitting by the campfire at night and the old man tells the boy about the battle that goes on every day within him—actually within everyone—a battle between two wolves. One wolf is good and kind and the other is evil and full of anger. The two fight for control of the soul of the human they inhabit..."

"So, which one wins?"

He sipped his scotch slowly before speaking softly. "The one you feed," he said.

Our steaks arrived at last, one sizzling and the other floating in a pool of blood. We ate slowly and in silence, oblivious to the laughter and activity around us.

CHAPTER THIRTY-FOUR

Y ou know I only agreed to talk with you today because my secretary was under the impression that you were interested in buying a whole life policy, and now that you've told me what it is you really want, I kind of find myself feeling like I'm being conned here. You've caught me at a bit of a bad time, as I am actually really busy this morning taking care of some paperwork concerning an accident over on the highway a couple of nights ago. You might have heard about it—no? Well, I guess a couple of my customers' high school kids got busted up pretty good drag racing or something, according to the police report anyway. One dead, one in a coma and another maybe won't walk ever again. Bad for business, but we'll make up for it with a hell of a premium increase on the kids' families—what the hell were they doing out there racing around anyway? Crazy kids.

So anyways, we've got to keep this pretty quick. I've got a golf league match this afternoon, but my old Uncle Arthur is acting up again in my knees. You probably heard I was a pretty damn good fullback in my day—made 3rd team all-conference my senior year. I could've gone to college like old smarty-pants Preacher boy, but I decided instead to go into business for myself and have never looked back. I built the Turner Agency into what it is today and I'll bet even my old man would be proud of how successful I've become if he was still around.

But, what the heck. I was thinking of giving the golf a pass this afternoon anyway. My knees are aching pretty good, damn it anyway. Do you play? I can hit it a country mile, but can't keep it on the fairway. It's like hook, slice, hook, hook, slice and I'm back in the woods or the sand or the water. My smart ass golfing buddies call me Jock Cousteau, because I'm in the water about as much as that scuba diving frog was. I don't care; the nineteenth hole is the only one I care about, if you know what I mean?

But anyway, that don't make much difference after all, and I really ought to toss your ass out of here for lying to my wife, but I say, what the hell, you seem like an alright guy, who maybe just doesn't know yet that he needs a new insurance policy—just kidding. But if it helps with your book—I get a free copy or two, don't I? And I get to pick who plays me in the movie, right? Not some prancing gay boy like that Johnny so-and-so who's in all those action movies. Hell, that fluff ain't never been in a fight in his life, 'cept maybe a cat fight-rawrrrr-rawrrrr—with one of his sissy closet queen Hollyweird pals. No, I'm thinking more rugged, like a younger Burt Reynolds, but bigger like a Schwarzenegger, and with better hair. Although I have to admit I've lost a little hair lately. No gray as you can see, but I am getting thinner on the top. Gained a bit of weight too—I tried my old jersey on the other day and let's just say I have not retained my football physique. I could run like the wind in those days; nobody could stop me; I'll bet I still could. I'd sure love to give it a try. Say, maybe you'd like to try to tackle me; we could drive over to the park and let you give it your best shot...

Aw, well, if you ain't into it. Yeah, I admit that may have put on a few pounds; sitting here at a desk all day doesn't help none. And all those dinners at the country club—well, I always was a sucker for rich people food: steak, lobster, cheesecake, chocolate fondue. I know that stuff ain't any good for you, but I figure you're only going to live as long as the good Lord wants you to, so you might as well help yourself while you still can, right?

And the added flab hasn't stopped my success with the women either—a well-fed man, is a rich man, and it sure didn't stop me from landing my new one. You ran into her out front—yup, my secretary—a real looker right? Her name's Prudence, but I call her "Number Four"—a real sweetheart—bucks like a cowgirl in bed, though I better not let her hear me saying anything about that. Yeah, I trade them in when I get tired of them, just like I do with my cars. You probably saw my Caddy out front—nice, huh?

Yeah, it is true that the economy sucks around here, but the insurance biz is always good no matter what. People ain't never going to stop worrying, and I'm just the guy for them to give their money to, to help them, of course, to ease their minds about the unexpected disaster possibly waiting for them around every corner, like a car crash. I tell you it's a great thing I got going, aside from the occasional weeping and wailing when somebody gets hurt or dies, but the money rolls in steady, and I got a nice house on the golf course, a boat and a cabin and a garage full of toys.

Of course, I'd have a lot more if I could just keep my pants on. I got what they call a wandering eye and that's got me paying plenty in alimony and child support. But hell, it keeps me busy working to make more money all the time, and that ain't a bad thing. I always was a hard worker, you can ask my coaches, and, well, maybe not my teachers—I wasn't too big on book learning, not like that lazy ass Preacher you want to talk about.

Yeah, that's the part you want to hear about. I heard what happened to him and I've got to tell you that I am not surprised—no, not one bit. You know, I didn't used to be as nice of a guy as I am now: I've mellowed out, but back then I was a bit of a hard ass. I took stuff like God and America seriously. I still do, and it just burned me up back then to have Jesse dragging that know-it-all wimp's sorry ass around with us.

Don't know what he ever saw in that sneaky little weasel; the creep was probably a communist. I know he sounded like one with all his "love thy neighbor crap." "Love they neighbor's wife" is more like it. And the loser never played any sports—I mean real sports, for the school, not just intramural or pickup games. I guess Jesse never did either, but that was more because the coaches didn't want his smart mouth affecting the rest of us. But, I just don't trust people who don't play sports or join the military—never have.

You see, I'm of the belief that things like sports and war promote manhood and values, discipline and the rules of fair play, all important stuff you need to succeed in life, but some stinkin' rats just won't stay on the ship. In any case, he was tall, but pretty skinny. I suppose maybe he could've been a tight end if he would've 'roided up like the rest of us. But no, he was into the Bible. I mean, don't get me wrong that was okay, I guess—and his frou-frou books like the *Count of Crisco Oil* or whatever it was. Thinking all the time... whew, tires me out just thinking about it. And you know what they say about thinking too much: it makes you crazy—case in point. And then there were all the drugs of course...

Well, I guess we were all into that, but that was just the times, right? And I don't see any harm in it anyway: a toot here, a snort there, same as a swig of whiskey, or a sixer or twelve-pack while you watch the game—to each his own as far as I'm concerned.

But when that punk came back home and slipped some bullshit to Jesse about how they could make some big bucks mixing up crank and pushing it, well, suddenly they got all high and mighty and started thinking they were hot shit.

And remember, I wasn't as nice a guy back then; I kind of razzed some people who deserved it. Like the song says: move it on over 'cuz the big dog's moving in. If you want respect, you've got to throw your weight around and let them know who the alpha is; and well, Preach was one I gave it to pretty good—when Jesse weren't around anyway. Not that I was scared of the runt; I could've taken Jess or his big brother Jake, or... maybe not... definitely not Jared— that boy had something seriously wrong upstairs. Did I tell you he used to bury kittens up to their necks and then run the lawn mower over them? Well, I never saw it, but they said he did.

But I admit that I liked hanging with him: Jesse, that is. He was a hoot and a half, always up to some crazy plan—made life in that dull town almost bearable with his kooky antics. I probably shouldn't tell you about when we smashed all those mailboxes over by the lake, or the time we egged cars, or when we climbed up and painted the statues on the courthouse green—they still haven't figured out who did that one. Or the time he threw all those M-80s into a mine shaft and I almost died laughing: he was always pulling stunts like that.

You know that was the same mine shaft where they found poor Little Pete's body. They said he shot himself because he was depressed. Bullshit! I never saw that goober without a big old grin on his goofy face. You must know most folks figured Jesse shot the kid, that was the rumor anyway; shot him dead just for fun and then threw his ass down that hole for kicks. Said it happened at a party out on his daddy's land, but I don't know nothing for certain because I wasn't there at the time. I was probably working that day bagging groceries. Those jokers wouldn't know anything about hard work would they?

And that fucker, Preacher, after he got kicked out of college for jacking a cripple, he started huffing and puffing around town like he was tough or something. Tried to get in my face one night at the bowling alley; I nearly pounded him senseless, but the loser wasn't worth my time of day. Plus, he and Jesse were known to be packing heat those days and I wouldn't have put it past the clown to have shot me down in cold blood just because I gave him a wedgie in 7th grade or something.

In fact, I wouldn't put it past that psycho, Preacher, to have been the one who shot Little Pete. It's always the quiet ones you gotta watch out for, right? Everybody says it, and I believe it after knowing him. I mean Jesse was wild, but he wasn't a killer as far as I know; but that other one—shit, Preacher had what they call a lean and angry look. His eyes weren't as crazy as Jesse's, but they were cold, like he hated everybody—like he was evil, truly evil.

Well anyway, like I said, I didn't really know him all that much because he wasn't into sports that much, and we really didn't hang out, except with a bunch of other people drinking and partying like young people do. But I do hope I was able to give you some useful information for your story at least. And, what the hell, as long as you're here, we could always take a few minutes to take a look at your insurance needs. As a writer, I'll bet you are self-employed and probably could use a good comprehensive policy.

CHAPTER THIRTY-FIVE

I didn't see him coming, but I heard his heavy footsteps approach and sensed his bulky presence behind my back.

I'd taken to laying low when I wasn't with Jesse or his brothers, but damn if my washing machine didn't choke and I had to take a trip to the laundromat by myself because he was down in Green Bay with a "client." Now, I'm not someone who has to have the freshest clothes at all times, but even for me there comes a point when you gotta do what you gotta do. I suppose I could have washed them at Jesse's place, but that seemed like it was taking things a bit far: sharing his woman was one thing, but washing my clothes there seemed a bit too far beyond the normal bounds of friendship, even for me.

It seemed safe enough. You know, I've always found a sense of comfort in a laundromat: all that lovely, comforting humidity and the clean smell of detergent; and the implied domesticity of the whole scene, what with all the divorcees and unfulfilled ladies from the trailer court checking me out. I would have brought Jenny with me, but things were pretty hot at the moment, and I couldn't be seen with her in public, so I was just sleepwalking through it all, trying to figure out things like spin cycles and the proper way to wash a load without having to bother with separating darks from lights, when I heard the door open and his heavy tread come clomping through the door.

"Hey there, Pete," I called cheerfully without turning around.

"Preacher," he said in a flat voice.

I turned around; his fat face was not smiling. His frame was the size of a family-sized refrigerator and his abundant presence blocked all of the sunlight from the door.

Quickly checking all of the exit routes, I calculated that if I left all of my clothes behind, threw a detergent box at his face to distract him, and pounced with a sudden burst, I could stretch out my arm and possibly reach one of those little metal carts and shove it into him as he pursued me, tripping him and causing him to fall to the ground; and if everything went just right, I might just make it out alive. That was a big if; I decided to let him have his say.

"What's up?" I asked as innocent as I could.

"I want to ask you a question and I think you know what it is that I want to know."

They hadn't found Little Pete's body yet, at this time, but word was around town that Jesse had had something to do with the kid's disappearance.

"Shoot," I said. Bad choice of words.

"You know where my brother is?"

"Nope, can't say that I do." I turned back to my washing. I was going to make a remark about him checking bars, jails and/or flophouses, but I didn't think humor was an appropriate choice in this particular instance. Besides, I had liked the kid myself. Didn't dislike him too much anyway.

"You heard that he's gone missing, didn't you?"

"Yeah, I heard that."

"Well, you were a friend of his, weren't you?"

"We hung around a bit."

"You and that Hawkins punk were pals with him. They tell me you've got him running dope for you."

A couple of the ladies within hearing distance decided folding shirts could wait and that a trip to the bathroom was in order.

"Who's they?"

"I got my sources."

"Pete, I don't what anybody is saying, but I don't know nothing—"

"You don't know nothing?!" His voice rose in anger. He gave the impression of a bull about to charge.

"Maybe we should take this outside—" I gestured. If I could make it to my car...

"You want to take this outside?!" Another poor choice of words. He was riled.

"To talk."

"What is there to say, Preacher? You either know where he is or you don't; but I think that you do know where he is."

"Jesse—" I started.

"Yeah, where is that little prick? I'm going to snap his neck like a twig the next time I see him."

"—and his brothers," I lied, "are picking me up here in a few minutes, if you'd like to have a word with them."

That stopped him for a minute. He was big and angry enough to take on two of us, but four, including the psychopathic Jared...

"Bullshit." He knew I was lying. "Jared's working at the lumberyard until four-thirty, and I saw Jake's car leave town headed toward Iron River twenty minutes ago." His eyes caught sight of the row of industrial strength dryers spinning on the wall and he started to grin. "You're a smart guy, Preacher: a college guy. So how long you think a guy would last in one of those? Plenty of room inside. You'd fit perfectly. Bet it would get real hot in there." He walked slowly over, keeping his eyes on me and with a click opened one. "Hey, here's an empty one, want to give it a whirl?"

What I wanted to do was to make a break for the door. Sweating, I tensed, ready to make a grab for the bleach bottle. Maybe tossing a bit of that in his face would slow him down, although I doubted it. I reached out slowly and...

I sighed in relief as, outside the window, I saw a cop car pull up. Junior leapt from the driver's side and strode through the door in a hurry. One of the ladies working at the place must have made a phone call; I could have kissed her cigarette-stained lips.

"How's everything going, guys?" Junior smiled sweetly through his pudgy lips as he walked toward us. "Now what are you boys doing, folding some sheets? How domestic, are you thinking of moving in together? Let me know, I'll buy the happy couple a gift. Maybe a houseplant?"

Pete snarled. "I'm asking some questions about my brother, since nobody else around here seems to want to do anything about it."

"Now Pete, settle down, settle down. You know very well that we are utilizing all of our resources in an attempt to find your little brother and bring him home safely. We, in the community are all concerned about his whereabouts."

Pete scoffed as Junior continued: "Little Pete was known to run in some pretty wild circles, and it may well be that he has simply decided to take an extended vacation from town. In fact, it wouldn't surprise me a bit that he got sick of all the bullshit around here and got the hell out. I wouldn't blame him a bit if he did. Who knows? If I had the choice, I might take it myself."

"Preacher knows where he is. Him and that Jesse Ray Hawkins."

"Now Pete, we've interviewed Preacher here and concluded he knows nothing about the location of your brother, and the same goes for Jesse and all of the Hawkins boys. And you know I cannot allow you to harass the innocent citizens of this town over unfounded rumors and misguided—"

"But Stan Jacobsen said—"

"We know all about Stan Jacobsen's stories. In fact, I spoke with Stanley at great length only today about the rumors he has apparently been spreading. When I pointed out his error in repeating hearsay, he admitted that he had no firsthand knowledge of anything, especially your brother's whereabouts, and would stop all this troublesome nonsense immediately."

"But, he told me—" Big Pete deflated like a balloon.

"You have to stop listening to every little thing you hear, Pete. You miss your brother, and I can understand that, but listening to every confounded story will not help find him. These people like to talk so much that they don't even know what they are saying half the time." He softened his tone and put his hand on Big Pete's shoulder, maneuvering the distraught man's large body to the door.

"Listening to the nut jobs around here will... well, it will make you crazy, Pete. You have to let it go, relax, and realize there are some things you have no control over. Just let us do our job. Your brother will show up. They always do. Just go home. Forget about it. I will personally guarantee that I will do everything in my power to find your brother. Just go home. Go home."

He pushed the defeated giant out the door. Pete lumbered down the sidewalk with his face downcast. As Pete climbed into his truck and drove away, Junior turned to me and slipped me a pistol.

"Here's that gun I said I'd give Jesse. Looks like you need it more than he does."

I slipped the pistol into my waistband under my shirt. Exiting,

Junior turned and whispered with a snarl: "And get your goddamn washer fixed."

CHAPTER THIRTY-SIX

"I'm going to have a baby, Preacher."

She sprung it on me one night when we were together in her bed. My mind was a bit clouded and it took me a minute to register what she said.

"What's Jesse got to say about it?" I finally answered.

"I haven't told him."

"I don't blame you. He isn't going to be happy paying for another kid."

"That isn't why I haven't told him."

"What do you mean?"

"It isn't his."

We held our breath as car lights illuminated the room through the bedroom windows. The car roared away into the distance.

"Jesus," I whispered.

CHAPTER THIRTY-SEVEN

Merrick, Gwynn and Teague dismounted and walked their horses quietly to a clump of trees where they hid and waited impatiently until the brakeman and conductor ran past them to the front of the train to where the tree trunks blocked the track. While the railroad crew was busy studying the roadblock, Merrick and Teague slipped quietly out of the shadows and climbed up the steps and aboard the express car coupled directly behind the engine. Gwynn held his position in the trees, guarding the horses and watching the action, as the men up front struggled to move the downed trees.

Holding his breath, Gwynn relaxed as the seconds passed uneventfully. The money in the train was already in his hand as he dreamed of the farm he planned to purchase in California. He already had big plans for raising a bumper crop that he believed he could sell the rest of his life in relative comfort: turnips.

A cry suddenly filled the air, followed by a gunshot, shattering Gwynn's dream, bursting the mountain-sized turnip he had imagined like a balloon. Running back toward the express car where the shot originated, the engineer, conductor and brakeman shouted: "Flynn! Is everything all right?" Sighing, Gwynn stepped from the shadows, rifle in his hands.

"Down on the ground!" he called out in a confident voice. The men's expressions turned to panic and, faces pale, they sank to their knees and proceeded to lie down supine on the damp earth. Gwynn held the upper hand, but as the screams and cries continued coming from the interior of the train car, he trembled inside, knowing something had gone wrong: especially because it was Teague who was crying out.

Inside, Teague lay slumped on the ground, groaning and wailing in pain, holding a gaping wound in his stomach, as sticky blood oozed through his fingers and onto the wooden floor. Merrick held his pistol aimed at a small built, older man with a drooping gray mustache, who wore the uniform of a railroad guard. In turn, the bantam-sized man held his revolver in direct opposition to the robber chief.

"Put the gun down and open the safe," Merrick said slowly.

"You just put your gun down or I'll shoot you down like your friend there, you son of a bitch" retorted the feisty veteran. "I think you understand now that I am not bluffing."

"Aiiiiii, bloody hell," Teague screamed in agony from the floor.

"Shut up," Merrick hissed. To the little man, he said, "You shoot me, I shoot you."

"That's right. You're a right bright fella, aren't ya?"

"You're willing to die for your job?"

"I do my duty."

"You'd pay with your life for the company? What have they ever done for you?"

The man shrugged. "My wife will get my death benefits. I've lived a good Christian life; I'd leave this bloody earth with no regrets and enter the Kingdom of Heaven willingly."

"Shoot the bastard! He shot me!" Teague screeched as his body writhed in sharp contortions. Merrick ignored him.

"You did your duty, grandfather. No one would blame you if you stepped away now. I'd even give you a share—"

The old man spat on the floor. "Don't think you can bribe me, you stinking devil. You know you can't get away with it. The Pinkertons will catch you, or a vigilante mob will find you. In either case, you'll be hanging from a tree soon enough and your soul will burn for eternity in Hell. It's not too late to repent sinner—"

Merrick charged, slamming his weighty body into the expressman's ribs. The man's gun retorted with a blast into the coach floor, grazing Teague's ear on its path, causing the prone man to shriek and curse a stream of insane gibberish.

The wiry little guard found himself tightly encased in Merrick's burly arms, with a cold steel gun barrel pressed against his temple. Merrick nearly broke the guard's arm, twisting it until the old man at last groaned and dropped his gun with to the floor with a clatter.

Teague stretched to grab it, his fingers just touching the metal, before Merrick kicked it away to the far corner.

"Now, that we have more of a common understanding, old man, tell me the combination," he whispered in the man's ear.

"Go to Hell, spawn of Satan," the guard replied, choking.

"Things could get rather unpleasant for you, old timer. It would save you a considerable amount of pain if you would just cooperate and allow us to be on our way."

"I do not fear you, for the Lord is my shepherd. He will deliver me from evil. Do what you will, you blackguard, but be assured that I will never talk."

"I don't doubt that," Merrick muttered.

"Arrrrrrrrrrrr!" Teague rolled over on the sticky floor.

"What's going on in there?" Gwynn's voice came nervously from the outside.

"No problems," Merrick called out. "We have everything in hand. Do you have everything secure out there?"

"Yes, we are all just having a bit of a picnic."

"Anyone out there married?"

"Answer him," Gwynn directed the men with his rifle.

"I am," sputtered the conductor at last. The other two nodded their heads.

"Wee ones?"

"I've got a newborn at home. Greene there has three youngsters, and Mulroney's got a half dozen or so."

Merrick paused. "Kill one of them," he finally said without emotion.

"Which one?"

"Take your pick. Maybe t'would be best to start with the youngest."

The conductor started bawling loudly. "You can't kill me, my wife... my baby..."

The others joined the chorus.

"Tell your friend Mr. Flynn here to give me the combination and we'll spare you."

"Flynn, Flynn, please give them what they want," the prisoners cried out.

"Go to Hell," the old guard sputtered. "All of you."

"Shoot one," Merrick said.

Gwynn aimed the rifle. The sound of a gun blast echoed; the cries intensified.

"Bastards!" Flynn gasped.

"Which one did you kill?" Merrick asked.

"'Twas was just a warning shot," Gwynn replied.

"I am quite displeased with you, brother. I expect you to follow my commands to the letter. When I say blow the head off of one of these fine gentlemen I expect you to do it. Now, will you please do as I say and shoot one of these loving fathers and dutiful husbands? We will have their poor widows and little fatherless children soon put to weeping and wailing at their fathers' funerals if this bloody little rooster here doesn't drop his sermonizing and get us our goddamn money."

"Aiiiiii," moaned Teague. "Kill them all! The bastard shot me, damn him!"

"Shut up," snarled Merrick. "Do you hear me, brother?"

"I do indeed, and I apologize for my error. I have my gun here ready and have decided, upon further reflection, to start with the oldest fellow here. One shot should be enough to turn his brains into a heap of pudding. He has enough children to keep each other and their mother company, and so I expect he won't be missed as much."

"Sounds like a wise choice."

The engineer shook violently, and he and the other men pleaded desperately to the guard: "Show mercy, Flynn. Give them what they want. For God's sake, Flynn. It's only money. Think of our wives and children."

"—or maybe," Gwynn continued. "I should in fact shoot the youngest. Only one child there, and a newborn. Less time for pleasant memories to have been made there, and a widow young enough to find another—"

"Flynn, have mercy!"

"Damn you all, I've taken an oath!" Flynn shouted.

"Every Christmas, missing their dear ol' Daddy Dear..." Merrick whispered.

"Shoot them all, damn you!" Teague screamed one last time

from the floor before his eyes rolled back and he collapsed in a heap.

"Or maybe let's just say that we split the difference. You say you've got three at home?" Gwynn kicked at the brakeman. "Boys or girls? And a pretty wife no doubt. Shame she'll spoil her pretty face crying her eyes out over a dead man in a ditch half eaten by wolves—"

"For God's sake, Flynn!"

"What'll it be old man?" Merrick said calmly. "You know the company has insurance. And like you said, we will never get away with it anyway. The Pinkertons will undoubtedly be on us before breakfast, so what's the problem? Surely you wouldn't be doing your Christian duty by allowing us to kill these innocents for filthy lucre. Think of Jesus in the temple, Mr. Flynn. What would the savior do?"

"I gave my word of honor, damn you all," the old man sobbed, and then spirit broken at last, turned and opened the safe. Merrick handed him a sack, and with the bandit chief's gun trained on him, the old man reluctantly filled the bag with all of the bills and coins from the recesses of the safe.

When the bag was filled, Merrick reached out took it, and then, keeping his eyes on the little man, backed toward the door. Flynn angrily turned away and faced the corner. "Go ahead, shoot me in the back," he grumbled. "You have ruined me. I'll never find another job after this."

"There are fates worse than that, old timer."

Flinging the bag over his shoulder, Merrick bent down and grabbed Teague's limp arm. The wounded man opened his eyes and groaned. Kicking open the door, Merrick dragged his wounded partner out, Gwynn looking on in disbelief as Teague's body tumbled out, down the stairs and onto the ground, in limp, bloody heap.

"What happened?" he gasped.

"The honorable Mr. Flynn is a worthy adversary... and a loyal company man, and you blokes all owe him your lives."

"He can't ride?" Gwynn asked, pointing to Teague.

"No."

"He'll slow us down. I say we leave him."

"Bastards!" Teague snapped, coming to again with a snarl.

"Now brother, we know we cannot do that," Merrick said softly.

Pulling the horses out of the trees, they hoisted the injured man, whose voice grew weaker as he alternately cursed them and begged them not to leave him, onto the saddle in front of Merrick.

"Good day to you, gentlemen, it has indeed been our pleasure," Merrick said with a grim grin and swung his legs into the saddle, as he and his brother turned and spurred their horses up the ascent.

"You won't get far, especially with your man there," the brakeman said regaining some heart. "They'll hunt you down and string you up good."

"I appreciate your concern. However, as it is now, I suspect, somewhat too late for second thoughts, I believe we are rather inclined to take our chances," Merrick called back over his shoulder.

Sunlight filtered down through the leaves like streams from a river of gold, as the soft breeze blew fresh and cool, and the trail lay straight ahead, with only Teague's labored breathing and moans disrupting the calm. They eased forward confidently.

A retort of gunshot to their rear, as a twig snapped off a branch near Merrick's ear. Startled, the horse reared, loosing Teague's drooping body from Merrick's grasp; the injured bandit fell screaming in pain, hitting the ground and sliding halfway down the bank to a stop.

Gwynn cried out as a bullet hit him in the shoulder. Merrick yanked the reins and spun around in time to see the little expressman charging forward with his pistol firing, his face a radiant red, the old man shouting in fury: "I do my duty! Let no man tell you that Seamus Flynn doesn't always do his duty!"

As the train crew scrambled to the safety of the engine cab, a bullet hit a tree trunk splintering a piece of the bark that ricocheted off Merrick's head and into his eye, stunning him with pain and half blinding him. The money bag fell out of his grasp and onto the bank. Lower on the slope, Gwynn struggled to control his horse with one arm, getting both of them tangled in the grasp of a cluster of low hanging branches. The little guard, firing wildly, striking Gwynn in the thigh and wounding his horse, which whinnied and bucked with huge fright-filled eyes.

Merrick slid down out of the saddle and reached for the bag. A bullet hit him in the hand as he slipped and fell to his knees. The old man stopped firing and reloaded as he stepped closer to get a better shot at the kneeling outlaw. Merrick grasped at his gun, but his hand was now a useless appendage. He fumbled for his pistol with his other hand, but came away with nothing. His gun lay above on the slope; his holster was empty.

Grinning widely, the old man approached, pointing the revolver with shaking hands. "I hope you leave a widow and orphans yourself when I send you to Hell," he chortled.

Suddenly a shot rang out and the expressman's eyes glazed over as he tumbled limply to the ground like an unstringed marionette, a dark crimson stain appearing on his chest. Merrick looked back and saw Sam riding toward him with a smoking rifle in his hands.

"No!" screamed Merrick. "Go back, Sam."

Out of the corner of his eye, Merrick saw a rifle barrel emerge from the engine cab and take aim. A flash and the young rider was struck and fell to the ground where he lay as still as death.

CHAPTER THIRTY-EIGHT

I leaned back comfortably in Jesse's office chair, enthroned behind his dilapidated wooden desk in his shed, and called the shots, while the two dummies stood gaping sourly at me across the desk. I called this particular meeting late at night and they clearly weren't any too happy about dragging themselves in for a little chat. They grumbled and scowled as I asked them to close the door behind them.

"So what's this about, Preacher?"

"I heard from Jesse," I lied.

"No shit? It's about time," Jake said, an actual show of relief was displayed in his skull-like visage.

"So where is the punk?" Jared's dull eyes registered a glimmer of thought. I had his interest as well.

"Green Bay, like I said before," I answered coolly.

"You never said that," Jared snarled.

"You said you didn't know, Preacher." Jake stared at me, searching my eyes. I stared back.

"I said I wasn't sure."

"You said he was probably in Green Bay with some whore."

"Yup, that's where he is." I coughed and settled my nerves. "I couldn't tell you before—he made me promise not to, but now he's got something new in the works." I paused for dramatic effect. "And he needs you guys to get down there and help him out."

"I knew it; the little shit's got himself in trouble."

"No, nothing like that. He just needs you guys to show up and help him out on a little project and things will be cool."

"Still sounds like he's in trouble."

"He said it wasn't anything serious."

"He needs muscle?"

"It didn't sound like it. Said it was some deal. Lots of money involved too."

That perked them up even more.

"What's the story?"

"Don't know; he didn't say."

"Those Mexicans cockroaches again?" Jared leered.

"Maybe. It's something... nothing serious. He said he just needs a hand."

"Really?" Jake was thoughtful. "Then how come you're not going?" I tried not to flinch.

"It's a private party, family only. I wasn't invited. He said I was supposed to stay here and make sure things keep going here. Just send you and Tweedle Dee."

"What the fuck for? Seems like he'd need all of us if it's big deal, doesn't it?"

"Well, we got a shipment coming in from the Canadians the day after tomorrow. I've got to take care of that."

"I suppose."

"Sounds goofy to me," Jared snapped and rubbed his head with a massive paw. "Not that you're worth much in a fight anyway."

"How the hell do I know what he's up to? Who knows why Jess does the things he does?" I was sweating. "Maybe he wants me to watch his bitch?" I shouldn't have said that. Nerves and all, but I knew I shouldn't have brought her into it.

"Seems like you've been doing plenty of that lately as it is," Jared snapped, glaring threateningly and flexing his burly biceps, huffing and puffing, pumping up his already substantial body to gargantuan proportions.

"All I know is he needs it to be quiet. So, just the two of you."

"I hate fucking Green Bay. How about you go and I stay and walk his dog?" Jared snarled.

"Fine. I don't give a shit," I didn't have to pretend that I was angry, "but that ain't what he said. He also never said anything about cutting me in on any of the money. So let's just fuck up whatever his plan is and you can stay home and be left out. Yeah, maybe that's a better plan; maybe he'll give me your share?"

"Settle down, Preacher," Jake said evenly. They pondered in silence.

"You know," I said calmly, "maybe he's just looking out for his brothers. Like you guys always did for him. You know, blood is thicker than water."

"Ain't thicker than oil," Jared interjected. We ignored the comment.

"I don't know. Did he say we were supposed to arm up heavy?" Jake asked, his carnivorous face now brightened with greed.

"No, he said no big deal; you probably don't even need any guns or anything. I suppose if you want, you can pack, just don't go overboard with dynamite or bazookas or anything. He said not to worry; it's just an easy day's work. He said drinks and dinner are on him and to bring a stash."

"Nice! Sounds like a party. The kid's been acting funny lately, disappearing and all, but it'll be good to see him again. Not that I blame him for skipping town. First Jess knocking Jenny up and having to support the bitch and her brat, and now the heat's been getting hot and heavy around here with Pete throwing his fat ass around about his brother gone missing and all—can't say I blame him for taking a vacation. So when did he say we got to be there?"

"Tomorrow night at nine. I wrote the address on the paper for you. He said to meet him around back... in the garage."

"The garage! What's that all about?" Jared asked.

"Hey, maybe he found that motor for your Charger that you've been looking for, Jared. You got a birthday coming up. Is that what he's up to, Preach? Is Jess pulling some stunt?"

I just smiled. "I really can't say, guys." My eyes sparkled with the secret. "Just act surprised, OK?" I said as they left, excitedly jabbering between themselves in anticipation.

They drove away and I walked outside whistling. The night was cool and crisp and clean and the stars twinkled winked in the sky above. Inside my heart, I danced and played my lyre.

CHAPTER THIRTY-NINE

Surrounded on all sides by a twinkling drapery of frosty darkness, we passed the bottle of cheap wine around, feeling that warm glow in our stomachs grow with every slug, as a steady shower of diminutive quavering crystallized raindrops descended upon us, lightly frosting the world with white dust. Jess sat on the frozen ground, and as I stooped down and handed him the roach, he held it at angle to his lips, and drew the last of the toke, held it in with a groan, before exhaling a vaporous cloud into the chilly air. My head was swimming. I had been drinking beer and smoking dope for over a year now, but this sweet wine was like drinking soda pop and we had downed a bottle already.

Snickering at our own jokes, we hunkered down together with our backs against a pallet of two-by-fours that blocked the biting wind and, feeling contented even in the frigid atmosphere, we monitored the rows of stacks of lumber in assorted lengths as if we were feudal lords proudly surveying a conquered kingdom. Jared had a job lugging boards around the lumberyard and made us a copy of his key to the gate—he and Jake and a couple other stooges were going to meet us there later. They had incautiously mentioned that they were bringing along a surprise and we anticipated that it might be a bottle of tequila or some of that killer Jamaican smoke that we had heard intriguing rumors about.

I was disappointed Jenny wasn't with us. I hadn't seen her much lately and she had been strangely distant the last couple months since she dropped out of school. I hesitated to mention it, but ventured a query, "Where's Jen tonight?"

"Aw she's home. Says she's not feeling good. Who knows with women what's on their minds?" I didn't know it then—not having seen her in weeks, but she was quite a ways along now with Jeremy's pregnancy. "Hell, forget her," he continued, "We'll have more fun without her anyway. Which reminds me..."

He reached into his pocket and pulled out a plastic bag. "Happy birthday," he said with a smirk and tossed it to me.

"Oh man you shouldn't have," I peered closely at the gift in the half-light to see it. "What is it?"

"Check it out. I special ordered it for you. Had to trade a shitload of weed for it, but it was worth it... for today you are eighteen, and at long last my friend, you have finally, and against all odds, become a man."

I was touched. I opened the baggie and poured a small pile of orange barrel-shaped pills onto the palm of my hand.

"Careful, that stuff ain't cheap you know."

"I don't... what is it?"

"It's orange sunshine, you idiot... LSD... acid... take you to the moon and back without even leaving the lumberyard."

I had a sick feeling in my guts. "Whoa. I don't know about this, Jess..."

"Hey, you only turn eighteen once. We've got to make tonight special."

"Well..." I squinted at the tiny shapes arrayed in my hand. "I guess you're right. How many do I take?"

"Better start with just one—"

They looked so small and harmless. What could it hurt? I popped a handful.

"—or not..." Jesse grinned. "You better have left some for me."

I had. I had split the dozen and he swallowed the rest.

"None left for the rest of the lugs, but hey, you snooze you lose. We don't have to tell them, and what they don't know..."

My heart raced with anticipation as I wondered what it would feel like and whether it would happen like a flash or it would just come along real gradual, and would I even notice when it did? Well, it didn't take long, and although it happened pretty gradually, it still came on like a flash, and guess what? I did notice.

About twenty, thirty minutes later I started to feel like I was floating, separating from my body, though still somehow attached. It was crazy: I felt like I was outside my body and watching myself in action. In the distance—diffusing, expanding and receding in rippling palpitations, I watched in amazement as the lights from the town melted into watercolors flowing and cresting, undulating like a beautiful shimmering tide of a sea that swelled and merged with the swirling Milky Way. The wine was long gone, so we started in on some beer, but the act of drinking itself suddenly felt weird, like I was reaching out and pouring the liquid into a bucket instead of down my throat. But—you know me—I kept on drinking, even though I wasn't tasting anything, because it seemed like the beer slowed me down some and helped to anchor my feet to the ground, which was good because I had a serious fear that I might at any minute lose control and follow the colored streams of light and go spinning off into the infinite sweep of the sky.

The bulky shapes of the pallets of wood around us magically revealed themselves as crouching animals in the shadows, but we weren't afraid of them: it seemed natural that they were there, and we were pleasantly surprised that we had discovered their unexpected existence in the everyday world of things we were usually oblivious to. We smiled at the awesome intricacies and impressive ingenuities of mysterious, omnipresent creation, while wondering, lightly troubled, why we had never noticed these hidden treasures before. Whatever our previous ignorant state, we found that we now had shed our veil and were newly initiated into the arcane arts and secret knowledge of the universal architecture. My jaw dropped as, across the road, the trees suddenly morphed into huge heads with unblinking eyes and leafy crowns. It was funny; it was so amazingly funny. I looked at Jesse and his eyes were glowing like two flashlights in the dark and his smile sliced nearly through his face almost cutting it in two. My own face felt the same way. Laughing, laughing loudly, yet soundlessly; we couldn't stop laughing, though in retrospect nothing was really funny. It hurt to laugh so long and so hard, but we couldn't stop.

All around us the town seemed ridiculous to us in its mundane resplendence. A few lonely vehicles crawled through the streets like electric insects on paved jungle vines. Inside their mausoleums, people slept, or watched TV, or made love, or maybe said their prayers, before sliding into their nightly coma, only to awake just to find their flimsy little artificial lives begun anew. All these little tentative souls, entities, flickering, sparking in tandem, connected together, playing their roles like gears and pieces in a clockwork mechanism that, although it seemed so monumental, was deliriously puny in the context of the immense universe. Running around like ants, so unaware, so innocent, playing their mindless parts under remote control in a frantic, futile attempt to keep the whole house of cards from blowing away, without even realizing the obvious fact that someday, someday... it would be all gone except for the cockroaches, the mud and dust and ice and the stars: if we were lucky, the stars. It all amused me so.

Jake and Jared and a few other ghouls suddenly tumbled in from the darkness like a line of wandering minstrel show buffoons, dragging their surprise in tow behind them: Connie Kulczyk, a pretty, but mildly retarded girl a couple of years older than me. A tough chick from the old neighborhood, she used to join us in our fun and games occasionally, before she dropped out of school and moved to Escanaba with her mom for a couple of years. She was back in town now, living with her dad, and it was rumored that she would put out in exchange for a couple drinks and some reefer. Connie had a full figure, large breasts, thick lips and big round cow eyes. She was cute, in a slutty sort of way, but she clearly wasn't all there, and she had a temper and a vocabulary of curse words to rival Jesse's old man. Somebody told me she was that way because her mom was drunk the night she was born, but that was just another of those stories. In any case she hadn't been right her whole life.

"We heard you were a virgin, Preacher," Jake said proudly, "so we brought you a piece of ass. Some real prime rump steak." He slapped her with an audible smack on her ample bottom.

"Ow," she said and giggled and punched Jake on the arm. "Get me a beer, dummy. I got some catching up to do."

Jared pushed me forward. "Here's your mystery date, Connie. You remember, Nate, don't you?"

Connie was busy swigging down a tall beer. She eyed me with wary anticipation. "Sure. Hi Nate. You going to be my boyfriend tonight?" She brayed like a donkey and drained her can. "Give me another one, I'm thirsty."

The boys roared and Jake handed her another beer that she put between her ripe ruby lips and guzzled down with gusto. Jake handed her a joint and she took a big drag that caused her to cough up a storm.

"Hell, that's some real good shit," she said laughing and snorting, "you trying to get me buzzed or something?"

Jared kicked at Jesse, who was still seated on the ground watching the scene without comment, smiling like he knew a real smutty joke, but didn't dare share it. "What's wrong with you?" he snarled.

Jesse tried to say something, but his mouth just opened and he said nothing came out. He knew the Truth, but he could not find the words to say.

I knew how Jesse felt. His brothers were drunk and stupid and earthbound, they couldn't understand what we saw and now understood. We were a part of the cosmos, while they were insects to be crushed beneath our feet. One of the clowns smashed a bottle and Jared clobbered him for making a mess. It was the Stooges. It was comedy.

In the background I became vaguely aware that Jake and Connie were arguing. "Come on, damn you, give me another drink!" she demanded.

"Uh uh, Connie, you gotta take care of the birthday boy first."

"Oh OK," she rolled her eyes. She hurried over to me and grabbed my hand. "Come on Nate, I don't have all night. My Dad will skin me if I'm not home by midnight."

The guys all laughed and hooted as she led me away, stumbling and slipping across the glazed ground, back away behind one of the wood piles. I watched the scene as if it were a movie. But the gangly performer on the screen wasn't me. It was just some collection of skin and bones held upright and together by unseen strings—a crudely fashioned puppet that she pulled along hurriedly by an arm that was barely attached to my body. I watched as the arm stretched as if made of rubber, yanked along by what looked like a doll—a grotesque molded plastic doll, made of parts and pieces that didn't seem to have been properly assembled at the factory.

Apparently the speech mechanism was faulty as well, as the harsh voice chattered away relentlessly, though I found the blurred torrent of words hard to follow. Taking her coat off, she laid it on the ground and embraced me in her clutches. I half-heartedly tried to participate, but my disconnected hands fumbled uselessly. While struggling with her bra, I searched her back as well for an off switch to stop the noise, instead, only finding folds of fat, giving me the sensation that a pair of insect wings would suddenly emerge from the grub-like body beneath her shirt.

Annoyed at my inexperience, she snarled, "Goddamn it, hurry up," and hurriedly removed her shirt and bra and crossed her arms, shivering, revealing a bulging torso that was pale and segmented. Her hard plastic shell had melted and her underbelly was made of a soft and pliable material. Removing her jeans, she lay down on her coat and pulled me violently into her soft, gooey flesh.

I panicked. I couldn't breathe with the thick pale walls closing in and absorbing all of the oxygen. I felt sick. She told me to hurry because she was thirsty, but her voice echoed as if it came from a broken loudspeaker erected within a tunnel located at a great distance from the lumberyard.

Insect-like feelers unfurled and undid my fly and reached inside: there was nothing. How could I tell her I wasn't there? It was someone else's genitalia she rubbed with increasing abandon, like a girl scout frantically trying to start a fire in a blizzard, struggling to prevent herself from freezing to death. I felt nothing but an uncomfortable shame in the knowledge that she was embarrassing me, and although I couldn't stop laughing, the laughter hurt. I felt sure that the joke was on me, and that everyone, including Jesse, was in on it.

"How's it going over there?" Jake howled. "You finding everything alright?"

"Want me to bring you some flour?" Jared added.

Connie laughed too and called back angrily, "Shut up!"

Working quickly now, as though employed on a factory assembly line, she removed my coat and shirt and I became aware of a tingly feeling that I presumed meant my earthly body was possibly cold, but this new feeling was just another remote sensation that afflicted an alien entity far, far away. The frost on the ground extended up through that frozen body and hovered in the air all around us, combining with our breath and painting smoky spirals in the dark. The girl in the movie worked furiously to revive me—but

I felt nothing but remote and undecipherable signals. The doll grunted, snorted and grew madder with every passing minute and at the crude remarks that flew in our direction from the rude boys the longer it took. Her mind was already thinking of the tequila she had been promised and she spat out her frustration towards me with contempt.

"Shut up and quit laughing, you fucking dummy!" she snarled with frustration. "What's wrong with you anyway? Ain't I pretty enough for you?" She grabbed at her breasts, and stroked and massaged them.

"I..." my voice was as empty as the wind through my soul.

"Don't I turn you on? Or are you just queer? That's it; you're a fucking queer boy."

Her insistence momentarily brought me back to reality, and I felt the pressure weigh on me like a mantle of chains. Here was my first and possibly only chance to ever experience sex... with another person that is. A real live girl. One who would let me do whatever I wanted. The fantasy that I had dreamed of for so long. Yet...

Fat rubber tire lips pouting, watery eyes hurt and angry loomed in my vision, but suddenly her face disintegrated and changed from her broad bovine appearance into the impish image of my mother as she appeared in the single dusty photo of her my father kept in a corner of the living room in my home.

"Come on, you asshole!" she mocked from my mother's sly and taunting mouth. "I told you I ain't got all night." She rubbed herself upon me, and all I could feel was her immensity collapsing, crushing my body.

The rubber spider gripped me tightly to its udders encased in its damp and sticky web. The mother who left me alone and unloved. Who never looked back, who never cared. Struggling to get away, her sweaty skin sticking to me despite the chill. I remember... I remember feeling like I couldn't breathe, that I was being smothered. I struck out wildly, in all directions, frantic for escape. She laughed and taunted me like it was a game and clutched me more tightly—pinning my arms like a straitjacket. I screamed at her to leave me alone.

I wrenched my arms free and slapped her. She only giggled in reply. I struck harder, repeatedly, and she told me to stop, that it hurt. She struck me back, her fists popping off a fleshy balloon that registered a flicker of pain far in the depths below somewhere. By now the gang's curiosity had been raised and I sensed a crowd surrounding us.

They say I had both hands clenched around her throat and was laughing hysterically at the top of my lungs, but I don't remember that at all. Based on the black eye and bruises I received, I frankly suspect I got the worst of it. After all she wasn't any shrinking violet and was a pretty rough female, not that that justifies my behavior. Many hands pulled me off of her and Jared angrily tossed me to the ground like an empty puppet made of papier-mâché. I hit my head on a skid and blacked out, and... that's about all can say. Until...

#####

When I awoke, I found myself staring into the face of a shimmering angel, one who looked upon me with a love and concern my own mother had never seen fit to provide me. I swam across that dark and terrifying void and ever onward toward two gleaming brown eyes. The delicate pink lips that haunted me moved softly and spoke with gentleness.

"Are you okay, Nate?" Jenny's whisper brought me back. She was the only one who could have; I know that for a fact: I was gone, never to return. How can anyone know what I felt? I was cold and alone, complete with the universe, in glorious, deathly nonexistence until... her melodious murmur burst forth upon my spirit in a chorus more beautiful than any earthly music. She brought me back to the world and back to her, and in doing so, she made me live again.

The rapture stirred within me, enveloping me in pure unadulterated love as she gathered me into her arms, and in doing so, blessed me, caressed me; and as she glowed brighter than a thousand suns and I felt her lips press on my forehead with sublime reverence, and I found myself bathed and cleansed completely within the shining presence of her saving grace. And within her abiding love for a poor, wretched and even dangerous sinner, I knew God.

CHAPTER FORTY

It took some doing, but I finally got Jesse alone in his shed/office late one night. He sat on his chair and swiveled and smoked in the semi-darkness, while I tuned in the classic rock station. Leaning against the rough wooden wall, I nervously kept an eye on the yard through a crack in the door. I didn't want anyone sneaking up on us.

"What's the big secret, Preacher? You been sleeping with my girl?" He said it like a joke, but his eyes were cold.

I let it slide and started in slowly and methodically. "You remember that story we used to talk about—the train robbery?" My voice sounded surprisingly calm, just as I had rehearsed in advance.

Jesse took a drag and blew out the smoke. "Yeah, what about it?"

"I might have found something."

"What do you mean?" He sat up. The lure was working, now to set the hook.

"I was fishing over on the Michigamme the other day—"

"Never knew you to be much of a fisherman."

"I've been doing it a bit lately, since you've been gone so much. Gets me out of town, away from Big Pete."

Jesse snorted and lit another match. "So, were they biting?"

"Not much."

"Figures. So what about the train money?"

"I'll get to it. Anyway, I got my old man's canoe—you know he doesn't use it— anyway I'm out by myself doing some fishing and things pretty well suck; it's raining off and on, and the mosquitoes were just nasty, and no, the fish weren't really hitting on anything. Probably getting their fill of the skeeters."

"He's still got that canoe? Surprised it still floats." He blew out a cloud of smoke. "Fishing blows, man."

"Anyway, I was working the reeds out by this one island—"

"Boring. Ice fishing too. Just an excuse to get plowed."

"—because somebody said there was maybe some bass hanging

out there."

"Those bass are sneaky bastards," Jesse giggled.

"But, I just put on a new spinner—"

"Rubber worm. You use a rubber worm to catch bass, dummy. Everybody knows that."

"Well, I was using a new lure that they recommended at the bait shop. Some bright and shiny thing. Cost me plenty too. Said the bass couldn't stay off it—"

"Rubber worm. Never known it to fail with bass—"

I paused. "Do you want to hear about this or not?"

"Ok, ok."

"Anyway, I was casting near the shore and got my line caught up in the trees."

"Bummer dude," Jesse laughed. "That's why I hate fishing; it's always something."

"Some branches were hanging out overhead and I just snagged one. Yanked and yanked, but it was stuck good; I couldn't get it loose. Normally I'd just cut my line and say to hell with it, but the lure was brand new, and like I said, it cost me a bit, so I pulled the canoe in and parked it on the island."

"Don't tell me you dumped the canoe? Remember that time we tipped over in it and got drenched? Your dad was pissed because we skipped school and sunk his boat."

"Naw, I can handle a canoe when I don't have a drunken idiot standing up in it."

"Yeah, I suppose that doesn't really help." He passed me the pipe, but I shook my head and continued.

"But, like I said, I was alone and figured I'd just climb up the tree, only it wasn't so easy. I tried getting up in it, but the branches were too high, and it wouldn't support me. I was just about ready to give up and then I found something weird."

"What do you mean, weird?"

"On one of the trees, someone carved a bunch of numbers and symbols."

"Like 'Jimmy Loves Susie' stuff?"

"No, this was old and real strange. More like triangles and crosses and numbers. I think it's a map in code."

Jess was standing by now, his attention complete. His eyes shone greedily. "You think it could be—?" I just had to reel him in.

"Who knows, but I'm thinking it might be; what else could it be?"

"It would make sense. They could have buried it on the island."

"That was before the reservoir was there, but it would have been higher ground. They could have made a map to where they hid it, but none of them ever made it back."

"So the money could still be there?"

"And we could be the ones to find it."

"Did you at least write down what was carved there?"

"Didn't even have a pencil with me."

"Damn. We should go back there with tools and metal detector. Can you find the place again?"

"I can find it."

"Maybe tomorrow morning we can—"

"I'm thinking we should go tonight."

"What do you mean? Like right now?"

"Yeah, why not?" I tried to act nonchalant.

"Well it's fucking dark out for one thing, you shithead."

"That's what flashlights are for."

"But tomorrow—"

"We'd have your brothers and every other idiot in the town tagging along with us. I don't feel like sharing it with any of those greedy jerks."

"You got that right," he said thoughtfully. "But Jenny—"

"You especially don't want her to know. You know women, next thing you know she'll have you buying another house and all new furniture."

"That bitch can go to Hell if she thinks she is going to spend our money on diapers and refrigerators and shit," he sputtered. "We've been dreaming about finding that stash ever since we were kids."

"She's asleep isn't she? Just leave her a note saying you've gone to Green Bay on business. She doesn't have to know a thing."

"Yeah. OK. No shit. Let's go check this thing out. You really think this could be it?"

"I've got a feeling about it, Jess. It's our destiny."

"It's funny, isn't it," Jess said as we walked toward the darkened house.

"What's that?"

"What her face is going to look like when I give her that trip to Paris she has always been talking about."

"Yeah," I said brightly, but my thoughts were grim.

CHAPTER FORTY-ONE

She leaned in so close I could almost taste her chewing gum. Spearmint.

"What are you reading?" she asked with a frown.

Sunlight Degas'd down through the branches and leaves above us like a French Impressionist painting of a lily pond hung upside-down by accident in a gallery, as we sat in the shade of a grove of trees on a hillock above the river. Below, Jesse and several friends screamed and laughed as they swung out on an old tire and jostled to knock each other into the water below. I had been involved in the action earlier, but soaking wet, and tired of being the primary victim, had slipped away to mope and read in solitude, at least until the gang tired of the game and wanted to go get a pizza.

Now my sanctuary had been invaded, although this time rather pleasantly, and by a most beguiling enchantress in a wet, form-fitting tank top that displayed a delicious pair of savory peaches dangling invitingly just out of my reach. I was never very fond of sharing my current reading material; people often get the wrong idea. I once had a well-meaning neighbor donate an entire library of white supremacist literature to me because they saw me reading a biography of Hitler, but in this case, I was pleased to make an exception for my Jenny in the vines.

"It's called *Lost Illusions*," I said. "It's by a French guy named Balzac."

"That's bullshit. Ball sack! You made that up." She reached for the book, but I held it away at arm's length.

"Uh uh, you have to be pretty special. I don't let just anyone touch my Balzac."

"Well I am special, aren't I?" She was.

I held it out and she grabbed the book out of my hands.

"You read some weird stuff, dude. Hey, you weren't kidding. The guy's name really is Balzac. So what's it about?"

"Well... it's kind of complicated—"

"And I'm too stupid to understand?"

"No, but there are a whole bunch of Counts and Madames with French names and stuff and it's kind of hard to keep it straight—"

"So why are you reading it?"

"Well... he's a really great writer and... I guess because his characters seem so real... they are so lifelike and... you really care about them and... well, the story is really interesting; I mean, you can't even turn a page without being blown away by the stuff he comes up with. Every page, just full of... amazing insights he has... about stuff... like life."

She looked doubtful. "Life in France?"

"Life everywhere. Life in France—even in Balzac's time, the early 1800s, it's crazy, but it was still pretty much the same as it is now."

"I don't see too many guys wearing powdered wigs in Crystal Falls these days," she smirked.

"Well yeah, fashions change, but the stuff that is real is always there."

"You're so deep," she taunted. "Like what is real?"

"You know, people trying to be good and make it in a world filled with a lot of bad stuff like hatred, wars, envy, cheating, stealing, murder, lust.... man's inhumanity to man."

"And women."

"Yeah, and of course, love..."

"Yup love..." She twirled her butterscotch hair between her fingers. "I guess it's always been that way, huh? Never going to change. If it's been going on since this was written in the 1800's, nothing is going to ever change."

"It's been going on since the Bible times, even before."

"I have to tell you, I know you dig it, but the Bible freaks me out," she said and sat down. "All that creepy stuff about people turning to salt and talking snakes and other funky shit. Brrrr..."

"Oh come on, you gotta love those stories: Daniel in the lion den, Jacob's ladder, Moses and the Red Sea."

"Actually, I always thought the men were pretty fucked up; like Noah getting drunk and flashing people, Jacob's brothers selling the little shit into slavery, or even worse, Lot getting it on with his own daughters."

"Yeah, that was pretty weird."

"The women though... they were the real heroes, like Esther and Judith and Delilah, Deborah... I especially love that Jael chick driving the tent peg through the Canaanite general's head. Now that's wicked cool."

"How do you know about that stuff?"

"My mom, remember. She's a total Bible freak."

"Some crazy shit, yeah I admit, but great stories. I love that old crap... Did you ever read any Greek mythology?"

"Just what we had to in school."

"Man, I love those ancient stories. Hercules, Ulysses, Orpheus and Eurydice, Jason and the Argonauts—"

"The Minotaur. Ugh. Gives me nightmares."

"You know those stories too!" I was overjoyed.

"The princess who strung the yarn through the maze and saved the hero."

"Yes, yes!"

"And then he dumped her and left her there."

"Uh yeah, you're right. I never thought about that," I remembered doubtfully after a pause.

"You wouldn't. A typical guy—treating his woman like shit." Jesse's voice could be heard laughing below. He called out, "Hey Darlin', you coming back?"

"In a minute," she shouted back down to him.

"So you read much these days?" I asked, anxious to keep her around.

"Not really. Magazines mostly. Gossip stuff. I don't much care for fiction—it's just a bunch of made up stories. I don't see the point. I don't want to read about life, I want to live it."

"We need both beauty and bread, you know."

"Beauty and bread, huh? You make that up just now?" She cocked her head and gave me that questioning look. She was paying attention... to me!

"No, guy by the name of John Muir said it, or something like it."

"Who is he?"

"Was. He was a naturalist, a nature lover, I think he founded the

Sierra Club."

"A tree hugger? Figures. So you need beauty huh?" She teased. Blushing. "Sure. Everyone does. 'Beauty will save the world.'"

"You're an idiot," she said and hit me on the arm.

"Ow," I said, flinching.

"Don't be a wimp," she teased. "So, if you need beauty so much, why aren't you down with us in the sunshine instead of wasting your time reading up here alone in the shade?"

I shook my head. "Don't you see? It opens up a whole new world to you when you read."

"What's wrong with this world?" She motioned around us.

"Nothing, but there is more—"

"What are you talking about? Ghosts, aliens, Santa Claus, Jesus Christ...?"

"You don't believe there's anything else? Anything extra special... spiritual even...?" I sputtered.

"I don't know. I kind of came to the conclusion that I don't fall for anything I can't see, hear, taste or touch anymore. It is what it is, and that's all there is to it. Guess seeing my momma get crazier the more she prays sort of taught me that one."

"But if this is all there is... what's the point?" I replied bitterly. "I wish I could make you understand."

"Maybe you could," she said smiling coyly and touching my hand. "So you never told me what the book is about other than a bunch of French dandies prancing around."

"There's a lot of things going on, more than I can go into, but I guess the main plot line would be a young man wants to be a writer and he goes to the big city—Paris that is, and once he gets there, he is cheated and abused by all these nasty folk and, as a result, he loses his innocence and the illusions he has of life as being fair and good."

"You may have a point about it relating to life after all," she said after a thoughtful pause. "Sounds depressing, but... hey, will you loan me your copy after you're done?"

"I'd be glad to—"

"And I won't tell Jesse that you let me have your ball sack," she giggled as she swayed like a slender willow in the wind as she made her way back down the path to the water's edge.

CHAPTER FORTY-TWO

C... U... N... T... That's right, you asshole. Throw away that planchette, I don't need any Ouija board to say what I want to say, and believe me, I am pissed off like you won't even believe. So the punk hated me enough to kill me. It figures. You help somebody out and what do you get. That's what I get for being a good Sumerian or whoever the hell that it was Nate was always preaching about. The prick. Probably always was plotting behind my back the whole time. So he was in love with Jenny—I knew that was the case, I just knew it. Steal a man's woman? What a friend. He'd probably still be hiding in the shadows if it wasn't for me. Hiding and drinking like his old man. What did I ever do but look out for the little shit.

Fancy college boy, the fuck had it easy. Yeah, his mom left him, but at least his dad didn't knock him around. I had the street smarts. I had to show that kid how to tie his own shoes. I taught him how to jump trains, how to be tough, how to be a man. *Castle bars* he said; turns out they were more like prison ones.

He probably tells you all how holy he is. Fuck that, I've seen that boy in action and trust me, he is anything but holy. Let me tell you something, he can preach all he wants, but let him tell you about that time in the lumber yard with the retarded girl. Hell, he was so drunk we had to pull him off her. He was out of his head. We thought he was going to murder her right there and then. Jared wanted to clock him and leave him in the snow, but I said no and dragged his ass to Jenny's and saved his sorry hide. Had to pay the fat girl to keep her quiet, but does he remember any of it? Meanwhile, he claims he had a vision and found God or something. Bullshit. I knew that would never last.

And all that crap he always goes on about not being an addict... I don't even know where to begin on that pack of lies. Shit, his old man was a drunk and his old lady was an Indian—what the fuck do you think? He couldn't not be an addict if he tried. I've seen Preach passed out in in a puddle of his own piss and vomit. Hell, I've seen that creep do every drug known to man and then some. He even scares me sometimes with his careless attitude toward the shit. You've got to be in control, like me.

Yeah, I've knocked Jenny around a bit—so what? She's a big girl; she can take care of herself. And believe me, she can give as good as she gets. I've got the scratches and bruises to prove it. She damn near stabbed me to death with a kitchen knife and smacked me pretty good with a baseball bat one time. Even pushed me down the stairs another time and nearly busted my ribs when I hit the basement floor. So I smacked her upside the head—that's what love is all about after all ain't it? A death match, for better and worse. We always ended up fucking after we were done. To tell you the truth, I think she digs it—the violence. Tell that to the little prince, Sir Galahad there: his angel likes the rough stuff. She'd never love a pussy wimp like Preacher; he'd bore her to tears.

But what is worst of all is this crap about me killing Little Pete. Look, I admit I was there that day, and I was pretty well fucked out of my head, but I'm pretty sure I'd remember if I did what Preacher says I did. That kid pissed me off, true, but shooting him? I talk shit all the time no doubt, and I've had to whack a couple knuckleheads around a bit, but killing ain't usually my way—too messy for one thing.

I think I was in the bedroom with some chicks getting plastered and next thing I know, I hear some screaming and Pete was acting up and I had to go out and settle him down. I probably did threaten the little bastard with my gun—so what? That doesn't mean I did it. I might have set it down on the counter and gone back to partying. Yeah, that's probably it. I was with some redheaded chick and her kooky tattooed friend we picked up hitching, and who I never saw before or after, and the next thing I know I'm helping Preacher toss Pete's body down the mine.

He kept saying how I had finally done it—finally popped some lowlife in the melon like I always said I would—and how I was so fucked up that I didn't even remember it, and man, that is pretty fucked up; and pretty soon half the town is telling me they saw me do it. But then I started thinking maybe it wasn't me that did it at all. That maybe it was our not-so-innocent-anymore Preacher boy who pulled that trigger and then spread the word around town and messed with my head and made me think it was me that did it. I mean, I liked Pete. And Nate... I still remember a time when Nate and I were sitting out in the woods and he was talking about how he wondered what it would be like to pop some kid in the head. Then that time when we borrowed the canoe, when he was talking about what it 'd be like to be dead and all. Gave me the creeps, I must admit. Still does.

Guess the best thing to do would be to ask Little Pete himself when I see him. I suspect he probably isn't going to be too happy to see me in any case. Haven't run in to him yet; maybe he's gone on, I don't know. I just don't...

CHAPTER FORTY-THREE

The sun's last light disappeared over the crest of the Porkies to the west as I pulled into Finn Town. The ghost town looked deserted and I didn't see Big Pete's red truck anywhere; he must have parked behind the trees at the far end of the abandoned mining settlement. Breathing hard, I focused only on the task ahead of me.

Though I walk in the midst of trouble, thou wilt revive me: thou shalt stretch forth thine hand against the wrath of mine enemies, and thy right hand shall save me.

I knew my time was short. I figured he'd have Jenny in one of the rickety buildings that lined the road, but which one was uncertain. For a moment I considered sneaking around the back on foot and peering in windows where I could, but I was sure that he had heard me coming and seen the dust I was kicking up as I tore up the road in Jesse's Trans Am. He was probably watching me now.

I pulled over quickly, spraying a cloud of dust into the air as I parked, and climbed out of the driver's seat. The air was cool, so I slipped on a jacket, and self-consciously felt for the handle of the pistol tucked into the back of my jeans. He'd have to know I wouldn't give her up without a fight, so the subterfuge was probably without value. But it made me feel better anyway: force of habit.

Yea I walk into the shadow of death...

I started down the road cautiously. If Pete planned on putting a bullet in my head with a hunting rifle I was probably in his sights right now.

I fear no evil...

I watched for movement in the shadows. The remnants of a curtain moved in the window of one house. I paused. The wind blew and it flapped again. I kept striding ahead.

Suddenly in the farthest cabin a light blinked on. A sign? A lantern signaling me, bringing me closer into a trap. As I approached, I heard a voice call out.

"Take the gun out of your back pocket, Preacher!"

"I'm not carrying," I replied halfheartedly.

"You're a lying SOB. I've been watching you with binoculars and I know you have a pistol stuck up your ass. Throw it away."

I turned and pulled the gun out and tossed it back down the road. Maybe not as far as I could, but he seemed satisfied. It wasn't going to matter anyway.

"OK. Come on in."

Looking up, I saw Pete's huge frame filling the doorway. He didn't seem to be armed. He was however, holding a hatchet. Taking a deep breath, I advanced cautiously toward him, hoping the orange blade was merely rusty and not stained with blood.

He moved aside and I stepped into the room tentatively, expecting a sudden blow striking the base of my skull. Cards were spread across a table—he had apparently been playing solitaire. A half bottle of tequila, some junk food wrappers and an ashtray full of butts, led me to conclude that he had been here for some time.

"Nate?"

A low moaning voice emerged from the back room. I moved quickly into the dusty backroom and saw Jenny, wrists bound together crudely, lying jacent on a sleeping bag. I fell to my knees on the dirty floor and held her, whispering, "Jenny, I'm here. Everything is going to be all right."

I heard the lumbering steps and felt the looming presence of the giant behind me and braced again for the blow, but instead he spoke quietly: "I didn't hurt her, Preacher. You know me. I'm a good guy. I'd never hurt anyone. Only... you know... what happened to the kid. I can't let that go."

"I... I... need water..." Jenny croaked.

"Get her some water!" I demanded.

"Sorry Preach, I kind of forgot to bring any, and there ain't any running water around this place. She can have a sip of this if she wants." He brought the bottle of tequila up to his mouth and took a swig and held it out for her, laughing.

"Let her go," I said. "She's not a part of this. She doesn't know anything. Let her take the car. You can do what you want with me."

"Oh, you're a real hero, Preach. Nice, save the girl. You didn't save my kid brother when you had the chance. I got it all figured out. You stood there and watched and let Jesse kill him."

"Preacher didn't have anything to do with that," Jenny said in a croaking voice, and motioned to Pete to hand her the bottle. She took it in both hands tied together at the wrists and tried to drink.

"Dude, you got to cut her loose."

Pete nodded and cut the rope with a knife. Glaring at Pete, the girl rubbed her wrists, before taking a long pull on the bottle.

"I didn't want to hurt her. You know I didn't. I like you Jenny, but... you gotta quit dicking me around. You gotta tell me what happened. I need to know, or so help me I'm going to..."

"OK Pete," I took a deep breath. "Here's the truth: it was an accident. Accidents happen. I hated for it to happen to your brother. I liked the kid. He was a twerp, and a loud mouth, but he had a good heart and I hated to see anything happen to him. I swear I did."

"He was a good kid, wasn't he, Preacher?" the ox muttered, choking up and wiping tears from his eyes.

"Yeah, Pete. Sure he was."

He was swaying on his feet, thinking of his brother.

Now was my chance. He had been drinking and was not suspecting a sudden attack. I was quicker, but it was close quarters and he outweighed me easily by a hundred and thirty pounds. It was suicide. And Jenny was weak. Again, in my mind, I felt the hatchet splitting my skull and decided to be patient and play the hand out. Maybe we could negotiate our way to freedom after all.

"But Pete," I argued softly, "killing us ain't gonna bring him back."

"I know, I know." The hulking figure slapped a meaty palm against his sweaty forehead and rubbed his red eyes.

"Just let Jenny go and then you and I can have a drink or two and talk about the good times. The good times we had with your brother."

"Like that time we were at that party—"

"Yeah that time."

"And Junior's old man came and broke it up and kids were climbing out the windows and—"

"Half the guys got caught, but you and I and Jesse and Jake hid behind the shed and they didn't see us."

"Landon got caught halfway out the window."

"Yeah, those were crazy times, weren't they?"

"That was always his luck, you know: he always got caught."

"That's the way it is, isn't it? Some people just don't have any chance. But Pete, you can't go back and change things now. It's over and done with. He's gone."

"You are right, he never had a chance. He always was goofy."

"Come on, Pete. Let's go sit down and have a drink, ok?"

"I don't know, Preacher. Maybe..." The anger suddenly raged again. "But that fucking Jesse Hawkins killed my brother and he's going to pay for it. I don't care if it was an accident or not, he will pay, yes he will. I don't know where that little creep has run off to, but I'll bet between the two of you I—"

Jenny suddenly sprang up like a coiled rattler striking, smashing the bottle into Pete's temple, both bodies falling into a heap on the floor by my feet. I grabbed Jenny, extricating her from beneath Pete's mammoth torso and bolted through the door, pulling her along like a rag doll. Stunned for a moment, the behemoth clambered to his feet, blood running in streams down his forehead between his eyes, roaring in agony before charging after us like a wounded bull.

We scrambled out the front door, Pete crashing through the room behind us, upending the table and sending playing cards everywhere. We had a few seconds head start, but Jenny was weak and stumbling, I dragged her as we ran. The Trans Am was at the end of the road. If we could make it.

Jenny looked back over her shoulder and uttered a muffled scream. Dodging to the right, I tumbled to the ground, knocking her down, as the hatchet whirred through the air, just clipping the side of my head and slicing my ear off cleanly in the process as we fell forward into the dust.

Pain flashed through my head as the extent of injury registered in my brain. Hurriedly, I pulled my shirt off and wrapped it around my head, staunching the bleeding somewhat. *At least, he's unarmed,* I thought. But then the clack of the chambers punctured the night and we turned and looked up to see Pete advancing with a shotgun: he really wasn't that stupid after all.

No way we make it to the car now. But my pistol. Where did it land when I threw it? I grabbed Jenny and we ran, blood running down my neck and shoulders and shoulders, bare chest, scanning the ground for a glint of the shining metal in the moonlight.

"Preacher," the giant rumbled angrily as though descending a beanstalk, "you know Jesse killed my brother. Either that or maybe you killed him yourself. And you are going to tell me the truth and then you are going to tell the police the whole story—if there is anything left after I get done with you!" An explosion resounded as he fired a warning blast into the air and we dove to the ground again.

"And not that fucker, Junior! I know he's in on the whole thing," he shouted to the heavens. Reloading the shotgun, he walked rapidly toward us. Jenny jumped up and yanked me to my knees and we struggled forward, half stumbling, half crawling, through the dust, blood spurting from the side of my head and soaking my shirt.

"I'm not a killer, Preacher! But you gotta tell me where he is," our pursuer bellowed, driven by rage. "Don't make me do it, Preacher. I don't want to kill you, but I will do it, so help me. Now tell me where Jesse is!"

Suddenly, ahead, lying on the ground by the side of the road, I spotted it: the pistol. Behind us the shouting became hysterical as the hulking stalker arrived at our heels.

"This is it—your last chance to tell me. Where is Jesse, Preacher? Where is he?" He stood looming over us, shaking with anger.

There was one last opportunity. Shoving Jenny to one side, I dove forward, fingers reaching out and grasping for...

A crunch as a heavy boot stepped on the gun and crushed it into the gravel—the boot belonging to a shadowy figure who had emerged, limping out unnoticed, from the darkness behind one of the cabins. Standing with his foot firmly on my gun, holding his own pistol pointed at Pete, tall and as frightening as a totem pole depicting the visage of an angry, grimacing slayer god demanding sacrifice, erected by a fierce tribe of pagan cannibals—Jared spat his words out as though forcing them through a rabid foaming mouth.

"That's what I'd like to know," he snarled as if uttering a vile malediction, and glared at us with his crazy evil eyes.

CHAPTER FORTY-FOUR

He was alone now and had been for months, traversing the criss-crossing trails, solitary, haggard and often hungry. While in the distance, sometimes in the calm center of the evening, he heard the howling of other packs, their voices carrying mournfully across the wide expanse of the night, reminding him of his own clan; and, longing for companionship, he would take up the cry, hoping the strangers would slow, or even halt their movement long enough to allow him to catch up with them, maybe even to join in with their group, to travel with them, feed with them, perhaps to even find a mate; but in the end, he was unable to reach them, to force an encounter, and so he traveled in solitude like a wayward spirit under the planchement of leaves and stars.

Already skittish from the blasts of the guns of the hunters, and the baited traps he had only just managed to avoid, the black wolf's desperation grew with every failure to capture his prey. Having missed out on several squirrels and birds, he lashed out aggressively in pursuit of a rabbit, which, at the last second, slipped through his paws and darted into its burrow unscathed. Shaking with fury and exhaustion, the wolf padded softly along the moonlit pathways, panting, attempting to garner enough energy for one last hunt before daybreak and another restless sleep with an empty stomach.

When the twig snapped, the wolf's ears twitched and focused immediately on the sound, his body preparing for action. His bright eyes searched the darkness like a spotlight, inspecting the underbrush for movement, while he sniffed the air, catching the unmistakable scent that led him to discover the shine of a pair of small eyes neatly hidden, nestled in the tangle of branches, concealed behind a drawn curtain of overgrown vegetation. A jerking movement disturbed the boughs, as a larger figure stood up with a start. The mother's action alerted the fawn who stood up shakily as well; both paused momentarily, ready for flight.

The black wolf's mind did the calculation: alone, he may not have the strength to pull down the doe, but the fawn... Its body would satisfy his desire; the energy gained would be enough to get him through another week or more. Before he could act, the doe's sleek muscles twitched, and she and her fawn bolted. The wolf followed, voraciously, rocketing straight into a breach in the copse, penetrating their refuge in an instinctual, finely-focused and inexorably determined attack.

Rain began to fall, lightly at first, but increasing in volume as a storm blew in, bringing with it thunder and lightning. Charging headlong through the suffocating forest along the snarled maze of concealed trails, the wolf chased the elusive pair, already tasting the flesh and blood dripping heavily from his salivating jaws. Fleet, ghost-like, the deer fled frantically, bounding over fallen trees and boulders as if the impediments were not there. Driven by the primal need to feed, the rapacious canid's powerful strides made up distance on his quarry—pitiless, his famishment spurring him inexorably forward in relentless motion, crashing over, under and through all obstacles in his path.

The deer suddenly slowed as they reached a crossing. The tawny neck now within his grasp, the wolf readied to pounce, uttering a guttural growl of triumph, the sweet perfume of death filling his senses, his jaws gaping wide, baring a row of gleaming cuspidated daggers poised to tear open the fawn's pulsing throat.

A wide pavement pathway stretched out ahead, and with it, headlights and the roar of an approaching engine, which intervened, interrupting and delaying the conclusion—the end game of the night's final performance.

A panicked pause, caused by the rapidly advancing machine, halted the wolf's attack, and he watched with cold interest as the approaching vehicle swerved to miss the deer, swayed erratically, and with the shrill and sickening shriek of skidding rubber on wet pavement as accompaniment, spun like a tipsy ballerina, crossing over the highway and into the far woods, where it collided with a tree with a loud boom, echoing into the dark heavens like the bursting of thousand hearts.

Slinking quickly away, back into the untamed shadowy regions from which he came, the black wolf retreated rapidly away from what he recognized to be the adornments of human civilization.

CHAPTER FORTY-FIVE

I know I did him wrong—Nathan that is, but how was I supposed to know what to do? I was on my own, wasn't I? Let's sit over here in the sun room under the palm trees. Here, let me just move my puzzle out of the way. A forest scene—you see, I've nearly finished the mountains. Reminds me of home—not that we had peaks like this in the U.P.—this picture must be somewhere in Switzerland, but the trees are nice to look at anyway.

Ah, do you feel that Gulf Coast breeze? Ha, fooled ya! It's just the air conditioning. The beach is only a few miles from here, but think I've been here for a couple years and we've only been to the beach twice. Gets so damn hot down here that sometimes I even miss those winds we used to get swooping down from Canada, can you believe that? So I mostly just sit in the A.C. these days freezin' my balls off. Honey, can you bring us some iced teas? Do you take any sugar or lemon? No? I'm afraid I've become accustomed to the sweeter things in life now that I've cut back on my drinking. Isn't that right, Janet?

I must admit that I haven't been back up north in nearly a year, and I don't know when, or even if, I'll get back there again. I don't want you to think that I don't feel bad about what happened to the boy, but some things are just too painful to even contemplate.

I let him down, I know I did, but those years, everything was so... out of balance... unstable. I mean she left so suddenly, and... I had no experience with children. Well yes, I was a teacher, it's true, but I mean raising one of my own... When Nate was a baby, I felt like my whole body was one big thumb: changing diapers and kissing boo-boos was not exactly my forte after all. Had to recruit some of my lady friends—sorry Dear, to help with some of that motherly attention he needed.

But hell, I did my best and tried to do the right thing for him, but you know Nate always was a little... odd. I loved him for sure, but there always seemed like there was something dark and unknowable about him. He had his mother's wild blood, no doubt, but most of the time he was so quiet that he just seemed like a little ghost lurking in the corners and the shadows.

He wasn't ever into sports; I guess that's okay, but I always thought it would have done him some good—maybe channeled some of his unresolved issues into productive activities. Not that he was a bad kid. He had some of the typical teenage angst—he stole my canoe once, but mostly he was a good, studious young man. Mature for his age, and I was very proud of him getting into college. I figured he'd go on and pass up his old man and find a career in something worthwhile, because he had brains. But for some reason—maybe it was my fault—we just never really... connected. Maybe I saw too much of his mother in him, or he was embarrassed by the mistakes I made while he was growing up, but whatever the case, I loved the boy, but I can honestly say I never felt I really knew him.

And although I truly do feel bad about how things resolved themselves, I can't say that I blame myself. I've learned over the years that you really can't take too much responsibility for how your kids turn out. Too much depends on genes and internal chemistry. Janet had one daughter—out of three—who ended up as a hooker. She was murdered, stabbed to death, on the streets in NYC fifteen years ago—don't tell her I told you that when she comes back—but, the point is, Janet is just an absolute peach of a woman and I can't believe she did a thing to make her little girl turn out so bad. In my case, Nate's mother and I were too different—she was like an acid and I was a base; I never should have gotten mixed up with her; I should have known it would be a combustible combination and probably raise a stink.

You like that one? The kids in my classes used to get a chuckle out of it. I always tried to teach my kids about things like how molecules combine in different ways to form elements, while making it fun and easy to learn. You can't turn everything into Hamlet or Einstein's theories, or you lose them fast. I was a pretty good teacher back then and a great coach too. I could calculate out when to hit and run and what batters to walk and all that stuff. You know I had a few troubled years and got some people against me:

you can't fight city hall, you know. At least the kid had the spunk to take a swing at somebody. I have to give him credit; he was tougher than I thought, tougher than me probably...

Smart? Hell, that kid was so damn smart. Even from the start, he was reading everything. He lived his life in books. A lot of them were my books, schoolbooks from my college days, and I inherited a whole library from an uncle who lived up in Toronto. Crazy stuff: classic works, Shakespeare, *Don Quixote*, paperback Westerns and fantasy, history, philosophy and even some soft porn. I maybe should have kept a closer watch on what he was getting into, but I figured any reading was better than none. In retrospect, maybe letting him read scary stuff like *Faust* and *Titus Andronicus* before he was ready was a bad idea. It probably contributed to his morbid fascination with guns and knives and torture chambers. It's funny, his first favorite, if I remember right, was Edgar Allen Poe's *Tell Tale Heart*, and when he read *Tom Sawyer* the first time, he admitted that he skipped right over the whole first part of the book with the Becky Thatcher gunk and whitewashing the fence and all, and went right to the graveyard scene.

Janet, would you mind filling our glasses again? Thank you, dear. No, I'm sad, but I won't take responsibility for Nate's actions. I had my problems with the bottle, as I'm sure you've heard, but I was sober when it mattered most. Uh uh, it was that crowd he got mixed up with: those Hawkins brothers were bad apples—everyone knew that; and that girl Jessy just turned his head and toyed with him until he couldn't take it anymore. I blame her the most for sending him down his spiral. Just a bunch of young people with no respect for any laws or authority, raised on television and rock music to hate everything and everybody. And then there was the drugs. Now liquor of course isn't any good for you I admit, but it is legal at least. But those chemicals in LSD and crack cocaine... I've read up on the subject and can tell you that they cause changes in brain function; bad changes that will turn you into an addicted zombie.

His mother? She wrote to him you know. Oh yes, for several years afterwards—even sent a few Christmas and birthday presents, but I hid them away and burned them, and he never knew. Not out of any hurt feelings on my part mind you, I just figured it was better for the boy: she'd only end up hurting him again. I'll tell you, I walked around half-jumpy myself for several years afraid she might show back up, but she never did. No, she stuck it out up in Fairbanks or thereabouts. Was one of the only women working on that oil pipeline. Tough as nails. Heard she died of cirrhosis when Nate was ten or eleven; never told him about that either. I figure it's better to avoid such things as much as possible in life, and he seemed to have enough trouble getting by as it was.

Janet, do you think we could have a touch of that good rum in the iced tea? Just a touch? Mmmm... better. Yes, I have pretty much quit the stuff, but the day is so fine and with the waves sparkling like that and with the breeze and my lovely wife... and just a touch of rum to top it all off. Yes, it is almost like a dream. By all rights I should be home eating TV dinners alone, or sitting in the Lakeside, bumming drinks and listening to fish stories and worrying about how the local baseball team is doing, but my luck took a turn when my beautiful angel here took pity on me and rescued me from my previous life.

It just goes to show you what happens when you live your life the right way. I always tried to do right and never hurt anyone or make waves and just go with the flow, and now I've been blessed and rewarded for it. I tried to tell Nate, but communication is a two way street and you have to be open to listen. It's a tough thing what happened to Nate, but in the end you dig your own grave.

CHAPTER FORTY-SIX

"I'm telling you, panda bears ain't bears, dummy."

"You're full of shit."

The wipers squealed across the windshield as the rain drizzled to a stop.

"Look it up; I saw it on TV."

"It's panda BEAR, stupid."

"That's bullshit."

"Oh yeah?"

"Yeah, it's wrong. Like dolphins aren't really fish."

"Like hell, you say."

"They aren't. Hey, give me a hit, you Bogart."

"Fffffffff.... mmm.... fuck you."

"Anyway, like I was saying; pandas are—ffffffffffffffftttt—"

"Bears."

"Uh uh... fffffffoooooo... Listen to what I'm trying to tell you, you moron."

"Indians aren't really Indians."

"That's what I'm saying."

"Because they aren't from India."

"Now you're getting it. They're from America. But Columbus thought he landed in India."

"Duh, Native Americans."

"Right."

"'Cuz, they're natives."

"Will you let me finish?"

"But pandas... that's just wrong. They look like bears."

"Well yeah, but they aren't. They are actually—get this—big ol' raccoons."

"Wha..ffffff... you're shitting me."

"No shit."

"They do kinda look like coons now that you mention it."

"Don't they?"

The brothers' laughter filled the front seat of the car as they exited the highway and drove south along a secluded stretch of frontage road north of Green Bay. The rainstorm had finally ended, and Jake snickered as he accelerated the vehicle furiously forward through deep puddles of standing water—spraying plumes of muddy water into the air on either side of the car—as they traveled deeper down the road that made its way into a rundown industrial area that was dark and empty at this hour.

"I ain't never going to look at one of them things without seeing a big ol' coon looking back," Jared said with a chuckle.

"Yeah, ain't that something," Jake replied and turned the car off of the main road and onto a back road leading east toward the lake.

"Next I suppose you're going to tell me possums are just miniature kangaroos or something."

"Big rats is more like it. You know, you should watch some of those animal shows; they're pretty cool when you're buzzed."

"Naw, I only watch wrestling, boxing and war movies and football of course, even though those pussies in the NFL wear pads. I prefer Australian rules football myself. So where is this fucking place anyway? I gotta piss like you wouldn't believe."

"It shouldn't be too much farther; should be coming up soon on the right. It's on a dead end road in the middle of nowhere; Jesse sure knows where to lay low."

"Panda coons," Jared snorted. "We gotta tell Jess about that one."

It took another twenty minutes and two wrong turns before they finally found the address. It was like Preacher said: the garage was at the end of a narrow and bumpy dirt road. Jake pulled in and parked behind the dilapidated building like they had been instructed. The cratered lot was filled with cars and trucks—some working, some not, and littered with car parts strewn about haphazardly, while the ramshackle building itself was quiet—seemingly abandoned, but for a light burning inside. Trudging through a maze of overgrown weeds, rusted metal, mud puddles and oily mounds of gravel, the brothers approached the back door.

"Preacher said knock three times on the door," Jake said, yawning.

"Screw that asshole Preacher anyway for sending us out here. You go ahead; I'm gonna take a leak first. Get Jesse to step out here and I'll surprise him and jump his ass like a motherfucking panda coon," Jared said as he retreated around the corner and—with a groan of relief—unleashed a torrent of urine against the back wall.

His older brother pounded his fist on the metal door in a triplet pattern that echoed loudly within. The door opened and Jake stood frozen.

"You?!" he just had time to utter before a double-barreled blast exploded into his chest, sending his body backwards and to the ground in a bloody heap.

"Idiot!" Jesus' voice screamed from inside. "You were supposed to wait until they were both inside."

"Sorry," stammered the burly man holding the shotgun. "I just..."

"Never mind, get the other one before he gets away!"

As distressing as such an extraordinary incident would seem to any normal human being, the shock of the event he had just witnessed hardly fazed Jared in the least, as a lifetime of combat training had prepared the hulking primate for just such an occasion. The brute knew what he just witnessed, that his brother and best friend, Jake was dead, nearly cut in two, and knowing there was no time for sorrow or regret, his rage took over. His torpor vanished in a millisecond, and his lizard brain sprang instantly to life, although featuring an important distinction that separated Jared from the rest of humanity: there was no flight or fight choices to be adjudicated in Jared's brain—there was only fight.

Without any hesitation, the beast emerged, and reaching out, clasped the powerful fingers of his left hand tightly around the shooter's neck, crushing his windpipe, while his other hand ripped the revolver from the belt behind his back and began firing indiscriminately into the cavernous interior of the garage.

Shouts of pain emanated from within in response, along with a barrage of gunfire. The return fire slammed into the back of the man with the shotgun, whose now lifeless body Jared used as a shield. Astonishingly quick, he pulled the shotgun from the dead man's hands and flung the body forward forcefully, scattering the group of people inside. With one hand, Jared swung the shotgun to the right and cracked a man's jaw, the wounded man falling to the floor unconscious as others dove for cover. Jared's wide set eyes moved like a fly's—catching the entire scene from periphery to center and instantaneously calculating his odds. Ten to begin with; four down already. One of the men on the ground started back up, but Jared's heavy boot caught him in the face.

The movie seemed to move in slow motion now for Jared: a table upended, chairs scattered, the shapes of people scrambling in to the shadows amidst torrents of angry shouting in Spanish. In seamless motion, he wheeled and fired a bullet into the kneecap of Jesus, who fell to the floor screaming. A bullet struck Jared's shoulder and passed through: he barely flinched. *Don't they know I'm immune to pain?* he thought. Annoyed, he turned left and fired into the face of the shooter, a thin man wearing a Dallas Cowboys ball cap, who slumped against the wall and slid down to the floor, leaving a trail of blood and brains. Jared thought he recognized the dead man's face before the gunshot erased his features forever. *Chavez? Orlando Chavez?*

Another shot hit Jared's thigh, burning as it cut through his flesh, causing him to forget trying to remember when and where he had seen Chavez before. He stumbled and grunted in pain this time, but recovered instantly, the painful sting redoubling his fury and he waded forward relentlessly into the crowd, even more enraged, his unstoppable motion surprising and frightening his attackers with its speed and ferocity—sending bodies retreating and falling backwards over one another like a row of dominoes. Bullets whizzed past him, hammering the walls as he dodged and wove his way like a boxer in the ring, pummeling one opponent to the ground, fatally kicking him in the temple with a steel-toed boot, turning and, in one motion, smashing another man's nose with an uppercut, sending the nasal bones back into his brain and killing him immediately, lashing out in rapid bursts of violence, punching, kicking and shooting as his adversaries fell one by one.

Whirling, his limbs striking savagely in every direction, the homicidal brawler suddenly spotted another familiar and frightened face cowering in fear. With a grim smile, and without any feeling of pity, he aimed and fired a shot into Jesus' nephew's stomach, and watched with a sense of satisfaction as the boy cried out and collapsed in the corner, holding his sticky midsection. Jared tasted the scent of smoke and blood in the air and it aroused the fury in him. He raised his face to heavens and howled. *Only three left now*, he thought and smiled: he liked those odds.

His gun now empty, he wrenched up a chair and smashed it over a man's head ruthlessly, breaking his skull. Another tried to escape through a window, but was pulled back in by the talons of a shrieking, raging animal that was no longer human except in appearance. In the end, after gently encouraging him to talk and tell him all he wanted to know—as Jared beat Jesus' face into a bloody stain on the floor with a table leg, he saw only one face in the intensity of his vengeful madness.

It was Preacher's.

CHAPTER FORTY-SEVEN

Merrick's feet sank into the soft ground as he stumbled up the hill toward the fallen boy, pausing only long enough to grab the money bag as he flew by at a run. Another bullet fired from the cab of the train and struck the boy's horse, and the animal fell, tumbling down the brush, kicking its legs out frantically. Gwynn threw a rope down to the wounded Teague, who grimaced as he grabbed it, and then pulling with all his strength, dragged the battered man up and over the ridge.

Sprinting toward his wounded nephew, Merrick bent and grabbed the boy at a run; his horse ran ahead of them, following Gwynn. Another pop, as a bullet smacked the ground near Merrick's churning legs, sending dirt and pieces of rock flying. The boy's eyes were blank, but he was breathing. His shirt was stained with blood, and he cried out weakly as his uncle lifted him into his arms. A quick glance showed the bullet had gone clean through the chest; Merrick hoped this was the case.

Another shot rang out as they reached the summit and, tumbling forward, fell over the top of the embankment. Merrick's horse returned to his master and the man climbed up, struggling to mount with the boy hanging limp in his arms. Behind them they could hear the voices of the train crew shouting; he doubted that they had the courage to follow them. Spurring their horses to a gallop, they sped for home, ignoring the cries of their hurt companions as best as they could.

Back at the cabin, the women's tears flew freely, but they stifled their shock and hurried into action tending the wounded. Hours passed as wounds were cleaned and dressed as best as they could and the men were fed and caught a few fitful minutes of rest. It was determined the brothers would survive their injuries, although it was feared that Merrick would be permanently blinded in one eye; but Teague and young Sam were another story.

Merrick knew they needed to find a doctor fast, preferably one who wouldn't report them. The locals were company men or easily bribed alcoholics and could not be trusted. Someone remembered that there had been a fellow over in Eagle River that claimed to be a healer the last time they had been through, but no one was sure that he was still there and hadn't been run out of town by now. It was their only chance.

As evening approached they quickly ate supper and decided that they would gamble on finding the medicine man. There was no time to bring the man back, so they loaded the boy and Teague into a wagon as comfortably as possible, and started off toward the setting sun with Gwynn seated and driving. Merrick painfully mounted his horse and followed. The road through the woods was rough, and darkness was already beginning to fall, but there was no other choice. The women stayed behind to care for the other children, and with the plan to tell the Pinkertons, if by chance they arrived, that the men had been gone away to Canada hunting and fishing for the last several weeks. Merrick would send for them later once everyone was safe. His wife kissed him goodbye, while his widowed sister offered no recriminations for the state of her son. She knew her boy would do what he would do: somehow, Merrick felt that was almost worse.

Clattering along down the heavily rutted road, the men found the going was even slower and harder than they had expected. The wounded woke and screamed out in torment as the wagon bumped along the heavily grooved and hilly path. The brothers tensed with every shout, sure that someone would hear them. Their eyes watching the road behind them intently, as they bounced and banged slowly onward; their suspicions that they may be followed creating panic with every rustling sound heard coming from the woods. They did not believe their pursuers would be on their trail yet, but they also knew the anger of the company would be terrible. Yet, so far at least, they saw no one; the woods and road remained empty of any humans, as the sun set before them, long shadows stretching out like gallows ropes strung taut by the advancing presence of nightfall.

At the advent of dusk Teague awoke and began gasping and shouting deliriously. "Where's my money? My money, Merrick. You promised," he wept and screamed in a high-pitched voice like a colicky infant.

"Shut up, damn, it," Gwynn snapped anxiously.

"Ohhhhhh it hurts." the wounded man continued. "Give me my money, damn you. I earned it! You know I did!"

"And got yourself shot, and damn near got us all killed," Gwynn muttered.

"Just let me have it. Let me have it. You promised!"

"Give him a bundle," Merrick ordered flatly.

Snarling, Gwynn handed the dying man a bundle of bills. "Now shut up and give us some peace. Look how the lad beside you is holding his tongue like a man, and he's hurt far worse than you are." He said this without mentioning that the unconscious boy was extremely pale and near death himself.

Teague shivered and pressed the bundle tightly to his chest.

"It's mine. I earned it. Going to buy a boat..." Teague shivered and fell into unconsciousness, marked only by a deep rasping sound rising from his throat.

Rattling onward, they traveled haltingly for hours through the thickening darkness until a wheel hit a rut hard, and, with a sickening sound, cracked in half, causing the wagon to list forward and the wounded men to scream out in pain. Cursing, Merrick and his brother spent nearly another precious hour as they strained to fix it; first placing their injured as gently as they could on the ground and then raising the wagon up and onto a crude jack made of stones. Removing the wheel, the pieces crumbled in their hands.

With no way to repair it, Merrick climbed back on his horse and spurred him back to town, where he roused the sleepy blacksmith and purchased his cooperation by paying a premium for two wheels with some of the proceeds of the robbery. Waiting nervously in the dark for Merrick to return, the boy groaned occasionally under the blanket on the ground, and Gwynn took off his own coat and added a layer of covering to the young man's thin body. He reluctantly built a small fire and paced its circumference, shivering, enraged in his helplessness. Merrick returned at last and, the new wheel now attached they pressed on at last, worried that time would run out, and that if they were to ever make it to Iron Mountain, it would be too late.

"Merrick, we have to face facts..." Gwynn spoke at last in soft tones.

"I agree, dear brother."

"Perhaps we should split up. You take the money and hide it somewhere safe. I will continue on with Sam."

"And Teague?"

"I think we had best— Wait! Do you hear horses?" Gwynn interjected. Merrick stilled his horse and cocked his head, listening.

"No, I hear nothing," he pronounced. The night air was quiet as the grave.

Teague suddenly lurched upward with a series of ear shattering screams, before collapsing with a ghastly gurgle and was still, his eyes open and staring without comprehension at the stars above.

Gwynn felt Teague's neck. "I think our beloved comrade Teague has left us, brother."

Merrick sighed. He had no great love for the dead man, but he still felt some remorse. He knew Teague had done terrible things, but he had had a hard life and done what he had to do to survive. Now what to do with his body? Did they drag him along or dump him like rubbish by the side of the road? Without his weight, the wagon might move faster and give them a better chance to save Sam. There was a clearing by the side of the road ahead. Maybe a shallow grave could be dug quickly enough. Or, better yet, perhaps just cover his body with leaves...

Dragging the dead man out of the wagon, they carried his slack body to the tree line, laying him on the ground in a hollow spot, where they hurriedly began covering him with some loose dirt and brush. "Some words, and be quick about it," Merrick demanded, as he reached down for the bundle still clutched tight in Teague's fingers.

A twig snapped.

The brothers looked up with a jolt, startled to discover a ring of armed men on horseback ranged in a half circle around them. Among them, Merrick recognized the ruddy face of the blacksmith, and cursed silently to himself that he did not kill the man when he had the chance.

A large man with a bushy black beard and several gold teeth

walked his horse forward and dismounted. Merrick recognized him as Otis, the leader of the company's guards. The captain was known for his ruthlessness in keeping order and his brutality in squashing dissent among the workers: Merrick and Otis knew each other well.

"Ah Merrick, I hoped we would meet again. You seem somewhat unpleasantly surprised to see me," the burly man said with a smirk.

Merrick said nothing.

"And just what is that you are you hiding there, Mr. Merrick? Could it be some of your ill-gotten gains?"

"We're burying a dead man," Gwynn spoke up. "If it is any of your business."

"Indeed it is, my good sir. Your business is indeed our... business," Otis said. The men on horseback chuckled.

The brutish man kicked aside a few branches, revealing Teague's contorted face.

"Well, well, the bluff Mr. Teague has met an untimely end, has he not? A Christian burial is not to be his reward then? Just a ditch and a handful of dirt and leaves for protection from the wolves? You're a harder man than even I thought, Merrick."

He laughed in a deep voice and was joined in his merriment by a chorus of laughter chortling from the band: a hard assortment of company men and townsmen, accompanied by a few bounty hunters, trackers, joiners and witless stragglers seeking monetary recompense as well as the opportunity to satiate their blood lust with the thrill of the hunt.

"The company sends its regards and congratulates you on your... initiative," the dark browed giant continued in a booming voice. "They spared no time or expense in speedily sending us down here via rail and horseback to follow your trail before it could get cold and have generously promised us a considerable bounty upon our catching you."

He paced back and forth at a leisurely swagger, while the grinning crew on horseback chuckled and leered among themselves.

"I am actually rather disappointed that it was so easy to find you. This was sloppy work Merrick, even for you. You were just too sloppy and too slow. But then, getting yourselves all shot up by a tetchy, broken down old cocker probably wasn't a part of the plan."

Merrick felt his blood rise. He was sweating although the evening was cool.

"All that blood spilled. You left us a right easy trail to follow. Right to your family's doorstep."

"They knew nothing," Merrick hissed.

"They did, but they didn't talk... at first. We really didn't need their cooperation; we just wanted to tie up all... loose ends. We pride ourselves on maintaining a truly professional operation. Like a well-oiled machine, so to speak." The men snickered. Otis turned and faced his audience, gesturing grandly like a Victorian-era illusionist on a gas-lit stage. "Be assured that they were dealt with promptly and efficiently and then we were off, hot on your trail. Your blacksmith friend here was quite helpful in that regard and found us shortly after your unfortunate incident with the wagon wheel. Bad luck again, that. I am surprised you hadn't noticed; we've been shadowing you for the last several miles."

"You dare not have harmed my wife—" Gwynn jumped up. Otis' gun was out and he fired into Gwynn's foot before he could strike a blow. Crying out, he fell to the ground.

"Easy there, Gwynn. Why complain, dear man? She is beyond feeling any pain now... and you will soon join her, although... I will not deny that there will be some pain involved for you in the interim."

"The company knows what you are doing?" Merrick asked.

"The company knows everything... and nothing. We have our orders. They don't need to know details. Face it, you messed with something bigger than yourself Merrick, and, like all rodents and insects you and your kind are simply pests in the company's eyes to be crushed underfoot."

"You can't just kill us. We have the right to a trial. It will be in newspapers."

"Oh it wasn't us. We were nowhere near here when it happened. It must have been vigilantes." Otis chuckled. "A lot of them running around these days: 'Knights of the Golden Dawn,' or something of that sort. You fellows killed an innocent guard, who was a good and loyal company man; the good folk of the area demanded justice be done. They must have gotten to you before we could, and... you know the rest of the story."

The boy moaned from the wagon. Merrick gritted his teeth. Otis motioned his men to pull the unconscious Sam from the bed. One held up the bag full of bundled bills.

"Here's the money, Cap'n."

"Bring it to me, Dobbs. Merrick here will be pleased to know that these funds will pay for a long weekend for us all at the whorehouse in Escanaba."

The men cheered.

"The company doesn't mind you spending their money, Otis?" Merrick asked.

"Ha! You don't get how it works, do you? Allow me to explain in terms even a simpleton like you can understand. You blood-thirsty train robbers hid the money somewhere around here. Buried it in the woods. We looked high and low, but never found it. It probably never will be found. Maybe you had an accomplice, someone who got away to Mexico. Sounds nice so far, doesn't it? The miner's families will have to wait to get their pay, until the insurance company pays the company for their loss. A nice little profit for them, eh? Even after our little celebration in town. We get that as a bonus. Yes, I'm afraid you picked the wrong side, Merrick: the company takes care of its own."

"No," Derrick whispered.

"Cheer up, son," Otis patted Merrick on the back. Merrick tensed his muscles. "You just gave the company you hate so much a considerable return on their investment, while giving us cause to remove an annoyance, all through your... misguided actions. See, that makes it a win-win situation for all of us. Well... perhaps not for you and your family..."

Merrick launched himself upward in time to take the full force of the butt of Otis' pistol striking his nose and shattering it.

*****

When he regained consciousness, hours having passed—hours spent absorbing such pain as he never knew existed, Merrick was seated astride a horse, arms tied behind his back and with a thick, scratchy rope lacerating his windpipe raw. His arms, legs and several ribs were broken, breathing was difficult, his face was bloody pulp, he could taste blood upon his lips, and searing pain throbbed through every cell of his body. Through the blood and swelling around his one still functioning eye he imperceptibly detected the sun gradually rising over the rim of treetops on the ridge to the east.

Next to him, Gwynn's face was a mass of red and purple that was hardly recognizable as a human face. He tried to speak, but all that came out of his toothless mouth was a gurgling stream of blood. His long golden curls were tinted red with matted blood.

On the other side, Sam whimpered: "I want to go home, Uncle. Right now."

"Yes, Sam," Merrick said softly through puffy lips. "We're almost there, nephew."

"What about the other one?" asked one of the men motioning toward the trees.

"Hang a dead man?" Otis scoffed. "Don't waste the rope."

As the voices of the men faded in and out around him, Merrick struggled to concentrate, to hold on to consciousness, and to life itself. Squinting through his one slitted eye he could just make out a cluster of white flowers in one of the trees above, and he forced himself to focus on a particular one near the center. He examined the flower closer with the full force of his powers of attention: white with four petals, slightly curled at the edges; a yellow center lightly tinged with green.

His thoughts veered momentarily to the face of his wife, his brother and his nephew, but he blotted them out with his examination of the beauty of the blossom before him. Through tears, he almost forced his broken face to smile. It was perhaps the most beautiful flower he had ever seen. In his mind he watched, with a recaptured sense of wonder, as a small blue butterfly circled the blossom slowly in the dawning sunlight before landing softly on its nexus...

A shout, the lurch of the horse from between his legs. Then, the crushing tightness, choking, legs kicking and thrashing, gasping for breath, shit and piss running down his legs, heart bursting, fighting for every last second of consciousness as the full weight of his heavy body caved in his throat, cutting off the flow of blood and air, taking him at last, after nearly twenty terrible, interminable minutes of struggle and intermittent blackouts, into a full and total acquiescence to the final tranquility of eternal oblivion.

As the party of men stood around, smoking and making jokes about the final frantic twitches of their handmade marionettes, they failed to notice a prostrate figure in the shadows behind them suddenly stir and, emerging quietly from under the leaves and brush, crawl desperately with a jerking motion across a few painful yards of ground to the base of a large boulder.

With trembling hands, Teague reached out and patiently placed the bundle of bills in a cavity under the rock, laboriously pushing dirt and rocks over the hole until it was well hidden from sight. He then turned and crawled slowly toward the cool, green depths of the forest that he never reached.

CHAPTER FORTY-EIGHT

There is a darkness here. It lies all over the town like a thick shadow encasing everyone in its evil spell. You cannot touch it, although it covers you, slithering down from the skies with the wind and sunlight, the rain, the snow, the air; erupting up from the ground, growing like stalks of noxious weeds and rising like smoke in double helix shaped filament through cracks from the burning underbelly of the earth. Wrapping around the heart of each and every one of the unlucky inhabitants, permeating itself into every small corner of their meaningless lives, it carries the stench of death with it. But make no mistake, it is quite alive, worming its way into the bloodstream—an entity too small to spot even under the strongest of microscopes, like a virus, the real sickness of living that drives men into fury and the seeking of solace in whatever they can find to take the pain away, even temporarily.

The infection, for lack of a better word, is hastened by fears and loneliness and the drive for power, for knowledge, for immortality—dragging the seekers, the shy and confident alike, deeper into the depths of their addictions, whether it be drugs or alcohol or sex or religion or money or books or blood— anything to momentarily muffle and mute out the almost constant drum beat chorus that reverberates in their heads and gives them a few moments of peace. I do not blame them; I have my own addictions, chief among them is a pair of sad brown eyes and rose petal soft pink lips, and I would be angry and indignant to be judged for my weakness when all are truly guilty in and of themselves and through no fault of their own. Guilty of nothing more than being born to die.

And despite our noble thoughts and intentions, we, the knights of the golden dawn, are discovered at last to be in league with the demon, the dragon, who we must love, and only pretend to hate, even as we dance for its amusement. Promoting the illness as if it is the cure; approving of segments of it because we know we can never truly control it; knowing that, if handled properly, it can help maintain the flimsy structure we have erected on this shaky ground, yet understanding it can never be contained by chains or put back inside its box. The darkness that destroyed our fathers and so many before them is one that is sanctioned and sold by the pillars of our community, who ignore the sallow looks and sunken eyes, the hollow, haunted faces of those poor souls whose only dream upon waking is the relentless pursuit of blank and sweet nothingness.

Trade in your booze for religion, whether it be saying High Mass or chanting *Hare Krishna*, and you find another crutch; maybe a more positive one, but hardly the choice for those monkeys seeking the excitement of what we call life, glorious life. Like toddlers fastened by a leash, angrily we chafe under the yoke of placidity and turn into temerarious maniacs, wrecking cars and marriages and other people and the world itself in the process. But what is life if we are not expected to explore, to feel, to experience?

Whether it is the local bar or convenience store pushing beer by the six pack, or the doctor prescribing pills, or the hunter blasting away his prey, or the choir singing hallelujah—even as they wash the stains from their hands—or good old boy Junior with his strawberry shakes and Chamber of Commerce meetings, or even us—Jesse and me cooking up some more goodies for the naughty kiddies, it is just another route of escape, another way out of dealing with reality, even with other people: those we count as our friends, our husbands and wives, brothers and sisters, parents and kids, neighbors and strangers, but most of all ourselves, the people whose faces we see in the mirror as those cursed and abandoned orphans who are rotting, decomposing into crumbling flesh even as we watch with the horrified eyes of an abused child.

We stumble, falter, and lose our way. The needle spins in all directions, never providing the route we need to attain the exit, while the abyss is vast, endless and inevitable. From the shade, the snake coils, but does not strike; it just tightens its grip and slowly squeezes until we breathe no more.

CHAPTER FORTY-NINE

Jenny and I lay prone on the side of the dirt road in the deepening darkness, a crazed giant of a man carrying a smoking shotgun standing in our wake, while on our opposite side, aiming a pistol at waist level like a gunfighter, snorting and gnashing his teeth, glared the beast formerly known as Jared. The behemoth and Jesse's loathsome brother faced each other, holding their guns pointed at each other above our heads.

Taking advantage of the unexpected surprise, we jumped to our feet and ran. Reaching the car wasn't an option, so we dove into the forest, sprinting down the trail, leaping over boulders, overgrowth and fallen branches as the winding path dipped into a swampy hollow before rising abruptly up a heavily wooded hillside. Crashing through the bushes behind us, Big Pete and Jared pursued, shouting insanely in spasms of agitated indignation.

The trail ascended the bluff overlooking the dam and the wide flat lake far below, the water shimmering like a mirror in the moonlight from our vista. Hearts throbbing, legs aching, we hastened along the top of the promontory. Jenny, slipping on the loose rocks, fell, sliding to the edge of the cliff, her motion sending a rockslide cascading over and off the overlook and plunging down the steep descent of the bluff. I reached back and helped her regain her footing, and we fled upward, rapidly rising higher on the mountainside, the ferocity of our pursuers below increasing as they slipped and toppled on the unsecured detritus.

Ahead, at the summit, rising tall into the onyx sky, the outline of an abandoned industrial building materialized like a desolate medieval castle—its windows exhibiting the skeletal remains of frames—lacking bars, and missing the stained glass that could complete its transformation into a cursed cathedral only suitable for black masses. Scrambling, we picked our way through the craggy terrain to the entrance of the scarred stone structure, crumbling and overgrown with tangles of verdant vegetation—a black wolf slinking off out the other side upon our approach.

Inside the four walls of the roofless edifice, the stars above trembled like a vibrant candelabra against an inky dome, floating above what appeared at first glance to be a demolished, disintegrating courtyard of an ancient fortress or palazzo, its recess littered with shattered hunks of stone and scattered mounds of debris, punctuated in intervals by vertical copper pipes and steel reinforcement and throughout by thick foliage, the vines of which gripped the edifice, actively engaged in the insuppressible return of the land to the peaceful chaos of nature, erasing every sign of this brief, unhappy occupation by humans on their petty crusade for copper and gold.

Exhausted, we stumbled slowly across the uneven plaza. Jenny suddenly grabbed my arm, frantically stopping me. "Wait," she cried, as my foot stepped into emptiness and I teetered over the void before falling back. Sunken in the center of the room was an immense open drop. In the dark, it was impossible to gauge its depth, but we quickly surmised that the bushes that filled much of the abyss were in reality the tops of the trees growing up from deep below. Exhausted, we sat down hard on the concrete floor and awaited the arrival of the inevitable, contemplating the visions of phantasms and ghosts from hellish days long gone by, wondering who the victims were that were sacrificed on these stony altars and to what bloodthirsty gods.

The duo arrived in tandem, entering at opposing entrances at either end of the structure, surrounding us, out of breath and apoplectic. Spotting us huddled together, they advanced toward us from either direction.

"This ain't any of your business, asshole!" Big Pete bellowed in rage, finally catching his breath.

"Hell if it ain't," Jared curled his lips into a snarl.

"Preacher knows where Jesse's run to. You know he does. That boy don't go anywhere without telling his shadow. You were supposed to let me talk to these two without you and your brother interrupting things." Pete's hands trembled, but his eyes had cleared and he no longer sounded slurred.

"Yeah, I know, but well, Pete, I'm beginning to think maybe you were right about a few more things than you realize, so maybe I can give you hand here. What do you say, Preacher? You know where my kid brother has run off to? Or maybe you just got another errand you want me and Jake to run?"

"Jake?" I queried, suspecting the answer.

"Oh he's here. Don't you worry. He's in the car... what's left of him anyway. Kind of funny isn't it, you look a little surprised to see me, Preacher. Yeah, we ran into your little welcoming committee alright, and Jake got himself turned into hamburger from a sawed off shotgun. But those spics never met anyone like me. No siree. They're going to have some trouble putting the pieces back together when the stink gets too bad and someone finally opens up the doors.

"You are probably wondering how I knew you were up here in Finn Town, but you see, Jake and me had a little chat with Pete here before we left and he mentioned his little plan to talk turkey to you and Jesse's little slut there. Let's just say we weren't overly concerned about either of yours' health and gave him the green light to go ahead." He flinched, and I noticed the wound on his shoulder and the wrap around his leg.

"You're hit," I said.

"Yup, they winged me, I guess." He swayed a bit, tired and weak, before the anger came surging back. "Nice of you to notice. You're like that ain't ya, Preacher? Always thinking about the rest of us. Always so concerned."

"Jared, I didn't know anything about an ambush. Jesse said—"

"You didn't know nothing, did you? So why did Jesus tell me you did? And why all the running?"

"It wasn't you, Jared, really. But I had to get Jenny away from Pete. He's gone crazy—"

The wounded ogre rolled his eyes. "I'm beat all to hell, Preacher. I just had to make guacamole dip out a whole mess of Mexicans and then drive halfway across the state with the body of my brother Jake soaking my back seat with blood and guts. Now, I gotta go on a hike up Mount fucking Everest chasing a couple of creeps, and to top it off, I have to deal with the tub of lard here. So excuse me if I'm not my usual pleasant self. Now, I want an answer: where's Jesse, Preacher?"

"I really don't know. Green Bay—?"

"No, I'm pretty sure he ain't in Green Bay, and I am also pretty sure you already know that. But Preach, I can guarantee that before this night is over, you will tell me where he is."

"Truly dudes, I really don't know—"

"Seems like Preacher knows lots he ain't telling," Pete blurted out, overcoming his shock. "You know I ain't got nothing against you, Jared. And I'm sorry as hell to hear about Jake, but for me... I just want to know where Jesse is."

Jared pointed his pistol at my head. "What you say you just quit fooling around right now and tell me where Jesse is? But Pete, you motherfucker, you don't need to know nothing about his whereabouts, until I get it all sorted out. So you just get your fat ass back down the trail until I say so."

"The hell I will. I ain't moving."

"You know you won't get anywhere near Jess. I won't let you."

"He killed my fucking brother."

"You don't know that for a fact, Blubber."

"Stan Jacobsen told me—"

"Stan's a liar."

"Let Jesse Ray tell it then. Let's see him tell me to my face he didn't pop the kid in the melon and been bragging about it ever since."

"He never said nothing to me," Jared announced, his teeth glinting.

"Whatever the case, Preacher ain't leaving here in one piece without his telling me where your fuckhead brother is hiding."

"Well, okay, I guess maybe we can agree on something there, Pete. I suppose it wouldn't hurt to pool our resources and work on this problem together. You ever watch wrestlin'? Maybe it would be a fun idea to get a little tag team action happening. What do you say we have some fun with old Preacher here and see if we can use our imaginations to find a way to loosen his tongue?"

"Sounds okay, I guess."

"And you gotta promise to lay off my brother Jess until we find out what really happened," Jared added. "If he did what you say he did, I'll let you rough him up a bit for being so stupid." Coughing, he spat on the ground, his spittle blood red. "Killing that pussy ass brother of yours—if he did, is fucking idiotic. But you gotta admit Pete, that loony tunes brother of yours was a fucking wasted case."

"He was still my brother."

"Yeah, I know. I know. Don't worry, I'll let you get some good whacks in, big guy. He has to understand that you can't just go around killing folks for no reason other than they're dumb asses. In the meantime, why don't you just get up here, Preacher, and take what's coming to you like a man for once, instead crawling around on the ground like a fucking worm."

He reached down and pulled me up by my collar. Jenny cried out as the butt of his pistol smashed into my face, knocking out a couple teeth and sending me back to the ground with blood pouring out of my mouth.

I tried to get back up but he kicked me in the ribs and I collapsed again.

"I'm just getting started, Preacher. Why don't you make it quick and easy and save yourself some pain?"

I sat up painfully with my bleeding head in my hands and tried frantically to think my way out. I spit a mouthful of blood out from between my lips. "Fuck off," was all I could come up with.

Angrily, Jared aimed his gun at my forehead.

Jenny cried out, "Jared, stop it!".

"Hmmm, I'll bet he'd talk for her," Jared leered. "Maybe that's the answer. Hey Ox, you get any sweetness from baby here yet? I'm not real big on sloppy seconds, but..." Bending over, he eyed the prostrate girl trembling at my side. "Course for her, I might make an exception."

Jenny slid closer.

"You for real?" Pete's eyes bulged.

"Why not," Jared laughed. "Mix a little business with... pleasure. Consider it part of your payback." He quickly walked over and, reaching down, violently grabbed a handful of Jenny's hair and yanked her upright as she cried out in pain. "What do you think Preacher, you up for a little show?

Jenny sobbed. I growled and coiled my body to spring. Instead, thinking quickly, I stammered, "I think Pete should be first."

"What did you say?" the lummox asked, as Jenny gasped.

"Well, I only think it's fair, don't you Jared? After all, it was Pete's brother wasn't it?"

"Fuck you!" Jared barked.

"No, I think Preacher's right. It's only fair. It should be me first."

"I already told you, fat ass, I don't—"

"I don't give a shit what you say. I'm the one who grabbed her, I should be first."

"You had your chance and you did nothing with it. It's my turn now."

Jared threw Jenny back to the floor hard. "You are all assholes. All of you!" Jenny cried, her eyes smoldering in indignation.

Pete licked his lips as he stomped forward toward us to the very edge of the chasm. We held our breath as he teetered on the ledge for a moment with one foot suspended above it. His eyes suddenly widened as he felt the pull of gravity and tried to pull back, when, with a sudden, heart-rending crack, the lip of the stone floor crumbled and fell downward into the yawning gulf"

"You bastards," Pete screamed as the surface fell away beneath his heavy foot, and he fired the shotgun wildly in our direction as he plummeted, the explosion spraying us with pellets, some of which struck Jared in the face, instantly shredding it into a torn and bloody mess.

Jared staggered forward toward us with his gun ready to fire, blinded by loose strips of bloody flesh and burning buckshot and howling like a wounded beast. "You're dead Preacher, you fucking bastard! You and that cunt whore are both going to pay for this!" The enraged monster towered ominously over us like the statue of the *Commendatore* come to life from Don Giovanni—reaching both arms out as—seeking to drag us down unto the depths of Hell.

A gunshot suddenly flashed from a lower window, striking the thug with a solid thud in the center of his weighty back. Two more shots slammed in rapid succession into the back of his wide torso, and the curses stopped at last. A strange gurgle came from his still snarling mouth, as our attacker's eyes rolled back, shining red in the moonlight, and his body tottered precipitously, a black stain spreading rapidly across his chest and midsection. Raising his bloody face to the sky, the dying man attempted one last howl—a horrifying blend of a wolf caught in a trap and a boar in a slaughterhouse—a shrieking wail that forced its way from the depths of his body and out through his lips, trickling slowly into haunting gasping groan as his wracked body fell forward.

The two of us leapt out of the way at the last moment, as the dead body of Jared landed between us with a crash, and settled on the lip of the precipice. Turning toward the doorway nearest the window from where the shots were fired, we held our breath with apprehension as we watched the entrance of the unknown gunman.

A black form cloaked in a rain poncho stepped from the darkness, revolver pointed at Jared's inert body.

"Get out of here," Junior said in a whisper.

I pushed Jenny toward the exit, and retreating without hesitation out through the closest door of the malevolent temple, I looked back over my shoulder and watched in horror as the deputy bent and slid the heavy body slumped on the ground over the edge of the pit and down into the nothingness below.

CHAPTER FIFTY

I preferred her to scepter and throne and deemed riches nothing in comparison with her

She wasn't at the diner when I went in that morning. The girl at the door said they sent her home because she was sick, but I didn't believe it. There was something funny going on—like they knew something and didn't want to let me in on the whole story. The usually genial cook, clearly upset about something, kept sending evil glances my way as he slammed the plates down, bellowing angrily that an order was ready. The grizzled, gray-haired waitress, refused to look me in the eyes as she asked me what I wanted in a cold and distant voice.

With a sick feeling in my stomach, I skipped breakfast and, after guzzling down a quick cup of coffee, headed out. Figured I'd just stop by and check in as it was on my way. Not that I had anywhere to go.

I drove slowly by. The house was dark and quiet with the shades drawn. Jesse's car was absent, so I pulled into the driveway and shut off the engine.

Beyond health and comeliness I loved her, and chose to have her rather than the light, because the splendor of her never yields to sleep.

It took nearly ten minutes of knocking before she finally answered and let me in. The house looked like it had been ransacked: broken glass, splinters of furniture and garbage was strewn everywhere. The aquarium stood in the center of the room filled with dark, rancid and filthy water and the bloated corpses of a few remaining dead fish floating on top. But as bad as the place looked, she looked even worse. Her greasy hair hung down in limp and fraying strands, and she was shrouded in a worn out T-shirt and filthy sweats, her pale skin contrasting strongly with the dark purple shiner that ringed one eye.

My whole body shook at the sight of her and I struggled to

maintain my feelings as my anger rose like molten magma filling the crater of a volcano. I put my arms around her; she was trembling.

"That bastard," I said, choking. She started to cry softly.

"He didn't mean it—" she sobbed and tried to push away.

"Bullshit," I said and held her tighter.

"It was my fault. I was ragging on him."

"That's no excuse."

"I pushed him too hard. I was pretty strung out and said some stuff I shouldn't have. Being a bitch like always." She struggled to pull free.

For in her is a spirit intelligent, holy, unique, manifold, subtle, agile, clear, unstained, certain...

"He shouldn't hit you, Jen," and I held her like I would never let her go.

"I deserved it, Preacher. You should've heard the shit I was saying. I don't blame him."

"I don't care what you said, he shouldn't have hit you." I looked at a broken toy fire engine in pieces on the floor. "The kid see what went down?" I asked quietly and let her push away.

"Jeremy? He woke up while we were... and... Yeah, he saw it. Saw the whole thing. He was crying, and Jesse... he said he was going to use a belt on him. I mean, Christ, the kid is still just a baby..."

"Is he okay?"

"My mom came and got him earlier. He's staying there for a few days until things settle down."

"What did she say?"

"She said I should learn to shut up and that I probably got what I had coming to me. Lord knows my dad and Al have knocked her around a bit over the years."

"Doesn't make it right, Jen."

"I don't blame him. I get mouthy sometimes."

...she penetrates and pervades all things by reason of her purity...

"It doesn't make it right. He's out of control. " I shook furiously. "Somebody has to stop him. Somebody needs to make him stop."

"Preacher, Nate, don't do anything." She looked at me fearfully with her eyes wide and pleading.

"He can't get away with this. He can't hurt you. I won't let him... anymore."

"He had every right. I was fucked up and getting on him about fixing some of the stuff around here. You know like the upstairs toilet. The thing's been running for weeks now and now it stopped working and we have to go to the bathroom downstairs. I said some awful things; I can't even remember what all I called him; but it was all my fault."

"I won't let him hurt you again," I said through gritting teeth.

It is mine to avenge; I will repay. In due time their foot will slip.

"Don't do anything, Preacher. Let it go. Please, just let it go. He's gone off with his brothers and if you make trouble, you'll just get hurt yourself, because as bad as Jesse is, those two are even worse. You can't start a war with them; they will skin you alive and feed what's left of you to the rats." She raised a hand to my face and stroked it; the wrist and arm were both covered with violet bruises.

"I'm telling you, Jenny, that I won't let him hurt you again."

Their day of disaster is near and their doom rushes upon them.

"It ain't your call, Nate. It's just the way it is. We gotta live with it."

"Then what can I do?"

"Just hold me. Ok? Please. Hold me."

I did. And one thing led to another until, for the first time, we made love. Softly, slowly at first, building to an outburst of violent thrashing.

For she is an aura of the might of God and a pure effusion of the glory of the Almighty.

I remembered her moans and how she sobbed afterwards and how I dressed and made my way back to my car before her boyfriend could return with his meth and his guns and his brothers. I remembered her soft moist lips kissing me goodbye and driving a burning stake into my heart.

*****

I remembered my promise to her on that day several months later as I sat behind the steering wheel with Jesse beside me as we drove into the darkness in search of buried treasure.

"This is dumb," Jesse said petulantly.

"What's that?" I answered.

"Driving out to the reservoir in the middle of the night, chasing some stupid fairy tale. Let's go back and catch a buzz and come back in the daylight."

"Shit, we can't turn around; we're already over half there." *Damn*, I thought—I should have been more excited and less cool about it, but I could only do so much with my emotions. I had to maintain a balance. "Besides, if you want a buzz," I said brightly, "check in the glove box. I saved up some of our best stuff for a special occasion."

"Fuck yeah? Nice, Preacher." Jesse found the goods and scrambled to fire up a hit. He passed it to me. I shook my head. I wanted to be clear. "Not while I'm driving. You go ahead. I'll catch up in a bit. I've got a bottle of Chivas in the boat too."

"Right on, bro! Just like the old days," Jesse said with a grin.

"Just like the old days," I agreed grimly.

A few miles further, I pulled off near Way Dam and headed down a bumpy dirt road to a secluded spot, where I pulled the car into a course thicket of trees. We walked down a brushy trail to where I had the canoe tied up at the water's edge.

"Hey, you were right—just like the old days." Jesse said happily. "So where's this island?"

"Not far," I said and together we slid the boat into the dark and quiet water. Digging our paddles into the waves, we propelled the canoe together with regular strokes out into the lake, working together in tandem, as we had done once before. Soon we entered deeper water and paused, drifting for a moment under the stars.

"Which direction are we headed?"

"We follow that shoreline for a ways, then head out further northeasterly. It's not too far."

Jesse blew on his hands. "You said something about a bottle?"

Reaching down into the bottom of the boat, I pulled out a bottle of our beloved blended whiskey and handed it to him, and he laughed and took a swig. "Woo hooie," he shouted and cracked a beer to wash it down.

"Shhhh," I said and motioned for him to be quiet.

"What the fuck for?" He took another gulp and hissed with pleasure. I said nothing. He tried to pass me the bottle, but again, I shook my head. "Suit yourself," he said and took another mouthful. "You okay, Preacher? I thought you said it was going to be like old times?"

"I want to get there first. I've got to keep my wits so I can find the place again. Don't worry, I'll have some soon enough."

"We've got to celebrate finding all that money," he said, smirking. I smiled darkly in response.

I turned us toward the bank, and we paddled smoothly for a while alongside the shore, before I steered us back out into the vast expanse of the reservoir. The atmosphere on the lake and surroundings was opaque, with only the lights from a few scattered cabins and campgrounds appearing in scattered, disparate locations around the shoreline.

In the distance we saw the light of some lonely fisherman's boat trolling across the water—some straggler desperate for one last catch. I hoped we wouldn't run into anyone out here, let alone a DNR ranger. I held my breath momentarily, but the light moved into the distance and disappeared, leaving us alone in the blackness with only the wind and lapping of the waves on the boat and sound of our oars striking the water. I watched the sky and made occasional corrections to our direction, keeping us on the course I had prepared.

"You sure this is the way?" he asked, his voice huffing.

"Where's the North Star, Jess?" It always annoyed me that people didn't know which direction they were going. The answer was always there in the sun and stars. I always knew what direction I was going, even when I didn't know where my destination was. But I knew both tonight.

"I never did figure that stuff out." He drank again. "That's why I've got you, to help me navigate things. I'm good at the action stuff; you're good at figuring out how to get there. A pretty good team, you and me—"

"And Jenny," I added softly.

"Eh, women," Jesse waved his hand in the air, "they ain't nothing but trouble." He took another drink and lit up the pipe. This time he didn't offer it to me, but lit it again for himself. "Ah," he let out a breath. "That's the feeling. Almost better than sex."

We paddled in silence for a time. A solitary loon cried out across the expanse. Finally, I could see the dark mass of the rocky, forested island approaching. I directed the flashlight on the edges, seeking for the particular inlet I was looking for. At last, a small marshy beach nestled beneath a bower of beech and pine came into view.

"Is this it?"

"This is it."

Pulling the canoe onto the beach, we tied it in place and clambered up the ridge. Jesse was wired from the meth and ran around in circles shouting. I let him burn off some energy. Finally, he slowed to a stop and, sitting down, opened and swilled down a mouthful from the bottle.

"So where is it, Preach?" he asked hurriedly, wiping his mouth. "Come on, I've got to get my hands on that loot."

"We have to dig. Over there. I marked the spot."

"What? Are you sure about that?

"Yes."

"You didn't say anything about digging. So what happened, you figured out the code on the tree?"

"Yes."

"Well, ain't you just the smarty-pants. But we didn't bring a shovel—"

"I left one here the other day."

"What for?"

"I was digging for worms." I pointed at the bucket on the ground in which several earthworms could be seen wriggling. "Here, I started digging already." Grabbing the shovel from against the tree, I dug out a spade full of dirt from the shallow indentation that already existed and tossed it into the darkness.

"Why didn't you tell me? We could have brought another shovel?"

"I wasn't sure."

"But now you are?"

"I think so."

I only dug a few shovelfuls of the soft dirt, before he grabbed it away from me like I knew he would. "Gimme that thing." He was amped with energy, and we took turns digging—he taking more turns than me, until we were at an appropriate depth. While he was engaged, I quietly stepped into trees and opened the vial I carried in my shirt pocket and surreptitiously poured its contents into the bottle of whiskey.

"How deep are we going to go, Preacher?" he called from the shallow indentation.

"Not much further. Let's take a break and have another drink." Reaching into the hole, I handed him the bottle, which he greedily snatched from my hand, taking a massive swig and snorting. He was sweaty and thirsty, but driven by gold lust and meth, he immediately started back in digging.

"Hey!" he said and reached over and pulled something from the earth. "I found something."

"What is it?" I asked, surprised.

"Aw, just an old rusty compass." He tossed the thing to me and I caught it. The broken needle flopped crazily.

"Must have been a tourist," I said with a chuckle.

"Yeah, everyone around here knows those things are no good in Iron County."

Sticking the rusted artifact in my pocket, I watched with anticipation as Jesse went back to work, excavating even faster now. Finally, he paused and said with a sigh.

"I don't think you've got the right spot, Preacher; we should've hit something by now—a chest or something, don't you think."

I did not respond.

"Maybe you should let me see these marks in the tree. I'll bet you got it wrong. I'll just—" He tried to climb out of the depression, but his legs wobbled and he slid back.

"Whoa, I'm feeling a bit..."

It took him a moment to notice the pistol I held pointed at him. His eyes focused, his face went pale and he looked confused.

"Preacher, what's up, man?"

I stayed silent.

"Seriously dude, you've got to put that thing away. Come on, where's that tree you were telling me about? We got to get that money before anybody else finds it, like you said."

"I lied," I said flatly.

"What do you mean?" He swayed a bit. The chloral hydrate added to the Chivas was taking its toll. He started to get angry.

"I mean there isn't any treasure."

"What are you saying? We've been talking about this shit for our whole lives..."

I shook my head.

"Are you telling me you dragged me all the way out here in the middle of the fucking lake, in the middle of the fucking night, just to fuck with me? You goddamn S.O.B., I ought'a bust your skull." He staggered forward, but I cocked the pistol, and he stopped, swaying side to side.

He started to laugh. "Preacher, I don't know what you're up to, but I have to admit you got me good. It's a good joke. I get it. The jokes on me. Come on, let's have another smoke and drink and... uh... I ain't feelin' so hot." He doubled over and started puking.

I stood silently watching.

"You've got to cut me some slack here, Preach, I'm sick..."

I watched wordlessly and calculated the time it would take to fill the hole back in alone.

"So what is this, Preacher? Did you slip me a Mickey or what? Afraid to take me on in a fair fight? That figures. You always were a pussy." He slid to his knees. "So what's next? You going to kill me? Me, your best buddy? Not even going to give me a fucking fighting chance?"

"Like you gave Little Pete a chance?" I croaked quietly.

"Fuck you." His voice was getting weaker now; his heart was pumped up—his body fighting the knockout drops with all his might. "You never gave a shit about that little turd. No, no, no... this ain't about Pete at all, is it, Preacher? I know what this is about. This is about that cunt—"

"Her name is Jenny, you bastard."

"Jenny..." he laughed and thought for a moment. "Well you know what, Preacher: what do you say I give her to you?"

"What do you mean?"

"Just what I'm saying, Nate. She doesn't mean anything to me.

You just take her. Just... don't... shoot me, okay?" He laughed nervously. "I mean, we've been friends forever. Hell man, you're my best friend, my castle bars or whatever. Come on, what do you say?"

I weakened. "So you say I can have her. You say that now, but what about tomorrow?"

"I swear, Pre... Nate. We can still be the three amigos and hang, but—"

"What about your kid, Jess?" I said softly.

"The kid?" Bewilderment filled his eyes for a moment. "Well, I don't know, but I'm sure we can work something out. I'll teach him to fight and you can... take him fishing." He laughed and grinned his seductive grin. "Come on, let's let bygones be bygones." He held his hand out for me to pull him out.

That smile, and in it I remembered all the times we shared: his eyes shining in the moonlight at the lumber yard when we laughed from high above at the simplicity of the world; his arms raised in triumph in the canoe when we conquered the river; his tears as he asked to spend the night again; his shoes approaching under the bathroom stall. I threw the gun away and reached for his hand.

Raising the shovel abruptly he screamed: "You dumb fuck!" and swung the shovel hard against my head, knocking me a good one. Dazed, I stumbled backwards, and stepped into the bait bucket, my foot wedging into its slimy interior; and twisting and tripping fell hard with a thump to the ground. Lurching out of the depression, with eyes ablaze, the meth in his system pumping adrenaline through his bloodstream, overcoming then effects of the poison, Jesse advanced fiercely with the shovel raised. Scooting away backwards across the sandy, rocky soil, half-stunned, I kicked the bucket off my foot and retreated, Jesse in pursuit, wailing: "You think she'd ever have you, Preacher?"

He swung violently and the air whooshed past my jaw. Rolling to one side, I scrambled into the jagged brush, Jesse staggering after me, brandishing the shovel blade like a broadsword, swinging it wildly in my wake.

"You think... you think she loves you?" he snarled savagely.

The shovel blade slammed into a tree, as Jesse howled with laughter.

"You really think that... that stupid bitch... would ever... love... you?" A swoosh of air as the blade just missed my chin. My heart thudding turbulently, my body spinning, flailing, tumbling through the scraggy brush, I rolled over the rim and down the bank to the water as he burst through the foliage in pursuit shouting: "And you're going to... you're going to... kill me... for her? For that stupid—"

His voice coming closer, laughing, the shovel slicing the air in an even more dangerous cadence, and I thought of my favorite story when I was a kid—*The Pit and the Pendulum*—and I felt sick, sick unto death. Death was upon me, and I would die as the coward I had always been in my brief life.

Panic overwhelmed me. There was no one to call upon for rescue; I had to fight my way out myself. I could not cry out for Jesse; Jesse was gone, but... what would Jesse do? That was it. Think hard. How would Jesse fight his way out of this situation? I reached out and felt my hand close around a mossy rock, and, filled with the rage deep within me, driven by the inspiration that Jesse had given me to do whatever it took to win the fight, and remembering the bruised and battered face of the one I loved who was abused by my adversary, the one I had promised to protect—I leapt to my feet, and with all my strength, threw the stone at his face, shouting as I did: "Her name is Jenny, and you will never hurt her again, Jesse! I swear you won't ever hurt her again."

The rock slammed into his forehead with a nauseating smack, and he fell to the ground with a thud that seemed to reverberate through the night, harrowing the island down through the earth even unto its fiery core, before trailing off into calm, pure and remorseless silence. I crawled up the bank and, picking up another rock, climbed onto his chest, and raising the stone in my fist, I hit him again and again with it, crying: "Do you hear me, Jesse? Do you hear me?" until his face was red and nearly unrecognizable.

Breathing heavily, my eyes wide at what I had done, I hastily dragged his body to the grave and rolled him into it. His breathing was shallow and he let out a gasp as I layered the soil over his inert form.

He made a pit, and digged it, and is fallen onto the ditch which he made.

"Kuuuuhhhhhnn..." I thought I heard him whisper, but it might have been the wind.

My brother's blood cries out to me from the soil.

Ascendant over the eastern hills, the sun's rays colored the horizon above the trees on the far shore with a silky gauze of rosy pink mist as I pulled my grandfather's canoe out of the water for the last time and headed home; cold, weary, covered with dirt and blood, my mind empty, barren and dark—the needle of the compass in my pocket clanking uselessly against its glass face.

CHAPTER FIFTY-ONE

Stumbling down the path away from the ruins, Jenny and I hustled back over, across and down the rocky, uneven downgrade, back past the cabin where Pete had imprisoned her; while in the northwest, a rumbling and occasional flashes of lightning signaled the arrival of an incipient storm. Passing through the ghost town, we reached the parking area where I shoved Jenny forcefully into the passenger side, jumped into the driver's seat of the Trans Am, and tore off into the night, sending a shower of dirt and gravel into the air behind us.

Rain, which had started as a light spattering, grew heavy within minutes; the wipers moving back and forth methodically, as we sat shivering in silence. The road was hard enough to see in the darkness with the wipers on full shooting streams of water in both directions, and my head hurt bad, throbbing from where the hatchet had removed my ear. I touched the side of my head and felt the gaping hole and almost threw up. Blood, mixed with sweat and rainwater oozed from my wet hair into my left eye. I felt weak and tired and yet, despite my pain and exhaustion and my body aching all over, I was deliriously happy: we were free.

Jenny stretched out beside me, limp and soaked with sweat, her breathing heavy. She nursed the red marks on her wrists, rubbing them tenderly as the car bounced jarringly down the scalloped dirt road.

I drove the car hard with a fury away from the ghost town, Jared and Junior and Big Pete and memories of Jesse and the things that I had done. Turning off the heavily washboarded lane onto the main road, we sped east down the empty highway, the tires sliding on the wet pavement on each curve we spun around. With every mile I drove we were putting more and more distance between us and the past. There would still be questions, inquiries, inquisitions, but I was sure we could weather them: anything was possible now.

I had proved it: I could take care of Jenny and our child. I'd even learn to love Jeremy and raise him right. We could break the circle.

Jenny looked out the window and moaned slightly. She was thinking of him. I didn't care: she was mine. No one could stop our love now. But she looked at me and I saw the tears in her sad eyes. She was crying for him. Offering me a shy smile, she reached over and touched my arm gently with her fingers in thanks.

And I knew. She would never love me. Not like she loved him.

"Can I have a hit, Preacher?" she asked in shaky voice.

Shocked at her weathered face, I closed my eyes and pictured her again as before when I was back at the river with a book in my hand, and the little junkie slut dying beside me was transformed into my golden girl again—glowing, innocent, angelic, full of the spark of life. *We could go back. We could go back there again.* Tears lingered in my eyes, mingling with the sweat and blood that ran down my cheeks. *We have to go back.*

I opened my eyes and pressed the gas pedal harder to the floor and felt the engine respond with a roar—the car was nearly flying over the road, taking us home.

"You don't need a hit. You won't need a hit again. We're going home now, Jen," I said, smiling through my bloody lips. "You're safe. He can't hurt you anymore. No one can hurt you."

Shaking, she turned away and, staring at the darkened landscape as it hurtled by, suddenly said in a soft voice. "Preacher, you have to tell me where he is."

"Who—?"

"Don't act stupid, Nate. You know who."

I paused. "He's gone Jen."

"No."

"He'll never hurt you again. We're free to be together now."

"No Preach—Nate. I need to know. Where is he?" her voice raising.

She grabbed my shirt forcefully. "Where is Jesse? Tell me where he is?" Gripping me tightly, grasping my arm, her nails dug into the flesh. "I mean it. Tell me where he is," she suddenly screamed.

"Jen, I..."

She stared at me with those shining fawn eyes and she knew.

"No," she moaned.

"I—"

"You didn't..."

"I had to... save you..."

"No, no." Tears burst forth down her face. "I never wanted..." She convulsed into gasping breaths before abruptly striking out with her fists in an outburst of anger, hitting me in the face and arms, as I struggled to protect myself and maintain control of the speeding car.

"I took care of him just like I'll take care of you," I said weakly.

"Noooo..." she thrashed and wailed.

"It's alright now, Jenny. Please. You're safe. He's... dead."

"No, no, no!" she shrieked hysterically, ripping and clawing at my eyes. "No, he can't be dead. I... love him!"

A slight movement ahead. She glanced down the road, her eyes suddenly widening in horror. Pointing, she screamed violently.

Looking up, I saw the dark outline of two shapes ahead emerging from the forest. The first was a shadowy figure of a deer on the side of the road that entered the corner of my vision. The doe paused momentarily, and then looking behind her, she and her fawn rushed, as if pursued by some demon, onto the road and directly into our path.

I stomped on the brakes. Foolish. The wet road; the half bald tires planing. Struggling furiously to control the car, I swung the wheel frantically and we skidded with tires shrieking toward the pair of deer—who froze and turned to look at us, their large eyes shining in the headlights as we approached. Cranking the wheel hard, we spun to the left and across the white line through the opposite lane and into a dark barrier of trees.

The wipers slapping in the rain; the sharp points of Jenny's nails digging painfully into my arm; the echo of Jenny's voice screaming... screaming; the eyes of the frightened deer brightly glowing, growing nearer, then receding; turbulent motion—that sickening, frightening feeling of being out of control; then metal on impact, imploding, thundering in my ears as impenetrable darkness curtained down all around me, thrusting me headlong into a vortex of permanent silence.

CHAPTER FIFTY-TWO

It wasn't all that hot that day—whatever anybody else tells you, but of course everyone was bitching about it. We had all the windows open in the trailer and the fans going, and there was a bit of a breeze. Anyway, I'm always cold—cold-blooded I guess, so it wasn't bothering me any. It never gets that hot around here anyway, but the losers wouldn't shut up about it, and it was pissing me off. That and Jesse in the backroom with those two sluts he dragged in off the highway who looked like a couple of cheap whores who'd do anything for a high. The fucker shut the door in my face and laughed his ass off while I banged on the door mad as all hell.

Sure, there were a couple of town folks there that day partying, but nowhere near as many as claimed they were. In fact, Chuck Larsen and his girlfriend were the last ones to leave and they took off because we had such shitty reception out there and Chuck had money on the game. So it was just me and Preach and Little Pete hanging out and waiting for Jesse to get done showing off.

Preacher was zoning in and out in the recliner in the corner, Pete was babbling to himself on the couch and I was hitting it pretty heavy in the kitchen. I'd never mixed the crank with tequila before and it wasn't settling too well. I just knew that Jesse was in there screwing both of those girls. The fucking bastard—father of my child—love of my life, and he was nothing but a lowdown, cheating, scumbag prick.

That's how my life was—no future, only years of bullshit and loneliness to look forward to. Jesse was going to leave me; I knew it in my heart. He was going to pick up and leave with those two skanks—leave me to raise that hellion kid of his alone. Alone with only the two dummies, Preacher and Little Pete, to keep me company. I'd lose our house; have to move back in with my mom and stepdad.

Pacing around the room, I thought that I could hear muffled laughing behind the door and my anger rose. The brunette had a nose ring and a butterfly tattoo on her arm. I wanted to slice it off her. There was a carving knife in the kitchen, but, even better, Jesse's pistol was lying on the counter. I could scare them. Scare them away from my man.

Pete saw me pick it up and knew what I was doing and he bounced across the room to stop me. He always was a goofy kid, but he had a good heart and was always looking out for me. I brushed past him and screamed at Jesse to come out. I thought I could hear him tell me to fuck off in a real drugged out voice, and then he laughed even louder and the two trashy cunts joined in, so I pounded on the door and yelled that I was going to kill him.

God bless his soul, the little jackass Pete jumped in between me and the door and tried to settle me down, but I wasn't having any of it and waved the gun at him and told him to get out of my way—that I'd kill him too. He reached for me; I guess he thought he could help this time. The gun went off, I don't know how. And Pete was smiling. He was smiling that silly smile of his like he was the village idiot, before he just kind of slumped to the floor, his blood splattered all over the door.

One of the girls opened the door and screamed. Behind her, lying on the bed, I saw with the darkest dread imaginable—Jesse passed out cold—three days straight partying had finally done him in: the shot hadn't even stirred him. Panicking, the girls in the room, knocked the window out, climbed through it and ran off down the road. We never saw them again—fortunately, they didn't call the cops.

I began to sob as I now realized that it couldn't have been Jesse's voice I had been hearing mocking me from behind the door after all; it had all been in my head. Fucking drugs.

Preacher had been awakened by the shot and came staggering down the hallway, saying over and over: "Jesus Christ, Jesus Christ." He saw what I had done and then we looked at each other and then at Jesse on the bed and then he took the gun from my hand...

...and he put it in Jesse's. "Why did you do it, Jess?" he said in a whisper as he shook Jesse awake.

"Wha... wha... I never... I couldn't... did I really...?" my poor uncomprehending lover sputtered as he struggled slowly to alertness and then to the horror of what he was told he had done.

"Don't worry Jess, we'll take care of this—won't we, Jen?" Preacher glanced at me quickly to follow his lead. "It was a mistake. He pushed you. It doesn't matter; he was just a fuck up. He forced you to. We'll help you clean up."

Jesse sat on the bed, head in his hands, muttering: "I don't remember, I don't remember," as Preacher and I wiped up the blood and wrapped Little Pete's body in plastic.

Suddenly sober, I looked at my good friend—my unexpected savior—Preacher, in a completely new light.

CHAPTER FIFTY-THREE

The leaves are changing colors these days in Crystal Falls. I know this because if I move my eye as far as I can to the right I can just catch a glimpse of a branch of the tree outside my window whose dark green palette is modulating into an attractive shade of burnt orange. Soon the snowflakes will be falling and covering up the streets of the town and all its crimes and secrets, including my own, will lie hidden once more and forever. And I will be here, safe and hopefully forgotten, if not forgiven.

They tell me I wrapped the Trans Am around a tree on my way back into town that night. I don't remember it very clearly. The roads were wet, and the tires no doubt needed replacing. Maybe I was tearing it up, racing to a wondrous future I had imagined with the woman I love. The woman I've always loved. I was in a coma for nearly three months and they say I'll never walk again, or hold a lover in my arms.

It's been a couple years now and it's really not so bad here. The food is bland, but the staff is usually pretty friendly. I've got books on tape, even a Bible; I listen to music—mostly Mozart; I'm learning French; and I don't spend even one minute feeling sorry for myself. Well, most of the time anyway. I'm tough now, Jesse taught me that. Nothing and no one can hurt me. I've hardened my heart and could stand on my own two feet now... If I could stand.

About a year after the accident, my old man married a woman who talked him into moving down to Cape Coral. Good for him. He's still drinking, but at least it's the happy kind. He's been talking about coming back up to visit sometime, but I told him not to worry about me and to just enjoy what time he has left. He sends a postcard once in a while, and I smile thinking of him and how he really was a pretty good guy who just wasn't ready to be a father, but only had the best of intentions for me. And I get to feeling bad that I let him down.

A couple of guys I knew visited me at first with all the latest news, but I guess I'm a bit depressing to be around, so haven't seen many of them recently. The whole incident where the three Hawkins boys and Big Pete all disappeared was big news for a while, but nobody really found it all that strange, since the two clans had been feuding over the whole Little Pete killing and all, and there are so many dark places to hide around here, so the story has pretty much faded away as time goes by and is just one of those weird tales we tell to scare the tourists about not going into the woods.

Nope, Jesse Ray's whereabouts are no longer of any interest. Most folks figured Big Pete could have beat him to death and buried the body, never to be found; or maybe one of his drug "buddies" collected on a debt; or just maybe, he found that treasure we were looking for after all and just kept on running. The town has moved on, and I guess that means I'm free and clear. The biggest news is Junior has taken on all of the business and looks to be a lock to follow in his daddy's footsteps and be the full-fledged sheriff of Iron County someday soon.

And Jenny...

She, when the just man fled from his brother's anger, guided him in direct ways, showed him the kingdom of God and gave him knowledge of holy things... She preserved him from foes, and secured him against ambush... She did not abandon the just man when he was sold, but delivered him from sin. She went down with him into the dungeon, and did not desert him in his bonds... Showed those who had defamed him false, and gave him eternal glory—

The soprano suddenly interrupts my thoughts; her voice leaping and pirouetting upon a towering leafy trellis in birdlike trills as my Angel, shrouded in sunshine rises from the waters below, crying out:

Voi avete un cor fedele...

Well, I guess you know that Jenny's with Junior now. Yeah, he keeps her under his thumb with drugs, and she, in turn, plays the part of his devoted girl. From what I hear she even wears a frilly dress and goes out dancing the polka with the fat boy and his mom and all the old ladies. Heck, I suppose she deserves a little fun, if you can call it that. She was thrown from the car when I hit the tree, you know, and is just lucky to be alive. Of course, she lost the baby... our baby. She stopped in once to tell me the news about our daughter and asked if she could have that copy of *Lost Illusions* I loaned to her long ago back, She said she'd come back, but when she left, I knew I'd never see her again and, as it turns out, I haven't. That's the way it is. That's the way it should be, I guess. I should have never tried to change her nature.

Little Jeremy's growing like a weed, they say. Spends his days throwing rocks at cars and terrorizing the other kids. They tell me he's the spitting image of Jesse. I can only hope he will find himself a better future.

And me...

Sometimes I find myself descending down into a dream of shadows. In the dream, I drive fast, rocketing along a dark road, the wipers incessantly in motion and... I can't see the sky. For once, I don't know where I am. The moon and stars have hidden themselves behind a canopy of rain and clouds and I can't find any light at all to guide me. I don't know where I'm going and I feel like I am falling...

The seasons pass here in Crystal Falls, people are born, people die: it never changes. Time stands still here in the U.P. and we like it that way. Strangers, the dark- skinned and city folk with their big city ways aren't welcome, but if you're a friend, we've got some pasties in the oven, a cold one in the cooler and an extra seat at the card table. There's bingo at the Legion, the community theater's presenting *Annie Get Your Gun* and it'll be grouse season soon.

Around here it's back to the most basic of human instincts—kill or be killed—hunters and prey. Pick up your muskets and tackle, deer are running, the wild turkeys are in the bush, and there are muskies as big as your arm down in the cool, dark depths of the Michigamme.

Well, better get myself ready. It's almost time for the church ladies to come and pick me up for my annual outing. The older one is a bit of a sour puss, but the younger one has a touch of sadness and some flecks of brown in her pretty green eyes that makes me want to make her smile and take that darkness all away.

In case you're wondering, they're coming to dress me and take me out for my big speech to the incoming students at the high school. I get to tell them all about my life of sin—well, maybe only part of it, and how it all came to a crashing end due to my driving in an intoxicated, drug-addled state. Sort of scare them all straight, I suppose, with my mangled and hideous appearance. Junior helped set it up. Part of my rehabilitation. I do a good job because it gets me out of my room, but I don't believe a word I am saying. I guess I never really did.

I lie. I question what I have done every day and will for the rest of my life.

J'ai commenc sur une existence terrible.

I ask why I have been forsaken, and I hope with all my heart that if the lame can walk again and the blind may see that I may be forgiven...

And let me ask in faith, with no doubting, for the one who doubts is like a wave of the sea that is driven and tossed by the wind.

Yes, but... but...

How long, Lord? Will thou hide thyself for ever? Shall thy wrath burn like fire?

Remember how short my time is: wherefore hast thou made all men in vain?

I'm sorry... sorry... But... could I ask you for one favor before you go? Can you help me take a sip of water? My mouth is parched from the telling of the tale. Yes, just hold the cup and place the straw between my lips? Thank you, that's better.... now, have I told you enough yet? Have you heard what you wanted to hear? I'm afraid there really isn't any more to tell. Well, you are welcome and thanks for coming.

Oh, and before you go—I have to tell you, we had a pretty crazy thing happen recently. One of the nurses here told me that she saw on the news a few weeks ago that some scientist from one of the colleges back east was out our way, looking for fungus or something, and ran across a few tattered bills from the 1890s hidden under a stone out in the woods. So I guess you just never know.

Well, my escorts have arrived at last; I heard them coming down the hall. My remaining ear works better than ever. And what a pleasant surprise, my sweet little shy one is wearing a blue dress today the color of the Pleiades just like I remember them looking so long ago in the night sky.

Winking at her with my one remaining eye, she blushes and looks away from my disfigured face, and I smile and whisper to her in a seductive drawl:

"Hey Darlin'."

THE END

Praise for *Crystal Falls*

Mr. Walseth is extremely good at the art of storytelling, and I can't wait for his next read. Well researched...Well written...Well read. Walseth's voice kept me mesmerized. He has an incredible storytelling ability.

Wow! Read this book in a day, Loved the character development and the way Brad tells the story of their lives right up until the end (of the book). Masterful storytelling and beautifully written. Hope there is a sequel.

Do yourself a solid and get this one, it's a good one.

More Great Releases by Brad Walseth

Bone Lake
Nearly twenty years after the events in *Crystal Falls,* Jesse and Jenny's son, Jeremy Hawkins returns from several years' incarceration to find his mother has recently gone missing. Jeremy soon suspects his stepfather, the brutal and sadistic Roy "Junior" Pultz, who is now the sinister, drug-trafficking Sheriff of Iron County. Upon his homecoming to a place he swore never to return to, the prodigal son uncovers buried secrets, finds unexpected love and faces demons from the past while racing against the clock to rescue his mother from a horrible fate.

The Courier
A broken man, Jerry Markley, finds himself in deep trouble when the plane he is riding in is hijacked and crashes in the rugged Copper Canyon Region of Mexico, leaving him just six hours to make it back to the U.S. border with the heart he was delivering for transplant to save a little boy's life. Facing numerous obstacles, including rough terrain, deadly wildlife and a band of ruthless killers who are after the heart for their own purposes, the courier must overcome all in a frantic bid to help the boy and find redemption for his own dark past.

Praise for *The Courier:*

I loved this book, I couldn't put it down. There were a few different stories going on that all ended up tying together. The stories and the details with in them made me laugh and cry. There were many unexpected and exciting turns that kept the book interesting the entire time. The suspense and action were awesome. I was also really happy with the ending. Wonderful book!:)

A hit from the very beginning. Lots of action and twists within the story. One of those books you don't want to put down.

The Courier is a compelling story of redemption.

ABOUT THE AUTHOR

Brad Walseth is an American novelist, screenwriter, musician and photographer currently living near Chicago. Born and raised in the mountainous region of Western Montana, Brad worked in a lumber mill, played in rock bands and hitch-hiked around the West. before graduating from the University of Montana with a B.A. in English Literature. Brad worked for several years in radio and television before relocating to Chicago, where he attended Northwestern University and worked as a stockbroker, a postal clerk and as a corporate communications writer. During these years, Brad's short stories and reviews began appearing in publications nationwide, while his several years of rock journalism on the groundbreaking music website Concertlivewire.com led to his starting JazzChicago.net, where he juggled responsibilities as publisher, editor-in-chief, photographer, primary writer and interviewer. Brad was co-host and producer of the popular radio show, "Jazz, Chicago Style," while also working as an award-winning magazine writer/editor. One of Brad's screenplays, a "mockumentary" about a garage band who burn down their garage and have to become a carport band ("Hug the Shrugs"), was made into an independent film in 2004. Brad's first novel ("The Courier") was recently translated into Spanish. "Crystal Falls"— a literary crime novel, was originally published by Satalyte Publishing in 2014. "Bone Lake," the sequel to "Crystal Falls" was published in April 2017.

Made in the USA
Coppell, TX
13 April 2021

53683011R00166